Devil's DEAL

MICHELE ARRIS

Crimson Romance
New York London Toronto Sydney New Delhi

CRIMSON
ROMANCE

Crimson Romance
An Imprint of Simon & Schuster, Inc.
1230 Avenue of the Americas
New York, NY 10020

For information about special discounts for bulk purchases, please contact Simon & Schuster Special Sales at 1-866-506-1949 or business@simonandschuster.com.

The Simon & Schuster Speakers Bureau can bring authors to your live event. For more information or to book an event contact the Simon & Schuster Speakers Bureau at 1-866-248-3049 or visit our website at www.simonspeakers.com.

Manufactured in the United States of America

10 9 8 7 6 5 4 3 2 1

Library of Congress Cataloging-in-Publication Data has been applied for.

ISBN 978-1-5072-0623-2
ISBN 978-1-5072-0477-1 (ebook)

Dedication

With love and giant hugs to my A-team.

Chapter One

"Coffee."

That one word was all Lucas had to say to his assistant, Kara, seated across from him in his limo. Her fingers flew over her iPad's keyboard as he forwarded an endless trail of to do's to her. As confident as he was that his driver and security guard, Isaac, would skillfully maneuver the car out of downtown Washington, D.C.'s gridlock, Lucas was just as confident that Kara would ensure his customary end of the day coffee craving would be met without fail.

"I've already found a location. Nuagé Café. It's just up ahead," Kara replied. She glanced up from her iPad, pressed the intercom button, and relayed the location to Isaac. Ten minutes later, the limo pulled into the busy plaza, taking up two parking spaces.

While Kara hurried into the café to get his coffee, Lucas stretched his tired frame with a rub at the back of his neck. He needed a break from marking up the terms and conditions of the fifty-page document he'd been working on for the past hour and a half. There were two others, just as lengthy, that he also needed to have ready for Kara to send out by morning.

Taking in the busy plaza around him, Nuagé Café was nestled between a bridal boutique and a vintage bookstore. Beside that was a pet grooming salon where he observed several patrons entering and exiting the place toting their pooches in fashionable handbags. Up the block, blanketing both sides of the busy strip, were Tiffany and Co., Saks Fifth Avenue, Neiman Marcus, Louis Vuitton, and a host of other high-end stores.

A recent transplant from California, he'd been in D.C. less than a month, but he now understood why Kara had suggested he consider the area when he'd mentioned to her that he was looking for a home to purchase. The location was just outside of the city and was littered with every convenience imaginable. Kara would be able to find anything he required without ever leaving the zip code.

Returning to his work, he quickly became distracted by the sound of a car's engine knocking and looked up as a Honda pulled into a parking space. It coughed out a last effort before shutting down.

His head pivoted, doing a double take. *Damn!* Warm honey—those two words sprung to mind as he watched the honey-brown-skinned woman fiddling under the hood of her car. She was talking to ... well, from the looks of it, she was holding a conversation with herself, chatting away.

She couldn't see him watching her through his tinted windows. Finding her behavior amusing, he sat back and crossed his arms over his chest.

Her hair, a thick mass of curls, was held back from her oval-shaped face with a thin, white hair band and piled into a disheveled updo. The short, khaki skirt she wore showed off long, shapely legs. *A tennis player. No, perhaps a runner.* Just then, a commotion coming from a small group of ladies standing over by the pet salon drew her attention. A dog had gotten loose from its owner and was now zipping around the parking lot. His mystery lady didn't hesitate, joining in on the chase to capture the fluffy, white, apparently freshly groomed Maltese. The animal darted under her car, and she instantly dropped down to her knees.

Lucas quickly sat up and slid closer to the window, getting a good look at her ass. "Nice. Real nice," he murmured appreciatively.

Moments later, she came up with the animal, whose fur no longer resembled puffy white clouds, and handed it off to its distraught owner who headed straight back to the pet salon, likely for a shampoo redo.

His mystery lady palmed her forehead, catching her breath, recovering from the chase. He chuckled at the dirt smudge her hand left behind. There was something adorable about it.

As she dusted at her skirt while muttering to her car, she gave a look over his way. *What the—! His breath caught in his throat. He'd expected brown eyes. He couldn't tell precisely the color from the distance and through the tinted windows, but they were nowhere near brown. *Hazel? Maybe. There was a pearlescent glimmer in her eyes from the sun's waning amber.* Lucas frowned. *Pearlescent glimmer ... sun's waning amber*—what a bizarre thing to randomly pop into his head. She had his brain spewing ridiculous verse like a besotted idiot. That thought had him moving away from the window, yet he continued to watch her. He told himself to look away, but he simply couldn't, and he fought back the sudden urge to get out of the car. At the very least, he could make her aware of the dirt on her face. He moved to the door, but she grabbed a satchel from her passenger seat and strolled off. His eyes locked onto her perfect ass in that short skirt, enjoying the gentle sway of her slender hips. She stopped midstride when she came upon another woman.

It's a uniform. She works at the café. The blonde she was speaking with wore the exact outfit—white polo-style shirt and khaki skirt—but with a short, black apron tied at her waist.

During their exchange, the blonde used her hand to wipe away the dirt smudge, and then the two approached the café.

His mystery lady pulled open the door and out walked Kara with his coffee. She held the door for Kara with a smile—an exquisite smile—and then she and her coworker disappeared within.

Lucas was still staring at the café's double doors when Kara entered the car and sat across from him. No woman in his circle of acquaintances, hell, not even Kara would have chanced soiling her perfectly fitted skirt suit to retrieve a dog under a car.

"Sorry for the long wait." Kara handed over the cup. "The place has both a dining lounge area and an on-the-go station with a very long line. It's quite a busy establishment."

Lucas took a sip. It was actually pretty good. "Has your mother gotten settled in?" he asked her.

"Yes. I still don't know how you got them to approve her application. It's one of the best living facilities in the country for treatment of ALS. There was a nine-month waiting list. And to cover the cost for twenty-four-hour care as well as private accommodations, I cannot thank you enough. I'm headed there this weekend to finish up the paperwork, but as always, if you need to reach me, I'll have my cell on around the clock."

"Kara, take all the time you need, and no need to keep thanking me." With everything she did for him, Lucas felt helping her care for her mother was the least he could do. "Let me know if she requires anything else."

He returned to his work as Isaac slowly brought the car into the line of traffic to exit the plaza.

"How's the coffee?" Kara asked. "The barista said they've won awards for their signature in-house brew."

"It's very good." Lucas took a last look out his window at the café. As he drank the strong, black liquid, he now knew what he needed to relieve his stress. The remedy was just beyond those glass doors, and it had nothing to do with the in-house brew.

Chapter Two

"Bails, that hottie's back. I gave him a menu. My section's full. I had Tina sit him in yours to keep him away from Kim. The man could hardly relax with her hovering over him like a damn buzzard. You should've seen her the other night."

"What? Who?" Bailey moved to the prep counter. She glanced back at her longtime bestie and roommate, Sienna, while grabbing table six's order of Thai chicken flat bread and roasted turkey with goat cheese panini, both with creamy tomato soup on the side.

"Mr. Hotnessss," Sienna emphasized. "He was here Thursday night—your day off. He came in just before close. I had your section. Girl, you should've seen Kim. She was prancing her butt by his table in that tight-ass shirt from the moment the man sat down. She should wear nipple pads if she's gonna wear her shirt that damn tight."

Bailey laughed. "Sie, leave Kim alone." She was used to Sienna going off about their coworker, Kimberly. Sienna felt Kim was lazy and only perked up in her duties when she spotted a man with potentially deep pockets stroll in.

Bailey retrieved two clean glasses from a stack, quickly added ice in each, and filled one with Diet Coke and the other with iced tea. She gave another glance over her shoulder at her friend and added, "Let Kim do Kim." She picked up her tray and turned around, unaware that Sienna was standing so close. Her friend had to leap back a step to avoid getting jabbed in the stomach with the tray.

"As for this Mr. Hotness, whoever he is, as long as he orders and eats fast, that's all I care about. I'm not looking to be here past my shift tonight."

She hated when Tina sat customers in her section close to the end of her shift. This time, however, it was Sienna she could thank for her possibly leaving late. All the same, she actually liked working at the trendy hotspot that practically stayed busy until close. The tips alone were worth the long hours she put in on her feet after having spent nine hours at her day job.

Professionals frequented the café late in the evening with laptops and tablets—sometimes both—to grab a bite and likely pick up where they left off at the office. It was a short stint from busy D.C., offered free Wi-Fi, and was considered a great place to network. A large, four-sided, weathered red-brick fireplace stood in the center of the dining area with comfy mahogany leather loveseats and chairs circled around it. Wide booths lined the walls, and tables were stationed about the floor with power outlets wired right into the tabletops.

"Sie, don't you have customers waiting? We're leaving on time tonight, so get moving."

With her tray in hand, she bustled over to the swing doors, backed against the right side, and entered the dining area.

Sienna was right on her heels. "He's at booth four," she muttered before rushing off to tend to her section.

Setting the plates and drinks before her customers, Bailey pulled two straws from her apron pocket and placed them on the table. "Is there anything else I can get you?" she asked with a polite smile. Both voiced *no thanks*, to which Bailey replied, "Enjoy."

She made her way to booth four where the man sat. His fingers were rapidly flying over the surface of the wireless keyboard that he had stationed in front of his iPad.

"Good evening, what can I get for you?" Annoyance pinched at her when he didn't acknowledge her standing there, instead choosing to continue working, texting, tweeting, or whatever it was that was more important than being polite.

I so don't need this. "Sir?" She barely fought back a snarl. *Does he think I got all night to cater to his butt? Some people think they're the cock of the walk.* She'd picked that saying up from her mom. *He may wish to work himself into an early grave, but I sure as hell don't intend to.* That saying, too.

Bailey was picturing her comfortable bed, wishing she could sleep in tomorrow. That was out of the question. Having only been employed at the interior design firm for three months, she couldn't risk being late.

Annoyed, she clenched her teeth to avoid saying something rude and turned to leave.

"Sorry, I didn't want to lose my train of thought," he said while continuing to type away.

His deep, throaty baritone made her toes bunch up in her sneakers. She turned back. He lifted his head; his steel-blue eyes locked steady onto hers.

Okay, Sienna, he's hot.

It was a stare down ... no, a stare at, at least on Bailey's end. She felt tethered to his stare, which he still hadn't blinked. *Damn.* He was truly a hottie—dark wavy hair, blue-gray eyes, lightly tanned complexion. And the man was big from what she could tell—the weight-room-scheduled-workout-regimen kind of big.

Her eyes roamed over the white button-down he wore with the sleeves rolled up his thick forearms, fitting snug over his bunching biceps and massive chest. Her gaze followed his movements as he planted his elbows on the table and linked his fingers. *Nice, big, strong hands. It could mean big ... Girl, get a grip!* It had been a while since she'd had sex. Well, more like three years. After getting burned by two cheating exes, one learned not to be so quick to hover a hand over the fire. But damn. This was a new record—the man had the crotch of her panties moist in under a minute with just a look.

What the hell is wrong with me? Sizing up this man, this stranger is downright wrong.

It's not like she hadn't served a good-looking professional man at the café before. They popped in aplenty, dressed in suits that cost more than what she made in a month, and drove cars that cost more than what she earned in a year from both her jobs combined.

The urge to look down at the man's shoes was tempting. She had a thing for men in fashionable shoes. Her mom always said nice teeth and quality shoes spoke of a man who took care of himself. That saying had never made any sense to her, since steel toe boots were the men's style of choice in the small town of Darlington, South Carolina, where she'd grown up. Nevertheless, she always found herself looking for those two qualities on a man. Shoes were the one vice she had herself.

Her curiosity building, she pulled her gaze away from the man's hypnotizing blue-grays to steal a look at his shoes. *Darn it.* They weren't visible under the booth. She brought her eyes back up. *Ding! Ding! Ding!* Perfect, straight, white teeth. He was smiling at her, throwing her off guard. She had to swallow air into her lungs to regulate airflow. His beautiful smile lit up his stunningly attractive features, taking her breath away.

"Did you drop something?" he asked and leaned to the side to look beneath the table, then brought his gaze back up to hers, but not before lingering on her bare legs for several heartbeats.

God, Bailey, so stupid. She was dissecting the man like a lab experiment, and he knew it. And he was still smiling at her. In place of air, she swallowed her embarrassment this time and placed the tray on the end of the table to grab her pen and pad from her apron pocket. "What can I get for you, sir?" He eyed her a moment longer with that enthralling smile, blinked—*finally*—and then took a look at his menu.

"I'll have coffee, regular blend, black, and, uh, what pie would you recommend?" He looked up and caught her once again attempting a look under the table. "It's not a mouse, is it?" A grin with a playful wiggle of brows.

"No! No ... I ... it ... uh, there are sixteen different pies and cobblers," Bailey hastily rattled off to mask her embarrassment. "The cherry cobbler is very popular, but I like the sweet potato. It reminds me of home." She regretted saying it the moment it fell out of her mouth. She preferred to maintain a professional distance with the customers—kind and very respectful, but never overly friendly. This man had her tongue all loose and parts of her body spiking a charge. She had to keep it together.

"And where might home be?" he questioned.

"South Carolina. So, it's black coffee—regular—and cherry cob—"

"I'll try sweet potato. South Carolina by way of ... somewhere abroad? Perhaps an island, given your lovely features."

Abroad? Her response was a faint shrug. She followed his gaze, slowly moving over her face, down her body, and then back up. Though she'd done the same to him, it pinched a nerve. His scan of her seemed to be more of an inspection.

Sienna often told Bailey that she'd pretty much lost her southern drawl from living up north for the past six and a half years, but she knew it wasn't so far gone that she sounded foreign, for goodness sake. It was clearly his way of trying to determine her ethnicity.

She was used to people asking her what she was mixed with, having inherited looks from her mother's side of the family, specifically her maternal grandfather's green eyes. She'd been told ever since she was a little girl that she was an *eye-catcher*, as her grandfather would put it. Both her parents were African American, but her eyes and curly hair would suggest she was biracial.

Her mother, even with Bailey's grandfather's help, couldn't pinpoint where exactly the race lines crossed along the family tree. There was some French in there somewhere, but there likely was a crisscross of a few races down the family line. Whose family tree was truly purebred these days anyway, so what difference did it make? *Apparently, it matters to this guy.*

He sat back with arms crossed over his remarkably broad chest. "Where in South Carolina are you from? I have an aunt that retired in Myrtle Beach."

It was that damn smile that was affecting her—his bright white grin and those perfectly shaped, pale pink lips. Frankly, their entire interaction was starting to unnerve her.

He's a bold one, this one.

"Nope, not Myrtle Beach and not an islander. I should get your order in." His casual nod was Bailey's window to leave. She didn't waste a second darting away.

As she headed for the kitchen, she gave a quick glimpse over her shoulder and caught him looking at her backside. That annoyed the hell out of her.

Typical.

Chapter Three

Sienna came up to Bailey at the coffee station. "Let me guess, that's for Mr. Hotness, right? That's all he had on Thursday night, too. Coffee and pie. How does he keep that ass tight on caffeine and sugar?"

Bailey's head jerked up from the cup she was filling with black coffee. "How would you know what his ass looks like?"

"Come on, you know he's packing it, girl." Sienna snorted. "And I got a good look on Thursday."

Bailey couldn't disagree. "Here, you take it to him." She pushed the tray over.

"Why? No, you do it. I'm at two to your one flirt this week," Sienna reminded her.

Kim poked her head between them. "I'll do it. He's cute as all get out."

"You need to tend to your own tables for once." Sienna turned her back to their coworker, blocking Kim out of the conversation. "Bails, his coffee's getting cold." With a wink, her dark eyes mischievous, she slid the tray back over.

"You're bad, you know that." Bailey smirked back at her best friend.

Like most of the waitresses, she and Sienna received their fair share of propositions from both single and married men. They turned it into a game, tallying their numbers at the end of the week.

The younger businessmen were the worst. Many were arrogant and felt entitled as if their financial position gave them carte blanche to any woman they sought. She'd become numb to it, unimpressed by their tailored suits and fancy cars. Besides, she knew all they wanted was a quick lay to ease the stress of their day to day—sex to take the edge off. She'd admit that Mr. Hotness got her panties moist, but she wasn't that weak.

Sienna often won the flirt game they secretly played. Men found her flawless, cinnamon-brown skin tone and tall, slender, runway model build very appealing. She wore her natural soft curls cropped short. Some days she'd mousse down the sides and spike the top. One might say her glossy, jet-black hair and dark slanted eyes suggested that she had some Asian in her. Sienna had never known her father, so it was possible.

Her looks would easily put Naomi Campbell to shame, but Sienna's passion was art. In college, every wall in their dorm room had been covered in her artwork. Now their current apartment walls displayed Sienna's masterpieces, and wherever there was a flat surface, one would find a Sienna original sculpture. It was why she worked as a docent downtown during the day. She could keep her ears open to possible opportunities to get her foot in the door to someday showcase her work.

The escalating voices of Kim and Sienna pulled Bailey out of her musing.

"I wasn't talking to you," Kim spat out at Sienna.

Sienna planted her hands on her hips and narrowed her eyes right back at her. "Shouldn't you be off clearing tables or something?"

"Who are you to tell me what I should be doing? How about you go do *your* job," Kim shot back.

Bailey wedged herself between the two ladies, looking from one to the other. "Stop before Joe fires both of you! Geez." Exasperated, she shook her head. Sienna and Kim were from the Bronx and both shared the I-never-back-down attitude.

"He's my customer; I'll take it to him," she told them.

Kim stood her ground a moment longer, then delivered another hard look at Sienna before turning with a theatrical swing of her long ponytail over her shoulder, its strands catching Sienna across the face on her exit out of the kitchen.

Sienna fanned away the hairs with a look of disgust. "Ew, Joe needs to make her tie that shit up. One of these days, I'm gonna snatch that horse tail right out of her scalp."

Bailey sighed. "Why you get worked up over her, I'll never understand. If you'd take the time to get to know Kim, you'd see that she's really sweet." Her tray in hand, she headed off with a look over her shoulder. "Really, you should talk to her."

Sienna sucked her teeth in obvious disagreement. "I already know her type. We work our butts off while she glides around the floor scoping out the men." She grabbed an empty tray to clear plates in her section and followed as she went on, "Why do you think Kim likes the five-thirty shifts? By six is when most of them start strolling in. You can always find her at the windows around that time to see who's driving what, so she'd know which one to schmooze."

She was still going on about their coworker as they entered the dining area. They both froze with trays in hand upon seeing Kim standing at booth four talking to Mr. Hotness with her chest exaggeratedly pushed out before him.

"Sweet, huh? See that? That right there is what I'm talking about." Sienna took a wide step, ready to charge, but Bailey touched her shoulder.

"Sie, I got this. Go finish up. I want to get the hell out of here on time tonight." Seeing Kim talking to the man, a twinge of jealousy crept just below the surface of Bailey's common sense.

"Bails, embarrass her ass. Tell him she has an STD or something," Sienna scoffed before she headed off to her section.

Bailey had no intentions of saying that. She walked over and subtly moved in front of Kim to arrange the cup and plate before the man whose eyes were trained on her every movement. "Thanks for keeping my customer entertained." She gave Kim a smile over her shoulder, and noticed how Kim had her hands linked behind her back, making her D cups even more pronounced in the one-size-too-small polo. Bailey thought of her own thirty-two Ds compressed in the confining sports bra she wore. *The poor things.* Her breasts had started sprouting early, around eleven years old. By age fifteen, her nipples were so overly sensitive, she often wore a compression bra to curtail the direct contact of them rubbing against fabric. The constricting garment also helped to keep men's lecherous eyes focused on their menu.

"I was telling him how much I liked his car. I happened to see it when he pulled in." Smiling at the man, Kim draped her ponytail over her right shoulder and twirled the end around her finger as she said to him, "I'm really into cars. I knew right off that it's a Ferrari 612 Scaglietti. V-12, I'm sure. It looks best in silver. You would think red, but no, silver's the way to go. You have exceptional taste."

Damn, the girl is good! Bailey watched Kim run her tongue along her top lip and end with a slight chew on the bottom one, giving the man an enticing smile. Kim also knew precisely when to slide in a bit closer to give him an *exceptional* view of her plump ta-tas.

Bailey had to hand it to her—Kim was good at her craft. However, the man didn't seem that impressed by Kim's knowledge of his car; he was more interested in his cobbler. He took in a mouthful, chewed, swallowed, and then sipped his coffee. Throughout, she noted that his eyes were fixed on her.

Her coworker was still going on about the car—engine specs, octane, and who knows what else. "Kim, we should give him his space." Bailey smiled politely at the man. "Enjoy your cobbler."

"Good suggestion on the sweet potato, Miss South Carolina. Is there anything else you would suggest I try? I'm open to anything you recommend ... that is, if you're one of my options."

Taken aback, her eyelids fluttered, and his words clogged Kim's jabbering in her throat.

In that suspended moment, Sienna walked up. "Kim, your customer at table twelve is asking for a refill. I told him you'd be right over."

"Uh, yeah, okay," Kim replied, looking just as thunderstruck.

Bailey could almost read the girl's thoughts—this obviously wealthy, very attractive man had bluntly opened a bedroom door for her to walk right in, but the Miss Upstanding Country Mouse that she was wouldn't take the bait. Kim would be partially right, Bailey thought. It wasn't that she was holier than thou by any means. It was more *been there, done that ... twice.* Her heart had enough scuff marks, thank you very much. Besides, he was probably not that good in bed anyway. All show, no action. *Who am I kidding? Look at him. I'd likely have an orgasm merely from the man's breath on my neck. Stop it! Bailey, pull it together!*

Straightening her spine to draw his attention to her breasts again, her coworker offered up another smile; her tone syrupy sweet. "Well, it was very nice talking to you."

Wow. All Kim received that time was a nod from the man. Her shoulders dropped, as did her bright smile, and she ambled away.

Bailey was unsure what to say to the man. He'd just propped her. She'd heard variations of this come-on from men numerous times before and was usually quick with a retort that made it clear she wasn't interested. For some reason, her brain blinked out on her.

But this was exactly the game she and Sienna played. It would count as two flirts for her for the week. She pursed her lips to strike. "You—"

"What's your name, beautiful?" he interjected and then took in another fork of the cobbler.

Beautiful? Seriously, am I supposed to melt and drop my panties over that? She could toss her pen in any direction in the cafe and hit a man like him: handsome—okay, maybe not as hot—wealthy, and offering up a big bowl of sex with nothing else on the side.

Typical," she murmured, shaking her head as she placed his billfold on the table.

"I—" he started.

"All of the options that are available to you can be found on the menu. Enjoy your cobbler." Not giving him a chance to utter another word, she walked off.

Chapter Four

Like most nights, Bailey had been kept busy, but tonight, the time seemed to drag on, draining her both physically and mentally.

She glanced over at Sienna entering the break room. "Hey, are you ready to head out?"

"Just about." Sienna pulled her backpack from her locker and stuck her tips into her wallet. "Here, Sir Hotness wanted me to give you this." She handed over a twenty-dollar bill.

"Stop calling him that. And twenty dollars for a twelve-dollar table bill? What do I look like to him, a beggar or something?"

"Why are you getting all bent? Girl, take the damn tip." The bill was dropped into Bailey's backpack. "It's not like he can't afford it. You said he propped you, so we're tied, right? He wanted some brown sugar to sweeten that black coffee," Sienna teased, and Bailey playfully shoved her friend at the shoulder. "You know I'm right." She rolled her hips and backed her butt up to Bailey, laughing.

Bailey closed her locker and grabbed her backpack from the bench behind her. "He gave me that tired-ass line as if I'm supposed to fall all over him because he called me beautiful. Please." She rolled her eyes. "You know I don't play that." Truth be told, she was kind of disappointed to see that he was just like all the rest. For some ridiculous reason, she'd wanted him to be different.

"You couldn't even go back to his table. What else did he say to you exactly?" Sienna asked.

"The usual weak crap they all say, thinking we're so desperate that we'd pant at anything they say. He had the nerve to ask me what I am. He didn't come right out, but I knew what he meant, like I had to pass some race checklist of his or something."

Sienna brought her chin up, lips pouted. "Well, you are a query at first glance," she said in a prim, proper tone. "And at least you know which direction to point your genealogy compass." Her dark eyes grew as hard as her tone was playful. "My loving mother was an ambassador of goodwill to so many partners, for all I know, I may descend from Attila the Hun."

"Don't say that," Bailey lightly chided.

"But, really, what's the biggie about it? Hell, all he had to do was get a look at that ba-dunka-dunk to know what time it is." Sienna reared back, eyeing Bailey's backside. "Show him you can drop it like it's hot."

Bailey smiled. "Oh, he got a good look all right." She fished in her backpack for her keys. "Like I said, I'm not that desperate. Let's go."

They left the break room, said their good-byes to their manager, Joe, and those scheduled to close, stepped outside, and headed across the parking lot toward Bailey's Honda.

Sienna spotted him first and elbowed Bailey in her side. He was resting back against a silver Ferrari with his legs loosely crossed at the ankles, talking on his cell phone. Her gaze dipped to his buffed, black leather dress shoes—double monk wing tips. *Very nice.* They made eye contact. He straightened and started moving toward them while continuing his phone conversation.

"Uh-oh, he's coming over." Sienna grinned and elbowed Bailey again. "Yum, yum, Bails, look at all of that. Mr. Olympia for sure."

"Would you stop with the names." Bailey immediately started to sweat. He *was* all that—tall, muscular, gorgeous with a casual swagger that oozed confidence. "What do you think he wants?" He was close enough that she could hear him giving demands to whomever he was speaking to on the phone—*enough with the excuses ... call me back with results ... get it done*, she heard him say before he ended the call. His autocratic manner didn't sit well with her.

"What does he want, you ask? One word, girlfriend ... you." Sienna pasted on a generous smile for the man now standing before them. "Good evening," she said.

"Hello," Bailey followed, managing to keep the irritation undercut by apprehension out of her tone.

"Good evening," he replied. "I would like to apologize to you for my rudeness earlier. It's not often a beautiful lady has me searching for words only to end up saying the wrong thing. It was in poor taste."

She shrugged. "No argument here, but it's whatever." Her tone was purposely cold as she looked up at the man's tall stature, while trying her best not to ogle his powerful physique.

"Wait. You were waiting out here just for her?" Sienna asked the man. "I'm touched and a bit creeped out."

"Sienna!" Bailey jabbed an elbow in her friend's side this time.

"What? Bails, we don't know him from Adam or," Sienna gestured a hand up and down the man's exceptional build, "Apollo in his case."

Bailey took a patient breath and rolled her eyes. "Sie, you're your own audience sometimes, you know that."

"Bails?" the man asked, looking between them.

"It's short for Bailey," she said, and his lips slowly curved upward.

"Ah, Bailey of South Carolina. I'm Lucas Marx, and I assure you, Miss Bailey of South Carolina, you have nothing to fear from me." He looked at Sienna. "I overheard you say you both got off at ten. I thought I'd wait."

"Walters. Bailey Walters." She accepted his outstretched hand, and Sienna did the same.

"Sienna Keller—pleased to meet you."

"My pleasure." His attention came back to her. "I'd like to get to know you. Have dinner with me."

Was that a command or a request? Bailey couldn't tell which. "Dinner? Now?" She glanced over at Sienna and then back at him.

"Of course not now," he responded with a relaxed smile in an attempt to relieve the slight spike of apprehension she was certain he could see in her eyes. "I meant tomorrow evening. Or we could meet in the morning for coffee."

"You like your coffee, don't you," Sienna commented.

Bailey fought not to elbow her friend again. "Here." She handed over the car keys. "Start it up."

"Good idea. You know it runs on a wing and a prayer these days. Good thing you had your boy, Kevin, work some of his mojo on it. We should be able to make it home." She grinned in response to Bailey's deep sigh. The girl's wit was turned on 24-7. "Nice meeting you, Lucas Marx."

"You, too, Sienna."

They both remained silent until Sienna was seated inside the Honda, and then he said, "If you're concerned about my character, we could meet here if you'd prefer."

"I have to work in the morning."

"I thought you worked nights, so—"

"You thought you had me pegged, that I was a desperate waitress, one who looked for generous tips chased with sexual favors." Bailey allowed her annoyance to show as she irritably pushed her pack's strap up on her shoulder and crossed her arms at her chest. "Do you always verify race before you decide if a woman is worth getting with, Mr. Marx?"

"No, I—" He frowned and looked away for a moment, then back at her. "You misunderstood. I appreciate your uniqueness, your beauty."

She blinked, surprised a bit by his compliment, but quickly regrouped. "Look, I don't hook up with patrons. It's late and I have to get up early. It was nice meeting you." She turned to leave, but he caught her forearm in a light hold. Her gaze dropped to his hand and then up at him. A slow grin crept into his cool, steely-blues as he held on a couple of seconds before letting go. "Have a good night, Mr. Marx." She pivoted, too startled by his warm touch to be vexed.

"Wait," he called and caught her wrist again, but only for a moment before reaching into the front pocket of his shirt. "I simply would like to get to know you. No pressure. Here's my card if you should change your mind. It's my personal line. You can reach me anytime."

Bailey took his card, turned, and went to the passenger side of her car, but then turned back.

"Your shoes."

"I beg your pardon?" His head darted down and back at her.

"Under the table ... I was trying to see your shoes. Very nice." She smirked at seeing his head cocked to the side before he looked down again, and then back at her. The right corner of his mouth curved up slightly once more. "Good night, Mr. Marx." She got in the car, and Sienna wasted no time peeling out.

Chapter Five

"Don't stop."

Bailey squirmed and rocked her pussy against his skillful tongue, her fingers snaking into the thick waves of his hair to the back of his neck, keeping his mouth sealed tight on her throbbing clit. His hands squeezed her buttocks as his tongue speared her sex again and again before returning to her clit.

"You like that, don't you?" Two thick stiff fingers thrust in and out of her clenching channel with precise, momentum before Lucas parted the folds of her labia and worked his tongue in slow circles, then pushed her legs back, spreading her wide, and devoured her with his mouth, slurping her cream, swirling his tongue in and out of her pussy, back and forth, not missing a single ounce of her flesh.

"Oh, yes, right there." She moaned as his hot mouth trailed a wicked path upward, licking her quivering body, and captured the peak of an achingly hard nipple between his teeth, while his fingers maintained a deep measured thrusting in and out of her soaking wet sheath. "Oh my God! Don't stop, Lucas, I'm going to come." The delicious sensation was so overwhelming, a low continuous hum reverberated every nerve ending throughout her frenzied body. The intensity grew with each thrust of his swift moving fingers, so harsh, so loud, so intense ...

Bailey jolted upright in her bed. Her breathing labored, she expelled a shaky breath as she silenced the blare of the alarm clock, then lay back down, pressing her head deep into the pillow. Her skin was clammy. The crotch of her panties was soaking wet. She was so close. *Ugh, I just met the man and now I'm dreaming about him going down on me. What the hell?* She left the bed in need of a really cool shower.

About forty-five minutes later, she sat on the edge of the bed to slip on her sneakers and hastily tied them up. She hadn't gotten much sleep. Her body had called it a night the moment she crawled into bed, but her mind was restless for hours. Then came the scorching hot wet dream she'd had. *Lucas Marx.* She couldn't stop thinking about the man. He'd actually waited for her outside the café, even apologized for that pathetic line. Truth be told, it kind of impressed her, even though he'd likely said it in the hopes of getting her on her back.

There was no denying that she was attracted to the man—her dream of him proved that—with his steady blue-gray gaze and sculptured physique that had her close to salivating. Heck, what woman wouldn't be? That said, she was very familiar with his type.

Remembering his card that she'd placed in her wallet, she reached across the bed for her satchel and pulled it out. The crisp white lettering was printed on black, heavy card stock. His e-mail and phone number were printed below an embossed red line at the bottom edge.

Having wasted enough time thinking and dreaming about the man, she stuck the card back into her wallet and went to her closet to get her new babies—a pair of black, Italian leather, peep-toe sling backs that she placed in her satchel. She'd saved for two months to buy the pair.

Having exorbitant student loan debt, she was very frugal with her money and could stretch a dollar. Except when it came to her shoes. They were her one weakness.

She checked her appearance one last time in the full-length mirror attached to the front of the closet door. Her gray pinstripe skirt was accompanied by Sienna's borrowed, red silk, sleeveless blouse. It coordinated nicely with her shoes' red under-soles.

Her hair was still slightly damp, but the curls were behaving with the help of the glob of mousse she'd worked in to tame them.

Deciding her appearance was as good as it was going to get, she left her bedroom and made her way to the kitchen.

"Good morning," she said to Sienna seated at the breakfast bar, eating cereal with a side of buttered toast and flipping through one of her art magazines.

"Morning, *chica*." Sienna grinned as she chewed. She ate another spoonful and chewed while saying, "Bails, you need to know something."

"What's up?" Bailey stole a bite of toast on her way to the fridge, grabbing from it a prepackaged salad. She then stepped over to the breakfast bar and gave a tug at the red blouse. "I borrowed this as you can see. I was going—" Her words lodged in her throat. *What the hell?* The sight of the individual coming toward her drew her pause. *Faith.*

"Good morning, all." Faith entered the living room wearing Sienna's robe. Her blonde hair was gathered and secured on top of her head with one of Bailey's hair scrunchies. She went to where Bailey stood catatonic and gave her a hug. "Bails, it's so good to see you."

Snapping out of her momentary coma, Bailey hugged her former roommate, while giving Sienna a perplexed look over Faith's shoulder, wanting an explanation. Painting on a smile, she drew back. "Hey, girl, Sienna didn't tell me you were in town."

"Surprise." Sienna grinned. "That's what I was about to tell you. She arrived early this morning. I had her sleep in my room. We didn't want our gabbing to wake you."

Faith went to the fridge and took out the orange juice carton, followed by a glass from the cupboard. She brought both over to the breakfast bar and poured as she said, "I hope it's not too much of an imposition for me to stay."

Bailey knew that statement was primarily directed at her; Faith drank her juice while studying her over the rim of the glass.

"I told Faith it was cool. Bails, you're cool with it, right?" Sienna subtly arched her brows behind Faith's back.

Bailey was indeed irritated that Sienna would have Faith stay with them without first discussing it with her. There was history there, and not all of it was *good* history.

The three had been tight as glue from that first day they'd met at freshman orientation up until their senior year. Faith sleeping with Bailey's boyfriend changed all of that. Bailey had returned a day earlier than expected from winter break and found Andrew and Faith in bed. Both claimed they'd been drinking and things just got out of hand.

Bailey wasn't stupid. She knew jealousy was part of the underlying reason Faith betrayed her. She'd heard from Sienna that Faith's boyfriend at the time once remarked that he had a crush on Bailey. He was drunk as usual when he'd made the comment. Faith took it to heart and cut him loose, but held the remark over Bailey's head.

Whenever Faith was rebounding, she'd get wasted and end up doing something stupid, like when she threw another ex's laptop and flat-screen TV out of his third-floor dorm window after she caught him cheating on her. *Birds of a feather ...* If it weren't for the guy's roommates pinning Faith flat to the floor, the poor girl she'd found him with would've been the next to take flight. She did manage to toss the girl's clothes out of the window before she was pinned down.

Georgetown was ready to expel Faith, but her father was a contributing alumnus and, most importantly, a respected judge. He wrote an apology accompanied by a really big donation, and all was right again in the Faith Sullivan world.

Though Faith's betrayal left a fissure in their friendship, Bailey got past it. As far as she was concerned, her ex, Andrew, wasn't worth ending their friendship, and Bailey soon discovered that Faith wasn't the only girl Andrew had slept with during their relationship. Soon after Bailey ended things with him, another girl approached her and said Andrew had gotten her pregnant. So, Faith sleeping with the scumbag sort of did her a favor.

What Bailey had a hard time genuinely forgiving Faith for was the night she and Sienna were awakened and pulled from their beds by a police canine unit. They sat side by side, handcuffed, as their apartment was searched for contraband. Bailey and Sienna insisted that the officers had the wrong address until they were questioned for information on a Faith Sullivan and her then boyfriend, Dale Carter. Turned out, Dale was maintaining a pretty large drug operation on and off campus.

Faith claimed she didn't know about Dale's drug involvement, even though she'd accompanied him on several trips to New York.

Dale was arrested and given twenty-eight months—it was his second offense. Faith was not charged. Dale signed a statement written in his own hand that stated Faith knew nothing about his purchase of and intent to sell an illegal substance.

Bailey still strongly believed that Faith's father somehow had a hand in Dale disconnecting Faith from his wrongdoings.

Though Faith broke it off with Dale after the search and seizure of their apartment, Bailey, and even Sienna, who always forgave Faith for every screw up she made, had had enough. They kicked Faith out, and she moved back home to Massachusetts. That was a little over two years ago. The last Bailey and Sienna heard about Faith was that she'd been keeping a low profile at her family's home in Cape Cod.

Even with all the craziness Faith had subjected them to, it was nice seeing her again. They'd really missed her. What concerned Bailey was that wherever the girl showed her head, trouble was usually not too far behind.

"Faith, how long are you in town?" Bailey asked her, and those cool, aquamarine eyes beneath sun-blonde winged lashes met hers briefly.

"I haven't decided." She finished her orange juice and poured another glass.

"Like Sienna said, you're more than welcome to stay here. We only have the two bedrooms now, as you can see." They all looked at one another, each reading the other's thoughts. Following the police raid, Bailey and Sienna were evicted from their three-bedroom apartment the very next day, their belongings literally dumped on the street.

"It may not look it, but the sofa's actually pretty comfortable," Sienna said as she rose from her barstool and brought her bowl to the sink.

Bailey stuck her salad in her pack and grabbed her keys off the counter. She strolled to the door, but paused with her hand on the doorknob at Sienna's call out to her from the kitchen.

"Don't forget, we're meeting Kevin and Diego at the club for drinks after work. They know it's our day off at Nuagé, so no excuses, *capisce?*" Sienna winked. "Kev said he and Diego will have some new songs in their set tonight. They played a sample for me the other day. It's really good."

"I guess I'll be there." Bailey sighed. The girl was aware that she was trying to limit her social involvement with her ex, Kevin, to prevent him from getting the wrong idea. Kevin would use any opportunity to try to sweet talk her into starting things up again between them. She tried to avoid that conversation at all costs.

Before the door closed behind her, Bailey heard Sienna add, "Oh, and I want Faith to meet Diego." That was also her friend's way of letting her know that she'd invited Faith and had already relayed the four-one-one on Kevin and Bailey's involvement. Thinking over how she felt about that on her way to her car, she spotted Kevin just as he was climbing out of a woman's Jeep. They made eye contact, and he gave her a nod. He said a few final words to the woman and then headed over to Bailey standing at her Honda.

They had attempted a relationship the prior summer that lasted about six months. Even after she'd told him she wasn't ready to have sex, that she'd recently dealt with a cheating ex, he still wanted to date her. So, for those six months, the poor man had coped with a constant hard-on, and she'd expected the next six months to be no different. It wasn't fair to him, so she ended the relationship.

It wasn't that she didn't find Kevin attractive. On the contrary. Bailey was initially awestruck by the man the first time they met when she and Sienna moved into the ground floor apartment across from him. She found his long dreads, which he kept dyed a warm shade of blonde and tied back from his masculine features, very appealing.

He'd said he was part Native American, Algonquian ancestry, which would explain his smooth, mocha-brown skin tone, dark chocolate eyes, and high cheekbones that complimented his African American broad nose and full, supple lips.

Kevin played both the guitar and the sax—a total turn-on. Bailey went often to see him perform with his band. They both loved the arts, exploring the museums, rooted for the Washington Redskins, and both favored the Yankees, except when they went up against the Nationals. It was sacrilege to do otherwise. But despite all their similar interests, something was missing. She didn't know what it was exactly, but had realized that friendship was all she could offer Kevin. Yet he didn't hide that he still wanted more.

"Hey, Kev."

"Good morning, lovely." An awkward twist curved his lips before he kissed her cheek.

"Thanks again for fixing my car." She tossed her bag on the passenger seat, got behind the wheel, started it up after a few pumps of the brakes, and brought down the window.

Kevin closed the car door and leaned in. "I didn't fix it. I put a Band-Aid on it. Among the many other problems, it has a slow oil leak. I added a can and put an extra one in your trunk. You really need to put it out of its misery, doll." Looking at her, he sighed and stood up. "Uh, about that woman, I—"

"You don't owe me an explanation. It's good that you're seeing someone."

"Bailey—"

"Kev, we've long since broken up, like close to seven months, and now we're great friends."

"That's your preference, not mine." His tone was rough, agitated.

"Kevin, let's not do this." Their sudden quiet stretched uncomfortably long. Breaking the tension, she shifted the gear in reverse. Thankfully, he relented with a nod.

"How about I meet you for lunch?" he suggested.

Bailey rested a hand on top of the one he had planted on the car door. Why couldn't she feel more for him? Kevin was handsome, educated, and he was always looking out for her and Sienna. He was the type of man to whom her parents would easily give their approval.

"I can't today. I'm swamped. Actually, I'm running late. I really should get going." She would've said yes to lunch, but knew he wouldn't let it end with just lunch. He'd somehow find a way to work in the discussion of them trying again. With that thought, she began slowly backing out. "We'll catch up later."

"You're coming tonight?" he called as she pulled off.

Her hand came out of the window with her thumb raised.

• • •

Bailey took the stairs from the parking garage up to the third floor. She made her way to Callaghan Interiors and was greeted by the receptionist intern.

"Good morning, Jason. Did you have a good weekend?" A mischievous grin formed upon his glossy pink lips. "That big smile on your face says you did." She returned one of her own.

"Girl, you know I did. Eight of us jammed at the Above and Beyond concert at Merriweather. It was fantastic. We—" The ring of the interoffice line cut into his weekend update. They both took a look at the telephone's display. It was their boss.

Jason grabbed up the receiver. "Yes, Sandra? Sure thing. I—" She closed the line before he'd finished speaking. "So annoying," he groused with an eye roll. "Miss Thang's all in a tizzy this morning, friend."

Bailey frowned. "Why? What's going on?" It didn't take much for their boss, Sandra Callaghan, to get up in arms over something or another. When things didn't go the way she wanted, she often behaved like a spoiled child by yelling, making threats, and even closing herself up in her office for hours.

"She's expecting a client." Jason irritably sucked his teeth. "Telling me to look sharp. What, like I don't always look the part?" He gave a tug on the front of his red plaid vest and perfected the cuffs on his black, long-sleeved, silk blend, button-down shirt.

"I better get going." Bailey didn't recall there being anyone scheduled on the calendar for today. She always checked, looking days ahead in order to be prepared.

As Sandra's assistant, being at the ready was paramount in keeping her job. She'd been told by several of the staff that she was Sandra's third assistant in the past four years.

Sandra was very demanding and could sometimes be downright vengeful when the mood struck her. Even so, Bailey wasn't intimidated. The woman was a kitten compared to her previous employer. She'd been hired as an associate designer right out of college, and from day one, her previous boss made her life a living hell. *Sink or swim*, he'd told her. A long list of unfinished projects had been dropped in her lap. Most of the clients were ready to cancel their orders, and several had already done so without notification. Bailey had worked hard and somehow managed to get the work caught up.

After seeing her design plans, she'd managed to convince a large number of the clients who'd been ready to jump ship to stay on board. Having done so well, she was promoted to lead designer.

Her glory was short lived. Years of poor management caused the company to close its doors, resulting in her being without a job for nearly six months.

Taking the assistant position at Callaghan Interiors was a severe step down, but it prevented her from defaulting on her student loans. It also got her in the door of another interior design firm. She was just waiting for the opportunity to show Sandra that she was much more than a note taker and carafe handler.

Bailey jogged down the carpeted hall, passing the swatches room where the lead designer, Brian, and the buyer, Melanie, were in deep discussion leaning over a table of print layouts and scaled furniture models. "Morning, guys," she greeted, and heard them return the same as she continued on down the hall to her desk. It was stationed just outside Sandra's heavy oak double doors, which were closed. *Thank God.*

Dropping her satchel on the floor, she rushed around her desk and turned on her computer to check her calendar, quite certain she'd done so on Friday before she left.

Remembering her salad in her bag that needed to go into the refrigerator, she toed off her sneakers, went back around to the front of the desk, and took the container and her shoes out of her bag, hastily slipping the pumps on her feet.

As she turned to head for the break room, her computer sang a trailed chime of reminder pop-ups and new e-mail messages. Her concern that she'd missed a scheduled client appointment overshadowed her crisp radicchio. With her lunch in one hand, she leaned across the front of the desk and fingered the keyboard in anxious pursuit of the day's events.

Chapter Six

"Give me a minute," Lucas said to Isaac who was standing outside of the car, awaiting his exit. Isaac nodded and closed the door.

"If you prefer, I could meet with Ms. Callaghan about the renovations," Kara offered.

They sat in his limo parked outside of the building where Callaghan Interiors occupied space on the third floor.

Lucas shook his head. "No, I may as well get the reunion over with. I wouldn't be here at all if it weren't for the fact that I would have to hear my mother whine about me not giving Sandra's company the damn contract." Seeing Kara's smirk in agreement, aware of his mother's penchant for pestering him, Lucas released a long breath to gather patience in preparation to deal with Sandra again.

The Callaghan's were longtime friends of the Marx family. There had been a time when Lucas's parents, his mother primarily, expected that he and Sandra would someday tie the knot. He didn't share in that presumption. The most he'd ever committed to with Sandra was a few nights of bed play. Simply put, he couldn't see himself shackled to a woman who was even more self-serving than himself.

When Sandra realized that sex was all she would get from him, she looked to challenge her hand: "Either we move forward or it's over." She gambled and lost.

Lucas understood that it wasn't that Sandra had fallen madly in love with him. Prior to her ultimatum, he discovered that she had her own agenda. Under her father Jack Callaghan's direction, Sandra thought she'd hook him into marrying her, and then she'd work to gain back control of her father's company, Callaghan Textile Manufacturing.

Back when Jack's company was struggling, Lucas's father, Logan Marx, invested and took majority ownership of Callaghan Textile. Jack wanted it back, and he'd tried to use his daughter to get it. One of her so-called best friends, Shelly, who shared an eye for Lucas, told him of Sandra's true intentions.

After Lucas cut things off, Sandra left California to avoid the gossip in her social circle. Her father funded her interior design business, creating a subsidiary to Callaghan Textile. As the reigning heir of his deceased father's legacy, Lucas now held the majority interest in Sandra's company.

His mother still knew nothing of the Callaghans' treachery, and she remains close friends with Sandra's mother. He saw no need to tell her about their scheme. It was business, and like his father, he'd handled it.

It was no surprise when Sandra contacted him to offer her interior design services. He'd made mention in the barest sense to his mother that his home was not ready as expected when he'd arrived. She wasted no time informing Sandra that he was in need of interior design expertise. Always the matchmaker, no doubt his mother was primarily hoping it would spark a renewed interest between Sandra and him. *Not happening.*

Shaking himself free of his thoughts, having stalled long enough, Lucas handed the folders he'd been reviewing over to Kara. "See to it that Gavin receives the duplicates of the changes I've made to the Paxton-Caldwell agreement. Make sure he's brought up to date on the others as well."

"Understood. Should I have a car pick up Ms. Callaghan on Friday, or will you be escorting her?" Kara asked.

"Friday?" Lucas tried to mentally pull up his calendar.

"The art event," she said.

"Still not clear."

"It's an event that is hosted annually by the National Art Gallery. New artists compete to have their work displayed in several art galleries downtown for one year. In addition, the winner is featured in several magazines, which gets the artist's name and photos of the art out to the public. The artist must be sponsored in order to compete in the event. That's where companies like yours come in." Kara pulled a sheet from her briefcase and handed it to him, but he waved her off. "Companies that have signed up to participate select an artist from the gallery's list to sponsor—their artwork unseen to keep it fair—and so as not to try to pick out the best to win. It's a major event in this area. Both parties benefit. The artist has the potential to sell his or her work and become widely known, and the sponsor gets to show its support for the arts. Ms. Callaghan asked if you would come out in support and if Marx Venture Capital would possibly sponsor an artist. I responded on your behalf as you instructed, but since we signed up late, I haven't received the list of artists competing yet."

Lucas rubbed at the tension between his brows. His plate was already overflowing as it was. "I vaguely recall. The date seemed much farther out."

"I'm afraid not. Will you be escorting Ms. Callaghan? She has called several times."

"Fine." Though his mother would be pleased, Lucas cringed a little at the thought. He stepped out of the car. "Be back in thirty," he told Isaac as he looked up at the building before him while closing the two buttons on his Gucci, single-breasted, dark gray suit. He was more than ready to get this meeting over, especially now that he was locked into spending the evening with Sandra on Friday.

Heading to the entrance, he addressed Isaac over his shoulder. "Make that twenty."

Entering Callaghan Interiors, he chose to head back to Sandra's office instead of waiting out front. The young man came from behind the front desk and pointed while rattling off the directions, as if venturing along the linear hallway was a very complex feat to undergo.

Reaching the end of the hall, Lucas froze in his tracks. Fate was a fickle bastard and quite creative. It had tested his patience more times than he'd care to count. It was one thing to be seated in her section at the café by chance, but to see her here?

He was facing her back, but it was definitely her. He would recognize that apple-round ass and those smooth, honey-dipped runner's legs anywhere.

She was leaning across the desk, her long, bountiful curls unbound and blocking her view of him standing behind her.

Balancing her weight on one spiked heel with the other leg slightly bent back, she once again gave him a tantalizing view of her from behind in a form-fitted, mid thigh skirt. That was exactly how Lucas wanted to take her—draped over his desk, a hand tangled in her thick curls, and the other squeezing that ass while he fucked her. His cock twitched and pressed against the inside of his slacks, begging for freedom. Getting a grip, he subtly adjusted himself and straightened the front of his suit coat before saying, "Good morning."

She spun around and just about lost her poise in those designer stilts at the sight of him standing before her.

"What the ... how did you—" Her winged, dark lashes fluttered like wings on a butterfly.

At that moment, the door to his left opened, and out Sandra came wearing a wide smile. "Luke, you're here! How wonderful!"

Lucas fought not to flinch. He hated being called Luke, and the woman knew it. Bailey's gaze jumped from Sandra to him and then back to Sandra, watching as Sandra threw her long, straight, golden-blonde hair over her shoulders and sauntered toward him with an exaggerated sway in her narrow hips. Sandra took hold of his upper arms, leaned in, and kissed his cheek, then drew back. In her stilettos, they were close in height, which made it easy for the woman to gaze warmly into his eyes.

"It's so good to see you, Luke. I've missed you." She affectionately ran her palms up and down his arms as she chose to give him another kiss rather close to his mouth.

"Hello, Sandra." He glanced over Bailey's way, her stare steady, head cocked, studying their interaction.

A man came up behind him and spoke to Sandra. Lucas took the opportunity to take a slight step back out of the woman's clutches.

"Good, we're all here," Sandra said. "Brian, this is Lucas Marx. He will be entrusting us to complete the renovations on his home." Sandra turned back to him. "Brian here is my chief designer, and Bailey Walters is my assistant. If you need anything and cannot reach me, you can contact her. She's a gem."

Lucas shook Brian's hand, then faced Bailey with his hand extended. Her cold, green gaze spoke volumes.

"Pleased to meet you, Mr. Marx."

"My pleasure, Miss Walters." He gave a light squeeze of her hand before he released it. Her finely arched brows pinched a fraction, allowing her relaxed, professional guise to falter. He got a glimpse of the indignation she hid behind it.

"Well, let us go to my office." Sandra led the way.

Lucas took the chair to Bailey's right at the small, round table. She gave him a narrow side look and subtly rolled her chair away, widening the space between them.

Sandra practically butted her chair to his and jumped right into the meeting. "Your assistant e-mailed me a layout of the property, along with the work that has been completed, and a list of what remains to be done. Brian will need to schedule a time with you to view the site. It's important we get a look at what's there to see if we can incorporate the current decor into our design plans." She smiled sweetly at him and then addressed Brian, "You are to clear your calendar for Mr. Marx."

Brian nodded. "What time-table are we looking at? Would you like to schedule a walk-through on—" His cell phone rang. He pulled it from his pocket and checked the display. "I'm sorry, I have to take this. It's the customs agent returning my call. It shouldn't take long, please excuse me." He exited the room.

Sandra's smile remained. "There's an artifact we've been trying to get cleared through customs," she explained. "While we wait for Brian, I want to thank you for agreeing to become a supporter of the arts, Luke. Kara phoned just before you arrived to tell me you'd signed up Marx Venture Capital. The art expo is a really great event. We'll have a wonderful time. I even found the perfect black dress to accompany these." She winked and pushed her hair behind her left ear, revealing a large diamond stud. He stared at the stone vacantly. "You don't remember, do you?" Her tone dropped a scale, clearly disappointed.

"Should I?" Lucas tried not to show that he didn't give a shit. He gave a glimpse over at Bailey and connected with cold, green daggers.

"I would think you should. They arrived as a surprise from you for my twenty-fifth birthday. Now do you remember?"

His response was a light shrug of a shoulder. He always had Kara send jewelry, and she knew what to get based on his level of interest in the woman. Earrings came in third before bracelet. A few had lasted long enough to receive a pendant necklace, and there hadn't been a woman worth considering that number one stone.

Lucas sat back casually in his chair, half listening to the woman on his right, for his mind was consumed by the woman to his left.

He chanced another look at Bailey; her gaze flickered from Sandra to him and then back to Sandra with a look crossing between astonishment and irritation. He shared those feelings. It annoyed him that Sandra would openly discuss their previous involvement in front of her assistant—in front of Bailey, of all people.

They all looked up when Brian poked his head into the room. "Excuse me. Sandra, can I see you for a moment? The customs rep needs to speak to you about the licensing."

"Uh, sure." Sandra turned to Lucas and lightly touched his forearm. "I'm truly sorry about this. I'll be right back." She stood up and spoke to Bailey on her way to the door, "Please give Mr. Marx—"

"Lucas," he turned to Bailey, "just Lucas."

"Please give *Lucas* a cup of coffee. He likes it black ... no sugar." Sandra gave him a playful wink and stepped out of the room.

"I'm aware," Lucas heard Bailey murmur as she rose from her chair and walked over to the sidebar. Returning to the table, she set the cup before him and took her seat, centering her attention on her portfolio.

Awkward silence.

"It seems we're having that morning coffee after all," he said. She cut a hard side look at him. Lucas countered with a half grin before taking a sip from his cup. He frowned and forced a swallow. "What is this?"

Flipping aimlessly through her portfolio, she uttered, "It's hazelnut, and *we're* not having coffee, you are." She swung her chair around, arms folded beneath her breasts, brows low, and legs crossed, squaring off with him as she whispered, "You've got some nerve trying to hook up with me last night when you have a girlfriend. The damn nerve of you!"

"Girlfriend? Do you always leap first, Miss Walters?"

"What are you talking about? Do I look stupid to you? It's obvious you and Sandra have a thing," she bit out.

He couldn't suppress his grin at her outrage. "I see those hot, green sparks are back."

She frowned, looking not at all amused. "What is that supposed to mean?"

Lucas's gaze roamed over her delicate features and wealth of curls on down, tracing the contours of her breasts outlined in the red silk blouse, the size appearing a bit weightier than he remembered from the night before. His eyes dipped to her smooth, bare legs. *Legs I'd like to have wrapped around my back.* He brought his gaze back up to her curls, lingering there.

"It's just as I thought."

"Wh-what?" She tensed and reared away from his hand reaching out toward her breasts.

His eyes came up, meeting hers. "Your hair." He lifted several locks and rubbed the silk strands between his fingers. "Beautiful." Her hair was tugged from his hold.

"Don't touch me," she hissed low and rolled her chair away.

On a sigh, he pushed the awful coffee aside. "You have it wrong here."

"You don't like the term *girlfriend*?" She whipped her head around, glowering. "Then let me rephrase—*fuck buddy*. What, Sandra's not doing it for you? Or are you looking to spice things up, splash some color into the mix? A threesome?"

Lucas cocked a brow and fought not to laugh at her palpable fury. "A threesome? You're full of surprises, Miss Walters."

Just then, the door opened, and Brian and Sandra entered, reclaiming their seats.

"We're sorry about that. Now, where were we?" Sandra cast a long look at Bailey, who was fumbling with her papers. "Bailey, did you refresh Luke's cup?"

"She offered and I declined," Lucas said, and he and Bailey exchanged knowing looks that had nothing to do with that god-awful coffee.

"Sandra, if Mr. Marx approves, Bailey could take this one," Brian suggested. "Mr. Marx, if I may say, sir, I've reviewed the specs on the work that's left to be completed on your home. Though there are some areas that are raw, and the completed work will need to be inspected, I feel that what's left, Bailey can handle. She has helped me on several projects and has really great ideas. She was actually the lead interior designer at her prior employer." Brian nodded to Bailey for support. "Your renovations would be a great place for her to demonstrate her skills. Her credentials are right there in front of you." Ignoring the heated look Sandra shot his way and the stunned stare Bailey did not mask, Brian slid the portfolio over. "See for yourself, she's very talented. If you would accept her as the lead, I can be her second if she requires my assistance, but I don't foresee it." He subtly winked at Bailey, who managed a weak smile in return. "If you give her a chance, you'll not regret it."

"I don't think that would be wise, Brian," Sandra chimed in. "I appreciate you helping Brian and all that you do, Bailey, but I don't feel this project is one where I would chance."

"These are very impressive," Lucas remarked as he flipped through her portfolio. He looked Bailey directly in the eyes and asked, "Do you feel you could fulfill all my needs, Miss Walters?"

With Brian chuckling at the double entendre, her eyelids fluttered, clearly discerning what he meant. "I think—" she began.

"I'm sure that didn't come out right," Brian cut in, still chuckling.

Oh, it came out just the way Lucas had intended. "Well, Miss Walters?"

"If given the opportunity, I'm confident that I can finish your renovations to your complete satisfaction and stay on budget, Mr. Marx," she said, her challenging stare upon him unwavering.

"I don't—"

Lucas jerked his head to Sandra, and she clammed up. He was sure her forehead would crack open from the severe frown she displayed. Unconcerned, he turned back to Bailey. "If you're free tonight, we can get together." Again, they exchanged a look, and he grinned a bit impishly. Her frigid stare said the chances of them *getting together* were about as likely as him getting out of his Friday evening meet up with Sandra.

"I can come by tonight, Mr. Marx." Clinically professional was her tone.

"Then it's settled." He stood up, and they all followed suit. "Be there at seven this evening. If you arrive before me, let yourself in and take a look around. My assistant will stop by later with the key." He headed for the door, but paused when Bailey called to him.

"What's the budget?" she asked.

"There isn't one." Lucas left the office with a smile. He'd just been handed his honey-dipped princess on a silver platter.

Chapter Seven

Bailey parked her car at the curb and got out. She didn't use the circular driveway for fear her car would leak oil on the pristine gray cobblestone.

"Be there at seven," she mouthed irritably to herself, recalling that same highhanded tone she'd heard Lucas use when he was speaking on his cell phone the night before.

Sighing out her irritation, she hiked up the long, stone pathway over to the security panel encased in pristine white brick and entered in the code that Lucas's assistant, Kara Kennedy, had given her. The heavy, black iron security gates slowly parted.

Stepping through, she trekked up to the foot of the grand curved front steps. A portico flanked by four twenty-foot-tall white stone columns protected and gave presence to a pair of stately arched, rich mahogany French doors with artfully designed iron grill inlays, set in rectangular, double-pane glass.

Bailey stared up at the massive white-brick structure and then looked around, admiring the three-tier fountain in the center of the circular driveway, to the immaculate landscape beyond. She would've expected him to be a penthouse in the sky kind of guy. "Why would one man need this much house?" she muttered as she climbed the ten stairs to the landing and pressed the doorbell that sang out a lengthy chime. *It's none of my business.* After a second attempt, receiving no answer, she pulled out the key from her bag and took a deep breath. "Bailey, you can do this." Turning the lock, she stepped inside.

The entryway floor was an ecru marble. A simple, yet artful, round floor medallion greeted those entering the home. A wrought iron chandelier dropped down a good thirty feet from the second-floor ceiling. Four Doric columns in an ecru shade, two on either side, balanced the opulent foyer.

Dark chocolate Brazilian hardwood stairs, with off-white stair risers and black iron rails, curved upward to the second floor on both the left and the right.

She scribbled in her notepad and marked up the specs as she moved about the house.

"Oh my!" Entering an enormous sunken great room, aside from the sparse furnishings in such a large space, a wall of glass with three sets of glass French doors greeted her, letting in an abundance of natural light. Outside, beyond the covered stone terrace, was an enormous swimming pool surrounded by strategically placed greenery and colorful flowerbeds. She went over and stepped outside to get a better view of the beautiful showcase.

A rock waterfall flowed into the deep end. A hot tub bubbled invitingly within its own botanical garden at the shallow end, casting a circled pool of blue luminous light.

To the right, beyond a large bed of rose bushes, was a fenced-in tennis court.

Off in the distance, mature evergreens and thick brush surrounded the property on all sides, offering privacy and tranquility.

Breathtaking. It was the only way to describe the exquisitely designed and impeccably landscaped grounds.

As she made notes to replace the outdoor low-end furnishings, she inspected the pool house across the way, then headed back inside the main dwelling.

Looking around, there was little that needed altering—the changes were primarily cosmetic.

It was interesting peering into Lucas Marx's life on such an intimate level, Bailey thought. In a way, she was getting to know him through his home. Not that she cared to get to know the man at all after what she'd witnessed this afternoon between him and Sandra.

He was handsome, she'd admit. She was shamefully attracted to him. She'd admit that, too. But she now knew that he was a womanizer, and dating her boss, which made keeping their involvement strictly professional very easy.

Getting back to her job, she noted that his color scheme suggested that he liked earth tones. An abstract piece Sienna painted long ago came to mind. It would work perfectly over the fireplace. Jotting a note to speak with Sienna about her artwork, she headed to the kitchen.

"Dear lord!" There wasn't a kitchen. The room lacked cabinetry and appliances, except for a small refrigerator stationed within a large wall niche. A center island that looked to have been under construction by the previous designer was merely a large, wooden square box. The stairs leading to the second level from the kitchen were bare wood planks.

Bailey hastily whipped out her measuring tape and went to work laying out a design plan. Soon she had a vision of the finished result in her head.

After a thorough review of seven spacious bedrooms, each with its own bathroom en suite, finding them all in order, she made her way to bedroom eight—the master suite at the end of the hall.

It was a surprise to see how well appointed it was and how warm and invited she felt in it. She'd expected ... well, she wasn't sure what she'd expected, but she surely didn't think she'd find an elegantly understated decor.

She could fall hard for a man who knew how to piece together a room such as this. Quickly erasing the thought from her head, she went over to the French doors/glass wall to take in the view of the pool below and looked out over the beautiful secluded acres. Then she gave the bedroom and connecting bathroom a full inspection. Both were nicely decorated in varying hues of dark brown, off-white, and camel.

Nothing for me to do here.

On her way out, she realized she hadn't checked the closet. Crossing the space to the double doors, she entered to find an area the size of Sienna's and her apartment.

"My goodness!"

Behind glass enclosures, suits—close to thirty or so, some with tags still attached—and shirts hung in pristine order by color, light to dark. Light sensors activated on as she moved past the glass. That element gave her an idea for the kitchen design.

Her eyes zeroed in on the neatly arranged racks of shoes. The tips of her fingers lightly brushed across several pairs of expensive, well-polished leather before picking up one shoe.

"Size fourteen." *Big feet, big hands, big ... Bailey, don't go there.* She placed the shoe back on the shelf, gave another quick look around, and decided that the closet was fine. On her way out, she noticed a sneaker haphazardly lying halfway underneath the black leather dressing chair. Looking around for its mate, she got down on her knees and found it wedged far beneath the shelf.

"Almost got it." The tips of her fingers brushed the heel. She dropped to her stomach and got under a bit farther. The darn sneaker was stuck tight under there. "I'll get you," she grunted.

"Brian was right, you're very thorough."

"Oh God!" Bailey gasped. That familiar male voice had her quickly rolling over to her back, feeling as though she'd have a heart attack right there on the floor. The organ was slamming against her ribs like a jackhammer as she lay sprawled out with Lucas Marx staring down at her.

"It … I …" Unable to speak articulately between shallow clips of air, she held up the left sneaker clutched in her hand.

"Good evening, Miss Walters."

Bailey tried to catch her breath, which was sawing in and out as though she'd just run a marathon.

His eyes dipped down and lingered on her skirt raised high up her thighs. She tugged it down and shot him a hard frown.

"May I?" He reached out his hand to help her up and then retrieved the stuck sneaker from underneath the shelf, placing the pair on the bottom shoe rack.

"So you tidy up *and* design," he said as he rested back against his dressing island with arms folded across his suited frame.

"I happened to notice the one under your chair. The other one was wedged tight." When he said nothing, not so much as a flicker in those blue-grays, Bailey cleared the knot in her throat and picked up her notepad from the chair. "I've just about completed my inventory of your home." Needing to escape his stare, she quickly left the closet. "This area is in perfect order. I find the furnishings and decor to be favorable, well-balanced for the space. I wouldn't change a thing in here."

Looking over at the custom size bed, Sandra popped into her head. He came up behind her, so close she could feel his body heat radiating against her back, and with it, his scent—a fresh, subtle woodsy and citrus mix. *Man, he smells good.* Bailey inhaled his scent into her lungs before turning to face him.

Towering over her, he had to be about six feet, three or four inches—and she thought of her shoes in her bag downstairs, wishing she was wearing her heels instead of her sneakers. Those extra inches would prevent her from having to crane her neck to look at him.

His eyes were staring uncomfortably deep into hers, causing her stomach to flutter. Needing to put some space between them, she walked over to the French doors and looked out over the landscape. "Your kitchen, I have some ideas I'd like to share with you on the type and style of cabinetry. Of course, top grade appliances and—" Hearing the bed lightly squeak, she paused, and turned around. He was seated at the foot of the bed. *When did he remove his suit coat and tie?*

"Come here," he said.

There was that bossy tone again. Annoyed, Bailey folded her arms beneath her breasts. "Come here?" She tried not to, but her eyes kept slipping downward to the broad expanse of his chest, on down to the sinewy outline of his thick thighs in his perfectly fitted slacks. *This is madness, Bailey, stop it.* "Come here? What do I look like to you, a Chihuahua?"

"You look like a woman I've wanted to kiss from the moment we met."

Her eyes popped wide and sprung up from admiring his exceptional build to see his gaze locked on her mouth. *Good gracious.* She inwardly groaned, hating that she was so attracted to him, loathing how just a look from the man once again heated the crotch of her panties. *Keep it professional.* It was becoming more difficult than she'd expected. He was incredibly sexy and gorgeous. *He's seeing your boss.* Recalling his interaction with Sandra earlier helped immensely.

Squaring her shoulders, she said pointedly, "Look, Mr. Marx, do you wish to go over my notes or not?"

"It's Lucas." He rested back on his forearms, the wondrous bulk of his frame spread out in an enticing invitation. "Come here, please."

Bailey walked over and stood directly in front of him to show he didn't intimidate her. *Liar.*

"Shoot, I'm all ears."

As he moistened his lips, his gaze traveled slowly up and down the length of her body and settled on her breasts. He was looking at her like a hungry lion ready to pounce.

Swallowing to remove the lump in her throat once more, she began. "Uh, okay. Well, as I said, I have some ideas for the kitchen, and the uh, the ... the ..." She shook her head and waved a hand out over his casual comportment. "I can't do this with you like that." *Looking all lush and sexy.* Her attention dropped to the lines on her notepad.

He sat up, which brought her between his legs. "Is this better?" His grin was sinfully wicked.

She glared at the maddening levity of his expression and didn't move when he inched to the very edge, coming face level with her breasts. His eyes were laser fixed there, not at all being subtle at his ogling of *her* body.

With a wave of a hand between them to make her point, she said sternly, "Let's get something straight, buster. This isn't gonna happen."

"Buster?" He chuckled. "Your southern roots are showing, love. I like it." He laughed more at seeing her scowl. "I find it very sexy."

That deepened her frown. "I'm not going to be your—"

"Fuck buddy?" he put in and smirked with a playful wiggle of his brows.

"I'm not going to be your anything. Your girlfriend, who happens to be my boss, gave me strict instructions to not 'screw this up,'" she stressed with air quotes. "I need my job, and I'm not about to jeopardize it for a quick lay."

"I hadn't planned on it being quick." He winked, maintaining his devilish grin, continuing to taunt her.

Bailey smirked, unable to hold it in. "You're impossible. It's not happening, Mr. Marx."

"Sandra is not my girlfriend," he stated with a hard-set countenance. "Our time together was brief. She wanted more. I didn't. End of story."

"Well, she clearly intends to revive whatever it was you two had, and I'm not getting caught in the middle." She held his stare, refusing to back down. "I have an engagement later. If you don't mind, I'd like to get started with my review."

"Where might that be, if you don't mind me asking?"

"In Georgetown. I'm meeting friends at a club there where one of them plays in a band." She would've sworn his right eye twitched in reaction.

"Would that be Kevin?"

She blinked, surprised. "How do you know his name?"

"Your friend Sienna mentioned him last night. Is Kevin your boyfriend?"

"What?"

"Or is he *your* fuck buddy?" A slow smile lit the cool pools of his eyes.

Bailey bit the inside of her cheek to avoid smiling at that. He was throwing her words back at her.

"So, which one is it, Bailey?" He leaned forward, his nose coming within a hair of her cleavage, and inhaled deep. "Hmm, you smell good."

She took a half step back. "Kevin is a good friend. We dated briefly. It didn't work out. End of story."

He rose to his feet and took a step forward, coming into her personal space. "So, I'm not seeing anyone, and you're not seeing anyone."

Holding her ground, Bailey took a quiet breath, allowing the sudden sputter of her pulse to settle. Then her eyes locked with his steady stare. "Mr. Marx, we have work to do. Enough of this." Her firm command lacked conviction even in her own ears.

He responded with a light stroke of his fingers along her left cheek as he slowly leaned in, the right angle of his jaw but a scant inch from hers, and whispered in her ear, "I want you."

Warm breath feathered against the side of her neck. A wet tongue followed the curve of her ear. *Sweet mercy!* Her pussy throbbed. The notepad and pen slipped from her hand.

"Mr.—" Her weak protest faltered as soft lips skated along the contours of her chin to her mouth. With his right hand secured at her nape, he tasted her unhurriedly, jockeying the rapid rise and fall of her sputtering heartbeat. The tip of his tongue teased her lips, licking the top, then the bottom before delving into the deep cavern of her mouth. Hungrily at first, then incredibly gentle. The act was so overwhelmingly sensual, she found herself encircling her arms around his neck and leaning into his hard planes, wanting to wrap herself around his magnificent strength. He freed one button on her blouse, then another, and slipped his hand inside, capturing her right breast through her bra. His thumb teased and fingers pinched the overly sensitive nipple with excruciating thoroughness. A powerful arm circled her waist; his fierce erection pressed against her stomach. They kissed, licked, nipped, tongues mating as their bodies rocked into the ever-rising sensations.

Feeling his splayed palm scorch a path up her inner thigh beneath her skirt and graze his fingers along her feminine lips through her panties, she stiffened, catapulting out of her passion haze. She managed to break away from his starving kisses and stepped back to dislodge his hands from her body. "We-we have to stop," she breathed heavily. His chest heaved out deep breaths, as his eyes smoldered with raw, unadulterated desire. There was no denying what she saw in his gaze, and what she'd felt rubbing against her lower belly. She'd let things get out of hand. This was wrong on so many levels. "We shouldn't do this. I'm sorry." It came out in a hoarse whisper as she quickly buttoned up, then picked up her pen and pad from the floor. "I should finish up the review."

His stare at her unblinking, he adjusted his erection in his slacks, forcing her to take note of the sexual frustration she'd provoked as he said, "All right, Miss Walters, you wish to discuss the renovations?" He inclined his head at the notepad in her hand.

"Yes, I would." There was a coldness now conveyed in his gaze. If she was being truthful with herself, she wanted to press him back on that thick comforter, straddle those muscular thighs of his, and fuck his brains out. Her throat was suddenly dry, her nipples ached, and there was a renewed warm pool of moisture between her legs.

"Bailey?"

"Yes?" Bailey blinked, her thoughts of him naked derailed, thankfully. "Yes ... I mean, let's get started." She began flipping through her notepad.

"No."

"No?" Her gaze followed him to the door.

"You're going to take me through each area that needs attention and explain how you intend to fix it."

She regarded his rigid demeanor. Gone was the playful teasing and bright white smile, having been replaced by the heavy-handed, all-business side of him, of which she was becoming quite familiar. It was as though what had taken place only a minute ago between them had never happened.

"Okay. If that's what you would prefer."

"That's what I prefer." Without another word, he left the room. She ran to catch up to him.

• • •

Bailey came home to an empty apartment. It was expected. Sienna and Faith were at the club with Kevin and Diego. She felt bad that she hadn't met up with them as promised and would get an earful from Sienna, and even double that from Kevin. She simply was both physically and mentally exhausted.

Following their groping and kissing session that left her body humming like a simmering tea kettle long after, Lucas had her go through every room in his home, and he asked a thousand questions in each. She even appraised his game room, home theater, fully functioning gym, full-size racquetball court and large sauna, and the garage where his silver Ferrari was parked alongside a silver Bentley Continental GT, a metallic black Porsche Cayman S, and a Buell racing bike that was perched up high on a wide ledge. *What does it matter whether the garage is painted dark gray or light gray? I mean really?* They stood in the space for nearly thirty minutes contemplating that ridiculous decision.

She started to think he was intentionally trying to keep her there. As the night wore on, she made mention again of her engagement, to which Lucas casually stated that Sienna would understand. She then spoke of Faith, Kevin, and Diego. At that, Lucas made it a point to remind her of her priorities. Through it all, he kept their interaction strictly business—not a tease, flirt, chuckle, or compliment came her way from him. His stare when their eyes met was ever deep and all consuming, yet his tone remained dry the entire evening. His behavior messed with her head.

The digital clock on the nightstand read 10:46 P.M. She didn't waste time peeling out of her clothes, sent a quick text to Sienna to say she wouldn't make it to the club, and then crawled into bed, easily dozing off with a picture of Lucas Marx and the sweet taste of his kiss front and center in her brain.

Chapter Eight

"What are your plans today, Faith?" Bailey bit into her toast and sipped her cranberry juice as she eyed Faith over the rim of her glass.

"Nothing much—catch up with some friends, I guess." Standing at the stove, Faith flipped the pancake and turned the Canadian bacon in the skillet.

"Good morning. Yum! That smells wonderful!" Sienna entered the kitchen dressed in her docent white button-down blouse and black skirt suit. She took the plate Faith handed her and sat at the island across from Bailey.

"We had a good time last night didn't we, Faith?" She stuck a piece of bacon in her mouth and gave a look over her shoulder. "You and Diego seemed to hit it off."

"Yeah, Diego is a cutie. He's an awesome drummer." Faith turned off the stove, brought her plate to the island, and took a seat on the empty stool next to Sienna. "Now Kevin on the other hand ... hot. Bailey, Kevin expected you to show up." She smothered her pancakes in maple syrup, adding, "He's really sexy, and I'm digging the blond dreads."

Bailey eyed Faith over her juice glass. The girl always had to size up every man she met.

"Kev did keep an eye on his watch until I told him that you'd texted and were gonna be a no show," Sienna told her. "We missed you, but I'm glad you finally got a design project. That's awesome, girlfriend." She reached across the narrow Formica countertop and gave Bailey a hug.

"I know I'd promised Kevin that I'd be there, but Lu ... my client is very demanding." Bailey had intentionally left out of her text to Sienna that her first assignment was none other than Lucas Marx's home. "I didn't leave his home until after ten. He—" she started.

"He!" Sienna and Faith burst out loudly in unison, and Sienna smirked, asking, "Is *he* hot? Will *he* make it difficult for you to keep your mind on your duties, Miss Walters?" she teased and Faith laughed.

Remembering the feel of Lucas's soft lips against hers, the sweet glide of his warm tongue, and his big, strong hand between her thighs, Bailey's core pulsed with unquenched need. Add to it the dream she'd had of Lucas's face burrowed between her thighs, if Sienna only knew how right on the mark she was with that one. That reminded Bailey. "I may have sold one of your art pieces."

Sienna jumped up. "Oh my God! Seriously?"

"Do you still have the one you painted in college? That large abstract oil painting of dark and light browns, with tan, burnt orange, and red splashes on black canvas?"

"I remember that one. It's beautiful," Faith said.

"I have all my work in storage. Does he really want it?"

Sienna's voice was skeptical. She'd sold a piece here and there over the years, but nothing to really speak of. To have someone even consider her piece was big, Bailey understood. "I have to show it to him first, but I'm sure I can convince him. It would work well with his decor."

"Yes! That's awesome!" Sienna did a happy tap dance, spun around, and then quickly sobered, hugging her again. "Bails, girl, thanks for looking out."

"Don't thank me yet. He has to sign off on it." As Bailey finished off her juice, she contemplated whether she should reveal the name of her client. *Why not? He's just a client, an assignment, nothing more.* "Here's the thing. My client is Lucas Marx."

"No way!" Sienna gasped around her mouthful of pancake. "How?"

"Why does that name sounds so familiar?" Faith asked.

Bailey got up and went to the sink to wash her plate and juice glass. "Apparently, the man is involved with my boss." She smirked at Sienna's trail of curse words. "He says their history is just that, history, but it's whatever." A shrug. "He's still trying to hook up with me, but I'm not jeopardizing my job by sleeping with him." *Kissing the man like a starved-craving addict doesn't count.*

"Wait." Faith left the kitchen and ran to Sienna's bedroom.

Sienna dropped back down on the stool. "Does he think you're gonna spread your legs if he gives you the work on his home? The bastard." She stuck a piece of bacon in her mouth, chewed, and wagged her fork between them. "I don't want him to have my painting. It's good you turned his ass down, too. Who does he think he is? You keep that shit strictly business. Don't go there with him and end up losing your job."

Bailey dried her dishes and utensils and put them away, then went over to the island. "Lucas was just as surprised to see me working at Callaghan's as I was to see him standing there. It wasn't his idea to put me on the project. It was the lead designer, Brian. Sandra wasn't thrilled about it, but since Lucas gave the okay, Sandra wasn't about to go against his decision. As for your art, you're not passing up this opportunity. Your work is spectacular. Who knows, some of his rich friends could see it and want a Sienna original." Bailey and Sienna looked over as Faith returned carrying Sienna's laptop.

"Look." Faith set the computer on the island between them. "I knew his name was familiar. It was the case my dad was involved in—Marx Venture Capital, MVC, almost ten years ago. It was Logan Marx that I remembered. He's Lucas Marx's father ... or was. He's dead now. The case had something to do with unfair business practices by MVC. My dad was caught up in that mess involving this guy." Faith pointed to the picture on the screen.

"Yes, I remember." Sienna looked at Bailey. "You don't know about the case?"

Bailey shook her head. "No, what happened?"

"In a nutshell, MVC was essentially strong-arming companies, stripping desperate owners of their business by acquiring them at low cost with an understanding to keep them on, but then they'd turn around and sell, leaving the former owners with nothing—something along those lines. It was alleged that Faith's father got bought off, which resulted in Logan Marx and MVC being absolved of all charges."

Faith frowned. "It wasn't true. My dad didn't break the law."

Sienna lightly touched her forearm. "Sweetie, I didn't say he did. I was merely explaining to Bailey what happened." At Faith's nod, Sienna tapped Logan Marx's image on the screen. "Anyway, that was this guy's deal, not Lucas's. He shouldn't be blamed for what his father did. I sure as hell wouldn't want to suffer for the sins of my mother, that's for damn sure."

Thinking of Sienna's drug-addicted mother and all that she'd endured because of it, Bailey took her friend's hand, and gave it a light supportive squeeze.

Sienna clicked a link and read the article. "It says here that at twenty-eight, *Fortune* and *Forbes* named Lucas Marx the fourth youngest millionaire CEO." She clicked a *Vanity Fair* link next that pictured him in an article with a crown hovering just above his head. The title read, "Multi-millionaire Playboy Heir Lucas Marx May Soon Wear the Crown *Billionaire* ... Stay Tuned."

"Look, it says, 'Following Logan Marx's heart attack and subsequent death, the son took the reins of Marx Venture Capital (MVC) and restored the family name to its former glory in a short span of three years.'"

"Yes, but see this." Bailey directed their attention farther down the article. "It also says, 'It would seem the powerhouse, Lucas Marx, is a force to be reckoned with, both in the boardroom ... and the boudoir.' Typical," she scoffed.

Faith clicked on another article headline showing Lucas's picture in an inset shot on the cover of *Fortune* with the title "Man on a Mission." "That's your client? Damn, Bails, he's super smoking hot. You get to decorate his home?"

Bailey clicked back to the previous article and stared at a younger Lucas. The image showed him leaving the courthouse in step with his father and a third man, Logan Marx's attorney, it read. She then clicked another link that had Lucas's name highlighted following the words *HIV/AIDS Awareness Celebrity Fundraiser*. It showed Lucas speaking to a reporter with his arm around the waist of a tall redhead. The article stated he was a big contributor to the HIV/AIDS Foundation, along with a host of other charities. All of his business achievements and philanthropic endeavors were nice to know, but Bailey was more interested in the redhead standing beside him. Like Sandra, she was your typical tall, slender, beautiful armpiece, exactly how Bailey pictured Lucas's type to be.

The Internet showed him with several different women, all having attributes similar to Sandra and the redhead. It had Bailey wondering why he was interested in her. She wasn't unattractive, but she surely didn't fit the mold Lucas apparently liked.

"Hey, if you don't want him, I'll take him."

Bailey's head shot up to Faith with eyelids instantly narrowing to slits. *She didn't just say that!* After everything with Andrew, the girl should know better.

She closed the laptop, grabbed her salad from the refrigerator, and gathered her things to leave. It was either that or she'd slap Faith hard where she stood.

"Really, Faith?" Sienna shook her head.

"I was joking, Bails." Faith trailed behind her. "I wouldn't have said it if I'd known you were interested."

Fuming, Bailey spun to face her. "I never said I was interested! I'm working for the man!" she shouted. "This opportunity is very important to me. I don't need to be concerned that you'll somehow mess it up by trying to fuck him." She was angrier over the fact that she felt territorial of Lucas than Faith's stupid-ass comment, but she wasn't about to tell her that.

"Sorry, Bailey, I didn't mean it. I swear." Her arms stretched open for a hug. "We're okay? Bails, it was stupid. I'm really sorry."

She stared at the peace offering. The girl always knew how to push her hot button.

Sienna stepped in between them. "She didn't mean anything by it. It was a joke. Given the history with you two, a bad one." She shook her head at Faith again. "But no harm intended."

Bailey took a breath, letting the irritation wane, then nodded, and stepped into the embrace. "Yeah, we're good."

"Well, now that that's settled, we have to get to work. You know that hunk o' junk of yours needs to warm up even in summer," Sienna teased in her usual way to lighten the atmosphere on her way out the door.

Bailey watched Faith bounce about the kitchen, tidying up. "The spare key is in the drawer to your left. Be sure to lock up."

"Will do." Faith's straight white teeth gleamed. "Hope your day goes well."

"Same to you." Bailey headed out wondering if this was the calm before the Faith storm. And when the tide hit, would she need a life jacket?

Chapter Nine

"What do you mean they want to negotiate the offer?" Lucas shifted his eyes to his assistant standing beside him and bit out firmly, "Negotiation is not an option." The elevator doors opened. He stalked down the hall to his office.

"I reiterated your terms and your intent to not lay off Paxton-Caldwell Laboratories' key researchers once the deal goes through." Kara rushed ahead to open the door, his stride not missing a beat.

Lucas sat down behind his desk and grabbed the two contracts sitting in his inbox, which she'd placed in it days ago, still waiting for second reviews.

"Then what's the problem?" he half barked.

"Among other things, Mr. Caldwell said the terms don't guarantee that he and his partner will remain following the transition of ownership. They want you to nearly double your offer if you want to hold the majority. Both partners have highlighted the changes they're proposing." She handed him the document across his desk. "I've sent you an electronic copy of it as usual."

Lucas knew why Caldwell questioned his motives. Among other issues, under his father's tenure, MVC had developed a reputation for investing in companies that had great ideas, and some had patented technology, but lacked adequate funding to produce. Logan Marx would set the terms with him, taking majority ownership, and once the company prospered, he would sell high without any negotiation of job security for the staff and top managers.

Lucas had worked hard at erasing MVC's negative image. Now that he was running the company, he ensured fair terms in all his acquisitions. Nevertheless, some companies tried to gouge him, using MVC's past transgressions as leverage, knowing he would want to keep the company image favorable in the public eye.

Thumbing through the yellow tabbed pages, he stood and turned toward the windows. This cat-and-mouse game was nothing new. It didn't normally get under his skin. It was that damn green-eyed vixen dancing around in his head that had him riled. He'd lost sleep thinking about their kiss and the warm feel of her silky soft lips, the taste of her tongue. Her breasts would be a handful ... and mouthful for that matter. He could capture her tiny waist in one hand. And he'd love to run his hands up and down those smooth, toned legs of hers. Picturing her firm, plump ass, he bit back a groan.

Last night, beating off to that mental image he had of her bent over that desk was the only way he could clear his head to fall asleep.

What is Kevin really to her?

When Bailey had mentioned that she had plans to see her ex-boyfriend/*friend*, Kevin, Lucas made a point to keep her at his home for as long as he could. He didn't give two shits about the color of that damn garage. He'd asked her mundane question after question about the interior design specs, anything that would detain her long enough that she would be too worn out to visit and perhaps end up in bed with Kevin. Her fighting not to yawn in front of him was the only reason he'd let up.

She likely went to Kevin last night anyway. Not wishing to go there in his head, he looked out over the cityscape to the Washington Monument off in the distance, thinking over his next move regarding the woman. Like Paxton-Caldwell Laboratories, and so many other acquisitions before it where he'd come out the victor, Bailey Walters would be no different.

"I want you to get me info on a Sienna Keller. Start with Nuagé Café and Lounge where she waitresses." Lucas knew what he had to do.

"I beg your pardon?"

He turned around and met Kara's quizzical stare. "I want to know where she is at this precise moment. Find as much info on her as you can. Try LinkedIn, Facebook, whatever you can."

"Understood. What about the Paxton-Caldwell proposal?"

Lucas frowned. "I'm doing them a favor as it is with the amount I'm shelling out on the damn company. If it weren't for the guarantee of tripling my investment, I'd just as soon pull my funding, and then all their asses would be looking for a job. You make it clear to Caldwell that I'm his company's only chance for survival. Either they agree to the terms or I walk. And where the hell is my general manager? Gavin's plane was due in last night. These proposals are piling up. Have him—"

"Good morning to you, too." Gavin ambled into the office still wearing his blackout sunglasses. "Damn, man, I could hear you howling through the walls." He ambled over to the bar, poured a glass of water, and spread out his long frame comfortably on the leather couch. "I took an earlier flight last night and went downtown. My brain is still in stasis, so if you don't mind." Lowering his sunglasses down the bridge of his nose, he gave Kara a glance. "Miss Kennedy, you're looking beautiful as ever."

Lucas looked between them. Kara's earth-brown hair was pulled into its usual neat bun atop her head. Not a hair was out of place as her russet-brown eyes homed in on her work.

"Good morning, Mr. Crane," she said without looking up from her iPad.

Gavin tipped his water glass to her, and then set his sunglasses on the side table. "Who knew, D.C. has some pretty good hang spots."

Lucas shot him a narrowed glare. They'd been best friends since the age of six. Even back then, if there was mischief to be had,

Gavin would be at the center of it. His Irish roots were forever front and center whenever he saw an opportunity for a good time.

"You're not in the city a minute and you find a bar?"

The man shrugged as he insouciantly sipped his water. "I would've phoned to see if you wanted to join me, but I met this smoking hot Brazilian on the flight. She was in town for some sort of photo shoot and wanted to blow off some steam beforehand." Grinning, he blew out a breath and shook his head. "Man, she was ..." He gave a glimpse at Kara, who was frowning back at him.

"Give us a minute," Lucas told her.

Kara stood up. "Here's the list of companies and the artists participating in the event on Friday. I've checked off the few who are still unsponsored and will pick from the list on your behalf later today." She set the paper on his desk and left the room.

When the door closed, Lucas said, "You should've been reviewing these instead of out scouting pussy." He rounded his desk, went over, and tossed the two thick proposals onto Gavin's stomach.

"Hey!" Gavin jumped up, spilling his water on his suit coat. He placed the glass on the coffee table in front of him and brushed at the water splotches on his tie. "Damn, Lucas, was that really necessary? Maybe I should've called you last night. Haven't fed the snake lately, brother?" he teased.

"Fuck you." Bailey's tantalizing body bent over the desk and her spread out on his closet floor: the images danced around on a reel in Lucas's head.

Gavin chuckled. "I'll pass on the offer. I only do females."

Lucas's glare narrowed more as he took a seat in the leather armchair. "Gavin, I want updates."

"As for these," Gavin picked up the documents and fanned the pages, "I reviewed the copies Kara sent over, and I've sent back your counter offer to each company. The Cali office is effectively functioning smoothly. The management team I've set in place is well suited to keep things running efficiently. As we discussed, I will bounce between here and California every other month or so to check in. Now, about getting your dick wet. The woman I met last night has a friend. She—" There was a knock at the door and both looked over as Kara stepped inside.

"Excuse me. I have that information you requested." Kara handed off a paper to Lucas.

"What information?" Gavin's head pivoted between them.

Lucas cut him a hard look, to which Gavin shrugged as he rose and went to the side bar for coffee. The man knew when not to push his luck.

"I've also e-mailed the information to you." Kara stepped back as Lucas stood and moved past her to his desk for his iPad.

Reviewing the data, a half grin formed. "This is good." Not only did Kara pin down where Sienna worked during the day from her LinkedIn profile, she'd prepared a report that listed Sienna's home address, her e-mail, cell phone number, and the college she'd attended along with a host of other useful information. There was one particular fact about Sienna that stood out. Lucas retrieved the paper from his desk that Kara had given him earlier, listing the names of the artists participating in the art expo. Sienna's name wasn't on it. "Perfect." He smiled. "I'll pick the artist. Have Isaac in front in ten."

Kara whipped out her cell phone.

"Lucas, what's going on?" Gavin asked. "One minute you're chewing my head off, and now you stand there grinning like a school girl winning at hopscotch." He looked at Kara and was met with silence as she left the room.

With his iPad in hand, Lucas grabbed his cell phone off his desk, strode over to Gavin, and planted a firm hand on his buddy's right shoulder. "We'll catch up later, my man." Smiling, he slapped Gavin on the back and walked out.

Chapter Ten

"I believe she's here." Lucas rose from his chair.

Widening the door, Sienna stepped into the office and drew up short in obvious surprise. Linking her hands behind her back, she tilted her head slightly, giving him an inquisitive, pronounced stare before addressing her manager. "*Mrsss*. Blake." She placed stress on the Mrs. "You asked to see me?"

A rush of blood flooded Patricia's face as though she'd been caught with her skirt up. In a way, she had. Lucas gave a glance at the woman's skirt, which she'd skillfully bunched up to expose an ample amount of upper thigh as she recrossed her legs.

"Sienna, Mr. Marx would like to speak with you. He's welcome to use my office and to take as much time as he needs."

Turning to Lucas, Sienna said, "Good morning," and extended her hand.

Lucas looked away from the woman that had been sizing him up like a prized cut for the past ten minutes to address the lady of interest. "Good morning, Miss Keller."

He displayed a smooth grin that had her eyeing him curiously. She then said to Patricia, "I have two tours on the schedule this morning, and my ten thirty has arrived early."

"This won't take long, Miss Keller." Lucas turned to Patricia. "Mrs. Blake, thank you for the use of your office. It was a pleasure meeting you."

"Please call me Patricia." She smiled and stood up. With her eyes never wavering from his face, she said, "I'll have someone cover for you, Sienna."

Retrieving her business card off the desk, Patricia took a step forward, narrowed the space, and handed it to him. "By all means, Mr. Marx, please stop by anytime." Her tone dropped in register, sweetly seductive. "I would be happy to give you a personal tour of the gallery."

Lucas stuck the card into his inside coat pocket. Now feeling inclined to reciprocate, he reached into his suit coat, made certain it was his white business card instead of his black personal card, pulled it out, and handed it over. "I'll keep that in mind."

Another gleam of white teeth. "I'll hold you to it." She fanned her flushed cheeks with his stiff card stock, then shook his hand, adding pressure while holding on several heartbeats longer than what one would consider respectable before releasing it, and left the room.

When the door closed, Sienna took the seat Patricia vacated and Lucas sat back down.

"She'll give you a personal tour all right. I thought she was gonna combust from the heat she was pumping out at you. The woman should be ashamed of herself. You do realize that ring she's wearing means she's married." Giving him a sideways look, her lip turned up. "I'm betting that doesn't faze you."

"Do you always say what you think, Sienna?" Lucas kept his tone inflectionless, but his fixed gaze suggested that she tread lightly.

"It has served me well thus far," she returned with poise, meeting his stare, looking completely unfazed.

Keeping in mind his purpose for seeing her, he sat back casually, releasing the buttons of his suit coat, his legs spread as though they were two friends about to chat it up. "Thank you for meeting with me."

"Sure. So, Lucas, to what do I owe the pleasure? I won't even ask how you found out where I work now that I have the four-one-one on you."

"Is that so?"

She crossed her legs and released a bored breath. "It is. According to the Internet, you're some sort of ridiculously rich investment mogul."

He shrugged. "I see you've checked up on me. I'll cut to it then. Are you familiar with the annual art contest that's held at the National Art Gallery?"

"Yes. Why?"

"I'd like to sponsor you."

She casually rocked her crossed leg and studied her neatly manicured nails as she replied, "First, I submitted my application again this year and was rejected, so that's not possible. And second, the deadline for submissions was weeks ago. I've tried for the past three years to compete in the event, and each year I receive a rejection letter. *Try again next year.* The damn letter always ends the same.

"Anyway, I heard that part of the contest was rigged. Most of the sponsors have already seen their chosen artist's work well before the event. They're not supposed to, but they do it to set the stage to win." Realizing what she'd said, she looked up from her nails.

"Hence." Lucas grinned.

She sat up and eyed him warily. "You want to sponsor me? Why? You don't even know me or my work. Bailey told me just this morning that you're likely to buy one of my pieces, but I haven't even gotten it from storage, which means you haven't seen it."

"Bailey said I would purchase your art?" Lucas found Bailey's confidence in her perceived ounce of authority over him intriguing.

"Well, she said you'd have to approve it, but she feels that this particular piece would look great in your home and that you would agree once you've seen it. She hasn't spoken to you about it?"

"No. I'm scheduled to meet with her tomorrow afternoon."

"Then how do you know that I would be interested in the art competition?"

Dismissing the question, he pulled out his wallet from his inside coat pocket, grabbed a pen from the desk, and wrote out a check for four thousand dollars, then handed it over. Several ticking seconds went by with her staring at his outstretched hand.

"Earth to Sienna."

Her gaze fluttered to his face. "What's that for?"

"I'm paying you for the artwork."

"But you haven't seen it."

"You said Bailey feels it would suit."

"Just like that?" Cockiness gone, she didn't mask her flabbergasted expression.

"Just like that," he replied coolly, still holding the check out to her.

"Okay, but four grand simply because Bailey said so?"

To make his point, Lucas reached back into his wallet, withdrew several bills, and extended it out to her with the check. "Six thousand should cover it." She rapidly shook her head back and forth and reared back. "Whoa, that's ... that's, Lucas, I can't take that."

"Think of it as a small investment." He smiled.

She finally reached for the money, but paused and returned a shrewd grin of her own laced with caution. Studying him, she asked, "This is for my artwork ... nothing else, right? I don't want you coming back saying I owe you favors or some shit later simply because you purchased my painting and somehow managed to get me in and sponsored me in the art competition."

"You can provide a receipt if you like." He winked lightheartedly. It did nothing to erase her wary stare.

"I believe I will." She took the money and the check.

"There *is* one small thing I do ask of you."

"See, I knew it." The funds were extended back to him.

Ignoring her outstretched hand, he leaned forward, resting his elbows on his knees. "You are not to tell Bailey we had this discussion and that I have entered and intend to sponsor you in the art competition."

"Now see—" She shook her head again, seemingly not on board with it. "She'll know something's up because she's already aware that I wasn't accepted again this year."

Lucas returned a light shrug. "Say the rejection letter was a computer glitch. Someone called you to correct the mistake."

Shaking her head more rapidly, she was beginning to look like a Bobblehead doll. "I don't know.

"Here, take this back." She moved to the edge of her chair and shoved the money and the check at him with determined force, but he merely maintained his smile.

"Sienna, if you tell her about this, she may play more into it than me simply using my influence to help you out. Like you said, the event is rigged to some degree."

"Maybe. You really like my girl?" She studied him with a scrutinizing eye.

"I'd like to get to know her if she would let me. There's one more thing I'd like you to do."

"Seriously!" Sienna exhaled an exaggerated breath. "I don't think that I can take one more."

"I want you to encourage Bailey to go out with me."

Her brows pinched. "I can't force Bailey to go out with you."

"I said encourage, not force." With a grin, Lucas sat back, adding, "You could tell her that I seemed like a nice guy." In a blink, his expression grew a bit stern. "There's a lot I can do for you, Sienna, both domestically and on an international scale. This art event is nothing compared to the connections I could offer you." He studied the play of emotions that crossed her attractive, smooth, cinnamon-brown features: They seemed to go from excitement over the possibilities, to concern over her devotion to her friend, and settled on wary of his intentions. "I only have to encourage her to go out on a date with you, not try to convince her to sleep with you ... that I won't do," she told him firmly.

"I can manage that on my own." Her eyes rolled upward. "She's dead set on not getting involved with me because she thinks I'm seeing her boss."

"Well, are you?" Narrow arms crossed beneath her small breasts, and her gaze upon him held firm. "If you are, this shit ends here." She flapped the bills at him. "And you can keep your money."

"Like I've tried to explain to Bailey, Sandra and I were only together for a short time."

He pulled out his card and handed it to her. "In case you need to reach me."

"The card you gave Patricia was white."

"Yes, the white card is my business line. You have my personal number." A nod. There seemed to be a small look of reassurance now brimming her eyes.

"All right, I'll try to *encourage* Bailey to go out with you."

Lucas held back a grin. "Remember, not a word to her about any of this. I don't want her to get the wrong impression that—"

"That you manipulated her best friend into helping you catch her by dangling the art competition."

"I wouldn't put it quite like that." They shared knowing looks; both understood that it was indeed precisely that.

"What if she still says no?" Her eyes fixed on him as he rose from his seat and buttoned his suit coat.

As he opened the door and looked over his shoulder, those dark orbs zeroed in.

"You won't disappoint me. Enjoy your day, Sienna." He strolled out the room.

• • •

Bailey grabbed her things from her locker. She looked over her shoulder at Sienna seated on the bench, staring out in space. "You're mighty quiet. Sie?" she called when there was no fired back wisecrack in response. With her backpack on her shoulder, she turned around, and waved her hand in front of her friend's face. "Hey you?"

Sienna blinked and looked up. "What's up?"

"What's up with you? You're quiet. It's not like you."

"Long day. Just tired and ready to go home.

"I hear you, same here."

"Uh, a rep from the art expo called me today to say I was accepted to compete in the contest this year."

"Oh my God, Sie, that's wonderful!" Bailey dropped down next to her on the bench. "I thought you said your application was rejected."

Sienna bent forward and retied her sneaker. "Yeah, they ... uh ... they said it was a computer glitch."

"Sie, that's fantastic! I'm so happy for you. Look at us. I get my first design project, and now you get a chance to show the world how great of an artist you are." Bailey hugged her. "Let's get out of here. I'm sure you have a lot to do. I have to work on my design for Lucas's kitchen as well as put together some fabric swatch samples for his sofas. I'm meeting him at his home tomorrow afternoon. He's a stickler. I want to be prepared." She stood up.

"About Lucas." Sienna cleared her throat. "I've been thinking. Would it be so bad to go out with him? What if he's telling you the truth about him and Sandra? I mean, we all have a past, right?"

Two of their coworkers entered the break room. Sienna stood up. She and Bailey said good night to them and walked out. They made their way through the dining area and exited the café.

"I'd be lying if I said I wasn't attracted to Lucas, but I can't jeopardize my job by seeing him. Sandra is hell-bent on getting back with him. She knows a lot of people in the interior design industry." Bailey unlocked the car, and they climbed in. She pumped the brakes a few times and started it up, saying as she drove off, "Sandra could make my life hell. I wouldn't be able to find a job anywhere if she found out that I was with Lucas. She can be vindictive, Sie."

"The man obviously doesn't want her ass," Sienna scoffed. "Why should you have to turn all of that big, strong, male hard body away?" She met Bailey's smirk and raised brow with her own. They both laughed. "I'm just saying why not get yours, if you know what I mean. If you ask me, you're due."

Bailey tried not to laugh, but failed. "Stop it." Her friend was right to some degree. When it came to the opposite sex, she was somewhat on the shy side. Prior to college, she'd only had one boyfriend.

Her parents were very strict with her to the point that they didn't even want her to go away to college. She still had a strained relationship with her dad for not returning home after she graduated.

"I just think Lucas seems like a cool guy, is all. He's definitely hot, that's for sure."

"I don't know." Bailey glanced over as she merged into the beltway traffic. "This morning you were in support of me keeping things professional with Lucas, even ready to deny yourself a sale of your art after what I told you about him and Sandra. By the way, I need to get that art piece from storage tomorrow. Why the change? With me seeing Lucas, I mean?" She glanced over at her again.

"I've been thinking, if Lucas is interested in you and you're attracted to him, then why not? When was the last time you went out with a man? Or even got some for that matter?"

Bailey drove along quietly, not wishing to discuss her love life or the lack thereof. She also knew that Sienna wouldn't let up until she answered.

Exiting the beltway, they traveled several blocks, turned into their apartment complex, and parked. The engine coughed out a sputter before shutting off.

"Well, when? And don't say Kevin because I know you didn't sleep with him." They both shifted in their seats to face one another. "And please don't say Andrew was your last because that would be really sad."

A sigh, Bailey answered, "You already know about the fiasco with Andrew." An even weightier sigh. "I wouldn't even call what we did sex." She shook her head over the memory. "My goodness, it was my first time. I was so nervous, and it was so quick and awkward afterward because I asked him if that was it. He got really pissed, which is likely one of the reasons why he got with Faith."

Sienna sucked her teeth and waved a dismissing hand. "Pish, Andrew's weak ass. A ten-second screw to take your virginity doesn't count as sex. Quite frankly, Faith saved you the disappointment of having to screw that loser again. But I know it wasn't Kevin either."

"No, not Kevin. He was the last guy I would say that I dated. Before him, I dated Craig for a short time, remember? We know how that turned out also. He got what he wanted, cheated, and poof ... gone."

A soft, warm hand enveloped hers, giving it a gentle squeeze. "That bastard wasn't worth the four months you wasted on him. Glad you had his ass wait three of those before you slept with him. I recall you saying he wasn't any better than Andrew."

"True." Bailey nodded. "There was Bruce Davidson last year, but that was only one date. We didn't have sex," she admitted. "He tried, but I wouldn't sleep with him, which is why it didn't go beyond the one date."

"Damn, since Craig? Let's see," tucking her left leg up underneath her in the seat, Sienna brought up her fingers and started calculating, "that means the last time you had sex, or a version of it anyway, was what, two years and—"

"It'll be three years next month," Bailey murmured with palms rubbing back and forth along the sides of the steering wheel in obvious embarrassment.

Sienna's eyes widened. "Double damn, girl, that long? I know I'm in a six months' dry spell right now, but nearly three years? How are you even able to function? I'd be climbing up the walls."

Bailey delivered her a playful punch on the shoulder, and they both laughed at her pathetic love life.

"You said you left Lucas's home sometime after ten o'clock the other night. How on earth did you not jump his bones? That man oozes sex appeal."

"It wasn't easy," Bailey sighed out, and they laughed again at her expense. "Like I said, I'm attracted to Lucas, and he doesn't hide that he wants to sleep with me, but I don't want to complicate things. If I didn't have to deal with the fallout of losing my job, and the likelihood of getting blacklisted by Sandra to all the other design firms, I might consider going out with him. But I'm sure he's only looking for a casual hookup, so what's the point?"

"They do it, so why can't we get a little casual somethin' somethin', you know." Sienna chuckled lightly, and then her gaze softened. "I do understand where you're coming from, but you really should consider, at the very least, a date with him. A man like that won't keep asking."

They got out of the car and headed up the walk.

"What if I chose the place for the date?" Bailey asked as they stood outside the apartment door. "Lucas and I could go somewhere where the chance of running into Sandra would be slim."

"Yes, you could just hang out at his place." Sienna opened the door with her key and flipped the wall switch that turned on the table lamp. "Get yours." She winked.

Bailey shook her head. "No, I'm not ready to take it there—the sex part, I mean. Lucas is so intense. Don't get me wrong, I've thought about it ... a lot," she admitted. "He's kind of intimidating. I've never met a man like him before." Dropping her backpack on the sofa, she released a weary breath and raked a hand across her forehead. "What should I do? Do you really think I should go out with him? It might be okay if I planned out where we'd go and set some ground rules with Lucas."

"That could work. Hey, it's been great seeing Faith, right?"

"Yes, it has. Is she here?"

"Faithhhh?" Sienna hollered and received no answer. "Nope, not here."

"Where would she go and stay all day? Everyone we know that she knows here works during the day," Bailey said as she slipped out of her sneakers.

"Who knows." Sienna plopped down in the armchair and did the same. "When Faith showed up at the club the other night, she was acting kind of strange. I assumed she'd downed a couple of shots or something to mellow out before meeting Diego."

Bailey cut her a side look.

"What?"

"You don't find it odd that Faith just suddenly popped up here carrying only a backpack, but said that she wasn't sure how long she'd be here?"

"That's Faith—unpredictable—you know that."

"That's always been her problem," Bailey returned as she stretched her tired frame. "I have a lot of work to do before I go to bed."

Their heads turned to the sound of the key working the door lock. Faith entered the apartment. Behind her was Dale Carter. Bailey and Sienna flew to their feet.

"Uh, hey, guys." Faith looked tentatively between them.

"What the hell is this?" Sienna barked.

"We're dating again," Faith explained with an anxious look between them. "It's not like it was. He's changed." She looked at Dale.

"Yeah, I've left all that shit ... I mean, that stuff I use to do. I don't do that no more," Dale said.

"I thought, thought you were—" Bailey started.

"Incarcerated," Sienna finished for her.

"Early release for good behavior. I been out about three months." Dale ran a hand over his dirty-blond hair and stuck his hand into the front pocket of his severely aged blue jeans. "I gotta job with D.C. sanitation, but I got other things working that's gonna be even better. And now that I got my girl back," he encircled his arms around Faith's shoulders from behind and kissed her cheek, "everything's coming together."

"See, he's changed." Faith smiled up at Dale. "I wanted you all to see for yourself. We're really good."

Bailey and Sienna could do nothing but stare at them. Subconsciously, Bailey rubbed her wrist as her mind took a spiral back to when she sat handcuffed and scared within a breath of a heart attack while the cops raided their apartment.

Faith turning into the man's arms pulled Bailey out of her nightmare. "I'll call you in the morning," Faith whispered, then let him out.

When the door closed, Sienna yelled, "What the hell is this? That man nearly got you sent to prison and nearly got us all tangled in his shit too, or have you forgotten? Oh, wait, that's right, you weren't the one woken up by a police dog's growling hot breath in your face."

Seldom did Bailey witness Sienna at this level of pissed off, especially with Faith. "Yes, Faith, Dale isn't good for you. You can do so much better."

"This is why I didn't tell you two that I was seeing him. Can't you all just give him a chance? He was released for good behavior. While he was locked up, he took classes and studied really hard. He has his G.E.D. now. Bailey, what was it you said to me back in college when I'd started smoking? That saying by that guy, Bill ... Bob ... I can't remember his name, but you told me, 'If you can quit for a day, you can quit for a lifetime.'"

"Benjamin Sáenz," Bailey supplied.

"Yeah, him. Dale hasn't been involved in drugs or anything bad for nearly three years."

"He's been in jail, that's why. And I say when the past calls, let it go to voice mail because it's got nothing new to say," Sienna argued.

Bailey almost chuckled at that. "Who said that?" Getting a shrug smothered in heightened frustration from her friend, she turned back to Faith. "Look, it's your life. Just don't bring us any drama."

"He's not welcome here," Sienna's voice whipped sharply. "If you want to see him, that shit's on you, but don't bring him here." Without another word, she stalked off to her room and slammed the door.

Bailey met Faith's solemn gaze, tears welling in her blue eyes. "I'll get you a pillow and blanket. The couch is really comfortable, you'll see."

"I can still stay here?"

Seeing a tear slide down her porcelain pink cheek, Bailey went to her and wrapped comforting arms around her. Faith had such a good spirit when she'd allow it to surface past the hellfire that kindled above it. Bailey tried not to hold the girl's poor decisions and transgressions against her. Feeling responsible for her mother's death and believing her father still blamed her for it, Faith had been through hell. That kind of guilt could do a number on anyone's healthy psyche. That said, Bailey released her and offered a small smile. "Let me get you the pillow and blanket." As she went off, she wondered if she'd also need to find herself a life jacket.

Chapter Eleven

Bailey used the key she'd been given to let herself into Lucas's home. She walked into the great room and was pleased to see Sienna's artwork had arrived thanks to the help of Lucas's assistant, Kara.

That morning, she'd called Lucas to discuss the painting, but got Kara, who insisted that she would handle getting the piece picked up from storage and delivered to Lucas's home for his review. After speaking with the woman, Bailey understood why Kara was his assistant. She was just as autocratic as Lucas.

She checked her watch as she headed into the kitchen. *He's late, but he expects me to be on time.*

Looking around the space, she couldn't wait to get started. The work was to begin as soon as Lucas signed off on her design plan. She gave the spec sheet one last check and headed back into the great room.

"Oh!" She skidded a step at seeing Lucas looking at Sienna's painting that rested against the wall.

"I didn't hear you come in. The military could use someone with your stealth skills. You move quiet as a mouse for someone your size."

"Sienna is very talented. This is exceptionally good."

"You like it?" Bailey walked over, and he faced her. She purposely wore a pair of five and a half inch espadrilles to avoid having to crane her neck when she looked at him.

"It would work perfectly over the fireplace. Sienna's a wonderful artist. She was accepted to compete in that art competition you're attending with Sandra on Friday." Feeling the twinge of jealousy return in her gut, she looked away from him.

"Play nothing into it," he said, apparently having read her expression. "We're merely business associates."

She brought her eyes back up to him with a twisted smirk upon her lips. "Whatever you say, Mr. Marx. It's none of my business."

He sighed and turned back to the painting. "You and Sienna are very close it seems. Are you related?"

"No, but we're BFFs, like sisters. We met freshman year at Georgetown."

He nodded, seeming only mildly curious, walked over to the sofa, and stared down upon it with a frown. "When do you expect I would have suitable furniture to sit on? And I'd like a flat screen above the fireplace that is tied into the security feed. Put the art someplace else."

"Okay." Bailey made a note and looked around to see where she'd relocate the artwork, deciding on the large wall it was leaning against.

"I can have a niche cut in where the flat screen would sit within and have it display an art feature when not in use. I have all of the furniture pieces on wait as well. I need your okay to move forward." She held up her portfolio, and he waved her off as he walked around and took a seat on the small couch facing the fireplace.

"Order what you see fit."

"You don't want to see it?" She spoke to the back of his head and got a mere shrug of a shoulder. Circling the couch, she stood in front of him. "I put a lot of work into this, stayed up late to find the perfect pieces for your home, got to work early to place them on hold, and you simply brush it off?" Her hand came down firm on her hip. "You kept me here late the other night, grilled me on every little thing. I was so worried that I'd screw this up and lose my job."

Looking up at her, he unbuttoned his suit coat and relaxed back with his left arm extended along the low sofa spine, once again appearing only mildly interested in what she'd said. "How's Kevin? If I recall, you were more concerned with seeing him that evening than doing your job."

Bailey gasped. "That's not true! And for your information, I was too exhausted after your grill session that the only thing I saw after I left here were the back of my eyelids. I could barely get my clothes off before I literally crawled into bed." His gaze did that familiar slow roll up and down the length of her body and settled on her mouth. She slipped her tongue along her lower lip, recalling the feel of his warm tongue tangled with hers, his kisses marking her down to the bone, which she'd savored with a greedy urgency.

"Did you manage the task? You could've called me to help." A grin stretched across his pretty mouth. "So you didn't meet up with your friend, Kevin, in Georgetown?"

"Nope." Bailey would have almost sworn that there was a gleam in his eyes at having foiled her night out with her friends.

"Sit with me." He patted the spot next to him, and she sat down. "Let me see them."

"What?" Her eyelids fluttered with a look down at her breasts, then back up at him.

"The items you want me to approve." He took the portfolio she had resting on her lap and began flipping through the pages. "I see your mind is in the gutter, Miss Walters."

"*My* mind is in the gutter? I have yet to note your mind to be anywhere else, Mr. Marx. I'm not as naive as you may think. I know seduction when I see it." She got a full grin and chuckle at that.

His eyes came up to hers, then went back to the book. "Apparently, you do not," he countered and closed the portfolio, then slid over to her. Her frame tensed up tight as a drum, and she pulled in her bottom lip, apprehensive of his intensions. He brought his hand up to her face, lightly skated the tips of his fingers along the contour of her left cheek, and then leaned in. Feeling his warm breath on her neck and expecting a wet tongue to rim her ear as before, her head snapped back so hard she almost got whiplash. He smiled. "I haven't attempted to seduce you yet, Bailey. When I do, I promise that you will consider it to be significantly different from all of our previous interactions."

Sweet geez. The smooth cadence of his voice mixed with his explicit pledge made her stomach clench, and her breath stalled in her throat. Bailey swallowed deep in complete intimidation, but did her best to mask it. "*When* you do? Pretty sure of yourself, I see. So you admit that sex is what you want from me?"

"To the point, yes. I won't lie to you, Bailey." His cool, confident stare held hers. "What heterosexual male wouldn't want you? You're very beautiful." The tip of his index finger lightly traced the outer portion of her ear and along her cheek again. "But it's not all I want. Like I told you when we first met, I want to get to know you. And you?"

"And me what?" Bailey removed his hand from her face and brought it back down to the top of the sofa. She liked the feel of his touch far more than she should.

"How often has the thought of sleeping with me crossed your mind?" he asked.

Laughter bubbled up within her and spilled over as she shook her head at his arrogance. He looked so sure of himself. Quite honestly, she'd thought about it numerous times, lost sleep over it, but she sure as hell wasn't about to inflate his ego any more than it was already.

"Unlike you, Mr. Marx, I'm not sitting up at night plotting a strategy to get you into bed. Now can we focus on my portfolio?"

"It's Lucas. I want you to say my name, Bailey. But you won't, will you. That would change the dynamics between us, makes it more intimate. You would then have to admit that the attraction is mutual. Instead, you maintain a formal distance and deflect whenever our conversation steers in that direction."

"That's not how it is." Looking away from his intense stare, she fiddled nervously with the hem of her skirt.

"No to which part? That you are equally attracted and want to sleep with me? You wish to keep a formal distance? Or that you deflect when our talks become too intimate?"

"Yes ... I mean no." Flustered as well as irritated, Bailey shook her head. "You're trying to rattle me, Mr. uh ... Lucas. If you're not interested in seeing the items I've selected for your home, then we're done here." Not five seconds from slapping his arrogant face, she jerked her portfolio out of his hand and stood up.

"Why do you fear me?" Looking up at her, he sat forward with his elbows on his knees, head cocked to the side, studying her. "Or is it that you fear your reaction to me?" At her quick look away, he grinned. "That's it, isn't it?"

Bailey had to laugh again at the enormous size of his ego. Obviously, the man was used to women drooling over him. "I don't fear you. I just know how this ends." She had been ready to take Sienna's advice and go out with him, but now ...

"Enlighten me since I don't share your clairvoyant gift." Seeing her eyes slit hot, he smirked with a look of enjoyment that he was getting under her skin. "Well, I'm listening, Miss Walters."

"You'll take and give nothing back. I'm not Sandra. You won't see me pawing and panting after you," she bit out. His brows shot up before slanting inward, looking both surprised and perhaps offended.

"You think I like that? That I get off on a woman's supplication? So you've defined me." He dragged his fingers through his hair and looked over toward the window wall.

Her remark bit deep, Bailey knew. She'd already made up her mind on the type of person he was without getting to know him. It wasn't fair. How had their meeting turned into this messy discussion?

"Lucas?" His name was said with purpose as she sat back down and laid her hand upon his that rested on the sofa. "I shouldn't have said that. It was out of line. I really don't know you well enough to judge you in that way. I'll admit that the little I do know about you comes from the Internet. My mom has a saying: Believe half of what you hear, see, and read about a person because there are always two sides to every story."

He looked at her then, and the hard lines between his brows slowly diminished. "I like how your southern drawl creeps in now and then. Really, I find it quite sensual," he said with a bit less suggestion to it. "Have dinner with me tomorrow evening. You can then decide if I'm worth getting to know."

"Okay, but I'll pick the place where there is less chance of running into Sandra." His eyes brightened, letting her know that she'd caught him off guard for once. "Sandra is never to know about this, Lucas," she said firmly, and that beautiful smile returned.

"I have no intentions of discussing anything short of the work on my home with Sandra. Even that can be discussed with you. So where to, Miss Walters?" Looking into her eyes, he brought her hand to his mouth and lightly brushed his lips across the back of her fingers.

Sweet mercy! His soft lips and warm tongue drew slow circles on her knuckles. It shocked Bailey how swiftly her nipples tightened and her sex pulsed over such a simple act.

"Where are you taking me?" he asked with a mischievous glint in his eyes.

Bailey reined in her growing desire for him in order to focus and gave his question some thought while lightly tugging her hand free to relieve the throbbing between her legs. "I know just the place. Be sure to dress casual and comfortable."

"You won't tell me?"

"It's a surprise," she answered with a grin. "You can pick me up at seven thirty. That should give us plenty of time."

"Miss Walters, whatever your heart desires, I'm at your command."

"Are you now?" Bailey smirked, and his head cocked slightly at the mischievous look she now gave him. "At my command, huh? We shall see."

Chapter Twelve

"Sie, do you really think I'm doing the right thing by going out on a date with Lucas?" With her cell on speakerphone, Bailey held it in one hand and held tank top number six in front of her before the full-length mirror.

"Sienna, tell her to stop worrying." Faith spoke close to the phone for Sienna to hear. The tank top was snatched from Bailey and tossed on the bed. "Bails, for the one hundredth time, what you have on is fine. You would think she'd never dressed for a date before," Faith yelled out for Sienna's benefit once more.

"She hasn't, not like this," Sienna said.

"You two are supposed to be helping me." Bailey grabbed up another blouse off the bed. "What about this one? It isn't cut as low. If I wear a bra—"

"Which one is it?" Sienna asked.

Bailey could hear the clank of plates in the background. "I'm sorry for bothering you at work, Sie, but I really need help with this. I have on the spaghetti strap, red floral chiffon top and navy-blue linen shorts, but I think the navy-blue stripe top covers my boobs better."

"No bra. Both have built-in support. What you have on is perfect. And wear those navy-blue wedged flip-flops you have, the ones with the little sparkly stones on them. Did you go to the spa after work as I said?"

"Yes, and that's why I'm running late. Sienna, I didn't need to do all of that. I feel terrible for the amount of money you spent. If you hadn't prepaid them, I wouldn't have gone," Bailey told her.

"I know you wouldn't have. That's why I paid in advance."

Bailey rubbed her forehead, her anxiety building swiftly. "This is becoming too much. It's not like he's gonna get to see my goods anyway." She was beginning to feel a bit overwhelmed.

"Bails, relax. And don't you always tell me that it's better to be prepared for a fire than, uh, I forget how it goes, but you get it." Sienna chortled. "Let me speak to Faith."

Bailey looked at Faith seated on the bed folding the pile of clothes that she'd previously tried on. "Here, Faith." She handed over the phone, and then went to her closet to get her flip-flops that were kept in their original box to protect the tiny faux sapphire gems sewn in along the band. Sienna had been shocked to learn how much Bailey had spent on the pair, given that the stones weren't real.

Slipping the sandals on her feet, she closed the door to check her appearance in the full-length mirror hanging in front. Her skin did have a nice glow to it. As well it should after all of the poking, tweezing, and yanking she'd gone through at the spa. She'd received what was known as the Signature Platinum Spa Package, which consisted of a facial a Brazilian bikini, underarm, eyebrow, and full leg wax, followed by a skin refinishing buff, and ending with a mani-pedi. She'd chosen a French white for both her hands and feet.

Hearing Faith say, "I'm on it," Bailey looked over at the bed. "You're on what?"

"I was told to make sure you don't back out of the date. Here." Faith handed the phone back to her. "You'll never be ready at this pace." She grabbed the hair scrunchie off the vanity and quickly arranged Bailey's hair into a ponytail. Faith then resumed her folding of the pile of clothes on the bed.

"If Sandra finds out ..." Bailey worriedly sighed deep as she grabbed her purse off the bed in search of her lip gloss.

"She won't," Sienna assured her. "Trust me, there's no way in hell Sandra would be caught dead at the event where you're taking Lucas. You haven't told him I hope?"

"No."

"I wish I could see the look on Sir Hotness's face when he gets there." Sienna chuckled.

There was a knock on the apartment door. Bailey tensed and looked at the clock on her nightstand. "I think he's here."

"I'll get it." Faith leaped off the bed and out of the room.

"I should finish getting ready."

"Bails, one more thing. I know you intend to take it slow with Lucas." Sienna's tone was encouragingly soft. "He's not Andrew or Craig, and not even Kevin. Remember that okay, chica?"

Faith returned. "It's Lucas's driver. He said to take all the time you need."

Bailey frowned and sucked her teeth. "Did you hear that, Sie? He sent his driver to retrieve me. He's not like the rest? He sure as hell is starting off like the rest, that's for damn sure."

"Let his first slipup slide," Sienna advised her.

"Yeah, yeah, we'll talk later." Ending the call, Bailey took out her tiny pearl studs from her jewelry box and hastily put them in her ears. She applied her pink lip gloss, grabbed the packed duffel bag from the floor, and then turned to Faith and gave her a hug. "I guess I'll see you later."

"Have fun."

Releasing one last calming breath, she headed out, still unsure if she was doing the right thing by taking this step forward with Lucas Marx.

Seeing Kevin approaching, Bailey paused on her way to the car.

"Hey, Kev." She caught his questioning look when he glanced from her to the parked limo, and then back at her.

"Hey, doll." Kevin drew her close and kissed her cheek. "So it's like that, huh?" He gestured with a head nod over at the limo.

"I'm going out with a friend."

"A friend that rolls high dollar, I see." Bailey figured her blush told him what she meant by friend.

Lucas got out of the car, and the harsh scowl that blanketed Kevin's face made her wince.

"I often wondered what was your type. Obviously, I wasn't it," he said as he held his glare upon the other man. "Now I know I would've never measured up for you."

Bailey gasped, offended. "Why would you say something like that?" Bitter resentment reflected back at her in his dark eyes. "It's not like that. You know how I feel about you. I care for you. We're friends."

"Oh it's exactly like that, Bailey."

"Kev, this shouldn't change our friendship." He didn't respond. "Can we talk later?" She reached for his hand, but he pulled it back.

"Talk about what? What else is there to say? You've made it clear. Crystal. I'm late for my set. I stopped by to get something from my place. You enjoy your night." He walked on and then turned around, walking backward as he said, "I have a show in Baltimore coming up. I was gonna invite you, but I wouldn't want you to have to slum it with me." With a head nod at the limo, he muttered, "Your boy's getting impatient. You better get going." He turned and strolled off to his apartment.

Hurt by his words, Bailey stood there staring at Kevin's apartment door contemplating if she should go to him to try to smooth things over between them. They'd always been good friends. She'd hate if they couldn't remain so.

Chapter Thirteen

Lucas sat patiently inside his car waiting for Bailey to join him to begin their first date. The operative word there was *first*—as if he would want a second. He mentally chuckled at the notion. It had been a long time since he'd *second* dated a woman that piqued his interest. And he'd never worked harder to get a woman to spend a few hours with him in his life. He typically considered an evening out such as this to be just that, one evening. If she didn't manage to bore him into a coma by the end of dinner, their involvement typically lasted three, maybe six months before he eventually became bored anyway. Yet, there was something about Bailey Walters that had him anxious, in fact, eager to spend a mere evening with her, while already looking forward to their next date and the one after that. His cell phone rang. "Yes," he answered without checking the display, absorbed in his thoughts.

"You had better not hurt her, Lucas. I swear if you do—"

"Hello, Sienna."

"I'm serious. Bailey is near and dear to me."

"You need not worry. I have no intentions of harming a single hair on her head."

"Don't play. You know I don't mean physically." When there was no reply, she snickered. "I hope you enjoy your evening."

"Of course, you know where we're going," he said dryly.

"Yes, I know, and don't even think to try to get it out of me."

Lucas sat up and slid over to see around Isaac's frame standing beside the door. "Sienna, have a good evening." He abruptly ended the call and would have sworn time slowed to a crawl to allow his brain to track every nanosecond of the most stunning vision that stepped out of the apartment. He was attuned to her every movement as she made her way down the walk.

Her ponytail was a thick mass of curls that bounced at her back with each sauntering step she took. Her high, plump breasts gently sprung up and down in the floral top she wore. Its sheer fabric caught the light breeze, revealing the solid red shell underneath and just a hint of her taut abdomen.

His eyes followed the synchronized sway of her slender hips, tracking every fraction of the movements she made in those navy-blue short shorts that sat low on her hips.

There was a healthy radiance to her honey-brown complexion, like that of summer wheat in a field bathing in the sun. Lucas gnashed his teeth, hating how ridiculous verses always popped into his head when he looked at her. But, man, how he loved the look of her satiny smooth skin. How he yearned to run his hands all over her, starting with her silky legs, the sleek, shapely form of her thighs and calves. No doubt those legs would wrap like a gift around him.

She was carrying a duffel bag. Isaac stepped to assist her, but she waved him off. Lucas allowed for a second the notion that her bag meant that whatever she had planned for them, it included her spending the night with him. He quickly pushed the thought away, not wanting to get his hopes up—or his dick for that matter.

Her stride slowed to a stop with a look over to her right. A cheerful smile was offered to the man heading her way.

Isaac stuck his head inside the car. "Should I handle it, boss?"

"No," Lucas replied. The two seemed to be very familiar with one another.

She turned her cheek up to accept the kiss from the African American man sporting the blond dreadlocks and carrying a guitar case. *Kevin.*

Seeing Kevin's hand intimately holding her at her waist, Lucas bit the inside of his cheek to tamp down his irritation, and surprisingly, his jealousy, assuming Kevin was the type of man she went for.

They once dated and were now friends, she'd said. The way Kevin looked at her, touched her ... *just friends my ass.*

Stepping out of the car, he worked at keeping his cool as he studied their interaction to try to determine for himself where Kevin scaled in that so-called friendship.

As the man went on his way, she stood there, looking as though she might follow. *Not going to happen.*

"Bailey," Lucas called to her. He walked up, took hold of the duffel bag, and led her to the car.

They both turned to the man jogging across the street toward them while calling out her name. He came to a stop before them. Lucas gave a side look at Isaac. His six-foot-six broad frame took a casual, loose side step, his relaxed demeanor belying his lethal readiness to step in should the situation require it.

"Bailey, hey."

"Uh, hey, Dale," she said, and he delivered a smile, showing dingy tobacco-stained teeth as he gave Lucas a once over. "Faith's inside." She didn't bother introducing them.

"I know, I just texted her." A short snort. "And yeah, I know, I know, Faith told me I'm not allowed into your crib. No worries." There was a hint of mocking in his tone. Sticking his hands in the front pockets of his jeans, jeans that had seen better days, he said, "You two going out on the town limo style? Nice."

"We should get going," Bailey replied with complete dismissal of the man's comment.

"Well, enjoy your night." Dale walked on.

"Yep, you too." It was said with little feeling.

She started to climb in, but pivoted to Lucas behind her.

"I have to tell your driver where to go." Stepping over to Isaac, she introduced herself before taking hold of his arm to have him lean down in order to whisper in his ear.

Lucas glowered over her body's close proximity to Isaac's. He was still battling with his jealousy over observing her with Kevin. The fact that the man lived directly across from her didn't sit well with him.

Seeing her with Isaac, he watched as a subtle smirk formed across the man's mouth as she whispered in his ear. She then drew back and said, "You can't tell him." Isaac nodded without hesitation. Seldom did Lucas see the man ever so much as grin. She had Isaac working facial muscles he hardly ever used.

Stepping back from his driver, she turned and offered a feeble smile before getting into the car. Lucas placed the duffel bag on the floor and settled in next to her. There was a crestfallen dimness in her eyes.

"Who was that, and why isn't he allowed inside your place?" he asked.

"My friend Faith's boyfriend. It's a long story, one I don't feel like getting into right now." She looked out the window in the direction of Kevin's apartment.

"I assume the other man you were speaking to was Kevin." He managed to keep the irritation contained. "Care to tell me what he said that upset you?"

"It's not important."

Deciding to table the Kevin issue for the moment and draw her attention away from the other man, he asked, "What's in the bag? Let me guess, your overnight clothes."

"No, but maybe we should stop by your place for you to change. I said casual and comfortable, Lucas, not a designer black button-down and tailored black slacks." Looking at his shoes, a pair of soft, black leather loafers, she pointed at his feet. "Those are really nice. Again, five hundred dollar shoes aren't appropriate for where we're going."

"Try eleven hundred. You have a thing for shoes?" He was glad to see a hint of a smile surface upon her lips. That damn Kevin chump had just about tainted the evening with whatever he'd said to her.

"Very. They're my one weakness. Sienna calls me the black Carrie Bradshaw." Seeing his puzzled look, she attempted to clarify. "You know, Sarah Jessica Parker—*Sex and the City*."

"If you say so."

She sighed and didn't say more.

"I am casual and comfortable." Lucas ran his gaze over her beautiful features, on down her tantalizing body. His palms itched to slide over her smooth bare legs. He took hold of a lock of curl resting on her shoulder and twirled the silky spiral around his index finger. "You look exquisite." Sliding over closer to her, he leaned in at her shoulder and came within a hair of her flesh. She took in a long breath and a slow release as he dragged his nose from her collarbone up her delicate neck to her cheek, giving her a light peck there, then drew back, his eyes meeting hers. "And you smell incredibly delicious."

"Behave yourself." She inched away. "Will you behave yourself tonight, Mr. Marx?"

"Behave? There has never been any fun in that." He winked.

Chapter Fourteen

"So where are you taking me? Surely you can reveal it now. Does it involve the two of us tangled together in cool sheets?" He playfully wiggled his brows.

The image that flashed in Bailey's head of Lucas's face buried between her spread thighs had her pressing her legs together to suppress the budding throb. *Man oh man.* The car's cabin grew warmer all of a sudden. She would swear the temperature rose a good ten degrees just then.

He was the one that smelled incredibly delicious. His combined scent of light cologne and clean male were affecting her hormones as some sort of addicting pheromone. Getting ahold of herself, she said, "I take it you don't care much for surprises."

"Only when I'm the one doing the surprising." Seeing her fan herself with her hand as she scanned the buttons on the console, he reached across her, and turned up the AC. "How's that?"

With him practically in her lap, she got another good whiff of his scent. Staring at his neck so close to her, she fought back the urge to lick his skin. *Get a grip, Bailey, damn!* His face then came in close, practically nose to nose, with eyes peering into hers.

"Are you comfortable?" he asked.

That low throaty voice stretched on in her head for long seconds. Sex. That was what his voice sounded like, that deep rumbling that followed after a good, long orgasmic release. *Heaven's mercy!*

"Th-that's better, thanks. So, you only like surprises when you're in control." Subtly, Bailey reared back and moistened her lips, biting down hard on the bottom one in chastisement for the erotic images that ran through her head of him spread out naked upon that custom size bed of his.

"I haven't had control where you are concerned from the moment we met." A half grin played at the corner of his mouth. He was baiting her, she realized.

"I beg to differ. You've been trying to control this thing between us from the very start." Just then, his cell phone that was stationed on the console rang. She released a subtle breath of relief when he moved away to check the display.

"It's my business line. It will go to voice mail. Is it working?"

"Is what working?" Imagining the many ways she'd like to explore his magnificent physique, she'd lost their trail of conversation.

"Do I hold the control here?" He playfully wiggled his brows again, and she rolled her eyes. "I better stop while I'm ahead ... if I'm ahead. With you, I'm never quite certain."

Turning away, Bailey pretended to look out of the window as she closed her eyes briefly and quietly exhaled. She was shamefully attracted to the man, to the point that all he had to do was smile, and she wanted to rip his clothes off. *What is wrong with me?* It had to be her three-year lack of sex causing her to react this way, she concluded. What else could it be?

"There were workers in my kitchen again this morning. I stopped by to view the progress," he remarked.

Composing herself, she turned her head back to him. "Yes, Kara mentioned that you're staying at a friend's. I know renovations can be a major inconvenience."

"His name's Gavin Crane, a longtime friend, and my GM."

She nodded. "I e-mailed Kara the work schedule, and she responded saying that she'd be there to monitor the work. When I stopped by this afternoon, the floors were finished, the appliances were on the truck parked out front, and most of the cabinets were in. This crew is very efficient. Sandra is paying them extra since they are being pulled from another job to work solely on your place, putting in overtime to get it finished by tomorrow." Talking business helped.

"It will be nice to finally have all of the renovations done. So far, I like what I see. You're very talented, Bailey. Your portfolio is impressive. You might consider starting your own interior design company."

"That takes money, and right now, my focus is on paying off my student loans. Maybe in ten or fifteen years, I'd consider opening my own business."

"I can help."

Her response was a rapid shake of her head. "Thank you, but no thanks. My mom often says that money is the demon to end all friendships."

"Say that again."

Puzzled, she frowned. "What? Which part?"

"I hear a hint of southern charm in your voice whenever you quote an idiom."

"There isn't." Bailey looked away shyly for a moment, mainly because *his* tone tended to take on a smooth pulse that curled her toes whenever he stared unblinking into her eyes.

"There is, and I like it." Smiling, he placed a light kiss on the back of her hand. "As for me assisting you in starting your business, it would be an investment into what I know to be a sure success."

"Nope, but thanks." That got things casually back on track. She crossed her legs and noted his eyes homed in, lingering there. "So, Mr. Marx, are you an only child? I would guess that you are." His focus was back on her face.

"And why would you think that?" he asked, but not before taking another subtle glimpse downward.

"You're used to getting your way."

"What do you call this? I've allowed you to dictate everything about this date of ours."

Bailey laughed. "Did you hear yourself? You've *allowed*." His frown had her head cocking back in laughter. She then asked, "Well, are you an only child?"

"I have a brother and a sister, Landon and Chelsea. I'm the oldest and Landon is the youngest."

"I guess I stand corrected. I read about your father ... his heart attack, several years ago. My condolences."

"Thank you."

He stared at her a moment, then chuckled lightly. She frowned, perplexed. "What's funny?"

"I was waiting for you to start in with the questions—the Marx family scandal. They all do."

Insulted, she glowered with stark understanding. "Comparing me to your other women, Mr. Marx, is not a smart thing to do on a first date."

"I simply meant that I'm often asked about the down and dirty details. And I don't have other women, by the way."

Yeah right. "Whatever you say. That brings me to ask, why me?"

"I beg your pardon?"

"Why are you interested in me? From what I've seen online, I don't fit the mold for you."

"Perhaps that's why you do fit."

When he didn't elaborate, simply sat there with those steel-blue eyes tightly shielded behind his unblinking stare, she let it go.

"That matter regarding your family's ordeal is your business, not mine. So we have Logan, Lucas, and Landon. I guess the letter *L* is very popular in the Marx family."

"It's a tradition on my father's side that the first born bear a name that starts with an *L*. However, it was my father's desire that both of his sons would have *L* names. Enough about me. I'll ask you the same question. Are you an only child, Miss Walters?"

He slid over, hooked his thumb beneath the spaghetti strap of her top on her left shoulder, and lightly stroked the pad across her skin. "You're beautiful," he uttered softly before his head lowered and his smooth lips feathered along her collarbone.

With her heart racing, Bailey tried to concentrate on not showing how much his touch affected her. It lasted all of one second as her strap was slipped off her shoulder.

"Uh, will I have to sit up front with your driver, Mr. Marx?" Bringing her strap up, she reared back and smirked at seeing the rigid scowl that washed over his face at the notion of her sitting with Isaac.

She tried to redirect them back to their casual, comfortable discussion. "I have a younger brother, Caleb. He graduated this past May from UNC. My parents, well, more my dad is annoyed because my brother has decided to take a year off before securing a solid job. My mom is just thrilled to have him living at home again. Oh!" Suddenly, the car swerved a sharp right, throwing her across his lap. Bailey gave a look out of the window.

"Sorry, boss," Isaac said over the intercom. "A group of teens rushed across the lane on skateboards."

"No worries," Lucas dimly answered back without pressing the intercom for Isaac to hear him.

He inhaled deeply through his nose, and Bailey turned to him. He'd sniffed her hair. His gaze shifted downward to her hand resting on his right thigh. The muscle flexed beneath her palm. *Goodness!* It was like gripping steel. That throb in her core started up again. Her cheeks warmed as she sat back in her seat. "Sorry." Her jumbled brain couldn't come up with anything better with the smoldering look he was now giving her.

"Don't be."

"We're here."

He looked out the window. They were in downtown D.C. near the Washington Monument. Scores of people littered the grounds watching a band perform on an outdoor stage. A jumbotron gave everyone a front row seat.

Not bothering to veil his displeasure, he looked at her with a frown. "An outdoor concert?"

"You don't like concerts?"

"I do, when it's held in an air-conditioned building, and I'm sitting in my nice, comfortable, *private* balcony suite."

"Well, you're in luck because the concert just ended." She pointed to the band walking off the stage. "I had no intention of us coming here for the concert." Getting a confused look, she said happily, "We're going to watch a movie. Thursday night is Movie on the Mall night. Every Thursday, from mid-June through August, a movie is played on the jumbotron." She waved a hand at her duffel bag. "I brought us a blanket to sit on." She then directed his attention back to the window. "See, everyone is cordoning off their spots." He looked around at the hoard assembling on the lawn. His grimace practically knitted his brows together. "Well, what do you think?"

"How about we go back to my place and watch a movie in my theater? Name a movie, any movie. I can get prereleases of any movie you wish to see."

"I want to see *Men in Black 3*. That's what's being played tonight."

"Really! Not even R-rated?" Still frowning, he shook his head as he looked out at the sea of people.

"It can't be R-rated. There are children present." Bailey observed him look out at the crowd with a shudder. "Not fond of kids?" she asked, and he visibly flinched at the sight of the children roughhousing upon the grass.

"You don't see yourself someday having little Lucas or some other *L* name running around that big house of yours? I assumed that's why you bought the property, given its size and location. Quite honestly, I would've pictured your taste to be some swank, downtown high-rise penthouse."

"I have several of those. I bought the Chevy Chase property because I like the location, six acres that would sell well. I certainly don't intend to fill it with rug rats."

So he doesn't like kids. That little Get to Know You was a bit disappointing.

"You said whatever my heart desired. I want to watch the movie here. Or we could call it a night if you like. I have to work tomorrow. I can get to bed early." She looked at Isaac standing in wait outside the door. "Shall we go or not?"

"I'm up for that, us getting to bed early, that is," he joked, and she playfully punched his shoulder. "How about we make a deal, princess? If I do this, you agree to go out with me again, and I get to pick the place, anywhere I choose."

Princess. Bailey couldn't help smiling at the endearment. He was very charming. That devilish look he was giving her was also her red flag to be wary, but the quizzical part of her was curious as to what he would have in mind ... other than the obvious. "Okay," she found herself saying.

"When in Rome," he uttered, picked up the duffel bag, got out, and helped her out. She came in close, ran her palms down his forearms to his hands, entwined their fingers, lifted up on her insteps, and planted a kiss on his cheek. His eyes brightened with a look of surprise by the intimate gesture. She then thanked Isaac for the drive, and he smiled widely with a nod.

"Let's find a good spot." Seeing Lucas's objectionable look out at the crowd, Bailey took his hand and led the way.

There were vendors selling popcorn and an assortment of food and beverages. Releasing Lucas's hand, she jogged over to a beverage vendor and asked for two bottled waters, then realized her wallet was stuffed in the bottom of the duffel bag. Turning,

Lucas stood behind her holding up a twenty. He gave the man the bill and said to keep the change. She scooped up the water bottles, made their way down the line of vendors, and stopped at a popcorn cart. Before she could say anything, Lucas stepped up and ordered a large tub—no butter. He handed the woman a twenty, and again, said to keep the change. Bailey grabbed a wad of napkins and turned to him.

"Ready?"

Lucas picked up the popcorn tub and looked out at the clutter of people. "Really, Bailey?"

"They don't bite. Come on."

She chose a spot far back and away from the crowd for Lucas's benefit, then took out the blanket and spread it upon the grass. "Mr. Marx, you're a very generous tipper."

He sat down beside her. "Is this how you spend your Thursday evenings off? Is that why Kevin was pissed? Did I take his place on the blanket?"

Bailey removed her flip-flops to get comfortable. "Kevin and I were here for—"

"Now I sure as hell don't want to be here," he muttered as he looked around at the crowd, his look of his displeasure absolute.

She sighed. "I was going to say it was to celebrate Sienna's birthday. There were twelve of us."

"I see." A wad of barbed wire cloaked those two words. Was that a hint of jealousy that she heard? "When does this thing start?" he asked.

"This *thing* should start any minute," she answered mockingly, and he met her eyes briefly before returning his attention to the crowd, looking very uncomfortable.

Night had come. The lights of the jumbotron flickered on.

Bailey regarded Lucas's bored comportment as he tossed one piece of popcorn in his mouth at a time. She faced him and sat back on her shins, wondering if she should just call the evening a bust. It was a mistake to bring him here. This was obviously not his cup of tea. "Have you seen this movie before?" she asked him.

His cell phone chimed. He pulled it from his pocket and checked the text message. "It's Kara updating me on a matter. And no, I haven't seen it." He was about to stick the phone back into his pocket when she took it from him and straddled his thighs with her back against his chest. Bailey brought his right arm around her waist and turned her face to his with a smile.

"Let's take a picture to remember our first date. Unlock it." He entered the passcode. She pulled up the camera app and held it out in front of them. With a tilt of her head to his, offering a big smile, she snapped the shot. Taking a look at the picture, she sighed, disappointed. "You didn't smile. The first pic is what counts."

He was about to wrap his other arm around her, but she gave him back his phone and got off his lap. She then began removing his loafers.

"What are you doing?"

"I'm making you more comfortable." She placed his shoes next to the duffel bag, and then massaged his sock-covered arches. "Better?"

Though he shrugged in reply, her fingers working his insteps seemed to take the stiffness out of his bearing.

She straddled his thighs again, coming face to face with him this time, unbuttoned the cuffs on his sleeves, and folded each neatly up his forearms. "How about now? Much better?" she asked as her hand slipped inside his shirt at his shoulders and began a firm massage of the tight muscles. The light express of breath he made eased her own tension.

"You seated on my lap, touching me, hell yes, much better." He took hold of her waist and tugged her to him. Her breasts teasingly brushed his chest. Their gazes held with his mouth a mere whisper from hers. "What now, princess?"

"The movie is about to start." Bailey gestured with a thumb over her shoulder as if she needed to show proof. "Oh!" Catching her by surprise, he effortlessly spun her around and maneuvered her to sit between his legs. "Lucas, what—" She tried to get up, but he wrapped a beefy arm around her waist, making it clear she wasn't going anywhere. "Lucas."

"Oh, it's Lucas now? Before it was Mr. Marx this and Mr. Marx that," he laughingly teased, tickling her, and she giggled and squirmed to get free. He held her close, sheltering her body within the solid form of his.

Bailey tilted her head back at his shoulder and looked up at him. So handsome he was. Unable to help herself, she placed a light kiss upon his cheek. "Popcorn?" With their eyes on one another, she fed him, and allowed her index finger to dip in and touch his tongue. Wearing a playful grin, he gently nipped and sucked the tip. A distinct shudder ran through her.

"A word of caution, princess. Be careful of what you start."

"Meaning?" she asked and chewed on her bottom lip at the sound of his voice taking on that familiar sexy pulse.

"I have a rather large appetite." He took into his mouth the full length of her index finger, suckled for long seconds, and then nipped and kissed her palm on up the underside of her wrist, his hot, compelling gaze upon her never wavering.

Her heavy pant could not be contained.

Good God!

Chapter Fifteen

Bailey was enjoying herself. She sat contently between Lucas's legs, resting back against his heavily muscled chest, taking pleasure in the feel of his strong arms secured around her.

Over the past two hours, they chatted throughout the movie, and each comfortably and without thinking, fed the other popcorn. It all felt natural—easy between them—as though they were longtime companions.

He'd been quiet for some time as he brushed his cheek alongside her left temple. She looked up intending to ask if he was all right, but lost her train of thought when their eyes met. They stayed like that, simply gazing with no words spoken as long seconds passed. Suddenly, as clear as the full moon above, a startling awareness seemed to glow bright between them.

Bailey moistened her lips as she stared at his pretty mouth, desperate for a taste, waiting—wanting—yearning for him to kiss her. *Kiss me, damn it.* Her eyes came back up to his with intent to be bold.

"I-I like being here with you." *Chicken.* She didn't have the courage. He was looking at her with such penetrating intensity, her heart sputtered, and a maelstrom of emotions welled up inside her. A deep inhale and slow release helped to calm her pattering pulse. *Am I seeing in his eyes what I want to see?* As afraid as she was to chance her heart again, one thing was certain: *I want this man.*

"Bailey, I've enjoyed being with you, too."

Was she right in her assumption? Unable to restrain herself a second longer, slowly, cautiously, her mouth met his. Her hand skated up hard muscular pecs and over broad shoulders, circling around his neck. His mouth opened—offering—his tongue chased—capturing, returning her kiss with heads angled sharply in eager need to deepen the kiss.

Her hand moved to the back of his head, silky, dark tresses slipping through her anchoring fingers as she turned in his arms enough that her right breast pressed into the solid wall of his chest. It seemed to spark a charge. Their kiss quickly turned urgent—greedy—desperate, awaking their pinned up desires like a lightning bolt.

He reared back somewhat and brought her nearly on top of him. Both hands moved in a slow caress along her spine to her buttocks and squeezed as he pressed her into the jut of his hips. That had her breaking their frenzied kiss.

"Bailey," he breathed out in hurried pulls with eyes heavy-lidded, his lust for her apparent.

"We ... we shouldn't do this here," she said, her breathing just as labored. "All of these people ..." She surveyed the crowd to see if anyone watched them. It didn't appear so; nevertheless, uncomfortable, she moved from between his legs. "We can't."

"You're right, not here." With his focus locked on her, he took out his cell phone. "We'll be at the curb in ten."

"We're leaving? But the movie isn't over."

As he moistened his lips, that hot, telling look of desire in his eyes was her answer. "Hell yes, it's definitely time to go." He stood up and hastily slipped his shoes back on, then crouched, and quickly guided her feet into her sandals.

Seeing that he was on a mission to get them gone posthaste, she grabbed the empty water bottles and popcorn tub and then sprinted over to a trash receptacle.

He made quick work of folding the blanket, shoved it into the duffel bag, and then turned to her. "Let's go."

She was tugged along this time.

• • •

Seated in the car, Bailey stared at him. "Lucas, the movie only had a few minutes left to go."

"I'll make it up to you. We'll finish it another time."

She followed his eyes like that of a predator roaming slowly over her body. "I'm talking ten or fifteen minutes at most."

"The way you kiss, trust me, I wouldn't have lasted that long." He slid over, took up her left hand, and planted a kiss in her palm. "Thank you for taking me out of my comfort zone. It's not often I allow my insecurities to be tested."

"You mean never allow, I'm sure." Bailey didn't object to his arm circling her waist to bring her next to him. He then brushed his lips feather light over hers and murmured, "I allow it with you." The tip of his tongue traced her bottom lip before he captured it between his lips, sucking her flesh.

She tried to remain in control by rearing back. He released her lip only to kiss her full on. His other hand cradled the back of her neck, holding her in place as his tongue practically slipped down her throat, ravenous in its exploration.

She managed to break the deep kiss once again, in search of much needed air. He simply dragged his mouth on down the arch of her neck, his warm tongue licking, tasting her skin along the way.

He was so much male, so intense, she didn't know how to react, totally out of her element with a man such as him. With that thought, it happened so fast, he brought her down to the seat and cloaked her body beneath his, positioning himself between her thighs.

She knew she should protest his aggressive actions, but the carnal desires stirring inside her, the cravings she'd had from the very first moment she'd laid eyes on him, controlled her actions.

Her right leg wedged against the seat hooked tight at his back, causing his erection to press at the apex of her thighs.

Man oh man! There was no way what she felt swelling up by the second between her legs could possibly be all him. A bolt of heat laced with fear shot up from her toes to her core with a slow pulsing taking root deep in her channel. There was also the cell phone in his pocket pinching her inner thigh. The slight discomfort kept her craving at a low simmer.

He drew back from kissing her neck and looked down upon her face. "You're so damn sexy, you know that," he uttered thickly. Cradling her nape, he took her mouth again, tonguing her deeper still, thoroughly, unrelenting, while stroking her between her legs atop her shorts, feeling the heat of her there swiftly intensifying.

"Bailey, let me have you," he whispered into her mouth and rolled his hips, massaging his erection against her hot center. A full-bodied shudder took hold of her. Her right leg clamped down even tighter at his back.

He ran his tongue greedily along her chin, up to the outline of her ear, and back to her mouth all as he stroked up and down her left thigh.

"You have the most beautiful legs I've ever seen. I've dreamed of running my hands over your silky skin, your beautiful body, touching, kissing you, Bailey."

"You're a leg man, Mr. Marx?" Bailey rocked her sex upon his incredibly rigid thickness as her sheath throbbed for the promise she felt to be had between her legs.

"I am now."

"Your cell phone is pinching me."

"Sorry." He pulled out the phone and tossed it behind him on the seat.

Short gasps escaped her as he slipped a warm hand under her blouse and glided upward to gently caress her breasts. Rolling the pebbling nipple between his fingers, he uttered through breathy kisses, "Damn, you're perfect."

Her moans grew louder as his other hand tunneled under the hem of her shorts, stroked, and squeezed her buttocks.

"We ... we should stop," she breathed out heavily before shutting her eyes and yanking him back to the starving demand of her mouth.

Ignoring her feeble words, he hooked his index finger underneath the silk string of her thong and circled her clitoris before dipping his finger inside her pussy. A smile broke out across his mouth against hers at the feel of how wet she was for him already.

"Oh yes!" she cried out and bucked her hips repeatedly at the slow roll of his finger in her sex. "Right there," she wailed shamelessly.

Her other leg came up and both wrapped high up his back, allowing his finger to tunnel deeper. In chorus, he rhythmically pinched her nipple and stroked her channel as their tongues danced and dueled, both wanting to lead in their devouring kiss.

At once, he tore away from her mouth and his synchronized movements abruptly stopped working her flesh. Peering up at him, she panted out, "What is it?"

"Stay the night with me."

"You're staying at your friend's."

"We'll go to my place." She nodded as a second thick digit was added to the one already buried deep inside her.

He released her breast, hit a button somewhere above her head, and quickly gave instructions to Isaac to head to his place.

The moment his tongue rimmed her ear, a feral cry escaped her partially opened mouth, and her nails bit into his back through his fine shirt, holding tight to him as she rocked her hips in quick momentum, matching his quick thrusting fingers and rubbing her clitoris along his length through his slacks, dry humping him, working to bring herself to release.

"You're so wet," he moaned as his fingers drilled her pussy in between his fevered kisses on her mouth and neck.

He abruptly released her breasts again. The music was turned up. Coldplay's "Paradise" resonated ear-piercingly in the car's cabin.

Moving to his knees on the floor, he brought her upright and forward to the edge of the seat. The crotch of her shorts and the silk string of her thong were pushed aside to toy with the swollen rosy bud of her sex. He pinched and circled the throbbing button, fingered her wet sheath with deep penetrating thrusts, in and out, again and again. A tug at her floral top exposed a breast that he hastily took into his mouth.

"Bailey, I want you," he uttered as he suckled, lightly bit the tight nipple, and then flicked it repeatedly with his tongue.

"Oh yes, right there!" She threw her head back and arched her back sharply in offering, so far gone, drunk from the pleasure that an intense prickling sensation reverberated up her spine. He was relentless. "I can't, please," she whimpered, unsure whether she was asking him to stop or pleading for more in between rolling her hips to take what she needed.

The prickling stopped and then started up again. She opened her eyes and blinked rapidly to clear the passion fog. It was his cell phone buzzing at the small of her back. Looking down at him between her legs, he was unzipping her shorts.

"Lucas?" Her voice was hoarse from the dryness of her throat brought on by heavy pants. He didn't seem to hear her, so focused on his task of pulling her shorts and panties down past her knees.

With urgency, his mouth clamped onto her mound with his tongue disappearing between the slit. "Oh!" She slapped a hand over her mouth to fight back a scream. The sensation of his tongue slowly circling her sensitive bud was mind-numbingly amazing.

She snaked her fingers in the feathery waves of his hair, raised her hips, and pressed her pussy to his mouth, wanting his tongue to cure the throb felt deep in her core. Understanding her need, he swiftly yanked off her shorts and panties in one fell swoop, sending her flip-flops airborne. "Oh shhh!" Bailey gasped, feeling sexually wanton and exposed before him.

"Tell me what you want, princess." He met her eyes as the tips of his fingers lightly brushed up and down her wet folds. "I'm waiting."

"Lick me. No teasing," she ordered without shame, and he obliged as he spread her legs wide and brought both of her feet up to brace on the seat. He ran his hands, followed by his mouth, along her inner thighs to her sex, separated her labia, and took her clitoris into his mouth, sucking hard as two fingers reentered her pussy, stroking deep.

"Yes, Lucas!" He threw her legs over his shoulders, cupped her buttocks, and buried his head between her thighs, lapping hungrily upon her.

With her legs spread wide, Bailey balanced her right foot on the door and dug her fingers in his hair to keep him right where she needed him. "Just like that, don't stop!" she panted and felt his tongue perform a rolling maneuver inside her, followed by long, lollypop-like licks from her vagina to her clitoris, up and down, over and around, to settle with a hard suck on her clitoris, repeating numerous times. The feeling was glorious. She'd never been so thoroughly eaten out and stroked before, so close, rocking faster upon his mouth and fingers, hanging on the precipice of an orgasmic explosion.

The persistent buzzing started up again. Bailey opened her eyes; Lucas's head was rapidly bobbing up and down between her thighs.

She retrieved the phone from behind her and read the display. The name Rachel lit up brightly on the screen. Seeing a woman's name quickly sent the blood from her nether regions back to her brain. It was his private line. His business cell phone was still cradled on the console.

Who's Rachel?

"Lucas?" she called to him while staring at the phone beside her. His head came up, his face from nose to chin practically coated in her juices, looking just as passion drunk as she felt. "Your phone." She sat up and turned off the music. He stared out as if confused by her words. "Answer it," she said. He spread her legs and brought his mouth back down. As he licked and sucked the lips of her sex, his hand snatched the phone from the seat. "What?" he growled into the phone, and then continued to lick and flick her clitoris.

"Is that any way to speak to your mother?"

Hearing Lucas's mother, as if she could see her through the phone, Bailey hastily grabbed her thong and shorts from the floor and put them back on in record speed.

"Why are you on Rachel's phone?" Lucas asked his mother. He licked his lips and accepted the napkin Bailey handed him from the minibar to wipe her cream from his mouth and chin.

"Your cousin is visiting with us here at the beach house. I borrowed her phone. I tried calling from my phone, but you wouldn't answer. I figured you'd pick up if you didn't know it was me. I see I was right."

Discovering that Rachael was a relative and not another woman, Bailey relaxed a bit and sat back.

"This isn't a good time, Mother." With the phone to his ear, half listening to his mother, he leaned in, and she allowed him to give her a peck on the lips, followed by another, that turned into full on tongues rolling together, so weak she was for his kisses. Tasting her heat on his tongue provoked her overstimulated body into a shudder of need. His free hand caressed her exposed breast with them kissing in short, hurried nips and licks.

"Lucas, are you listening to me? It's the least you could do," his mother huffed, practically yelling into the phone with full irritation in her voice.

Unable to help herself, Bailey nipped his bottom lip and tongued him in deep, sweeping thoroughness before uttering against his mouth, "Talk to your mother." He continued to kiss her in a fevered rush. She reared back and lightly gripped his chin to get him to look at her. "Lucas, talk to her."

"Is that Sandy? That's why I'm calling. Let me speak to her."

Sandy! She didn't just ... Bailey gaped. A giant tub of ice water had been pour over her, chilling her to the bone. That's what it felt like. He reached for her. "Don't." Annoyed, she batted his hand away and began looking around the floor for her flip-flops.

"Mother, it's not her," Lucas answered with his jaws set when she asked again to speak to Sandra. "Really, this isn't a good time." He attempted another kiss, but Bailey shoved him hard in the chest.

"Well, I called to ask if you were planning to bring Sandy as your date to your sister's wedding. I'm confirming the guest list, and I haven't received a commitment from you on your plus one. Sandy said she plans to talk to you about it when you two get together on Friday. Will she be joining you at the pre-wedding dinner as well?"

Hearing that, Bailey's eyes narrowed before she looked away. *But you say you're not seeing Sandra, that you're just business associates. Bullshit. I'm such an idiot. Men, they're all the same.*

He took hold of her chin and forced her to look at him. Holding her arctic glare, he said to his mother, "I'm not bringing Sandra to the wedding or to anything, ever. We're not involved. Are we clear, Mother?"

"But, Lucas, she said you two have a date scheduled, so I thought—"

"I'll call you tomorrow. Good night." He ended the call. "Are we clear, Bailey?"

"Whatever." Bailey straightened her top and crossed her legs. Her nipples ached, her pussy throbbed, and the crotch of her shorts was soaked, making her all the more pissed off that she'd let her guard down with him. *I'm so stupid.*

"Since my father passed, my mother tends to call me quite often. What's more, she always speaks loudly whenever she walks along the beach, as if the ocean waves prevent me from hearing her." A light chuckle.

Bailey looked out her window, crossed her arms at her chest, and delivered a clip answer back, "Whatever, Mr. Marx."

"I'm Mr. Marx again." A sigh. "I see we're back there then." He moved back to the seat and combed his fingers through his hair as he said, "Sandra and I aren't together. Our families have been friends for many years. To be honest with you, my mother would like to see Sandra and me become a couple again. It's not happening."

"Whatever you say." Bailey scanned the console. "Where's the button to talk to Isaac. I want to tell him to take me home."

Lucas frowned. "You're not coming to my place?"

"Nope."

"Why? We're a block away."

"Look, I'm tired and in no mood to play twenty questions."

He stared at her for a long moment before tapping the intercom and gave Isaac instructions.

They remained silent throughout the trip to her place.

Standing at her door, Bailey turned to face him with her key in hand and her eyes downcast, too annoyed, mainly with herself, to even look at him. He brought her chin up with the side of his index finger and her frigid eyes met his.

"I actually enjoyed the Movie on the Mall." His tone was soft, sweet.

Unfazed. "Yep," she responded dryly.

"Bailey—"

"It's late. I have to get up early. I'll stop by in the morning to check on the progress of the work. Your girl, *Sandy*, expects a report first thing."

He bent to kiss her mouth, but she turned her head, reducing him to a mere kiss on the cheek. "Good night, Mr. Marx." She quickly unlocked the door, entered, and closed it in his face.

Chapter Sixteen

Bailey came back inside the apartment. "Of all days, I don't need this right now," she grumbled on her way into the kitchen and washed her hands.

Sienna followed behind her. "Just let me ask Kevin to take another look at it," she suggested for the third time.

Faith came into the living room and plopped down on the couch. "Hey, Bails, I thought you left."

"My car won't start." Bailey turned back to Sienna. "And absolutely not. I told you what he said to me yesterday." She ripped off a paper towel and dried her hands. "He was wrong for what he said, but I understand his feelings. I'll catch the bus."

"You know the bus doesn't run near Lucas's place. You'll have to walk about a mile from the nearest stop to his house. By then, you'll be drenched. It's seven o'clock and already close to eighty degrees."

"I know. I'm clammy from fiddling around out there with that damn car." Bailey tugged at her silk blouse sticking to her skin. "I'll call an Uber. It'll cost me a fortune because I'll have to take it from his place into the city at rush hour, but I have to go over there to review the work. Sandra's expecting a report when I get in today."

"So his mother is team Sandy, huh? You said she's tight with the family."

"Yes, it seems that way, but it's cool. It helped me put things back in check."

"You said Lucas told his mother that he wasn't involved with her. Bails, you need to talk to the man. Place the whole Sandra issue on the table, lay it all out."

"There's nothing to talk about. He's taking her to the art event. From where I sit, that's involved. I know what he wants from me. I'm sure that's pretty much all he wants. I don't want to talk about him anymore." Sienna followed her to her bedroom. Bailey began removing her clothes, stripping down to her bra and panties. "I need to get my ride, but first, I need to take another shower."

"Let me handle your ride. You go get ready." Sienna left the room, but then poked her head back in. "You're still coming tonight, right? Don't forget, it's formal. Black tie formal."

Bailey gasped. "Geez, why didn't you tell me? I wouldn't miss it, but now I have to find something to wear." She stepped across the hall into the bathroom.

• • •

Lucas pulled up and parked in front of Bailey's building. He got out of his car just as Kevin stepped out of his apartment. It would seem they locked eyes on one another at precisely the same moment. Neither man balked from the piercing challenge as they passed each other on the sidewalk.

Standing at Bailey's door, Lucas kept hard eyes on the man that was doing the same to him. Kevin cut a contemptuous look over at Lucas's Ferrari before he climbed into the Jeep Cherokee that was parked beside it and drove away.

Just friends my ass.

He took a moment to settle the slight rise in primal aggression that seeped in him from the mere sight of Kevin. Lucas also prepared himself for *pissed off Bailey* to emerge as Sienna had warned him when she'd called. After the way things ended between them last night, he expected it.

He knocked on the door. A moment later, it opened, and he was greeted by an attractive blond dressed in a fluffy pale blue bathrobe. "Good morning, I'm Lucas Marx. I'm here to see Bailey."

"I know. I'm her friend, Faith." Her head turned. "Bails," she hollered over her shoulder, then turned back. "Come in. Have a seat." She beckoned a hand at the barstools over by the counter, and they both sat down. "Can I get you anything? I was about to have some tea."

"No, thanks."

As she added sugar to her cup, she said, "It's great to finally meet you." She crossed her legs, and the robe separated, revealing smooth pale skin far up the split of her thighs.

Lucas's gaze dipped and then came up. Her blue eyes glinted as she slowly rotated the spoon in her cup. Awareness bloomed when she didn't bother covering herself, merely rocked her crossed leg between his while giving him a long look.

Their attention was drawn to the voices coming from down the hall. Lucas heard Bailey say, not bothering to whisper, "What's he doing here?"

"Well, see, when I told you I'd handle getting you your ride—" Sienna said.

"You didn't. Tell me, Sie, you did not call Lucas? Why would you do that? Did you not hear anything I said last night?"

"You needed to get to his house, and you didn't want to ask Kevin for help."

Moments later, Bailey came into the living room dressed in only a purple towel and pink fuzzy slippers. "Good morning," she all but gritted, her expression as hard as marble.

Faith immediately hopped down from her perch and Lucas slowly stood up.

"Good morning, princess. Did you sleep well? I of course have had better nights." Lucas sent her a small smile and received the slight narrowing of her eyes before she shifted them to her friend.

"I see you've met Faith." A flicker of something he couldn't quite place surfaced in her expression directed at her friend before she brought her rigid gaze back to him. "Sienna told me she called you, but I don't need a ride. You can go now. Thanks for coming."

Even with the blistering look she was giving him, she looked absolutely irresistible in that getup.

When he didn't move, her glare was direct and candid. "Don't you have a company to run, someone to push around?"

"I was expecting to see you at my place this morning, thought we could talk." He wasn't at all affected by her vicious bite, though his leveled demeanor seemed to add to her irritation.

"Uh, Bails, you do need a ride," Sienna said, now standing beside her. "And sweetie, you need to put some clothes on."

"Good heavens!" Bailey gasped and looked down at herself. Clutching the front of the towel, she ran out of the room.

"Yeah, she's kind of worked up," Sienna told Lucas.

"I can see that."

"Lucas, you wouldn't be in need of an assistant, would you? I'm looking for employment," Faith said.

"Does that mean you're not going back home?" Sienna asked her.

Faith's head turned to him, and Lucas read the admiring gleam in her eyes as she said, "There are better prospects here than back home."

His attention shifted to Bailey entering the room now wearing a hot-pink dress with thin shoulder straps and matching, very high heels with tiny multicolored flowers crisscrossing the deep arch of her feet. He liked how the severe instep exaggerated the shapeliness of her calves. Her hair was pulled up, twisted, and pinned back from her lovely face. She kept her appearance simple, yet always pulled together well.

"You look lovely."

A slight flicker softened in her eyes before those glacial green orbs hardened back up. "Thanks." Dry as a bone. She whipped her head over to Faith. "He has an assistant. A very efficient one," she shot at her, apparently having heard their conversation from her bedroom. Lucas sensed an undercurrent of something going on between them.

"My assistant is irreplaceable, I'm afraid. However, I'll make some calls around," he said.

At that, Bailey snatched up her satchel and portfolio from the sofa, then turned to him, still scowling. "I guess I'm riding with you." She swung open the door and stalked out.

Lucas turned to Sienna. "Good luck tonight."

"Yeah right. I need to tell Bailey about all of this. You think she's pissed? When she finds out what we did, you had better bob and weave, pretty boy."

"Give me a couple of days. I first need to get back into her good graces. I don't think now would be wise." He glanced at the door that Bailey left wide open. "We'll tell her together." He turned to Faith. "It was nice meeting you."

"It was very nice meeting you, too, Lucas." Faith smiled, an overtly seductive smile.

Ignoring the gesture, as he closed the door behind him, he heard her asked Sienna, "What was that about?" Her head had bounced back and forth between them, having been left out of the exchange.

Thinking about all that Sienna would share with Faith, he headed to Bailey standing at his car, her arms tightly crossed at her chest, her features a turbulent storm. *I better get ready.*

Chapter Seventeen

Bailey was mutely humming along to Drake's "Furthest Thing, Unedited" until Lucas decided to turn the volume down. The music had actually helped tame her foul mood.

She side-eyed him, then turned her head back to her window. Like many things about the man, it was interesting to her that Mr. CEO would be a fan of a hip-hop singer.

Her irritation with him didn't stop her from appreciating his powerful build. Her nostrils pleasantly soaked up his familiar masculine scent, that blend of a light woodsy fragrance with a hint of an airy fresh citrus she'd come to love, and had been covered in his distinct, delicious bouquet the night before. She'd purposely climbed in bed to savor his scent as she slept dreamily into the morning before reluctantly showering him off.

His hair fell in dark, damp waves, shaping around his ears, and curled loosely at the back of his neck. He wore his black loafers from the night before with no socks, a stone-gray-colored T-shirt that hugged the sinewy sculpture of his chest and biceps, and his muscular thighs were encased in a pair of medium blue denims.

Why does he have to be so damn gorgeous?

"Are you attending the art event this evening?" he asked, breaking the silence.

"Yes," she answered with her focus kept out her window. "I need to find something to wear. I didn't realize until today that the attire is evening wear. I'll likely raid Sienna's closet. How I am with shoes, she's mad about clothes."

He nodded. "What's up with your friend Faith? You—"

Bailey whipped her head around, facing him. "Why? What exactly are you asking? Whether or not she's available?" Her temper spiked back up. "I saw you two, the way you were looking at her."

His head jerked over. "You're being ridiculous."

"Am I?" She uncrossed her legs and angled in her seat toward him. "You find her attractive?"

"Do I find her attractive? Yes. That goes for Sienna and the weather girl on D.C.'s five o'clock news. What's your point?" He briefly met her rigid stare, then brought his eyes back to the road.

"Typical. It's how you all are. It's not the first time, and it won't be the last. At least you're honest about it." Annoyed, her head turned back to her window with arms crossed tight at her chest.

"What is that supposed to mean? I asked about her because I sensed tension between you two, mainly you with her," he pointed out.

Her head swung back to him. "So you assumed I'm the one with the problem?" He sighed deep as if grappling for patience, which only fueled her vexation.

"Bailey, you're upset about your car, obviously still irritated with me about last night, and likely Sienna for calling me."

"Sienna shouldn't have called you," she bit out.

"I'll have my mechanic take a look at your car. You can take the Porsche."

She shook her head. "No way."

"Then take the Bentley or this one. It doesn't matter."

A sharp turn took them down the winding road to his home and onto his property. He quickly tapped in the security code to open the gates and rolled through as garage door three slowly came up.

"No, Lucas, I'm not driving your Ferrari or any of the others." She looked down at his hand shifting gears as he pulled in and brought the car to a stop. "I can't drive a manual vehicle anyway."

They got out of the car and headed for the door that led into the mudroom of the house.

"I'll buy you a car."

Entering the kitchen, Bailey took out her camera and began looking over the finished work. "You're not buying me a car." She bent down for a closer look at the floors and trim work, checked the cabinets, appliances, inspected the marble, snapping pictures as she went, and then left the kitchen to check out the great room.

The three sofas and flat screen were due to arrive soon, but the walls were painted a rich taupe as she'd instructed. The large area rug, tables, and armchairs along with the other accessories were in place. Sienna's artwork hung on the wall, and the fireplace's new black glass surround was completed. She walked over to the French doors and stepped outside to inspect the new outdoor furniture.

"You keep running from me."

His voiced startled her, and she jumped slightly at the feel of his massive body close at her back. Strong, capable hands rested on her bare shoulders. Then he ran his palms lightly up and down her arms. *I have dreamed of running my hands over your body, touching, kissing you.* Her mind replayed his words from the night before, and with it, those warm feelings of being wrapped in his comforting arms came rushing forth.

She stepped away, breaking the contact to avoid getting pulled back under his spell, and went over to the pool house. A few minutes later, she returned and saw that he hadn't budged from where she'd left him.

"I need to take a look at the patio furniture on your private sundeck." Hastily, she moved past him back into the house and up the stairs with him close behind her.

Entering his bedroom, she glanced over at the rumpled sheets on his bed on her way out the French doors, taking in a much needed breath to relax.

"Why are you so afraid?"

He spoke from behind her again. Bailey made some notes in her pad, snapped a few pictures, and then closed her eyes while taking another refueling breath before turning to him standing in the doorway.

Just then, her cell phone chimed a text message. Pulling the phone from her satchel, it was a text from Kevin that read:

Let's talk, dollface.

Kevin using the pet name he'd given her meant he was no longer upset with her. It brought a smile to her face. Her head came up to see Lucas's eyes shift from the phone in her hand to her face, giving off a wary look.

"Is Kevin the reason you keep pushing me away?" he asked with his gaze pinned on her cell phone. "I'm not seeing Sandra, so you can lay that excuse to rest. Your concern for your job may be some of it, but there's another reason why you won't let me in."

"Kevin and I are friends." She put her phone back in her satchel, stepped back inside, and he closed the door.

Lucas brought her chin up and lightly ran the pad of his thumb across her lips. "From the looks of it yesterday, there was much more between you two than mere friends. Was that text from your *friend*?"

Looking up at him, Bailey nodded and swallowed to soothe the dryness in her throat. Just being close to him gave her warm tingles all over. If he only knew the impact his mere presence had on her.

"Like I told you, we dated for a short time. We remain close ... as friends." He dropped his hand and stepped back, his warm gaze now replaced with a severe scowl and his features sealed tight.

"Friends, you say. You accuse me when it's you who should be admitting truths."

"Admitting truths? Like what exactly?"

Without another word, he went into his closet.

"I do care for Kevin, but not in the way that I believe you're implying." Did he think she would have allowed him to put his mouth and fingers on her most intimate parts if she was involved with another man? What type of woman did he think she was? More importantly, what type of woman was he used to?

She went over and stood within the doorframe of the closet where he was inside taking a pair of gray silk socks out of a drawer. He then moved over to his tie rack and hit a button that slowly revolved the rack until he stopped it to select the one he wanted. "I'll admit, Kevin wants more than friendship, but—"

"But you keep him at arm's length, pull him in when the need suits you, and then string him along when you tire of him." He laid out his dotted gray tie across the black marble island next to his silk socks. "I'm becoming very familiar with your technique," he uttered with a fleeting look at her over his shoulder.

"How dare you!" she snapped, and he turned around, stabbing her with a harsh look.

"I'm not into games, Bailey. Go play with Kevin." He turned away, then pivoted back. "You know what I think?"

Bailey bit her bottom lip to keep the angry tears stinging the back of her eyes at bay. "It's abundantly clear what you think of me." His dark brows rose subtly at that.

"This has nothing to do with my prior involvement with Sandra. That's merely the setup here in this game of yours with me. I think some chump screwed you over, and now men like Kevin and me are being hit with the shrapnel. The moment you start to feel something, you clam up. Cold-hearted Bailey Walters, she'll do it to them before they do it to her. I guess Kevin is comfortable with your leash."

"Don't you speak to me that way! We're done here." With jaws clenched tight to hold on to her restraint, she stated with a professional evenness, "Mr. Marx, your renovations are complete. The remaining items should arrive next week. Your assistant will be contacted at that time. I'll call an Uber and wait outside." She stalked off with the hurt and pain of his words spearing her chest. He rushed in front of her and blocked her path at the bedroom door. She kept her eyes downcast, holding on tight to her emotions while swallowing repeatedly to cure the sharp ache in her throat. "Move out of my way, Mr. Marx."

"Did I hit a sore spot?" His audacious attempt to touch her cheek, which was scorching from the heated depth of her anger, was slapped away. "I'm right, aren't I?"

"Get out of my way!" she yelled and tried to shove his muscular body to no avail. It was like trying to move a train. "Move, damn you!"

"Not until you admit it. Tell me I'm right, and then I'll let you leave. And trust me, I won't bother you again."

Bailey brought her eyes up to his, hating that he witnessed the angry tears he'd provoked. "You're partially right. Does that make you happy?" she gritted. With her eyes fixed on his, first in anger, then with a steadily increasing anguish, she told him, "My ex cheated on me with my then best friend, Faith. I forgave her, and in time, I allowed myself to trust yet another man, who ... yes, you guessed it, cheated on me, yet again." She blinked and hastily swept away the tear from her cheek that managed to escape. "But there's one thing you didn't get right, Mr. Marx. As afraid as I was to do so, I was falling for you, falling fast and hard, so hard that I cannot stop thinking about you. Oh, I tried damn hard, trust me. But you're in my head, my dreams," she admitted. "A man like you, I figured would be my downfall once again. It scares the hell out of me. That's the main reason why I pulled back, afraid that you would also hurt me." A heavy-hearted sigh left her. "I guess I can't seem to dodge that bullet."

She pushed and shoved him to get him to move. There wasn't even a ghost of a sway in his stance from the laborious effort. Giving up on it, she headed for the French doors, intending to leave by way of the stairs on his private terrace. Again, he blocked her path and stared at her with a look of astonishment blanketing his features over what she'd said. "Get out of my way!" she hissed angrily.

"Bailey—"

"Don't." She shook her head with full-on tears now, crying softly, unable to hold back. "Please, just let me leave."

"No." He took hold of her by her waist and tugged her to him.

She tried to shove his hands away, slapped and pushed at his chest as he walked backward until the backs of his legs hit the bed. He pinned her flailing arms at her side, the feeling likely short of being trapped in a straitjacket.

"I didn't know you felt that way."

"I want to leave! Lucas, let go of me!" Her voice raised several octaves as she struggled in his grip.

"Don't go. I'm sorry. I'm not used to these feelings I have for you. I find myself in a constant state of insecurity." Her fight eased up a bit. "I'm not usually like this."

"Rude and obnoxious?" she huffed.

"Okay, I deserved that. I'm possessive and even known to be selfish, I'll admit, but jealous over your relationship with your ex … it's a new beast for me to tame." Her eyelids fluttered in reaction to his self-deprecation. "I'd like us to start over." Tentatively, he released her, and she swiped angrily at her eyes with the heels of her hands. He brought her chin up with the side of his index finger. "Please look at me." A flicker, and her watery eyes met his. "You think we could do that? Start over?"

"No … I don't know." Upset, Bailey shook her head. "I can't get hurt again, Lucas, not by you."

His thumb wiped away the wetness from her cheeks, and then large hands cupped her face. "That's the last thing I would want to come out of this." Drawing her close, his cheek lightly brushed at her temple, and he said quietly, "I fell hard for you the moment I saw you talking to your car."

Bailey reared back with eyes wide. "You saw me? When? How?"

"At the café. I was sitting in my limo when you drove up in a cloud of exhaust." A tender kiss was placed on the side of her neck followed by a peck on the bridge of her nose.

"That was you?" He gave her a wink. "I've had that car since senior year of high school."

"I can tell." A chuckle, then his expression grew serious as he ran the pad of his thumb across her lips. "There's something about you, Bailey Walters. I'd like to explore this, you and me, if you're willing to give us a chance."

"I *am* concerned about my job. Sandra sees you two getting back together."

The back of his fingers gently caressed her cheek. "With or without you in my life, that will never happen."

Bailey wanted to trust his words, trust that he would not mar her heart. "I want to understand my feelings for you, too. I've never met anyone like you before. You can be a bit overwhelming."

"Me? Nah." He grinned a wolfish grin, drew her closer, and stroked her back in slow caressing circles. "Given the way you opened yourself to me last night as I tasted you, I would say you can handle anything I dish out." His eyelids grew heavy, desire coloring his voice. "I want to finish what we started in the car." As his hands searched and found the side zipper of her dress, lowering it slowly, he kissed her along her collarbone, one side to the other.

Taking a seat on the edge of the bed, he slipped the straps of her dress off her shoulders, allowing the garment to fall in a pool at her feet. She wore her strapless, pale pink lace bra and matching lace panties. His gaze roamed over her, as if cataloging every curve and angle. "God, Bailey, you're so beautiful." He lifted one leg and then the other to remove her dress and shoes.

"I can't."

His head came up to see her staring at his unmade bed. He glanced back at the rumpled sheets when she shook her head. "What is it?"

"Have you and Sandra slept here?" She inclined her head at the bed. "There?"

"Sandra has never been here. Understand, Bailey, there hasn't been anything between Sandra and me for quite some time." She nodded, and he reached up to her hair to remove the pin that held her twisted bun in place. "I love your curls." She assisted by pulling out a couple more pins, allowing her thick mane to tumble down to the middle of her back.

He sank his fingers in her hair and brought a thick mass to his nostrils, then kissed the center between her breasts as he released the front closure on her bra and dropped it on top of her dress at his feet. His hands slid up the backs of her legs, along her hips, over her buttocks, as though making mental marks of her curves, following the arch of her spine, on up the sides of her breasts, cupping and caressing.

Looking into her eyes, he cradled her face in his palms and took her mouth. His tongue leisurely tasted and explored for long seconds before he drew back and brought his gaze back to hers while continuing his stroking of her body as he said, "I've wanted to do this for so long."

Bailey touched her temple with her index finger. "Uh, you've wanted to talk me to death?" She laughed, followed by a shriek at his quick lift and flip of her onto the bed as if she weighed next to nothing.

He brought his massive frame down on top of her, secured her wrists together above her head with one large hand, and stared down at her bare breasts.

She'd never been a fan of her cup size and sensitive nipples. Now seeing Lucas moisten his lips as he stared at her breasts with the look of a hungry wolf had her nipples instantly pebbling hard.

His index finger circled the areola, one and then the other. That hand then ran all over her body, indulging his desires, becoming familiar with her form.

She liked that he was taken with her body, but what she needed right then was his mouth on her. "Suck one," she told him, unable to stop the words from tumbling out. He didn't waste time following her directive—his mouth clamped down on her left breast. "Yes!" A shuddering heat rushed through her at the feel of his lips, combined with the circling and flicking of his tongue and strong sucking.

He moved to the other breast, giving it equal treatment in between pinching and lightly biting the nipple of the other to keep it nicely peaked.

Needing to touch him, she got one hand free of his hold and found the hem of his shirt. Her hand slipped underneath and over the broad expanse of his back, feeling the heat radiate off his smooth skin.

Popping her nipple free from his mouth, he sat back on his shins between her legs to remove his T-shirt, followed by the swift removal of his jeans and boxer briefs.

Sweet heaven! The look of his sculptured physique made her breath catch in her throat. *Mr. Olympia.* If Sienna only knew how spot on she was.

Her gaze followed the well-defined muscled outline of his thick pectorals and bulging biceps, on down his rippled abdomen that was so ripped, she could strum a tune across it. *Two, four, six ... is there such a thing as eight-pack abs?* Her gaze went farther south to his trunk-like thighs. *Dear me!* Eyes bucking, she stared at his long, thick, jutting erection. Precome glistened the slit of the bulbous, ruby head. It was by far larger than the other two she'd seen, and quite frankly, much more than she likely could handle.

The pictures of the women she'd seen online seemed capable of taking him on. Her experience in the sex department was mediocre at best. How would she be able to satisfy a man like Lucas, keep him interested in her? Feeling insecure, it was necessary to confess her lack of experience.

He swiftly removed her panties, and then his head dropped between her legs. Bailey attempted to sit up, but he lightly nudged her shoulder for her to lie back. "We need to talk," she said.

As he placed a light kiss upon the crest of her mound, his eyes came up. "Now? You didn't want me to talk you to death, remember?" He brought his mouth back down to her folds and circled her clitoris with his tongue.

Oh my, that feels good.

"This ... this is important." She pushed his head away from her sex and inched back a bit in order to focus. He got up and sat back on his shins between her spread legs, but his hands continued to stroke up and down her thighs as if needing to keep the contact.

"It's about this, what we're about to do." Staring at his ridiculously large penis jutting out toward her, instinctively, she licked her lips upon observing the droplet of precome that rolled down the thick vein, the wet, ruby head eagerly ready to invade her.

"What is it?" He looked down at himself and then back at her.

"It's been a while for me." He nodded and went back to massaging her folds with his index and middle finger on his way down, ready to dive in.

"I mean a very *long* while for me," she emphasized. He froze and really studied her then. "Like three years long, and there have been only two, sort of, if you count an awkward ten minutes. The second wasn't much better," she murmured and looked away embarrassed.

He lightly took hold of her chin and turned her face back to him. "You and Kevin?"

"I never slept with Kevin. We kissed and touched a little, but that's all." Bailey watched his astonished expression transform into something short of genuine glee before he uttered, "Oh baby." Hastily, he brought her legs over his shoulders and dropped his mouth down on her. His entire demeanor changed, becoming near urgent in his quest.

His hands slid up the backs of her thighs, spreading her wide to tunnel his tongue deep inside her sex. "Oh my, my, my!" She trailed the words out on a quiver and bit her bottom lip to keep from screaming out as he kept his eyes trained on hers while he ate away at her pussy.

"I won't stop until you come on my tongue this time."

Bailey was too far gone to protest even if she wanted to, which she didn't.

Spread wide, he inserted two thick fingers inside her and used his other hand to separate her labia, exposing her clitoris. Loud gasps and deep pants escaped her as his fingers stroked in and out of her constricting channel. His warm breath brushed over her sensitive clitoris before licking and sucking her swollen bud in time to his swift thrusting fingers.

"Oh, Lucas, please! Yes!" she moaned, panted, and begged with each thrust and slow swirl of his tongue upon her.

Snaking her fingers into his feathery locks, she clamped onto his scalp and held him steady to roll her sex upon his mouth, directing his tongue where she needed it most.

She hitched a sharp breath and clenched her buttocks at the feel of him toying with the rosebud of her anus.

"Open your legs, love." He ran his wet fingers up and down the crease of her buttocks and massaged her puckering bud as his tongue speared her pussy, stroking deeper and faster. Then his mouth formed a seal over her clitoris and sucked vehemently, applying a consistent pressure. A hand came up and pinched her nipple. She moaned through her pleasurable pain, and her hips rocked faster and faster on his demanding mouth and fingers until her body tensed up, her back arched sharply, her thighs clamped around his head, and she screamed his name as her orgasm sent a shockwave of sensation from her pussy down to the very tips of her toes.

"Hmm, you taste so sweet, Bailey," he murmured, lapping up every ounce of her cream, slurping, and licking, running his tongue over and around, up and down from her clit to her vagina, careful not to miss a single spot of her quivering flesh.

Finally releasing her, he kissed his way up her limp, sweat covered body. His tongue circled her navel, laved along her stomach on upward to capture and suckle on a painfully erect nipple.

His lips moved up her moist, hot skin, kissed and licked along the column of her neck to her chin, and finally claimed her gasping mouth, exploring the cavern within for long minutes, and then drew back and braced himself on his forearms above her. Not an inch of her was spared from his glorious tongue's assault.

"You're delicious." His head dipped to the swell of her right breast, and she felt a nip from his teeth, followed by warm licks and gentle kisses.

A contented, lazy grin played across her mouth, visibly satiated. Bailey had never imagined oral sex could feel so good. Both her exes led her to believe the act meant a couple of quick licks and then done. They were more interested in getting to the main purpose of satisfying their own need. And even that was less than mediocre. But Lucas, as in his limo, didn't just pleasure her, he feasted on her, his mouth incessant, unrelenting, the caresses of his tongue precise, thorough, the nips of his teeth and soothing licks determined, the rapture reaching a level of mind-numbing euphoria she hadn't known existed.

"I need to get a condom."

Her eyes fluttered when he abruptly left the bed. He retrieved a strip of Trojans from the nightstand and quickly rolled one onto his exceptional length. Then he got back in bed and settled between her thighs.

Bracing himself on one forearm, he positioned his penis at her entrance and pushed in unhurriedly on a controlled thrust of his hips.

She moaned and bit down on her bottom lip to grasp onto some form of purchase. "Wait. I need a minute," she uttered behind shuttered lids, not sure how much more of him inside her she could take. It was too much for her. His member seemed to be thickening with each slow push forward.

"You're tensing up. Relax your inner muscles and take me inside you." He kissed her mouth softly as he pushed in farther.

Bailey inhaled slowly and exhaled just as slow as she concentrated on relaxing the muscles of her sex as he instructed. There was so much pressure that her inner walls strained to near bursting, trying to accommodate his girth.

He put his hand between their bodies and gently stroked her clitoris, reestablishing the heat deep within her core, easing the stress of his invasion. With each thick inch into her, the walls of her channel grew hotter, wetter, and began to throb, the pleasure rebuilding. One final thrust seated him fully inside her.

"Damn," he hissed low, "the way you feel wrapped around me, so wet and incredibly tight. I want to fuck you, Bailey. Can you handle that, love? Can I have you the way I want?"

Her heavy-lidded gaze came into focus and stared back at him. Bailey thought it was pretty clear that was what they were doing already. The large head of his shaft practically touched her womb.

Given the hot, carnal look in his eyes, he was asking permission to no longer be gentle. She tried to sound ten times more confident than she felt. "I'm here in your bed, Lucas. I can handle it." *I hope.* Apprehension had her swallowing hard when he brought her arms up over her head and had her hold on to the smooth wooden spindles of the headboard.

"Don't let go."

She nodded, yet her breath came out in quick, rapid pulls.

Holding still within her, he whispered her name repeatedly like a soft ballad as he nipped her earlobe, kissed her mouth, forehead, cheeks, nose, neck, everywhere, easing her into this sensory sexual journey.

Her inner muscles clamped down tight around him, and he began a measured rocking that quickly became aggressive surges, thrusting harder, faster, deeper with rotating hips.

Staring up at his concentrated expression as he took her body vigorously, she held tight to the bed spindles and rocked in time with his ever-quickening stride.

Bailey lifted her head from the pillow in need of his kiss. Oh how she enjoyed the taste of his kisses. Her tongue traced his lips before devouring his mouth.

"Damn, even the way you kiss could make me come," he grunted against her lips. "You're mine, now, Bailey." He bowed his back, and she arched hers to guide a breast into his mouth that he indulged for long minutes. Both hands splayed across her buttocks to hold her steady, forcing her body to take his brutal plunges.

"Yes!" she wailed, amazed by the way her body reacted to his, how overstimulated her pussy felt with him inside her. She'd never experienced this level of sexual arousal before. With each downward thrust he made, her channel throbbed, and when he pulled out almost fully, her inner muscles clenched tight around him, wanting to hold him deep inside her.

He took her mouth in a hungry kiss as his right hand slid from her buttocks to the back of her left knee and brought that leg up to rest on his right shoulder, grinding her balls deep.

She released the headboard, grabbed hold of his firm buttocks, her nails embedding in his taut flesh, gripping, imprinting, squeezing, and pressed down to her upward pumps and rotating hips. The feeling of it was incredible as she teetered on the edge of her orgasm.

Suddenly, he withdrew, swiftly turned her to her stomach, brought her up on her knees by a light tug of her hips, and entered her pussy fully in one smooth thrust.

"Stay open for me," he said and spread his knees between her legs, anchoring her pose as his strokes slowly built up momentum again. One hand grabbed hold of the top of the headboard for leverage. The other tangled in and lightly tugged on her hair.

Gripping the sheet tight in her palms, Bailey pushed her buttocks back to meet his unyielding strokes, welcoming every indelible inch of him. It astonished her that she would take pleasure in the animalistic pose he subjected upon her. The only other two times she'd had sex were nothing like this, not even close.

"Don't stop," she moaned, freeing her inhibitions as they fucked one another with a primal, ferocious intensity.

"I have no intention of stopping, princess." He continued his severe thrusts as he brought her upright on her knees with her back against his chest, their skin hot and slick from their combined sweat. He pushed her curls aside and licked a glistening bead from her left shoulder up her throat, snaked his right arm around her waist to her left breast, caressed, pinched, and rolled her pebbled nipple. His other hand found her slippery wet clitoris and circled it fiercely in time to his tunneling cock burrowed deep in her core. "Lucas ... so good," Bailey purred, enjoying every second of their joining.

She reached back to his nape and angled her head in search of his mouth, capturing his tongue with her own. "Damn good." He slowed his hips and eased out of her.

"No, don't stop." She gripped his thigh, disappointed that he would rob her of her orgasm. She was so close.

"I want to look into your eyes when you come with me inside you for the first time."

Bailey moved to her back, but was unsure what to make of his behavior. He was staring intently at her, his gaze never wavering as he slowly came down and eased back inside her. His thrusts now were slow, controlled, and she daresay ... loving. He never looked away.

"How is it, princess?"

"Wonderful. More than wonderful."

"We're good together. Always remember that."

She nodded and closed her eyes briefly, struck hard by the emotional depth she felt from his words and could see in his unwavering gaze upon her.

The tempo of his thrusts became determined, purposeful. As he continued to throw his hips against hers, he palmed her face and kissed her tenderly on the mouth—once, twice, and then a third before finally drawing back to reconnect their gazes.

She cried out on a full-bodied shudder as her sex contracted in wondrous ripples, her orgasm overtaking her completely. Short seconds after, he shouted her name, and his body tensed up as he delivered two good hard thrusts before she felt his penis pulse repeatedly, deep inside her. With one last magnificent shudder, he collapsed and buried his face in the side of her neck, kissing her there as the rapid beat of his heart battered against her breasts.

Minutes ticked by with them working to level their breathing. Then he came up on his forearms and planted a light peck upon her right temple. "I knew it would be this way with you, princess."

"So that's what a vaginal orgasm feels like." Bailey grinned with exhausted delight.

"You're saying you were a virgin in that respect?" He brushed back the damp hairs out of her face and administered gentle kisses to her mouth and cheek.

She hadn't expected him to be so affectionate. "I've never experienced lovemaking like that before. It was spectacular."

"So, essentially, I'm your first, and you're welcome," he said with a cocky smirk, and she playfully punched his shoulder. "It's *you*, princess, who was spectacular." He wedged his arms underneath her back and held her close.

Cuddling after was another thing she'd never experienced before. Both of her exes had departed immediately following the act.

Bailey twirled her fingers in his damp hair at the nape of his neck, saying, "As I explained, my experience is very limited in that department."

"Don't think I'm not thrilled to hear that. The not having slept with Kevin, in particular." He winked and received a quick peck on the mouth.

"As you said about Sandra, there's nothing between Kevin and me. We're just friends."

"Friends," he muttered. "I'll have to learn to become comfortable with that, I suppose." He rose up. "I'd love to stay in bed with you the entire day, but I have a meeting and you said you do as well."

"I do." Bailey could lie in his strong arms forever and immediately felt cold, empty when he slipped free of her body and left the bed, even though her flesh was scorching from their combined sweat and friction.

She heard running water. He returned to the bed and reached for her.

"I'll bathe you, princess." He carried her to the shower and then grabbed the shower gel from the shower wall niche.

She took it from him and sniffed it. "Hmm, this is why you always smell amazing, but I can't use this. It's smells masculine, too manly."

"Too manly." A chuckle, and he gave a light pluck at her chin. "Let me see what I can find." He left the shower and went to the cabinet. "How about vanilla?"

"That's fine." She stared at his beautiful body, admiring the gentle sway of his long, semiflaccid penis as he walked back to the shower. He was exceptionally endowed. It still amazed her that she'd been able to take in all of him.

To his word, he started to bathe her. "Lucas, I can do it." Her hand was batted away.

"I got this." He poured a liberal amount of the vanilla-scented shower gel in his palm, lathered up nicely, and began working the suds over her body. His hands moved over her breasts on down her hips, circled to her buttocks, slipped between her twin cheeks to her vagina, and stroked her plump folds. Soft purring moans escaped her as his fingers teased back and forth along the rim of her sex and over her overly sensitive clitoris.

"You might want to stop making those sounds, princess, or I'll be forced to take you again."

Bailey set lustful eyes upon him as she took hold of his cock and pumped the thick, long length of him. Instantly, his fingers sank into her sheath. "Hmm, that feels good." Looking up at him, she licked the rivulet of water dripping off his right nipple. "Don't make threats, Mr. Marx."

"Threats?" He groaned at her nibbling and sucking the tight bud before rolling it between her teeth as her hand continued to pump his cock, easily giving it renewed life. "I ... I never threaten, Miss Walters. Shit." Unable to withstand her taunting seduction, he shoved her back against the shower wall and lightly nipped her neck. "Vixen." Hastily, he wedged a knee between her thighs, brought her left leg to his hip, and thrust in deep, drawing out a sharp gasp from her at his swift invasion.

"Is this what you want?"

With the warm water pounding his back, he held her leg up at the crook of his arm and pounded her pussy, hearing her shrills, gasps, and pants echoing off the walls.

"Yes, Lucas, fuck me!" she shouted.

"I love to hear you talk dirty, princess." He brought up her right leg, spreading her wide, and gripped her buttocks tight as he drilled his cock in and out of her. "Damn, Bailey," he grunted into her mouth, their teeth hitting, tongues dueling, taking her with a feral hunger once again, wild and greedy.

"We ... we need a condom," Bailey managed to remember before her erotic high started to cloud her brain.

"Yes ... we do," he uttered, kissing her hungrily. Yet, neither was willing to stop thrusting for even a second to get a condom. Instead, they tightened their hold on one another.

"I'll pull out."

"Okay." She wrapped her arms around his neck, clinging tight as he worked her sex hard with her pressed up against the marble. In no time, her inner muscles clamped hold of his cock, her orgasm erupting cataclysmic from his quick pumps. He gave her two more hardy thrusts, squeezed her buttocks, and pressed her tight to his body as copious spurts of warm semen filled her channel.

"Lucas?" Bailey breathed out, and his eyes met hers looking a bit dazed, then quickly turned to alarm.

"Shit." Breathing heavily, he lightly pressed his forehead against hers. "Damn."

After minutes of them clinging to one another for much needed support, both released deep, sated exhales.

Bailey brought her legs down. "That was amazing," she said, as she tried to catch her breath.

"Woman, you're going to cripple me." He sat down on the shower bench with her on his lap. When his breathing settled, he took the vanilla scented shower gel and lathered his hands once more. "I didn't pull out. Evidently, it was easier said."

"I'll get on the pill. I haven't had need for it since I've been abstinent for three years. No need to worry ... about an STD, I mean."

"No worries here either. I've never gone without a condom ... until now." He gave her a peck on the mouth. "See what you do to me."

She finger-combed his wet hair back off his forehead. "I guess I got caught up, too. I never knew it could feel like that."

Lucas chuckled. "Woman, you have my brain rattling around in my head, unable to think of anything else, but you, and these …" He made a hand gesture at her breasts, and up and down. "This spectacular body of yours. I'll try to get through the ministration this time." Soapy hands ran over her full breasts, followed by his mouth latching onto a nipple.

"You think you can manage it?" Bailey smirked and shook her head when his hand then went between her legs, and he groaned. "I think I better do it myself or we'll never leave this shower." She got off his lap, moved to the opposite end, and turned on the dual shower heads there.

"I have to agree. Keep that sexy body away from me."

Giving him a look over her shoulder, she smiled at him seated on the shower bench, working shampoo into his hair as his gaze roamed over the contours of her soapy naked form. "If that is what you wish, Mr. Marx."

A wolfish grin. "That is what I wish, Miss Walters."

Chapter Eighteen

They sat in the limo in front of the building of Callaghan Interiors. Lucas couldn't stop enjoying her. All it took was for her to look at him, and he would be all over her like a man starved. He'd become addicted to her taste—her scent—her mere presence. No woman had ever affected him as intensely as Bailey Walters.

He'd spent the last five minutes with a mouthful of her magnificent breast, trying to persuade her to let him escort her to the art event instead of Sandra, but she refused to budge on the matter. "Say you'll come with me," he muttered around her succulent nipple.

"Lucas, you cannot show up there tonight with me, and right now, I really have to go. May I have my breast back? Sandra is going to have a cow that I'm late."

"If you insist." He gave her right nipple one parting hard suck before popping it free from his mouth.

"I don't want Sandra to know that we're seeing one another," she said as she tugged at her bodice to ensure the passion bruise he'd left on her right breast was fully covered.

"If that's what you want, I'll go along ... for now. I'll have a car pick you up tonight and drop you off at my place following the event. You have a key. Keep it. It's yours."

"You're sure? You don't need time to put out an all points text to your female groupies? I wouldn't want to turn the lock and for there to be an awkward moment." There was a teasing twinkle in her eyes.

Lucas shot her a severe look that said her joke wasn't received well. "I told you I don't have other women, Bailey. Don't believe everything you read on the Internet. Hell, it still says I'm a millionaire." He gave the press just enough string so they'd stay out of his business. If the bastards knew his actual net worth, he'd need more than Isaac on staff to keep the damn vultures at bay. "You're the first to ever have a key to my place."

"Fair enough." She nodded and asked with a playful grin, "Sandra will want to know if I met all of your needs, Mr. Marx."

"Well, I guess, Miss Walters."

"You guess?" A small lift of her finely arched left brow. "Are you saying I didn't meet all of your needs as promised?"

Pretending to think on it, Lucas straightened his tie. "Let's see. I did have to instruct you to keep your legs spread while I ate you out and to raise your cute little ass higher when I took you from behind. Let us not forget how I had to hold you up while I fucked you in the shower, Miss Walters. All will need to be revisited, I'm afraid. Be sure to put that in your report, madam." He laughed deep in his throat, and she punched his shoulder, laughing with him. She then leaned in and captured his nape, her thumb stroking the side of his neck as she said, "You're not funny," before she kissed him slow, long, and deep, their tongues mating for long seconds, and then drew back. "I guess I'll see you later." Her voice was as hot and sweet as that lover's kiss she'd just given him.

Lucas blew out a breath. "You most definitely will." His cell on the console rang. He looked at the display, then took her hand and planted a kiss on the back of it. "I won't be but a second, love. Don't leave yet." As he took the call, she captured his nape again and kissed him, snaking her tongue deep within, then quickly moved away from him. Lucas blinked, surprised by her boldness.

"I have to call you back." He closed the line, then looked at her. "Damn, woman, do you have any idea what your kisses do to me? If you keep that up, I'll have to take your sexy ass again. My turn. Come here." He wiggled his brows naughtily and stuck his hand between her legs.

"Stop!" she shrieked with laughter and slapped his hand away. "You stay over there." Grabbing her satchel, she slid over to the door to exit. "Until later, Mr. Marx."

"Definitely later." Lucas reached into his inside coat pocket. "Take this."

She looked at the black credit card in his hand and then back at him. "What's that for?"

"You said you needed a dress for tonight."

"I also said that I'd borrow from Sienna."

"Buy whatever you like."

"So that's how it is? We have sex, and now I get a credit card at my disposal." She frowned and shook her head. "Geez, I don't believe you. Is that how you see me? Like some *Pretty Woman* skank?" When he didn't catch the reference, she rolled her eyes. "Richard Gere and Julia Roberts." Again, he shrugged. "You have a home theater, for goodness sake. I don't want your money, Lucas, and I'm offended that you would see me in such a light."

He exhaled long. "Bailey, it's just a dress. You say no to my cars, no to me buying you a car when you clearly could use one, and now no to a simple purchase of a dress. I would like to help out my lady. It's as simple as that."

"I'm your lady?" Her eyes flickered. Then he watched her expression shift from irritation to a broad smile, her mood doing a complete one eighty.

"No. You're merely the only woman with a key to my place, the only woman who will share my bed at night, and the woman who will be my plus one at my sister's wedding."

"What? Lucas, I can't do that."

"Which one? The sharing of my bed or my plus one? Because the bed sharing isn't an option on either front."

That made her chuckle, and she shook her head. "I have to go, but we'll talk about this some more later."

She turned to leave, but he caught her wrist. "You're forgetting something." Lucas held up the credit card between his index and middle finger.

"Fine." With a sigh, she took the card and stuck it in the side pocket of her satchel, then waved a hand between them. "You and I, it has nothing to do with your wallet," she said firmly.

"I know. It's what I lo ..." *What the fu—! Staring at her, Lucas swallowed the hard lump in his throat, stunned that he was about to say that four letter word. She didn't seem to notice, given that she nodded and exited the car.

"Bailey?" he called. She stuck her head back inside. He slid over and whispered in her ear, "Don't wear any panties tonight, princess. It will be our little secret that your pussy is unencumbered, awaiting my fingers." A devilish grin.

Her green eyes met his, looking quite taken aback before she delivered a slow nod.

• • •

Bailey cringed at seeing Sandra and Brian standing at the window. By the hot sparks Sandra was shooting her way, and the subtle grin that Brian wore, she was pretty sure they saw her exiting Lucas's car. Better to hedge the truth. "My car wouldn't start. Lu—" She caught the barbed look Sandra tossed at her over the almost slip. "Mr. Marx offered me a ride. He was headed to his office."

Sandra eyes narrowed briefly. "Well, let us get started."

Brian move to the round conference table and took a seat. Bailey pulled out a chair and sat next to him. She took out her laptop and hooked up her camera to display the pictures she'd taken.

Sandra walked over. "Hurry it up," she voiced brusquely. "I have to leave to prepare for my evening out."

Bailey angled her laptop between them and updated Sandra and Brian on the renovations. Brian chimed in, giving his "That's great, well done, you've done well." Sandra stared at her with a shrewd eye while she casually or more like intentionally, Bailey was becoming to sense, twirled the large diamond stud in her right ear—the earrings Lucas gave her. Suddenly feeling disconcerted, Bailey began to worry if Lucas was telling the truth about his and Sandra's involvement being completely over. She was glad when Brian said, "Everything seems to be in order. I told you she could do it," which thankfully brought the meeting to a close.

"Sandra, don't you agree, a great job done," Brian said, undoubtedly noticing the way Sandra gave her a scrutinizing eye as well. Even a blind man would pick up on it, Bailey thought.

Sandra nodded. "Yes, everything seems to be in order." She sat forward with her elbows on the table, her fingers steepled. "There shouldn't be any need for you to go over to Mr. Marx's home from this point. As you said, you will notify his assistant once the remaining pieces are in. From here forward, I will see to it that everything is properly situated."

"Uh, okay." Bailey looked away from the woman's piercing stare.

"Bailey, you can help me on a new order. You'll love it. It's a twins nursery," Brian said, and they all stood up.

Sandra strolled over to her desk to retrieve her purse. "I have a spa appointment and will be leaving for the day." She headed for the door as she said, "I'll be able to get a firsthand look at the renovations tonight. Oh, and leave Mr. Marx's key on my desk." She smiled sharply at Bailey on her way out.

Brian shook his head. "That woman can be so juvenile at times."

"What's her problem?" Bailey pretended to be clueless when she already knew, since Sandra was standing at the frickin' window when she walked in. The woman would have a conniption if she found out Bailey had spent her morning in Lucas's bed, and that they were pursuing a relationship. The fallout would be catastrophic to her career path. She was more than certain now.

"She's all hot and bothered because she saw you exiting the car of the man she intends to screw tonight," Brian answered plainly. "Double standard if you ask me."

"Yes." Bailey tried not to show how the mere thought of Lucas and Sandra together made her head throb with jealousy. "I guess I'll go get some work done." She left the office, trying her best not to overthink it.

Chapter Nineteen

Lucas entered his office and found Gavin seated behind his desk. "Hard at work? It's about time," he mocked good-naturedly.

Gavin glanced at his watch. "It's almost noon. That's beyond late for you."

Lucas hit the speaker button on his desk phone and tapped Kara's set number. One ring in, she picked up. "Afternoon, Kara. Contact Smyth to get the name of a jeweler he trusts in this area."

"I understand. Which shall it be, a pendant necklace, bracelet, or earrings?"

His assistant knew not to even hint at ring. "I'll be selecting the item this time."

"Pardon?" Kara asked.

"What the fuck!" Gavin gasped out and sat up ramrod straight in the chair.

"Was I not clear?" Lucas walked over to the bar, poured himself a cup of coffee, and then moved back to the front of the desk, taking a seat on the edge.

"Very clear, sir," Kara replied on speaker.

"Have the individual come here with a wide selection for my choosing."

"I'll see to it."

"Thanks." Lucas closed the line.

Smiling, Gavin reared back in the chair and linked his fingers behind his head. "Someone's been busy out here on the East Coast. Who is she? By the looks of it, she tamed the serpent as well." He chuckled. "Thank goodness because after another day of you snapping and growling, I would've been forced to find someone for you."

"Get out of my chair. Don't you have an office?" Lucas rounded the desk. Gavin stood up and moved around to the front, taking Lucas's place on the edge.

"Well?"

"Well what? Lucas pulled up his e-mail on his laptop, not really paying close attention. His mind was consumed with thoughts of his blissful morning spent with Bailey and the parting kisses she'd given him that promised a repeat after the art contest tonight. His mind and body were still recovering from the sexual euphoria she inflamed.

He'd shouted her name during sex. He couldn't remember the last time he'd done that. And in the car, *what the fuck was wrong with him*? He'd almost said that four letter word to her.

"Details," Gavin pushed.

"There's nothing to tell." Lucas sipped his coffee as he continued to scroll through his messages.

"Like hell there isn't. When was the last time you personally selected a gift for a woman? And I don't mean your mother or sister."

Lucas shrugged.

"It was Stacey Pelligren in eleventh grade," Gavin recalled. "You were head over heels for her."

"Concentrate on your own love life. What's happening with the Paxton-Caldwell deal?"

"They're still holding out. They want an additional quarter percent and a two-year guarantee of job security."

"Give it to them."

Gavin's eyes bucked. "What! Are you serious? Now I know something's up, man. You never concede."

"Gavin." Lucas gave him an impatient look.

"I'm just saying." Gavin stood up and planted his palms on the desk. "Hey, just tell me her name."

If he didn't answer, he'd have to hear the man's mouth for hours on end. "Bailey. Now shut the fuck up about it."

"I was expecting a Tricksy or Lola," Gavin quipped.

Lucas couldn't suppress his grin. "Paxton and Caldwell should be here in an hour, and don't forget the art contest is tonight."

"I'm prepared and I haven't forgotten." Stretching his muscles while cracking the tension in his neck, Gavin remarked, "I was looking forward to us hanging out tonight, thought we'd tag team and shit, nail a couple of those artsy broads. Wait a minute. So you're not banging Sandra?"

"Fuck no!" Lucas frowned, revolted at the mere thought. "You know good and well that ended years ago."

"When I overheard Kara confirming the pickup time with her, I thought—"

"I'm her escort as a business associate, nothing more." Again, he scowled in disgust. "I wish I'd never agreed to it."

"Bro, are you really coming off the field with this new lady?"

Lucas looked up from responding to an e-mail. Bailey was nothing like any woman he'd ever met. It was indeed the reason he was so drawn to her. He found her startlingly attractive. Hers was a natural beauty. But, it was also that exposed innocence about her that intrigued him. "I want to see where it goes. She's ... different, special."

"I gathered that. I never would've thought you—" Gavin paused at the buzz of the desk phone.

Lucas pressed the speaker button. "Yes, Kara?"

"Mr. Alfred Deluca from Tiffany's will arrive at four."

"Thanks." He closed the line.

"I guess I'll go review my notes." Gavin headed to the door while teasing, "Oh, Bailey, smooch, smooch, kissy, kissy." He laughed at his own antics and dodged the sticky pad that jetted past his ear. "I'll be back in an hour."

"Yeah, yeah, until then, stay the fuck out."

Chapter Twenty

Bailey sat behind her desk, unable to concentrate on her work. She couldn't shake the mental image of Lucas and Sandra together, imagining him making love to Sandra in the many ways he'd been with her that very morning. She pressed her thumbs at her temples in an effort to stop the slideshow, unequivocally smothering in the images.

The very idea that Sandra would be on his arm later made the jealousy near unbearable.

Don't do this to yourself. He's not Andrew or Craig. He said there was nothing going on between him and Sandra.

She had to trust that Lucas spoke true. That said, she understood that Sandra had a different take on the matter. Recalling the woman's parting words, Bailey shot to her feet and sprinted down the hall to Brian's office. He was typing away on his computer. She knocked on the doorframe, and he looked up.

"Hey, Brian."

"What's up?"

"I was wondering if I could take the rest of the day off. Sandra's gone for the day, and my work is caught up."

"Go ahead. I say you earned it. You really did a great job on that project. Sandra will see."

That's exactly what Bailey was afraid of—Sandra getting a firsthand look by way of Lucas's bed.

"Thanks for supporting me."

"I know you have the skills and could do much more if given the opportunity." Brian crossed his arms over his chest and sat back. "I kind of wish there was more to that little car ride this morning than you needing a lift. That woman needs to be brought down a peg or two."

Feeling her cheeks warm, Bailey subtly looked away. She was such a terrible liar.

Brian jerked up in his chair and slapped his knee. "I knew it!"

She sighed. "We're getting to know one another. Please don't say anything to Sandra."

"Mum's the word from me. I mean why give the woman an aneurysm." With a grin, he zipped his fingers across his lips. "You do your thing. By the way, that tall, handsome, dark chocolate specimen who drives Mr. Marx around is hot." Wearing a winsome grin, he cocked his head. "Just saying."

Bailey laughed. "Don't let your husband hear you say that."

"Hey, a guy can look, but don't touch."

"I'll see you on Monday. Have a good weekend."

"You, too." He winked.

Bailey headed back to her desk to get her things. She trusted that Brian would keep his word. With that thought, she changed into her sneakers, then picked up the phone, dialed the spa where she'd gone earlier in the week, and was in luck to snag an appointment in forty-five minutes.

She waved bye to Jason and headed for the elevators. Stepping out onto the busy D.C. street, Sandra's words rang like cathedral bells in her head. *I'll be able to take a firsthand look at the renovations tonight.* Bailey then remembered that Lucas was having a car drop her off at his place later. Smiling, she patted the outside zipped pocket of her satchel that still held Lucas's key and credit card. With a pivot left, she headed one block up to catch the Metrorail en route to the spa.

Don't wear any panties tonight, princess. It will be our little secret that your pussy is unencumbered, awaiting my fingers. He was such an intense man. The naughty glint in his eyes had made her pussy pulsate in anticipation of the pleasure he'd give her.

As for Sandra, *bitch, you're not the only one who can seduce a man.* Bailey had learned what she was capable of that very morning.

Chapter Twenty-One

Lucas hadn't thought it would be this difficult. He sat on the couch with his elbows on his knees, looking over an impressive array of diamonds and gemstones situated upon white velvet cloths and neatly spread out on the coffee table before him.

What should he choose for Bailey? Emeralds would complement her beautiful eyes, but the rubies reminded him of the fire he ignited and brought out of her with his touch. There were also the traditional diamonds. She'd appreciate the simplicity of the stone.

His eyes came up to the jeweler. The man sat patiently in the leather armchair where he'd been stationed for the past forty-five minutes, watching him study the jewels presented before him.

"Mr. Deluca, my apologies for my indecisiveness. This is much harder than I anticipated."

"Might I make a suggestion?"

Lucas sat back. "Go ahead."

"Imagine the lady wearing something you like to see her in—a special cocktail dress or an evening gown. A certain fur, perhaps."

Lucas gave that some thought. All of the jewels would look stunning draped over Bailey's naked body. Quite frankly that was his favorite outfit. A thought occurred to him. "Just a minute." He went over and hit the speaker button on the desk phone.

"Yes?" Kara asked on the line.

"Find out what purchases were made today on my Amex card ending in zero, zero, three, three. I want specifics down to the color and style. I need the info—"

"Directly," Kara interjected. "I'm on it."

Within fifteen minutes, Kara phoned back with the information he needed. Lucas told her she could call it a day and to take off next week as well. Kara deserved a month off for all she did for him.

She, along with Isaac, had been in his employ for five years now. They were among the few people he allowed in his personal space, the few able to tolerate his demanding nature. Lucas recognized their value and compensated them generously for their loyalty and dedication.

About twenty minutes later, he walked Mr. Deluca to the door and shook his hand. "Ensure they arrive as I've instructed. Thank you for your assistance."

"Earrings in a trillion-cut sapphire and diamond surround, set in platinum with the matching pendant necklace and tennis bracelet, the trio is a magnificent choice. Mr. Marx, she will love them, I assure you."

Lucas nodded and closed the door behind Deluca hoping the man was right.

Gavin was right about the last time he'd picked out a gift for a woman—excluding his mother and sister—usually leaving the matter to Kara. This time, it was imperative that he do it and do it right.

Finding out what Bailey had purchased was the help he needed in picking the right stone. Smiling, he shook his head as he walked back to his desk. He'd given Bailey a credit card with no monetary limit and all she'd spent between a spa visit and a dress boutique was four hundred thirty-seven dollars. He sat down in his chair and turned to face the window, quite intrigued by her. She was truthful about not being attracted to his wealth. *Impressive.* That said, *what would it take to impress her?*

Chapter Twenty-Two

"What do you mean she left? Sienna, hold on." Bailey exited the cab in front of her apartment building. She draped the garment bag over her forearm in order to dig into her satchel for her wallet to pay the cab driver. "Thanks." She brought her cell phone back to her ear. "Sienna, you're there?"

"Yes. We had a stupid argument. Among other things, it was about that asshole, Dale. I overheard them outside the apartment ... okay, I had my ear to the door, but whatever. Anyway, I heard Dale say something about meeting up with some guys in southeast D.C. in Anacostia. You and I know that nothing good goes on near that end of town. Dale is just using her, but she refuses to see him for the scum that he is."

"Sie, of course he's using her. That's his M.O. We can't force her to listen."

"I called her cell, but she's not answering. Bails, I'm worried about her. Faith also told me her dad kicked her out."

"Oh no! Why would he do that?"

"Don't know. I asked, but she stormed out."

"We need to find her. I'll try calling her also, but, Sienna, you need to concentrate on the art competition. This is your night. You've waited years for this. Do you have everything?" Bailey pushed her satchel strap upon her shoulder and slipped her straight tresses behind her ears. She'd gotten a blowout for the evening. Her long mane about reached past her waist. "Lucas is sending a car for me. I can bring anything you need."

"I'm good. Everything is set up. We're all doing the whole howdy, how are you bullshit, sizing up each other's work and all that. Bails, when you get here, I need to talk to you about something. Hey, are you there? Bailey?"

"Sie, there's a guy outside our door. Are you expecting someone?" Bailey suspiciously eyed the young man that was seated on the ground next to her apartment door. They made eye contact, and he came to his feet. He was holding a package.

"Where's your pepper spray?" Sienna asked.

"Hold on." She pulled her pack off her shoulder and hastily dug around in search for her spray. As her mom would say, *you can never be too cautious.*

"Bailey Walters?"

Her head came up. "Yes?" She brought the phone back to her ear. "Sienna, he has a package. It's a delivery guy."

"Don't trust that. Find out what he wants, but keep your distance, and have that spray ready. Who hand delivers shit after five?"

Bailey addressed the man, "Can I help you?"

"Miss Walters, I'm here to deliver a package that must be placed in your hands only. Here's my identification." He approached her with hand extended holding his I.D.

"Did you hear that, Sie?" Studying the guy's picture on his badge, it read, *Falcon Express Couriers.* She'd seen the company's name on the back of the shirts worn by couriers zipping through D.C. traffic on their Bianchi Pistas.

"I heard. What is it?" Sienna asked.

"Please provide I.D.," the courier requested.

Bailey pulled out her wallet and showed the man her driver's license. She signed the electronic pad. He then handed over the package, said thank you, and headed over to a white Mini Cooper.

She went to her apartment, entered, locked the door, and went straight to her room. The hanger sticking out of the garment bag was hung over the door.

"What is it? I have to go soon. Hurry, open it," Sienna urged her.

"Just a second." With the phone to her ear, she sat down on the side edge of the bed and began tearing into the heavy brown wrapping, revealing a glossy robin's-egg-blue box. "Oh my God, Sienna, it's from Tiffany's!"

"Lucas," they both said in unison.

"Open it!"

Bailey opened the box and gasped, nearly swallowing her tongue.

"Bails, what is it?"

"It's ... they're beautiful." Gaping at the sparkling jewels perched upon white velvet cloth, she shook her head as if Sienna could see her. "It's too much. I can't accept this."

"Let me see. Take a picture. Hurry up!"

A snapshot was taken with her cell phone and sent off. "Take a look."

A moment later, Sienna came back on the line. "Oh my God, Bails, they're gorgeous! He must want you to wear them tonight."

"You don't understand. I slept with Lucas," she said as she brushed an index finger across the twinkling stones.

"What! Oh hell yes, now I understand fully. You put a hurt on big boy. You unleashed three years of pent up orgasms, and it blew his mind." Sienna laughed.

"This isn't funny, Sie. Sandra still wears the diamonds that he bought her."

"So what? Now tell me, was it worth the wait? How does he measure up to Andrew and Craig?"

Bailey pictured Lucas's beautiful body spread out on top of her, him behind her, his massive frame pressing her up against the shower wall, thrusting, and pounding his long, thick, hard cock inside of her. A warm shiver engulfed her entire body from the memory. "It was definitely worth it. Andrew and Craig don't come close to Lucas." She laughed shyly.

"Yes!" Sienna screeched.

"I need to talk to him."

"Bailey, he cares about you. That said, we need to talk."

"I have to go." Bailey's thoughts of Sandra and her twirling earrings bounced around in her mind. "We'll talk later. She closed the line." Lucas and she needed to have a conversation if he was really serious about having a relationship. This was what he did for the woman he was currently screwing. She refused to become Sandra.

Chapter Twenty-Three

Lucas electronically signed and sent the final agreement to Paxton-Caldwell via his laptop. He would respond to a few more e-mails before heading home to get ready for the evening.

The fact that he'd arrive tonight with Sandra instead of his beautiful lady left a bitter taste in his mouth and soured his mood.

Needing to hear Bailey's voice, he reached for his cell phone, but his desk phone rang. The display showed *Security* from down in the lobby. He answered the line, "Yes?"

"Mr. Marx, there's a Faith Sullivan here to see you. She says she's a friend."

Lucas could hear the skepticism in the man's voice. Curious of her visit, he replied, "Send her up." A few minutes later, Faith walked into his office with the strut of a pro, wearing a pink tank top, sans bra—her nipples practically poked a hole in her top—and a black mini skirt with strappy high heels. Her eyes were heavily inked in black eyeliner, and her hair was pulled up into a tight ponytail. He now knew why the security guard had his doubts. *Low rent* were the two words that came to mind.

She took a seat in the chair in front of his desk, sitting side-angled on the edge, exposing ample thigh.

"Faith, what can I do for you?"

"I thought I'd follow up on our conversation about possibly working for you."

Lucas's eyes dipped down at her crossing her legs and then back up. He got a good view of her ass peeking out at the hem of her skirt. Her legs and ass didn't hold a candle to Bailey's beautiful body.

"As I said, I'm in no need of an assistant, but I'll ask around. What experience do you have?" She got up, rounded his desk, and took a seat on top. He eased his chair back from her crossed legs that found their way between his. "Faith, what is this about?"

"I was thinking you could have two assistants. One for your business," she uncrossed and spread her legs to reveal she wasn't wearing any panties, "and one for your pleasure."

He looked at her bare, pink pussy and was repulsed. Seeing him looking, she spread her legs wider. He could scarcely mask his scowl of contempt. She was supposed to be Bailey's friend.

Bailey had told him that Faith had slept with her ex. Apparently, it was her intention to try that shit with him.

Forcing a grin that he didn't feel, he asked, "Are you interviewing to be my, what you might call, *pleasure assistant*, Faith?" The ring of his cell phone displaying Bailey's name had him hastily coming to his feet, feeling guilty for ... what? He didn't know why he felt guilty. He had no intentions of fucking the woman. In fact, he was about to tell her to fuck off.

"Get out," he growled. She looked surprised by the abrupt shutdown. By the third ring, he turned away from her, and answered the call. "I see you are indeed clairvoyant, madam. I was just about to call you."

"Is that so? Well, I'm calling you because I received the jewels. They're beautiful."

Lucas smiled, pleased with his choice. "I'm picturing my princess as she—"

"I'll be returning them to you," she interjected.

He frowned. "Why?"

"Evidently, Sandra was thrilled to receive your *thank you* earrings after you took her to your bed."

"It's not like that. I—"

"Lucas?" Faith called from behind him.

Lucas spun around. He'd forgotten about her, dismissed her from his brain that quickly. She'd removed her top and was resting back on her elbows, her perked pink nipples pointing skyward. *Shit!*

"Lucas, did I interrupt something?"

"Just a minute, love." With the phone pressed against his chest to muffle his voice, he whispered tightly to Faith, "Put your top back on and get the fuck out now!" Seeing the woman scramble into her top, he turned away from her, and brought the phone back to his ear.

"Hey, love."

"If you're busy with Kara, we can talk about this later."

"No ... I mean, it's—"

"This was fun. Nice seeing you again, Lucas." Faith giggled close at his back. He spun around so fast, he knocked into her, and she fell back across the desk, sending his desk lamp crashing to the floor. "I didn't ... sorry about that," she said as she tried to regain her footing.

He brought the phone to his ear in time to hear Bailey's sharp intake of breath.

"Is that ... you're with Faith?"

"Listen, Bailey, this can be easily explained."

"Don't bother. Bye, Lucas."

"Bailey, wait!" She hung up. Lucas set eyes on Faith, and she shrunk back. What she saw glaring back at her had her scrambling off the desk and running as if her life was in jeopardy. Raw, unmitigated rage filled with gross contempt toward her lit him on fire.

With her back pressed against the wall beside the door, her breath sawing in and out, he brought his mouth near her ear and spoke in a menacing, tight whisper, "You're going to see to it that this is made right with Bailey, or I will make you regret you ever met me." His jaw muscles were clenched so tight he was close to fracturing a bone. "Do you understand?"

She nodded rapidly. "I ... I was forced to do it. Please," she whimpered.

His anger churning, Lucas snarled, "Talk!"

Looking up at him, black mascara tears stained her cheeks. "My boyfriend is in some trouble. He owes money to these guys—a gambling debt ... and for some other stuff, but things got screwed up. He lost the money. When he saw you at the apartment the other day—" She paused, and her swallow was loud enough to hear.

The motherfucker had sized him up that day on the sidewalk. Lucas cocked his head, "Other stuff like what?" Not that he gave a shit.

"A pick up. The items got seized before Dale could complete the transaction. It wasn't his fault, but he owes these guys. I was to sleep with you, and then—"

"Then you'd have leverage. You'd go to Bailey if I didn't pay you off." Her head bobbed, and a growl of unmistakable fury vibrated up from his chest.

"It's the truth," she voiced timidly when he said nothing as he grappled for much needed restraint. "Dale took on the full burden for something I was part of. I owed him and wanted to help him. But everything has gotten out of control now. I don't know what to do," she cried.

Incensed, Lucas swung open the door. "I don't know what kind of shit you're mixed up in, nor do I give a fuck, but the fact that you would callously hurt Bailey by coming here and attempting this for some piece of shit boyfriend tells me the kind of person you are. Now get out."

"Wait! You don't understand!" Pants of breath made her pitch near panic.

"Stay the fuck away from me. We clear?" He didn't wait for her reply as he slammed the door in her face.

Infuriated, he raked his fingers through his hair. Bailey was already wary about starting a relationship with him. Those previous chumps she'd been with left her skittish, unable to trust. No doubt this shit with Faith would set him back to square one with her. He had to somehow repair the damage that bitch had just created.

Fuck!

Chapter Twenty-Four

"I'm going to need something a lot stronger than champagne to make it through the night." Gavin swallowed down the entire contents of his glass and then beckoned to a waiter for another. "I've been here ten minutes, and already I want to slit my wrists. How can you stand it?" he asked Lucas beside him.

"Why are you getting here so late?" Lucas glanced over at him.

"I got tied up on a conference call. I'll fill you in tomorrow." The waiter approached with a tray of filled champagne flutes. Gavin quickly snagged one and took a large gulp, then surveyed the room. "So how's it going here, besides insanely boring?"

"I've networked with some of the other sponsors," Lucas answered. "I guess that makes it worth it. Plus, my artist, Sienna Keller, is getting a lot of praise for her work. I've been asked by several if she's truly an amateur."

"I can see why. I walked by all of the displays when I got here. Her paintings and sculptures are really good. Given the mediocre competition I see in comparison, she has a good chance of winning this thing. By the way, she's smoking hot. Considering her name isn't Bailey, glad to know you're not hitting it." Gavin winked as he caught the sleeve of a passing waiter while tossing back his champagne. He placed the empty glass on the tray and said, "Thanks," then continued on, "You've been holding out on me, brother. What's the deal with you and her?"

"She's Bailey's friend."

"Good to know. My eyes have been playing cutout of her apple-round ass in that tight, black dress. It makes this shit bearable." They looked over at the artists standing beside their displays that were lined up along the far wall. "What's next here?"

"Now that the judges have done their review, all that's left is to announce the three finalists." Lucas did another sweep over the room in search of Bailey, but she hadn't shown. He had to see her and clear things up. The fact that she wouldn't come out to support Sienna told him just how deep in the shit he was sunk in with her over Faith's stunt.

He pulled out his cell from his inside coat pocket and sighed long. No missed calls or text messages.

• • •

Staring out the car window, Bailey refused to shed another tear. After she hung up on Lucas, she'd crawled into bed listening to the sound of her cell phone ring over and over—Lucas redialing nonstop. A short time later when he knocked repeatedly on her apartment door while calling her name, amid ringing her phone, she turned it off.

She'd cried in the shower and cried as she got dressed. The gown she'd purchased had been selected specifically with him in mind. At the boutique, she'd fallen in love with the rich indigo-blue, full-length evening gown, and already had the perfect shoes to wear with it tucked away in her closet—deep blue, strappy heels with a glittery beaded band across the toes.

The dress was strapless chiffon with a sweetheart shaped bodice and a side slit high up the right thigh. That feature in itself was why she chose the dress. Remembering Lucas's words to her before she left his car, she snatched up the gown knowing he'd appreciate its easy accessibility for his fingers. What's more, the fact that the jewels she'd received from him coordinated perfectly with the gown made her cry all the more.

The driver parked in front of the National Art Gallery and assisted her out of the car. Her straight tresses caught the breeze of the evening and whipped across her face as the slit of her dress billowed, exposing her bare legs. She had to grab hold of the fabric to keep from exposing herself. She wasn't wearing any panties, and not for Lucas's benefit. Simply put, the bodice through the hips hugged her like a second skin.

Looking at the glass doors in front of her, she took a deep breath to gather her nerves. If it weren't for the fact that it was Sienna's night, she would have just as easily stayed in bed for the next two weeks. Her heart felt so heavy in her chest, she could barely withstand the weight to stay upright.

At least this time she didn't have to carry the mental image of Faith's naked body on top of Lucas like the mental picture she had of Faith and Andrew forever in her brain.

In a moment, she'd have to face Lucas and somehow mask the hurt and betrayal to get through the evening. Better it happened now before she'd gotten in too deep with him. But that didn't stop it from hurting.

Showing up late was in bad taste, but she was in such a dismal mental state, barely able to move, that she'd stayed seated on the edge of her bed weeping and staring into space for nearly an hour. There, she'd tried to digest the reality that Faith had done it to her again.

You're here for Sienna. Releasing another lung-cleansing breath, she squeezed the beaded clutch purse in her hand for renewed strength and started up the steps to the entrance. Hearing her name, she paused and turned around. Kevin was heading toward her and Diego was paying the cab driver. Both were dressed in black-tie.

She was glad to see them, especially Kevin. His text had gone unanswered, with her being so preoccupied with Lucas and ending up in bed with him. Her heart constricted painfully, remembering those blissful hours spent in his arms.

Gathering herself, she forced a light smile. "Hey, Kev." She kissed him on the cheek and did the same to Diego. "You two clean up nice."

"Look at you! Wow, lady, you look killer!" Diego praised.

"Truly a vision," Kevin said.

"Thanks." Bailey caught the added weight carried in Kevin's words. "Kevin, I ..." She glanced over at Diego.

"I'll go check on our girl." Diego went inside.

Once the door closed behind him, Bailey said, "I'm sorry if I hurt you. I value our friendship and would hate to lose it. I really mean that. You're important to me."

"I'm sorry, too. Seeing you with that dude, I guess it caught me by surprise. I understand that you're gonna see other people. I don't have to like it, but I understand." He cupped her chin, with his thumb caressing her cheek. "I will always care about you, Bailey. I can't just hit a switch and turn it off."

Glum, Bailey nodded. Here was a man, a good man who was kind, honest, and trustworthy. He was always there when she needed him, and he obviously cared about her, yet she was grieving over the loss of her relationship with a man who in all likelihood had hooked up with her ex-friend. *What the hell is wrong with me? Was I dropped on my head as an infant?*

It was safe to say Kevin wasn't tardy because he was crying like a baby into his pillow.

With a hand on her hip, she said, "I know why I'm late. What's your excuse, mister?"

"Diego and I had to speak with the reps in Baltimore about the show we'll be performing in next week." Kevin proffered his arm to her. "Shall we, my lady?"

"We shall." It was like that with Kevin—nothing complicated, just simple, easy ... safe.

Chapter Twenty-Five

Bailey took in all the men dressed in black tie. She felt like a beacon in her indigo blue among the mass of women in black as well.

She and Kevin scanned the crowd and over to the wall of at least twenty-five to thirty artists' displays stretched from one end of the room to the other. They found Sienna with Diego about three booths in from the far right and headed over.

"Sorry I'm late." Bailey gave Sienna a hug.

"It's cool. They announced that the judging will take place in twenty minutes," Sienna informed them.

"Who's your sponsor?" Taking a side step, she gave a look at the company's logo printed on the easel: Marx Venture Capital. For a moment, Bailey's gaze studied her friend's features, not sure what she was looking for. "How did he manage that?" Her head turned to Diego and Kevin. "Can you give us a minute?"

Diego's cell phone rang. He stepped away to answer it.

"Would anyone like something to drink?" Kevin asked.

Bailey took his hand and gave it a light squeeze. "That would be great. Thanks." She waited until he was far enough away before she said, "Lucas was with Faith."

Sienna's eyes popped wide. "Oh shit," she grounded out. "Are you sure? When? How do you know?"

"After I spoke to you, I called Lucas and could hear Faith's voice in the background. It felt as though I was back in college when I walked in on Faith with Andrew." Deeply hurt, Bailey sighed. "It's over with Lucas, not that there was much to end."

"Let's not be hasty," Sienna cautioned. "You don't know for sure that he cheated."

"Not be hasty!" Incredulous, Bailey gaped, annoyance grating her tone. "Why else would they have been together? They'd only just met that morning. I saw how they were behaving with one another." She received a side-eye. "What?"

"You're doing that thing you do."

"What thing?"

"I know you said that you weren't into Kevin beyond a friendship. I get that, but you and I know that when he started wagging behind you too close, you cut him loose."

"That's not true." With arms crossed at her chest, she made an aggravated snort. "I know what I heard."

"It just doesn't sound like Lucas."

"How would you know?" she argued.

"Here you go, ladies." Kevin came up and handed them each a glass.

"Thanks, Kev," Sienna said.

"Yes, thanks, I really need this right now." Bailey took a sip with an unblinking stare at Sienna over the rim, apprehension beginning to flutter in her stomach. Was her friend right? Overwrought, she shifted her glass from one hand to the other, the weight of it all taking its toll on her.

"You all right?" Kevin stroked her back, settling his arm around her waist, his affectionate, concerned eyes studying her face. "What's wrong, dollface?"

"I'm good." Bailey attempted a smile and took another sip from her glass, trying her best to relax. She just had to get through another hour or so; then she could go home, and shut herself up in her room. She knew the drill. It's not like she hadn't been here before.

Chapter Twenty-Six

Getting an elbow nudge from Gavin, Lucas looked up from checking his phone for what felt like the hundredth time, pulled out of his dismal musing.

"Now that's a lucky motherfucker." Gavin blew out a low, appreciative whistle.

Lucas followed the man's fixed gaze and nearly fell over when he saw to whom Gavin was referring. He could feel the blood slowing in his veins, his lungs lacked adequate air, and the sudden rapid patter of his heartbeat felt as though it was trying to punch a hole in his chest at the sight of Bailey standing over by Sienna ... on Kevin's arm. When had she arrived?

He felt Gavin's nudge in his side again, but he couldn't speak. Hell, he could barely breathe.

Her curls were replaced by a curtain of lustrously straight tresses, gracefully flowing down her back, drawing many male gazes to the splendor of her stunningly beautiful face.

Her dress ... *merciful heaven*. He closed his eyes for a heartbeat and then brought them back to Bailey wearing a dress that was melded to the shape of her hourglass figure. It sketched out the tight roundness of her breasts to precision, narrowing to the contour of her small waist to form over her slightly flared hips and her firm ass.

As she took in the artwork around her, the side slit of the dress fluttered freely with even the slightest graceful stride she made, revealing a shapely right leg high up the thigh. Strutting in her heels gave even more emphasis to the way her perfect figure worked that dress.

Like Gavin beside him, Lucas observed how several men were caught in a trance. They all stared at the stunning beauty in vibrant blue. He wanted to gouge their eyes out, his best friend included. They were all plainly ogling her with lascivious eyes. It brought to mind what he'd told Bailey before she left his car. He bit the inside of his jaw so hard he tasted blood as he tried to keep his composure intact at the very idea that she was likely sans panties on Kevin's arm. And she wasn't wearing the jewels. Lucas saw blood.

"Damn, man, do you see that body?" Gavin blew out another faint whistle. "She's got equal front and back."

Sandra walked up behind Lucas and Gavin. "What is she doing here?"

"You know her?" Gavin asked without turning around.

"Of course I know her. She's my assistant." Sandra stepped over to Lucas's side. "Did you know Bailey would be here tonight?"

Gavin's head jerked over. "That's Bailey! Damn, bro." He looked across the room and shook his head. "Just damn."

Sandra frowned. "Lucas, what's going on? Is there something I should know? Are you seeing her?" Her inquisitive stare at him hardened. "Answer me," she snarled.

Lucas forced his eyes away from Kevin's hand stationed at the small of Bailey's back, bordering her ass and cut a glance to his right. "Sandra, who I see is not your concern." At that moment, Bailey's gaze collided with his from across the room. With a startled look of surprise at seeing him staring directly at her; she quickly turned away.

Looking affronted, Sandra gasped. "Bailey works for me. If there has been some sort of breach of professional conduct, she'll be terminated."

"If you fire her, I'll ruin you," Lucas growled, his eyes transfixed on Bailey.

Heavy lashes fluttered. "What are you saying? I thought we could try again. We're both out here on the East Coast now, away from the influences of our families. I understand what you expect. I won't pressure you. I can be that woman for you. Luke, give us another chance." She came in intimately close. "Let me stay the night." Stroking his forearm, her eyes softened. "We can have some fun like we use to."

"Drop the notion, Sandra," Lucas stated coolly, contrary to the blood simmering in his veins from seeing Kevin now affectionately caressing a hand down the length of Bailey's hair. Smiling sweetly at the man, she seemed to welcome his affections.

Hearing someone call Sandra's name, Lucas turned his head and saw a young man waving to get her attention. "Sandra, you're being summoned. Your artist needs you." She hardly gave the man a glance.

"Let me be there for you, Luke."

"Your artist, how about you go *be there* for him."

Her blue eyes narrowed, and her lips were thin as sheet paper. "I must say, Bailey's date is awfully sexy. Big, strong, African American man like that, I'll bet he'll fuck her good and plenty tonight. What do you think, Luke? I mean, from the way he's practically stroking her ass, I wouldn't be surprised if they disappeared and found a closet right here. On second thought, she was late getting here. That may explain her tardiness." She shrugged with a malicious grin and walked off.

Gavin turned back around. "Bitch," he murmured. "Now on to more important matters. What's the deal with your lady showing up with a date?"

"She said he's a *friend*," Lucas bit out. His eyes narrowed, fury welling up inside him as he watched Kevin now caressing Bailey's lower spine. Sandra's parting words began running on overdrive in his head. "If her friend doesn't take his hand off her, I'm going to break the son of a bitch's joint off." He stalked off toward them.

Gavin kept pace beside him and asked, "Did you get Bailey the jewels? She's not wearing any."

"Yes, I sent her the damn jewels, and I got fucking eyes, Gavin." Lucas sighed deeply for composure. He was unfairly taking out his anger on his friend. "Sorry about that, bro."

"It's cool. That shit Sandra said about Bailey and the dude ... don't let her fuck with your head."

"Bailey thinks I cheated on her with her friend."

"Not your artist, I presume. They look pretty chummy over there."

"Not Sienna." He gave Gavin a quick rundown of the ordeal with Faith as they made their way over to Sienna's group.

Patricia Blake stepped in his path. "Lucas Marx, you've just made my night." She lifted up and boldly kissed his cheek.

Lucas's gaze jumped to Bailey, and he felt her scornful glare slice deep into his jugular. *Shit.*

"Mrs. Blake, it's good to see you. Are you here with your husband? I'd like to meet him." He lacked the patience to deal with her.

"Actually, I'm going solo tonight." She smiled suggestively with a touch on his arm.

"That's too bad. Well, I was headed over to my lady. Please excuse me."

Her eyes fluttered with her mouth popping open and then quickly snapping shut. "Oh, I see. It was good to see you." She stepped aside.

Lucas walked on, dismissing her.

"Who was that?" Gavin asked and followed it up with, "Not important," when he didn't get an answer. "You said that you threw this Faith chick out, no harm, no foul. Hey, does Bailey have a sister? Twin preferably," he muttered out the corner of his mouth.

Ignoring Gavin, Lucas stepped before Bailey. His eyes shifted and met Kevin's challenging dark glare beside her, then dipped to the man's hand stroking up and down the side of her waist. The fact that she was allowing Kevin to caress her so intimately made Lucas near violent. "We need to talk," he managed through tight jaws.

"Lucas, this isn't the place for this." She looked around at their group, which was keenly watching. "This is Sienna's night. I won't do this here."

"Then let's step outside." He reached for her.

"Whoa, man, ease back," Kevin warned and gave a glance at Bailey when she took a side step. He tucked her back to his side. "You heard her."

"Take your fucking hand off her." Lucas's voice dropped to an ominous, grinding pitch.

"Lucas!" Bailey gasped; her winged lashes flickered.

Kevin came in dangerously close to him with brows set low. "You had better back the fuck up before—"

"Before what?" Lucas moved in even closer, his smile a dark warning. "Don't let this suit deceive you, my man."

"Lucas, Kevin, stop this please," Bailey said low with an anxious look around the room. "You two are going to cause a scene and ruin Sienna's evening."

"Guys, come on. Not here." Sienna placed a hand on Kevin's chest. "Kev." She nodded when he finally dragged his scorching glare away from the one Lucas was firing back at him to look at her.

"Like the beautiful lady said, not here." Gavin took hold of Sienna's hand and brought the back of it to his lips. "I'm Gavin Crane. My buddy here was rude in not introducing us."

Sienna stared back for a moment, giving Gavin a quick once over. "I'm Sienna Keller—nice to meet you. Now, if we could get these guys to dial it back."

Lucas took Bailey's hand and stepped back, bringing her out of Kevin's clutches. "If you would just talk to me, hear me out."

She and Sienna exchanged a look, a quiet understanding. With a sigh, Bailey allowed him to guide her over to a somewhat private—when the waiters and waitresses were not whizzing by—breezeway that led to the kitchen.

He jumped right in. "I didn't have sex with Faith. Let me make that absolutely clear."

"Then you admit that she was with you?" She crossed her arms beneath her breasts. "Was she at your house?"

"No. She came to my office with a proposition for sex, but I didn't touch her. I threw her out."

"That's not what it sounded like to me," she retorted. "Faith seemed pretty cheerful for someone who was about to be thrown out on her ass. I should've expected it. She's more your type anyway."

Lucas released a deep chest exhale to maintain patience with her. "You seem to have a presumption about my type of woman. How does Faith fit the ticket? Is it because she's white?"

She shrugged. "Not just that. I've seen the type of women you've been with, and none of them resemble me."

"Good. I've improved my standards." His grin was countered with an eye roll. "As for the jewels, I don't deny that I had Kara purchase earrings for Sandra during that brief time I was involved with her. *I*, however, selected the items I gave to you. Painstakingly, I might add."

The pinch between her finely arched brows softened. "They were very beautiful and went well with my gown."

"That's because with Kara's help, I found out what you'd purchased to wear tonight. I coordinated the jewels to your dress." Lucas came in close and palmed the right side of her face. His thumb stroked lightly along her soft cheek. "I was looking forward to you wearing them tonight and later when I took you to bed."

She bit her bottom lip in that sexy way he liked. "They weren't meant as some sort of token—compensation—for sex. The jewels were a gift to express my feelings for you."

Her smooth lips turned into his palm and planted a kiss. "I picked this dress for you." She flared out the fabric slit at her thigh and smiled shyly as he looked her over.

"You look stunning ... beyond stunning." Lucas tucked silken strands of hair behind her right ear, leaned in, and whispered, "Are you wearing panties, princess?" She chewed her bottom lip again while shaking her head. He came within a whisper of her mouth, ready to take her offering lips, but his eyes came up, distracted by the man walking up behind her. It was the other man who was with their group. "Can I help you?" he gritted.

Bailey turned around. "Oh, hey, Diego." She looked up over her shoulder. "This is my friend, Diego Gutiérrez. Diego, this is my boyfriend, Lucas Marx." She looked up at him again, and he smiled. Damn, how he liked the sound of that.

Lucas shook the man's hand. "It's nice to meet you."

"Diego's a fantastic drummer," Bailey cut in. "We have to go see him play."

"How long have you played?" Lucas asked him with hands resting on his lady's bare shoulders. "I tried to pick up the skill, but didn't put in the dedication."

"I've been playing since I could hold the sticks. My father played. When he saw I was interested, he taught me everything he knew."

"As Bailey said, we'll come to your show."

"Cool." Diego's phone rang. He answered it, and his forehead creased as he looked at them. "Yeah, uh, Bails," he eyed Lucas and then looked back at her. "It's Faith on the phone. She wants to talk to you. She said she tried to call you, but got your voice mail. This is her third call," he murmured.

Lucas stepped forward. "Good. She can tell you herself what took place at my office."

"Really?" Diego questioned. "You really want Faith to talk to Bailey? Dude, I don't think that would be wise."

"Let Bailey talk to her," Lucas insisted.

"You're brave."

Lucas turned to Bailey. "You'll see that what I said is true. I told her to clear this up with you."

Bailey took the phone. "Faith, what do you want?" The loathing she felt for the woman was palpable. "Yes, but the mere fact that you attempted that with Lucas is unforgivable. What? Now I know you're lying. Just like you tried to stir up trouble with Lucas and me, you're lying about this." Her eyes met Lucas's as she said, "They wouldn't do that. Sienna wouldn't. Don't you ever speak to me again." She ended the call and gave the phone back to Diego. Then her head swung back to Lucas.

Seeing those green eyes flicker third-degree flames, there was no need for Lucas to try to discern what Faith had revealed. "Now wait, Bailey."

"It's true, isn't it?"

Lucas reached for her, but she jerked back, rough and aggressive. "How could you?"

Fuuuck me! "Allow me to explain." He reached for her again, and once again, she stepped away.

"What is it about me that I habitually attract cheaters and liars?" she voiced in a self-addressing manor.

"Bailey, please."

"You," she pointed squarely at his face, "stay away from me." Pain mixed with disgust flashed across her features as she shook her head and then walked off.

Diego stepped forward. "You ever see a bad accident about to happen, but there really isn't anything you can do to stop it? That's what this looked like. That chick, Faith, got issues, man. I was hanging out with her one night and got the vibe quick on how whacked out she was. I advised her not to tell Bailey, to leave it alone, but dude, she was hell-bent on outing you. The woman wouldn't stop ringing my phone. She said Bailey had a right to know what you did."

"She doesn't give a shit about me. Her aim was to hurt Bailey." Lucas stepped out of the breezeway and observed Bailey standing over by Sienna. They were arguing at a whispered pitch.

Diego came up beside him. "Personally, I believe you. Like I said, Faith has issues, but I'm not the one you have to convince. Now if what she said about you bribing Sie is true ..." Diego ran his hand over his buzz-cut hair. "Not good, dude. I'll go see if I can help Kevin calm the ladies down."

Lucas followed and came up to Bailey and Sienna, who were still arguing at low volume. "Bailey, I'm to blame here. Sienna did nothing to—"

"Like hell she didn't!" Her anger acute, looking between them, she said in a harsh whisper, "You two were in it together. I was a joke to you both. Gullible, naive Bailey, twist her in any way, shape, or form you want."

"Bails, it wasn't like that." Sienna took in a breath, tears visibly brimming her eyes. "I'm sorry."

"You're not sorry. You wanted to compete in this event, so you used me, pimped me out to him." Her voice shook with eyes glistening from the onset of tears.

"I went to Sienna. She didn't—" Lucas started.

"You thought to use them both." Kevin glowered, then moved to Bailey's side and used the tense moment to put a comforting arm around her shoulder.

"You stay out of this," Lucas gritted in stark warning.

"People, they're about to announce the three finalists," Gavin said, breaking into the blended verbal melee. "Lucas, man, come on." He tugged him away from Kevin off to the side.

They all stood watching the art director at the front of the room, not a smile to be had among them.

The third-place artist's name was called, followed by the company sponsor.

Lucas looked at Bailey standing next to Kevin. He was bending near her ear, likely stirring the fire. "He'll make the situation worse."

Glancing over at Kevin, Gavin whispered, "When this is done, you'll handle it, brother."

Everyone looked on as the second-place artist and sponsor made their way to the front.

Lucas's eyes stayed glued on Kevin as he voiced to Gavin, "In dealing with the whole Faith shit, I forgot about the arrangement I made with Sienna. If Bailey would listen to reason, she'd see that I helped her friend and that what I did was in order to get to know her."

"That may be, but I don't think she's able to see anything positive about the situation right now. First, she thought you cheated on her with her friend, and then she found out that you bribed her other friend. Right now, the best bet for you both is to let things settle down a bit."

"That bastard will try to make her see otherwise." Lucas kept hard eyes trained on Kevin with Bailey. Just then, Kevin swept a tear from the corner of her eye. Lucas started to charge over, but was intercepted by Gavin blocking his path.

"They announced Sienna! Lucas, she won!" Gavin nudged him and Sienna came over to them.

"Lucas, we have to go up," Sienna told him dolefully.

Lucas blinked and looked around. Practically the entire room stared at him. He turned his head to Gavin beside him, who nodded and mouthed the words, *get moving*. He and Sienna made their way through the crowd to stand at the front.

He half listened to the art director offer congratulations to Sienna and hand her a plaque. The man then thanked him and MVC for participating and supporting the arts. Basically, he was thanked for his very generous contribution that likely paved the way for Sienna. She clearly won on her own merits. Her work was superb, but his substantial monetary generosity surely left a mental stamp with the organization.

The director announced to the crowd all of what Sienna had won. Lucas's attention, however, was fixed on Bailey and Kevin. They had moved off to the side. Kevin was still jabbering in her ear. She stepped away from the man and headed for the exit. Kevin was in step right behind her.

Lucas moved to go after her, but was blocked by reporters and photographers. He stood with limited patience next to Sienna, whose face wore a forced smile as they took photos and gave repetitive responses to several of the local news channels and art magazine columnists. Inside, he paced like a caged animal, wanting to break and run after his female.

Chapter Twenty-Seven

Seated across from Sienna in his limo, Lucas watched as she stared out the window at the whizzing traffic while dabbing her eyes with a tissue that was already soaked with her tears.

He'd possibly destroyed a friendship, a close bond between two women who were like sisters to one another.

"Sienna, I'm sorry about all of this." As if those words could fix the colossal turmoil he'd caused. Regrettably, there wasn't much else he could say. It was at least the fifth time he'd apologized. She didn't acknowledge him, but the tears seemed to flow freer down her cheeks each time he did.

He retrieved several tissues from the sidebar and handed them to her as long minutes passed listening to her soft cries, hating himself for being the cause of her grief. Suddenly, she looked at him. Silence, then a quiet deep breath before she turned back to the window.

"Faith thinks I'm overprotective of Bailey," she said. "She feels I shelter Bailey. I believe it was the reason she slept with Andrew, Bailey's ex. Faith argued that Bailey needed to know what the real world was like, that she need to be shown how the rest of the world functioned outside of her protective bubble."

Lucas scowled hard. "That woman is bad company. Why you and Bailey bother with her, I'll never understand." He didn't even want to hear the bitch's name spoken.

"Faith's mother was an alcoholic. She told me that one night she was at a party and her mother showed up drunk, staggering through the house, shouting for her. When she found Faith, her mother screamed that her father was having an affair. Faith said her mother always accused her father of cheating when she was drunk. Her so-called friends at the party found her mother's behavior amusing. Several even offered her more to drink for the entertainment. Faith managed to get her mother out of the house and into the car. She said the drive to her house was only four blocks, but they didn't make it home. Her mother grabbed the wheel, sending the car head on into a utility pole. Faith's learner's permit was scarcely a week old. She could barely control a car, let alone an inebriated mother. She was sixteen when her mother died. She blames herself for her mother's death and believes her father still does as well."

Lucas shook his head. "It can't be easy carrying that guilt, but I would expect her to be a bit more reverent to you and Bailey, considering that you all care about her despite the malevolent things she does."

"Bailey and I know Faith's deal. I, in particular, know what it's like to have a mother so wrapped up in her own shit that she forgets you exist." Sienna wiped away the tears that fell and sighed glumly. "Anyway, we try to cut her some slack."

"A lot of slack," Lucas muttered.

"There's some jealousy with her at Bailey, I know that. She sees Bailey as having had a perfect upbringing—the perfect home—perfect parents—and that I perpetuate it by sheltering her. What Faith doesn't understand is I haven't been protecting Bailey. Bailey protects me." She dried her eyes once more, her long sigh labored by anguish.

"I was raised from the age of twelve by my grandmother. Not because my mother wasn't around. Oh she was around, along with the current man she was sleeping with at any given time. My grandmother took me from my mother when I told her that my mother's boyfriend paid a visit to my bed." Seeing his jaws clench, she supplemented, "He came close, but he didn't get to do what he intended only because the bastard was too out of it to get it up. He beat me instead. Somehow he felt it was my fault his ass was limp."

Lucas scowled, wishing he could find the bastard and strike him down.

"Anyway, I took to sleeping with several hat pins punctured into my mattress. Whenever one of my mother's boyfriends came at me, I'd whip one out and stick the bastard hard," she said with a light chuckle. "They'd literally squeal like a stuck pig. That particular night I ran to my mother and told her that he came into my room ... he touched me. Like two of her previous boyfriends, he denied it of course, and she blamed me as usual. She always claimed that I wanted those pieces of scum for myself. I like to believe it was the drugs that prevented her from caring about me." She shook her head as though attempting to push the mental pain away and went on, "After that last attempt, I got the courage to tell my grandmother what happened. She took me in and raised me until she died two weeks before I graduated high school."

"God, Sienna, I'm really sorry." What she must have suffered, Lucas couldn't imagine. He felt even worse for possibly destroying her and Bailey's sisterhood. Bailey could be all she had as family. *Damn.*

Sienna lightly shrugged. "I made it through. My grandmother named me the beneficiary of her life insurance, but my mother felt it should've been hers. To keep the peace, I gave her a portion of the money and set to use the rest to pay for college. All was good for a while. I went off to school, met Faith and Bailey at freshman orientation, and we became friends from that day." She sniffled and retrieved another tissue from the sidebar, then continued. "At Parents' Day, my mother came, and so did Bailey's parents. Faith's father and stepmother were in Bali. They sent a guy down to deliver her a lemon-yellow, convertible Mustang. Freshmen couldn't get parking decals on campus their first year, but somehow Faith got one. Bailey's parents brought her a care package of everything you could imagine." Reminiscing, Sienna laughed softly. "Toiletries, heating blankets, snow boots, and a large box full of ready-to-eat can goods. We had Campbell's Chunky variety the entire semester." She sniffled and laughed lightly again, saying, "You would've thought Bailey was attending school in Antarctica and wouldn't have access to rations for months on end.

"My mother didn't bring anything, but I didn't care. I was just ecstatic that she showed up. She looked good, too. Not all strung out like she usually looked. History should've taught me to know better, though. She didn't come to see me. She came to ask me for more money. I'd given her thirty K in May. It was October, and she was broke. She claimed the guy she was with stole her bank card and cleaned out her account before he ran off. I'm sure she'd blown a good chunk of it on drugs. Who knows."

Damn. "Did you give her more money?" Lucas was immensely rapt in Sienna's life story. Now he understood why she was such a direct and strong-minded individual. She had to be in order to withstand her difficult upbringing and a pathetic mother.

"I was set to give her all of it, which meant I would leave school, return home, and find work because I knew that my mother would either run through it all or simply disappear. Either way, I would've needed to take care of myself. She wasn't big on sharing. At least I wouldn't have felt guilty anymore. The money should've been hers."

"On the contrary, it sounds like your grandmother was a smart woman. She made the right call in assigning it to you."

"Bailey convinced me not to turn the money over to my mother. I fought her at first. I told her she didn't understand, that she'd grown up with parents who loved and cared about her. I had

my grandmother, thank God, until she died, but my mother ..."
Her eyes misted. "Though she was a piss-poor excuse for a mother,
I felt obligated to her. Still do."

Lucas gave her a disagreeable look and she shrugged.

"I know that sounds crazy, but it's how I feel. Anyway, Bailey
said something that struck a chord with me: *If you educate a man,
you educate a man. If you educate a woman, you educate a generation.*
I believe she said it's by Brigham Young." Sienna smiled faintly.
"She's always quoting something or another."

"She does." Lucas grinned as the sing-song siren of Bailey's
voice feathered across his mind.

"Bailey told me point blank, 'Break the cycle, Sienna. You
can help your mother by completing your education. You don't
want to end up like her. Power within, not power over.' Bailey was
right."

"I would agree." She met his eyes and nodded to his nod.

"Bailey was also the one who got us both jobs at Nuagé so
she could help me, help my mother. I stayed in school, used the
life insurance money for my education and living expenses. The
money I make at Nuagé, I send to a PO box for my mother. I
assume she checks it. I haven't heard from her. That's usually
confirmation.

"Bailey insisted on giving me half of her paycheck from Nuagé
to add to what I send each month. This way, I don't cut into
the other funds and my mom won't hound me—bleed me dry.
Secretly, I was putting Bailey's portion in the bank for her to have
for a rainy day. She found out and wasn't happy, but with all the
repairs recently with her car, it came in handy."

Thinking of Bailey, recalling the hurt and betrayal he witnessed
in her eyes upon learning what he'd done, Lucas's chest twisted
tight. He released a subtle breath to tamp down the ache. "I have
to say you're very generous to your mother, considering."

"I have enough to live on. With my docent job and what's remaining from the other funds, I'm good." She brought her eyes back to the window. "I went along with you because I really wanted to compete in the art contest. It's what I've wanted for a long time, but it's tainted now." Her voice trembled, and more tears slid down her cheeks. "I'm turning it down. I'm going to give my award to the second runner up."

"Like hell you are." Looking at her, Lucas sat forward with his elbows on his knees. "I admit that my entering you in the competition was for my self-interest, but you won it, Sienna. Your work is outstanding. Don't allow my selfish actions to take away your dream. Bailey may be upset with the both of us right now, but she loves you and wouldn't want to see you deny yourself this opportunity to further your art career. Sienna, are we clear?" He stared at her until she nodded.

The limo parked in front of the apartment building. Isaac assisted Sienna out, and Lucas followed her up the walk. Sienna retrieved her key from her purse and was about to unlock her door, but they both abruptly turned around at hearing Kevin's door open across the hall.

"She's not inside." Kevin stood within the doorframe of his apartment delivering a smug grin to Lucas.

"Is Bailey with you?" Lucas took a wide step, ready to barrel through Kevin to get inside the man's place.

Kevin revved up sharply. "Where the fuck do you think you're going? Back the fuck up!"

"Is she with you? Bailey?" Lucas called out to her and glowered at Kevin when he got no response. "Where is she?"

"Wouldn't you like to know." A taunting grin. "I suggest you go find yourself another plaything to occupy yourself. You've done enough damage to these ladies."

"Kevin, is Bailey with you?" Sienna asked, on the verge of more tears. "Please, I need to talk to her."

Kevin shifted his eyes to her, and they softened. "No, Sie, she's not inside."

"Where is she?" Sienna cried.

"You were with her!" Lucas bellowed, his fury near its breaking point. "You know where she is!"

"Yes, and you don't." A cocky satisfied grin. He reached inside his apartment and brought out a Tiffany box. "She asked that I FedEx this to you, but since you're here—" Lucas snatched the box from his grip, brows pinched tight. "Your Amex and key are tucked inside. Go exploit some other woman." Kevin tacked on a snide laugh. "You thought your expensive gifts, your money, and power would keep her? I guess you can chalk that up to your arrogance. Bailey may have been impressed by it at first, but she came to her senses tonight, saw your true colors."

Fury churned and simmered in the pit of Lucas's gut. His eyes narrowed as he took a threatening step forward and was met in the middle of the hall. "You don't want to start this dance, my man," he warned. "Tell me where she is now!" His head pivoted to Isaac heading toward them to intervene. Turning back to the asshole in front of him, he gritted, "Where is she?"

"I suggest you have your man servant there take your ass on home," Kevin sneered.

Lucas took note of Isaac's right hand buried inside his suit coat, undoubtedly clutching the butt of the revolver he kept holstered beneath his left arm. He waved Isaac off, but Isaac hesitated as his intense gaze stayed laser marked on Kevin. Dark eyes shifted to Lucas. Reading the subtle head shake, Isaac pivoted and resumed his position by the car. Then, Lucas came in tight to Kevin, his voice dropping to a grating snarl. "You're going to tell me where Bailey is."

"You had better get the fuck out my face! I won't say it again!"

"Guys, stop it! I can't take this shit right now!" Sienna yelled through tears.

Lucas clenched his jaws, conveying a harsh grin. "Tell me something, Kevin. How long have you been in love with Bailey knowing she won't ever have you? It must be difficult for you."

"I could ask you the same question. I'm not the one trying to find her. I, on the other hand, know where she is," Kevin shot back. "You don't deserve a woman like Bailey. And as I held her in my arms tonight, I helped her see that she needed to be rid of you. When she returns, my arms will be the ones she come back to, not yours. You'll never have her ... my man," he mocked, triumph conveyed in the wide stretch of his stance.

Lucas smiled tight. "See, now that's where you're wrong." He came in close near the bastard's ear and whispered, "You may fuck her in your fantasy. I, on the other hand ..." Stepping back, he smiled in his success of having hit his target dead center. Kevin's face had twisted and screwed down tight with the clarity of those words reflecting in his eyes. The man's sinister glare was so blistering hot, Lucas felt it could have burned a hole straight through his skull.

He was given a millisecond to act. A tightly clubbed right fist aimed high came at him, which Lucas blocked with his left—the hand that still held the Tiffany box. A right jab met Kevin in the gut, followed by a blow to his left temple in quick succession, sending the chump barreling into his apartment door, landing across the threshold.

"Kevin!" Sienna shrieked and rushed over to him. She dropped to her knees, quickly checked his pulse, and lightly slapped his cheeks. "Kevin, are you all right?" His eyes were glassy. She checked his pulse again, then looked up at Lucas. He was pacing back and forth, trying to calm his rage. "Lucas, what the hell!"

"Sienna—"

"You should go." She lifted Kevin's head to her lap. He was slowly coming around. Looking up again, she urged, "Lucas, leave now."

"Please call me if you hear from her." Lucas walked back to his limo where Isaac stood, having witnessed the entire ugly scene. His expression stoic as usual, Isaac opened the car door, and asked, "Where to, boss?"

"Home." Before Lucas climbed in, Isaac muttered low, "He got what was coming to him." The comment surprised him. Isaac was always all business when on duty. That sounded personal. That stupid *man servant* comment must have hit a nerve.

Kevin was lucky Isaac hadn't intervened. The man was ex special forces. Five years ago, Isaac had taken the job as driver and security guard because he'd said he looked forward to the ease of it, and that looking after the safety of one would be a cakewalk compared to his previous assignments that sometimes involved watching over thousands in a hostile region.

Lucas shut himself inside the car. He'd done yet another thing that would cause Bailey to despise him even more when she found out.

He loosened his bowtie and rested his pounding head back against the seat. *What the hell is wrong with me?* Isaac was right about that asshole, but still, things had spun out of control. He was turning into a madman, surprised by his lack of restraint. And the words that came out of his mouth and set the whole thing in motion were despicable. What had she turned him into, a raving lunatic? The ring of his cell phone in his pocket had him jolting upright, pulling out of his mental chaos. He took it out, read the display, and let out the anxious breath that he hadn't realized he'd been holding in for who knows how long. Taking the call, he leaned forward with his elbows on his knees, closed his eyes, and put the phone to his ear. "Bailey, love, I'm so glad you called," he said softly.

"I'm only calling out of respect to you, unlike you toward me. This thing between us was nothing but a game to you. I guess you got what you wanted."

"It's not like that at all, and I do respect you. Where are you? Let me come to you. If we could talk about this, not over the phone, face to face where I could also show you how I feel about you."

"Are you kidding me! You have the nerve to suggest sex as a way to fix everything."

"No. I meant that if we're together, I could hold you in my arms, and we could discuss this rationally without anyone else but us. You'll see that this is all simply a misunderstanding."

"Manipulating my friend, paying her to deceive me in order to sleep with me, you see that as a misunderstanding? And that whole thing with Faith—"

"I didn't touch Faith, damn it! Didn't she tell you that?" he yelled and heard her gasp sharply at his outburst.

"I took a chance here with you, Lucas." She cried and sniffled through her words, "I can't trust—"

"Don't say it! I messed up, I know that, but don't say you can't trust me." Lucas leaned his aching forehead into his left palm. "Our relationship, the rules, I'm learning here, Bailey. We can work through this."

"What relationship? I was merely a conquest for you."

"Not true."

"This is too much for me. You're too much. I need time to think. Kevin suggested that—"

"Don't bring his fucking name up in this!" Lucas roared and heard her gasp again and cry out. He took a breath and tried to level his tone. "He's the reason you're not thinking about this rationally. He's manipulating you now. Can't you see that?"

"I do feel I need space, Lucas. Right now, I just don't see us working out if—"

Lucas hitched an anxious breath. "What are you saying, Bailey? One error in judgment and you're out?" His eyes watered, stunned that she would so easily end it. "It's that simple for you?" He suddenly felt sick. "I get it."

"Lucas," she sobbed. "I'm—"

He interjected again. "I've never had a purely monogamous relationship, never felt it was worth the aggravation. My conjecture was right." Pressing his thumb and fingers at his closed lids, he swallowed hard to lessen the ache in his throat. "I took a chance, too, Bailey. Hope Kevin gives you what you believe I couldn't. Have a nice life." He hit End on his phone.

"Boss, there's a car parked at the gate," Isaac said over the intercom as he pulled onto the cobblestone driveway and came to a stop behind the tan Mercedes.

Lucas stepped out of the limo to see Sandra exiting her car. *You've got to be fucking kidding me!* He hadn't a modicum of patience left to deal with her.

"Sandra, what are you doing here?" When he made no attempt to go to her, she walked over to him and cut a dirty look at Isaac when he remained standing outside of the car. Lucas thought of Bailey and how pleasant she'd been to Isaac.

"Luke, I—"

"That's not my damn name." He glowered, and she tensed, then smiled faintly with a nod. "Lucas," she stressed, "I want to apologize to you for my behavior earlier. You know me." Her chortle grated his stressed nerves like sandpaper. "I sometimes have a quick trigger." She glanced back at the house. "How about we go inside and have a glass of wine ... talk." A light palm came to rest at the center of his chest, and she stepped in close. "I know it was Shelly who told you that I was only using you when we were together. She called herself my friend, yet she told you lies about me because she wanted to be with you. It wasn't true. I cared deeply for you, still care for you. Shelly sought and succeeded in coming between us. As for Bailey, she could never be the woman you need. But I can."

Still reeling from his last words spoken to Bailey, Lucas removed her hand and took in a slow breath through his nostrils to hold on to his calm.

"Sandra, go home." Those were his only words to her before he got back into his car. Isaac climbed in, maneuvered the limo around the Mercedes, pressed in the code to open the gates, pulled through, and the gates closed behind them.

Chapter Twenty-Eight

Bailey stood on the side of the road waiting for her dad to show up. She should never have driven his truck in the first place. A typical twenty-minute round trip to the grocer for dinner rolls and milk had turned into a roadside tick-tock.

When her mom asked her to run the errand, she was glad to have something to do. It was her dad who insisted she take his truck instead of her mom's Subaru, since the truck's tank was full.

"Geez, Dad, where are you?" She checked her watch for the third time. Forty-five minutes had passed and counting.

At least now her dad was speaking to her again. She'd been home little over a month, and the first week she'd endured the silent treatment from him, followed by grunts in passing during week two, and now full sentences. She could only guess that he assumed that she intended to stay in Darlington. It was likely what brought about his decision to let go of his two-year-long crabbiness over her decision to remain in D.C. following graduation, instead of returning home as she'd promised.

Bailey had quickly realized that she'd outgrown Darlington, but what did she have to go back to in D.C.?

Sandra fired her when she'd phoned asking for a leave of absence to tend to a personal matter. She hadn't accrued enough hours; therefore, time off was not approved. What's more, Sandra made clear that if she didn't show up for work on Monday, not to bother coming back at all.

Joe at Nuagé was much more understanding. He told her she could take as much time as she needed and that her job would always be there. *At least I have that*, Bailey thought glumly.

Her watch showed another ten minutes had gone by. She glanced up and down the main road that led in and out of Darlington Square. She'd become bored out of her mind within the first week of being home. Nothing had changed. The same faces greeted her from six years ago. Most of the girls she knew from high school were married and had babies. The guys were no different. Many had wed their high school girlfriends.

And they're all doing a hundred times better than me. At that dismal thought, she peered over her shoulder at her satchel sitting on the passenger seat next to the dinner rolls and soon to be rancid milk that was fermenting in the ninety-degree heat for nearly an hour. The pregnancy test she'd purchased was buried at the bottom of her pack. *Lord, help me if I'm pregnant with Lucas's baby.* Fearing the strong possibility, she pressed her palm to her forehead, knowing that she could practically tell time by her cycle, which was exactly four weeks and five days late.

Ugh, why am I such a screw-up?

Just the thought of having to tell Lucas made her stomach lurch. He'd looked ready to gag at the mere sight of the children attending the Movie on the Mall, and she could guess how he'd react to the news of becoming a father.

It was killing Bailey to not have Sienna to talk to, especially now with the pregnancy issue hanging over her head. She wanted to call Sienna, but what would she say to her after how she'd walked out on her best friend at the art competition. It was rude and unkind regardless of how upset she was over what Sienna and Lucas had done to her. What's more, she hadn't answered any of Sienna's calls after everything happened. Things between them had been too raw. Now she longed to talk to her.

Lucas. Her heart ached and her stomach knotted tight whenever she thought of him ... which was practically every waking minute and restless night. She'd ruined that relationship as well. Sienna was right. Instead of talking everything out like he'd wanted, Bailey had run away scared, and he ended it. Why would he waste his time with someone who jets at the first sign of conflict? *No wonder Faith hates me. She's right, I am pathetic.* The tow truck pulling off on the shoulder behind her cut short her self-condemnation.

The waning sunset reflecting off the truck's windshield prevented Bailey from seeing the driver. She brought her hand above her sunglasses to aid in getting a better look at the man getting out of the truck. As he came out of the glare, she realized that it was Marcel Duncan, her ex-boyfriend from high school.

"Oh my God, Marcel, how are you!"

"What's up, girl?" He came up and gave her a hug. "I got a call from your pops about the truck out here. Sorry for the wait. I had another tow." He took a step back. "Let me get a good look at you. Still beautiful as ever."

"You're easy on the eyes yourself." Aside from the goatee, he still looked the same—tall, dark, and handsome. "You're driving a tow truck now?"

"I own it." Accomplished pride was heard in his voice. "I opened an auto repair shop over on Kingston Wood."

"Really! Congratulations. You were always great at fixing things. You're the reason I still have my Honda."

"You still have that hunk of metal?" He chuckled.

"Hey, leave my baby alone." Bailey playfully punched his arm. "It finally stopped running a few weeks back."

"It's really good to see you again, Bailey. You're still a sight to behold. That beautiful face of yours hasn't changed a bit."

"Thanks. I-I'm glad to see that things are good with you." Bailey nervously rubbed her moist palms up and down the sides of her jean shorts. The overly affectionate way Marcel looked at her made her a bit uncomfortable.

They chatted a bit more, and she was surprised to learn that he hadn't married as most of their friends had. Marcel was a good man. He'd make some woman a good husband.

In high school, a lot of the girls were jealous of her for snagging the quarterback. Several even tried to tempt Marcel to cheat on her. It was common knowledge that they weren't having sex. She'd been labeled Bailey "Chastity" Walters by her peers after she'd refused a kiss from a boy at a birthday party during a Spin the Bottle game. That title was held all through high school, but Marcel remained faithful to her. For that reason, she hadn't felt it was fair to have him wait on her for four years. Had she not gone away to college, would they have married?

"So, can you fix the bucket of nuts?" she asked to redirect his attention. Immediately, she thought of Lucas, reminded of what he'd said about her knack at deflecting when she felt uncomfortable. She touched her sunglasses to reassure herself that they were in place to hide the melancholy in her eyes.

"I'll take a look." Short minutes later, he called out from under the hood. "I think I found the problem."

"Really? That's great." Bailey waited at the rear of the truck, appreciating the distance.

She looked over when Marcel closed the hood. He retrieved the cloth hanging from his back pocket to wipe his hands as he walked back to her. With a playful smirk, she asked, "What's your diagnosis, doctor? Will it survive or suffer the same end as my Honda?"

"I'm afraid it'll have to spend a night at my garage. I'll hook it up."

"Okay. Let me get my satchel and groceries." She retrieved the items while Marcel maneuvered the tow and hooked the truck up to the wheel lift. He then came back over.

"Hop in. I'll take you home."

As she climbed in, she also wondered if it was fate at work with the truck breaking down and Marcel coming to her aid. Would they have made a point to reconnect if not for the truck?

• • •

"Had to tow it?" Bailey's dad asked as they stepped onto the porch.

"I'm afraid so, Mr. Walters. I'll take a look at it in the morning and give you a call," Marcel said.

"Good, good." He turned to her. "Marcel has his very own auto repair shop."

Bailey shifted the grocery bag in her arms. "I know." She smiled again at Marcel. "I'm really happy for you."

"He's doing so well that he's had to turn away business. Marcel, am I right? And you said that you were considering opening another location, didn't you?"

Bailey stared back at her dad's wide smile as he championed the man's accomplishments, a bit perplexed by his behavior. Again, she said to Marcel, "That's really great. Thanks for the ride. It was good seeing you." She hugged him and kissed his cheek, and he returned the same.

"You, too, Bails. Anytime."

As Bailey turned to head inside, her dad asked Marcel, "Have you eaten? We're about to have dinner. Why don't you join us?" She eyed her dad warily. Was this whole thing somehow orchestrated by him? *He couldn't have predicted the truck breaking down*, she told herself.

"If it's not too much trouble?" Marcel looked at her.

"Uh, sure, Marcel, please join us." Watching her father as he grinned and slapped the man on the back in the way a teammate would after scoring the winning point, she realized something actually had changed in Darlington.

Chapter Twenty-Nine

"Just call her. You know you want to."

Seated behind his office desk, Lucas's eyes came up from his computer and met his buddy Sean's gaze over on the couch. "Like I've told you, she made her choice, and I'm good with it."

Sean leaned forward with hands clasped. "You're good with it, my ass. Dude, you look like hell. You look like you could use about a month of continuous sleep."

"Thanks. You're so great at pep talks," Lucas mocked, his features tightening in annoyance. "Maybe you should give up that CEO chair over at Grant Enterprises and start your own counseling center." Sean Grant was his buddy from their prep school days. Notably, Sean was CEO to the renowned Grant Royal Hotels and Resorts found around the world. However, today, his chosen profession was being a pain-in-the-ass relationship consultant.

Sean chuckled, looking not at all bothered. "I'll consider it."

The office door opened, and Gavin entered. Dax filed in behind him.

"Great, another wise man and soothsayer," Lucas groused, now realizing what was going on. This was his intervention. *Damn them.*

"I call dibs on soothsayer." Dax grinned as he unbuttoned his suit coat, then dropped down in the armchair.

Daxton Pattarozzi completed their brotherhood pack. Like Gavin's role at MVC, Dax was chief operations officer at Grant

Enterprises. Lucas loved each and every one of them and considered them his brothers in every sense. That said, their hovering was annoying as shit right now. He just wanted to focus on his work, be left alone. He couldn't keep up with the countless emotions that continued to try to crash down on him. Work was his only refuge to hold the overwhelming feelings at bay.

"I see he's still biting off heads." A wide grin stretched across Gavin's mouth, he, too, looking unaffected by Lucas's petulance. Taking a seat on the couch, he said, "Sean, my man, I saw the press release on your purchase of the site to build a Grant Royal Hotel and Resort on the National Harbor. Congrats, bro."

"Thanks. Now I just have to waddle through the political red tape before I can break ground."

"Brutal shit, no doubt," Gavin said.

Sean gave a look at Lucas. "I've been trying to get our boy to get off his ass and call his lady." A small smile. "What's her name? Lucas wouldn't tell me."

"Bailey Walters, and he's got it bad, bro."

"I can see that. It's worse than Stacy Pelligren. Remember her? The man didn't leave his bed for a week."

"Yeah, and remember the love letter he wrote her?" Gavin cleared his throat, stifling a laugh.

"It was a sonnet," Sean corrected and pinned his lips together tight, resisting a smirk.

"Are you girls done gossiping? I'm not deaf," Lucas grumbled and could see all fighting back a laugh.

"Is this her?" Dax angled his cell phone toward Gavin to show the Facebook picture he'd found of Bailey."

"Yep, that's her."

Dax turn the phone toward Sean next, and they looked at Lucas and voiced in concert, "Call her."

Lucas sighed out his growing frustration, trying his best to ignore them.

Gavin strolled over to the bar and poured himself a shot of Patrón as he asked, "Where's Kara? She wasn't in her office? I need Sienna's tour itinerary."

With his eyes never leaving the computer screen, Lucas replied, "She's visiting her mother. I gave her the rest of the week off. She's been putting in a lot of hours with me over the past few weeks." His attention shifted briefly to the sidebar. "I see happy hour has begun."

Gavin raised his filled glass. "As it should. I'm Irish, every hour is happy hour." He swallowed the contents, then went back to the couch. "I thought I'd go to New York—the art tour—see how Sienna is coming along. MVC's in between contracts right now."

"Sienna's from New York, she'll do fine," Lucas said dryly.

"I know, but it would be appropriate to have an MVC rep there, you know, for marketing purposes." To Lucas's shrug, Gavin added, "Before Sienna left, we met for coffee. All she could talk about was Bailey and how much she missed her. That whole ordeal has been hard on her."

"You're not going to New York for MVC." Lucas eyed him. "Sienna's still resisting your charms?"

Gavin smirked. "I think I'm slowly rubbing off on her. Like I said, we met for coffee. Those dark eyes ..." He dragged a hand down his face and shook his head. "Man, she's smoking hot. I'm jonesing for that woman."

"Wonderful for you," Lucas muttered sardonically.

"Bro, you and Bailey have had well enough time to cool off. You know where she is. Go to her. Look, I'm going to say this and I know you're not going to like it. You're—"

Lucas shot him a loaded-barrel stare in warning. "Mind your fucking business, Gavin." He looked at them all. "I mean it."

Not backing down, Gavin sat forward, meeting his challenge as he said, "You're in love with Bailey, but you're too damn prideful to go after her. You made a mistake. Fine, it's done. Should she have stuck around? Absolutely. Now the two of you need to sit down and work this shit out because quite frankly, man, you're a … what was it Sienna said to you that day when she stopped by? Oh yes, a hot-ass mess."

"That he is." Sean nodded.

"Lucas, man, call her, text her, something. I'll bet she's waiting by the phone to hear from you," Dax said.

Silence. Then conceding to their persistent pestering, Lucas finally said, "She wants space."

"Space? It's been over a month. Fuck space," Gavin said.

Lucas sighed long. "Look, it's not like she's made any effort to reach out to me."

"Who called it quits, you or her?" Sean asked.

"I did."

"Then, shit, man, it's on you to make a move, not her," Dax put in. "You dumped her, and you expect her to ring your phone?" They watched as Lucas abruptly stood up, pulled on his suit coat, and headed for the door. "Where are you going?"

"Home to work out." He was done with their meddling.

"Isaac and I worked out with you this morning. You need to *work out* that shit with your woman," Gavin called out as Lucas swung open the door and stepped out with it closing behind him.

• • •

Bailey had never heard her dad jabber on with Marcel as much as he had throughout dinner tonight.

Back when she and Marcel were dating, her dad acted as though he disliked the boy, always kicking him out at nine o'clock on a school night, and precisely 10 P.M. on weekends. Now here he sat chatting up a storm with the man as though they were old buddies.

She wondered how her dad would react to Lucas. Would he treat him the same as he did Marcel, the man? He wouldn't have a problem with Lucas's race. However, he would take issue with Lucas possibly getting her pregnant out of wedlock. He was old fashioned that way. That was one of the reasons why he hadn't wanted her to go away to college, fearing she might get taken advantage. Bailey was sure her dad wouldn't want to hear that she was a more than willing participant in sleeping with Lucas.

Her head came up from rolling her peas around on her plate at another of her dad's loud laughing outbursts.

"Bailey used to love the festival, didn't you, baby girl?"

"Pardon?" She looked at her dad, over at her mom, who smiled, and then back at her dad. She'd missed the entire conversation.

"Marcel mentioned the annual festival going on in the square this week. I told him you used to love it." Charles relaxed back and hooked an arm over the back of his chair saying, "How about you two go for a spell? You remember how you used to love the bottle ring toss, baby girl."

Baby girl? Bailey hadn't been called that by her dad since she told him she was accepting her admittance to Georgetown University. As for the bottle ring toss, she hadn't been interested in that since age ten. It was clear to her now what her dad was up to and was curious if Marcel was privy to his scheme. Studying them both, still laughing it up, she would guess it was highly likely.

"Baby girl, what do you say?" Her dad eyed her as he resumed in the cutting and eating of a piece of his roast beef, chewing while wearing a rather festive grin.

"Charlie, Bailey hasn't been feeling up to par lately. She's still adjusting back to the climate here, dear."

Bailey gave her mom a faint, appreciative smile at her attempt to save her from the apparent date her dad and Marcel were concocting.

"Nonsense, Nena," Charles argued. "The fresh air would do her good. It's exactly what she needs."

Seeing her dad's hopeful grin directed at her, Bailey decided she'd give him this one. "It's been a while since I've been to the festival. It should be fun." She thought her dad's cheeks would split from the wide smile that formed across his mouth ... Marcel along with him. *Just this once.*

"How about tomorrow afternoon?" Marcel suggested.

"I don't know, Marcel, Bailey really shouldn't be walking about in the heat," her mom said. "It's been ridiculously hot lately. Maybe you two could go see a movie indoors where it's nice and cool."

"Nena, honey, they're young. A little heat will do Bailey good," Charles countered. "She needs to reaccustom herself to the weather here. What better way than a day at the festival?"

Bailey's eyes bounced between her parents. They were acting as though she'd just returned from the moon for goodness sake. As for the movie idea, that was definitely not happening. She could hardly watch television without images of Lucas and their first date, the erotic high he gave her in his limo, flooding her brain. A warm shiver ran through her at the mere thought of his mouth on those sensitive, intimate parts of her body. *Absolutely no to the movie idea.*

"I—" Her cell phone rang in her pocket. She pulled it out. *Sienna.* She skidded her chair back and jumped to her feet. "I have to take this."

"What about the festival with Marcel tomorrow?" Charles asked.

"That's fine. See you tomorrow, Marcel." With a quick wave to him good-bye, she hurried off to her bedroom and dropped down on the edge of the bed.

"Hey, Sie."

"Uh, hey, Bailey. I—"

"I'm so sorry for being such a jerk to you," Bailey blurted out. "I was wrong. I miss you, girl. I ... I—" She began to cry.

"Bails, I was afraid you still hated me. When you wouldn't take my calls …" Sienna broke into tears.

"No! I don't hate you. I could never hate you. You're my sister."

"I'm so sorry for what I did, and I miss you, too. "Kevin told me you went to your parents'."

"Yes. Sie, I wanted to call you. I didn't think you'd want to hear from me after I walked out on your award presentation. It was wrong of me. I'm truly sorry."

"Don't be. We …" Sienna sniffled and cleared her throat. "Bails, he misses you."

Knowing she meant Lucas, Bailey's tears became a river down her cheeks. "Did he say that?" She swept away the wetness with the back of her hand.

"Not exactly, no. He knows that you're at your parents'. I didn't tell him, but you know Lucas—if he wants something, he'll find a way to get it." They both knew what that meant, and the conversation grew silent for a moment. "He asked me if you were okay, if you needed anything. I haven't seen him much. I've been dealing with his assistant, Kara, when it comes to my art tour schedule. Lucas had your car towed to his mechanic a few weeks ago. That was the last time I spoke to him. He'd called to let me know."

Bailey gasped lightly. "He did that? I'll have to find a way to repay him." Touched by Lucas's kindness, she wiped away more tears. "He hasn't called me. I guess it's for the best. Granted, I still feel it was wrong of him to do what he did, but I understand that he was using the only method he knew to get what he wanted. Making deals, it's what he's good at, what he succeeds at. Of course he'd use his money, power, and persuasion." She stopped trying to clear the tears away. It was useless. They'd become torrential at this point. She grabbed a tissue from the box on her nightstand to blow her nose. As an attempt to change the subject, she asked, "When do you start on your tour?"

"I'm in New York now and will be here for the next couple of days, followed by L.A., and ending in Vegas. It seems surreal. I still can't believe I won. Lu ..."

"It's okay, go on."

"As my sponsor, Lucas's company has spared no expense. He had Kara set me up in the Grant Royal suites. Kara said Lucas is BFFs with Sean Grant, the man himself! Can you believe that? I also have a car and driver at my disposal. Lucas has been great. He even tried to make amends with Kevin for the K.O. He didn't want you to be upset with him over it. Kevin wasn't having it."

Bailey frowned. "The what? Did you say K.O.? Knock out?" Alarmed, her spine stiffened into a tight column.

"Shit, shit, shit," Sienna muttered.

"Sienna, what did Lucas do to Kevin?"

"Before you go off, in fairness to Lucas, Kevin provoked him. He was getting in Lucas's face, taunting him over the fact that he knew where you'd gone off to, but he wouldn't tell Lucas."

Feeling guilty, Bailey exhaled heavily. "I didn't want anyone to know at the time. I'm sorry about that. Sounds like whatever happened was also my fault."

"It's okay. Anyway, Lucas and I came back to the apartment to talk to you. Kevin opened his door when he heard us outside. He gave Lucas back the jewelry and then started in on him. I'm not sure what Lucas said that set Kevin off. I asked them both, but neither would say. All I know is Lucas whispered something to Kevin that, I swear, Bails, Kevin's eyes turned black as coal. Before I knew what was happening, Kevin swung on Lucas, but Lucas blocked the punch and delivered two solid rights, boxing style, that sent Kevin airborne. Kevin was knocked out cold, but he quickly came around."

Bailey gasped. "Oh my God! Is Kevin okay?"

"His pride is still bruised, but the black-and-blue bruise under his left eye is fully healed."

Astounded, Bailey shook her head. "I can't believe Lucas hit him."

"Honestly, Kevin made the first move. Your boy Lucas got skills." Sienna cleared her throat at the awkward silence that once again followed. "It's so good to hear your voice, chica. Are you coming back?"

"Well, I lost my job at Callaghan's. Again, stupid move on my part to leave the way that I did."

"You know I got you until you can find another one."

"I can't ask you to do that, Sie. Not again."

"You didn't ask before nor this time. I'm offering. I'll be away. You can have the place all to yourself if you need space to work through the whatever."

"Thanks. I don't intend on staying here, that's for sure. I think I've outgrown my hometown. I miss the Metrorail, us hopping over to Adams Morgan, and the clubs in Georgetown. Oooh, and the tapas restaurants."

"I miss us hanging out, too. Well, home is here when you're ready. Thanks for forgiving me. I thought I'd lost my best friend."

"Never. Sisters forever," Bailey assured her.

"I better get off to get some rest. Tell your parents I said hello and also that hottie brother of yours."

Bailey chuckled. "Will do. Enjoy your tour."

"Oh, by the way, Faith called me. She left a message that only said that she'd decided to return home to try to work things out with her father. He'd kicked her out upon discovering that she'd gotten back with Dale, that and something about some money being stolen, you know, the usual Faith soap opera. I texted her to let her know I'm here if she wants to talk. I haven't heard from her since."

Bailey's forehead crinkled in annoyance. "Sienna, I'm going to need some time before I can get past this one. Though Faith apologized, she made a play for Lucas. I don't know if I'll ever be able to forgive her for that." She let out a deep breath to try to dispel the bitterness she still felt. "I'm glad you let her know that you would always be there for her. I really mean that."

"Yeah, I don't think she has anyone else to turn to, friends that truly get her, I mean. Well, I'll say good night. Hope to see you when I return."

"Okay. Good night."

Bailey placed her phone on the nightstand, feeling a little better now that she'd spoken to Sienna. They were still best friends, and Sienna was starting out on her art expo tour. She couldn't be happier for her.

She undressed, put on her robe, grabbed her pjs—T-shirt and boy shorts—and then pressed her ear to her bedroom door. There was only the muffled sound of the TV mixed with the faint voices of her mom and dad chatting in the living room. Satisfied that Marcel had left, she quietly left her room, walked down the hall past her brother's room and into the bathroom that they shared. Caleb was out as usual. He'd show up well after everyone had gone to bed and would be off again before everyone woke up, off to who knows where.

Turning on the shower, she allowed it to steam up nice and hot before stepping in. Like each time before, the shower she shared with Lucas entered her mind. He supported her weight effortlessly with her pressed against the cool marble as he pumped in and out of her pussy until she thought she would faint from the mind-blinking pleasure. *I can't take this.* She rapidly shook her head to push away the image, as well as the melancholy that accompanied the loss she felt.

Hurrying through her ablution, she shampooed her hair, soaped, rinsed from head to toe, stepped out, dried off, moisturized, braided her hair, and put on her pj's, all in under fifteen minutes, wanting to be done with the task.

Back in her room, she flicked the light switch off on the wall, climbed in bed without thinking, and buried her head in her pillow, hoping that tonight she'd actually sleep through the night. That's what it had become. She couldn't eat, sleep, watch the television, shower, or do practically anything without thinking of Lucas. He'd become a part of her very being.

With the pregnancy test still in her satchel, she rolled to her back and placed her hand on her stomach, fearing Lucas had literally become a part of her. Shifting to her side, she fluffed up her pillow and tried her best to find a comfortable position, having had several restless nights, unable to shut her mind off. Every time her lids closed, Lucas's face appeared, and with it, the agonizing pain of sadness in her chest.

A groan choked her up as the familiar nighttime tears came forth, escaped her eyes, and spilled over the bridge of her nose, disappearing into the fine hairs at her temple.

"I can't get over you, Lucas," she cried softly, squeezing her eyes shut with the heels of her hands pressed over her lids, drowning in deep despair. "What am I going to do?" Turning to her stomach, she sobbed quietly into her pillow, her heart aching excruciatingly for him with no way to stifle the pain.

There was a soft knock on the door. Quickly, Bailey wiped her face on the end of her T-shirt, rapidly fanned her face with her hands, blinked several times, hoping it helped to reduce the redness, swallowed deeply, and exhaled a breath before saying, "Come in." Her mom entered and closed the door behind her. The lamp on the nightstand was turned on. Bailey brought the blanket up to nearly cover her head.

"You're in bed early. It's not even eight o'clock. I thought I'd check on you. With your father pushing poor Marcel at you, it's a wonder you're not in here packing. You picked at your dinner. I've noticed you haven't been eating much since you got here." The blanket was pulled away from Bailey's face. "And I see you've been crying again."

Again. Each night Bailey tried to keep her anguish confined to the center of her pillow. Evidently, nothing under this roof escaped her mom's eye.

"I'm just tired."

"Bailey Elaina Walters, you know I don't like it when you and your brother speak untruths."

Her mom didn't like to use the word *lie*, preferring words like untruth, falsehood, and even tall tale. "Sorry." She sat up and hugged her legs at her chest with her chin resting on the top of her knees.

"Sweetheart. We've always been able to talk. That hasn't changed."

Her solemn eyes closed as her mom fingered several unruly curly strands of hair out of her eyes that only fell back in her face. "I know." She pressed her forehead at her knees and sighed long. "I'm dealing with something right now, that's all."

"I gathered that the moment you unexpectedly crossed the doorstep several weeks ago." The hairbrush was retrieved from the dressing table. "Scooch up." Her mom sat sideways behind her and undid her braid to brush out the tangles. As she began the task, she remarked, "Your troubles involve a man, I take it."

Bailey understood she wasn't asking a question. "His name is Lucas." Her tears returned, and her mom handed her several tissues from the box on the nightstand. She blew her nose, then said, "He did something that hurt me. I got scared."

The brush stilled. Her mom looked at her with concern. "Was he physically abusive?"

"No." Getting a worried stare, Bailey assured her, "Honest."

"Was he unfaithful?"

"No, nothing like that."

"Well, then it's fixable."

"I messed things up, and I know that it can't be fixed. I'm just having trouble getting over him," she explained as she dried her eyes with another tissue.

"Maybe there's a reason why you cannot let go so readily."

"What do you mean?" She attempted a look over her shoulder, but her mom nudged her head forward so as not to ruin the braid she was working on. "Mom?"

"Perhaps there's still a chance to make amends."

"I don't believe so. I'm afraid to call him. He probably won't answer anyway if he sees that it's me calling. He hasn't called or texted me. That pretty much confirms it. I can't blame him. I allowed my fears of getting hurt to dictate my actions."

Coming within a couple of inches to the end of the braid, her mom brushed the strands smooth and then secured them with the hair band.

"You got out of the relationship to protect your heart. That's interesting."

"Something liked that." With an expressed exhale, her mom got up, and Bailey slid down underneath the covers.

"Yet your heart breaks over not having him."

"Yes." She sobbed and was handed another tissue. "I'm sure it's over. If … if you knew him, you'd agree. Trust me, he … he made it clear when we last spoke," she said through choked tears.

"If you look for people to disappoint you, you'll never be disappointed," her mom stated as she straightened the covers over her shoulders.

"What does that mean?" Bailey hated when her mom spoke in idioms. She'd grown up trying to decipher sayings. Yet, she found herself doing it at times and would likely speak that way to her own child. *Geez*, she inwardly groaned, thinking of the pregnancy test hidden in her closet.

"There's a fine line between having a problem and creating one."

Growing annoyed, she exhaled, "Mom, please, what are you saying?"

"What I'm saying is love hurts sometimes. It gets messy and complicated." With a kiss upon her forehead and a palm of her cheek, her mom added, "Don't be afraid of a little conflict and uncertainty. If you care for one another and work together, it will make your relationship stronger. Now I'll let you rest. You need it during this time."

"Huh?"

Her mom turned off the lamp, and her silhouette moved quietly to the door. "Let poor Marcel down gently, dear."

"It's Dad who's pushing this."

"I know. Enjoy the festival tomorrow, but don't give the young man any hope that you're interested in anything more. I love you."

"Love you, too." As the door closed, Bailey turned to her side facing the bay window, reflecting on their conversation. Tomorrow, she would take the pregnancy test and then call Lucas. Hopefully, the only thing of major importance to tell him would be her apology.

Chapter Thirty

"You forgive me, but you don't want this ... us anymore?" Bailey couldn't seem to get in enough air to her lungs. Looking up at his cold, steel-blue eyes, her knees buckled under her, forcing her to sit on the edge of the bed before she crumbled to the floor.

"I think it's what's best for us both. Your time away gave me time to understand that we're not right for each other," Lucas said.

It was over, completely and unequivocally over between them. Her mom was wrong; Lucas didn't want to reconcile.

"But I'm carrying your child."

"That's why I came when you called. I'll always be there to care for my child."

"You care nothing for me?" Bailey blinked to free the tears clouding her vision.

"You're the mother to my child, but beyond that ..."

She hastily stood up and fell against his chest, burying her tear-soaked face against his shirt. Her hands gripped his arms tight, desperate to hold on to him. "I love you, Lucas. Please don't leave me. I'm sorry. We can work through this," she pleaded.

"It's over." Lucas dislodged her from his frame and opened her bedroom door. "Have a nice life."

"No! Don't leave! Lucas, please!" She fell to her knees, sobbing, begging as he walked out of her life forever.

Bailey shot straight up in bed, her eyes blurry from both sweat and tears. She quickly turned on the lamp on the nightstand and scanned her bedroom in search of Lucas. Sweat soaked the fine hairs around her face and neck. Her heart raced violently. Her breathing was quick to near hyperventilating, and she needed to take deep, even breaths to calm her pulse. When she managed to stop gulping for air, she left her bed to change out of her sweaty T-shirt and shorts that clung to her skin. Returning to the bed, she sat on the side edge and recalled her nightmare that felt so stunningly real. Her mind tried to convince her that it was simply a dream. *Heaven help me.*

She brushed the wild, wet strands of hair out of her eyes and rubbed her hand over her chest at her heart where the pain could still be felt. *It's official, I'm certifiable.* She would swear all of it was real. Lucas stood before her cold and apathetic as though they were strangers. Even after she told him she was carrying his child, he showed not an ounce of feeling for her. That part of the nightmare had her rushing to her closet. Pregnancy stick in hand, she left her room and padded quietly over the carpet to the bathroom.

With only the nightlight illuminating inside, a splash of cold water on her face helped to relax and center her nerves. Staring at her reflection in the mirror, she told herself, *Take the test. No more stalling.*

Having followed the instructions to the letter, she now sat on the closed toilet lid waiting to see which direction would be her future. The time had long since passed to view the results, but she waited a good twenty minutes longer before she brought the stick close to the nightlight. As she studied the plus symbol in the small round hole of the stick, for a moment, she wondered if she was actually still in the dream.

The urge to throw up, mainly from shock, grabbed hold, and she hastily dropped to her knees, swung up the lid, and emptied the little contents she had in her stomach. Closing the lid, she flushed, pulled herself up, moved back to the sink to splash more cold water on her face, and brushed her teeth, followed by her resuming her seat on the lid, not sure what to do next.

Her life was spiraling out of control. What was she going to do? How was she to raise a baby on her own and without a job? Abortion? A constricting ache of a strange kind of loss pained her chest. *No.* With that said, she'd have to find a reputable pediatrician. *How do you even do that?* And she'd need a reliable babysitter, one who worked nights—she'd need to keep her job at Nuagé. *Huggies or Pampers? Studies suggest breast milk is better.* Minutes ticked by with her sitting there as thousands of thoughts rattled her brain on what she was now faced with ... alone.

With her head pounding and her stomach somersaulting, still deep in her own thoughts, she opened the bathroom door and took a step. "Oh!" She fell back against the wall with her stick flying from her hand, having collided straight into her brother's massive, hard chest.

"Geez, Caleb." On her knees in the dark, she ran her hands over the carpet in search of her pregnancy test stick. "You need to watch where you're going."

"You ran into me." Rubbing the sleep out of his eyes, Caleb followed her crawling around in the dimly lit hallway. "What are you doing?"

"Shh, be quiet before you wake up Mom and Dad. I dropped something. Weren't you going to the bathroom?"

"Mom might wake up, but you know that you can drop a grenade in here and Dad won't budge. Here, let me get the light."

"No!" Bailey shrieked at a whispered pitch as the hallway light flicked on bright, casting a spotlight on her pregnancy test stick sitting next to Caleb's left foot. He picked it up, studied it, and then her. She snatched it from his hand.

Caleb gawked. "What the fu—"

"Shhh." Bailey grabbed his wrist, dragged him down the hall to her room, pushed him in, and closed the door.

"Uh, does that symbol stands for what I think it does?" Caleb leaned back against the bedroom door with his arms folded at his chest. "I'm guessing it's safe to say Mom and Dad don't know."

Looking up at his unblinking amber eyes trained on her, Bailey nervously chewed her bottom lip while shaking her head in answer.

She was the older sibling, but like everyone in her family, Caleb treated her as his baby sister. At twenty-two, he was about as tall as Lucas and just as big.

Their skin tone was the same shade of tawny brown, but Caleb had their mom's amber-colored eyes. His hair was a just a touch coarser than Bailey's, and he wore it in a messy, curly fro when it wasn't tied back in a ponytail beneath a bandana.

She didn't sense any condemnation in his tone, but his eyes showed concern for her.

"I just took the test." Her tears fell. "Caleb, I don't know what to do."

He extended his arms, and she walked into his embrace. "It'll be all right."

"I have to tell the father, but he ... he ..." she sobbed.

"Relax." He stroked her back. "It's not the end of the world. You're grown, and as for the baby daddy, I can be with you if you need me when you talk to him. I haven't met the dude, but I don't like that he's got you in here crying over him every night."

"What?" Bailey drew back and looked up at him. "I'm not." Her brother's lips twisted in a smirk. *Geez.* And here she thought she'd been discreet in her misery.

"I messed things up so bad with him, Caleb, that this would only add to the problem."

"Well, he had better readjust real quick or his ass is mine. I don't like seeing you cry, not over a dude."

"He's a good man, Caleb, really. I'm the one that needed readjusting." She wiped her eyes on the end of her T-shirt. "I intend to call him."

"You do that." Taking her hand, he walked her to the bed. She got in, and he pulled the covers up over her, tucking in at the shoulders. "Let me know how it goes. I'm here if you need me, always." He kissed her forehead. "Get some sleep."

"I'll try." Her brother always knew what to say to make her feel better. "Caleb, thanks."

"Not a problem, baby girl. Sleep tight."

• • •

Lucas lay in bed with the television remote in hand, mechanically flipping through the channels. His eyes were on the large screen, but he really wasn't paying attention. His mind was cluttered with images of Bailey and his parting words to her.

He'd told himself after he hung up on her, essentially ending their brief relationship, that he was better off—she wasn't worth the frustration. By day three, the piercing ache in his chest, the emptiness he felt there made a mockery of his iron pride.

Giving a look at the clock on the nightstand, it was 2:20 A.M. Another sleepless night. His body was exhausted, but his mind was on overdrive.

He'd nixed coffee, switching to an assortment of spirits in the evenings, worked out twice a day, read contracts well into the night, did anything and everything he could think of to wear himself out. It worked. The moment he hit his bed, he was out. Then about an hour later, he was awake. Some nights, he managed to get in a few hours, but inevitably, Bailey entered his dreams.

It always started out the same, a blurred image that turned into full-on vivid color of her, of them together. Him between her thighs staring down at the gleam of her sex, wet and swollen from his tongue's abuse, her pretty pussy ripe and ready for his taking. He kissed his way up her velvety skin and entered her smoothly, fitting snug within her warm tunnel. Their bodies surged rhythmically in sync, their limbs tightly entwined, skin scorching hot and slick with the sweat from their efforts. The image then quickly switched to her on top with him lifting her up and down on his cock. Kissing her throat, his tongue followed the delicate curve of her shoulder, trailing down to suckle one luscious breast and then the other as he rocked his hips, twisting as he did, and hearing her gasp in awe at the feel of him thrusting inside her at different angles.

Just as his lips formed words to speak to her, he was pulled out of the dream awake. That's how it played night after night.

With a heavy sigh, he tossed the remote on the bed, got up, and headed downstairs. Entering the kitchen, the low ambient sensor lighting along the floor boards—an ingenious idea of hers—guided his path to the refrigerator.

Looking around his kitchen, stainless steel appliances— handcrafted cabinetry—glass backsplash—Egyptian marble counters. There was even a coffee station nestled within a small alcove. He was quite impressed by Bailey's interior design skills. Her exceptional talent was displayed throughout his home. He could see her someday very successfully running her own company.

Lucas peered through the glass door of the refrigerator at the assortment of juice bottles and opted for a bottle of water, then moved to a swivel barstool at the island. As he drank, he thought about what it was he'd wanted to say to Bailey in his dream before prematurely being pulled out of it. Was it an apology for the mistakes he'd made? *It sure as hell should be.*

Like Gavin pointed out, his pride was massive. At the faintest hint that she was calling it quits, he dropped her before she could do it to him. Had he not accused her of that very behavior?

What has my pride awarded me? He shook his head on a dry chuckle. *I love her.* Gavin was spot on about that as well.

He tossed the empty bottle in the recycle bin, went back to his bedroom, got in bed, turned off the flat screen, and closed his eyes where immediately the image of Bailey sprung forth. He knew what he wanted to say to her in and out of his dreams. The words had been lodged in the back of his throat from the moment they first made love.

Alone in his darkened room, he mentally worked on the words to say to her: *Bailey, I'm in love with you. It doesn't change what I did. I'm sorry that I hurt you, and I hope you will give us another chance.*

Lucas grabbed his cell phone from the nightstand. For the one hundredth time, he brought up the picture Bailey had taken of them on their date. His discomfort was visible in his expression. She'd smiled bright, and those brilliant, green eyes that first captured his attention sparkled, lighting up her beautiful face. *I miss you. I love you.* He quickly pulled up her number and was ready to hit send, but remembered the time. He also realized that what he wanted to say to her should be voiced in person. Instead, a quick e-mail was sent to both Gavin and Kara to let them know that he would be away for a couple of days on personal business. Within a minute, his phone chimed a text from Gavin, which read:

About damn time.

A couple of minutes later, Kara's text came in:

Give Bailey my best.

Had he really been that bad off?

Chapter Thirty-One

Lucas put the Mercedes in park and verified Bailey's home address on the mailbox at the curb. He wasn't sure what he expected to find when he set out from the airstrip in Florence, which was about a half an hour's drive to Darlington. The quaint, single story, white-brick house with black shutters sat back a good distance from the street and was quite picturesque.

A dark green Subaru and a blue racing bike with its front tire missing were parked beneath the attached carport on the left side of the house. Thick, healthy hanging ferns adorned the stately wide front porch. A swing hung from the rafters at the far right, and twin white rockers were stationed on the left.

Someone spent a lot of time tending to the grounds. The flowerbeds as well as the lawn were meticulously groomed. A smile came to his face picturing Bailey as a young girl playing in the yard while her mother worked in the garden.

He thought he could simply walk away from Bailey, consider her and their very brief relationship an afterthought, but that proved to be excruciatingly difficult for him. He couldn't function without her. After how he ended things, he hoped that she could find it within her to forgive him.

His night in bed was spent working on his apology. That, and the right words to convey his feelings in a way she would accept as sincere and that would convince her to join him on his plane back home.

Lucas exited the car and headed up the walk that split the front yard. Climbing the six red-brick steps to the door, he realized then that there was a glass storm door where he could see inside. The television was on, but the room was empty. Beyond the living area, he could see straight through to an eat-in kitchen and onward to a bright sunroom. The air around him was saturated with the rich aroma of something sweet baking, causing his stomach to rumble.

Bracing himself, he rang the doorbell. As he waited, he wondered what Bailey's reaction would be when she saw him standing at her door. No sooner had the thought flashed in his head, entering from a side hallway, what he got was an older, yet very well-preserved version of her.

With the exception of her amber eyes, it was as if he was looking at Bailey twenty years in the future. Her hair was a wavy dark brown with sparse strands of gray throughout, which she had twisted and pinned at the nape. Her honey-brown complexion was smooth with only subtle laugh lines, he noticed, as she smiled warmly at him on her way to the door.

The woman looked rather fit in her navy-blue T-shirt, khaki capri pants, and white canvas sneakers.

He took a step back when she unlocked the storm door and opened it a crack. "Good evening, I'm Lucas Marx, a friend of Bailey's from D.C." She returned a kind smile and shook his extended hand.

"Hello, I'm her mother, Nena."

"I'm pleased to meet you, Mrs. Walters."

"You as well, Lucas. I'm afraid Bailey isn't here right now."

"She wasn't expecting me." Lucas blanked his expression to mask his disappointment. Did he expect that Bailey would be sitting around pining for him as he'd been for her? *Pretty much.*

He pulled from his pocket his card. "May I trouble you for a pen?"

"Of course." She left the door and grabbed the pen she had tucked inside her *People* magazine, returned, and handed it to him.

He wrote the hotel information where he was staying on the back of his card, and then handed it to her with her pen. "Please give it to Bailey." She nodded while slipping the card into her pocket. He took another step back. "It's been a pleasure, Mrs. Walters."

"Would you like some lemonade? It's fresh-squeezed. My husband doesn't like the store-bought kind."

No doubt, she expected a yes with her widening the door open for him to walk through. "Thank you." He stepped inside.

She closed the storm door while commenting, "I prefer coffee. I know that it's near ninety degrees outside, but it's not as if I'm having it under the sun, so what's the big deal, right?"

Lucas chuckled lightly. "I actually would prefer coffee myself, if you don't mind."

She turned around wearing a smirk and placed a hand on her hip. "You're not just saying that to get on my good side, are you?"

"I assure you, I often drink coffee in the middle of the day regardless of the weather."

"Lucas, we've become fast friends." A wink with a cheerful smile. "Please call me Nena and make yourself comfortable. I'll be right back."

"I'd be happy to help," he offered. She was so warm and kind; he felt a sense of calm just being in her presence. He'd had some anxieties over seeing Bailey and meeting her parents, but just like that, Nena put him at ease.

"It's not necessary. Sit. Relax." She went off to the kitchen.

Looking around the space, it was a comfortable size, not overly spacious, but very inviting.

Moving over to an array of portraits set out on a credenza and those on the wall above it, there were several of Bailey and her brother at different ages. He picked up a baby picture of Bailey wearing a dress that just about smothered her in pale yellow lace. Like the woman she was now, she was a beautiful baby. He set the picture down and picked up one with her dressed in a track uniform and holding a trophy. There were several pictures of her proudly holding trophies.

"She came in second there." Nena placed the tray down on the center coffee table. "I have milk and cream. This one's cream." She lifted the yellow serving cup. "Have you ever had sweet potato cobbler, Lucas? It is minutes out of the oven."

Sitting the picture back in place, he walked over and took a seat at the left end of the sofa closest to where she sat in the armchair. "I tried it for the first time the day I met Bailey. She suggested it." He took the cup Nena held out to him. "I take my coffee black. Thank you."

Lucas noticed that Nena was looking at his feet. Her gaze met his, and she smiled. It brought to mind Bailey's fixation with shoes.

He took a bite of the sweet potato cobbler and groaned out loud. It tasted better than Nuagé's, and he hadn't thought that was possible.

"You like it, I see. Bailey makes hers with extra cinnamon. I prefer nutmeg. Have you tried hers?"

"No, I haven't." How much had Bailey told her mother about their relationship? His sister, Chelsea, always discussed her man woes with their mother. Given his offenses, Lucas hoped Bailey was a bit more selective.

"Tell her to make it for you. When you see that mine is better, be sure to tell her so." Nena chortled.

He laughed lightly with her, unable to help it. Her affable smile was contagious. He took a sip of his coffee and set the cup on the tray. "I should tell you, I care for your daughter very much, but we're not on the best of terms right now." Curious of her reaction, he studied her face while taking another bite, followed by another sip from his cup.

She rested her plate on her lap, reached over, and gave his forearm a tender squeeze. "You came to her. That's a start in the right direction. I know my Bailey can be quite stubborn, a handful at times. Whatever it is, try to maintain patience with her."

Lucas nodded. *She definitely knows her daughter.*

They ate, and Nena chatted about Bailey in between them watching two segments of *Judge Judy*. About an hour and a half and their second helping of cobbler later, the storm door opened, and in walked a man, presumably Bailey's father—he made up the family portrait hanging on the wall above the credenza.

Lucas stood up as the man approached Nena and kissed her cheek. He was somewhat tall with a slender build, his complexion a medium brown, and he wore his salt and pepper hair neatly tapered close.

"I saw the swanky car out front and wondered if my wife was entertaining a dignitary in here," he quipped. "She always has something or another going on. I never know what I'll find when I come home. If it's not her book club, it's her charities."

Nena smirked and sucked her teeth. "Oh, Charlie, stop." She set her plate and cup on the tray and then rose from her chair.

"It's true," Charles said. "One time I came home to a yard full of dogs and cats. Nena was hosting a spay and neuter fundraising drive for the pet shelter. It was bathe your pet day right there on the lawn. You should've seen her running around after those dogs, soaked to the bone. The animals gave her a bath instead of the other way around." Charles chuckled and shook his head. "She should know better than to try to bathe a cat." He laughed heartily. "It was a sight, I tell you."

Picturing it, Lucas held back a laugh to try to be respectful.

Nena smirked. "Lucas, ignore him. Charlie, this is Lucas Marx."

"Hello, Lucas Marx," Charles voiced cheerfully and shook his hand.

"It's a pleasure to meet you, sir."

"What brings you to the Walters' domicile? Please don't say it's another animal drive," Charles teased. "Ahwow!" he sang out at Nena's pinch of his arm. Laughing, he took a step back. "I better stand over here."

"You better if you know what's good for you." Nena chuckled, and so did Lucas, unable to contain it. He enjoyed watching Bailey's parents' playful repartee.

"Charlie, Lucas is Bailey's boyfriend from D.C.," Nena said.

Charles's eyes jumped from Nena to Lucas then back to Nena. "Boyfriend?"

Lucas read the disapproval on the man's pinched face. He'd been a bit apprehensive about how they would react to him being white. Nena was kind and accepting from the start. In contrast, the tendon now throbbing on the side of Charles's neck said he was definitely not on board. And all things considered, Lucas felt he no longer held the title of boyfriend.

"Bailey and I—"

"They had a spat," Nena hastily interjected. "That's why Bailey came home. Lucas is here to try to mend things." She nodded at him.

"A spat?" Charles didn't bother masking his irritation as he tossed a scowl between him and his wife, with Lucas catching the brunt of it. "Bailey's been here over a month and has never mentioned anything to me about a boyfriend or a spat," he bit out.

"She needed her mother, Charlie. She and I talked." Nena smiled warmly at Lucas as she reiterated, "He's here so that they can work on their relationship."

Shaking his head, Charles shoved his hands in his pockets in obvious displeasure. "I'm sure you're a decent fellow, Lucas, but Bailey evidently has decided what's best for her. If she felt that there was something to work out between you two, it would have happened a month ago. Even as we speak, she's out on a date with—"

"Charlie, enough! You weren't even speaking to Bailey for half of the time she's been home. It's no wonder she didn't tell you about Lucas." Nena's head turned to him, and her eyes widened at seeing that all the color had drained from his face. He could feel the lack of oxygen beneath his skin. "I didn't say where she was because I wanted to get to know you," she said softly.

Bailey's on a date. Lucas felt as if someone had taken a sledgehammer to his gut. The cobbler he'd eaten was slowly rising. Quickly composing himself as best he could, he extended his hand to Nena. "I should go. It's been a pleasure. Thank you for the coffee and cobbler." He turned to Charles. "Mr. Walters, it was nice meeting you." They shook hands, and then he moved to the door.

"Lucas, please stay," Nena beseeched, trailing behind him. "I really think it's important that you do what you came here to do." She followed him outside and called to him as he headed down the walk.

Lucas turned around. "Thank you again for your hospitality." Literally feeling sick, he wanted desperately to be gone from there. As he got into the car, he heard Nena say, "If only—those are the two loneliest words in the world. Remember that."

Even the idiom caused a churning nausea in his gut, for it reminded him of Bailey, and that was a name he wanted to forget.

Chapter Thirty-Two

Bailey and Marcel had only been at the festival a short time when she asked to return home. It was early evening, but she was exhausted from lack of sleep, and with the fact that her body was assiduously growing a baby, she felt close to passing out from fatigue.

That morning, bright and early, she'd gone out and purchased a different brand pregnancy test from a different pharmacy. After taking the test again, she discovered that she should never play the lottery. If she didn't have bad luck, she had no luck. Not only was she not part of the one percent of false positives, she was without a doubt pregnant, without the father around, and unemployed. *Ugh.*

She had enjoyed spending a little time with Marcel. It was as if they'd picked up right from where they had left off six years ago, excluding the boyfriend-girlfriend part. She liked Marcel, but not enough to consider anything more than friends. The whole baby on board pretty much sealed that door anyway.

The entire day, Marcel was behaving as though there had never been a break up—showering her with affectionate touches and playful tickles behind the ear. It was what he used to do when they dated because he knew she was sensitive there.

They ran into several couples from high school at the festival, and all assumed by Marcel's touchy-feely behavior that they were back together.

Bailey glimpsed over at him in the driver's seat, and his head turned to her wearing a smile that had been affixed to his face all day. *I have to put a stop to this.* Her weary sigh came out a bit louder than she'd intended.

Attuned to even her slightest gesture, he looked over and took hold of her hand that rested on her lap, his fingers stroking her palm. "Penny for your thoughts?" he asked.

There it is again, touchy-feely. She subtly pulled her hand free from his and pretended to fix her braid, with a look at him. "I hope you're okay with me wanting to call it a day so early. I know how much you look forward to the fireworks. I'm simply exhausted. I haven't been sleeping well."

"It's cool. You're not sleeping? Should you see a doctor?"

Yes, but not for the reason you think. "A good night's sleep is all I need. I plan to turn in early tonight. I'm sure I'll feel better tomorrow."

They pulled up to her house just as Caleb climbed off his motorcycle and headed inside.

Marcel took her hand in his again, affection glowing in his dark eyes. "Bails, I really enjoyed being with you today. I'm glad you're back. I hope we can spend more time together like this."

Bailey didn't want to hurt him ... again, but she couldn't let him think that they were getting back together. "I enjoyed spending the day with you, too. It was nice seeing so many of our old friends." She sighed lightly. "But, Marcel, we—" He brought the back of her hand to his lips. *Dear God!* "Marcel—"

"Bailey, I won't pretend. I would like us to reacquaint, but I know it's too soon."

"Marcel, I—"

"Bails, you're tired. We can talk more tomorrow." He palmed her cheek and leaned in, aiming to kiss her mouth, but she turned her head. The fluttering look of surprise in her eyes brought the atmosphere between them to an awkward pause, then he said, "Let me get you inside."

What the ... he tried to kiss me! She had to put a stop to this, but she was too drained to deal with it right then, intending to make things quite clear with him tomorrow.

Exiting the car, they made their way to the porch. Her parents' raised voices drew her to a halt. It was rare that they fought. The last time she could recall was when she'd decided to go away to college. Her dad was dead set against it, while her mom, though she would have preferred Bailey to stay in-state, had resigned herself to Bailey's decision.

They entered the house just as Caleb strolled into the living room carrying a plate of sandwiches piled high and a full glass of lemonade. As her mom and dad sat in the twin armchairs facing one another caught in a heated quarrel with the rectangle coffee table acting as their buffer, Caleb took a seat on the sofa between them and quickly started in on sandwich number one seeming without a care in the world. Listening to them, from what Bailey could tell, their fight was about her.

"Nena, enough on the matter! I've said all there is to say!" Her dad gestured a hand over to her and Marcel. "That right there is what's best for Bailey."

"You can't control her life, Charlie! Once you get that through your thick skull, you'll be happier for it!" Her mom's eyes met hers, then narrowed back on her dad. "It's not your decision anyway."

"What's going on?" Bailey looked between her parents for an answer, but Caleb piped up instead.

"They're arguing about you."

"I gathered that, Sherlock." She smacked her brother on the back of his head. He hardly flinched and took another large bite out of his sandwich.

"You two are back early." Charles glanced at his watch. "It's barely five o'clock. You'll miss out on a good spot for the fireworks."

"It's hot, and I'm tired," Bailey said and then asked again, "What's going on?" She looked at her mom when her lips pursed to speak, but her dad interrupted.

"How about you two sit and watch a movie," he suggested. "I've seen Caleb rent them right on the TV somehow. Don't you, Caleb?"

Caleb finished off his first sandwich and immediately started in on his second. With his mouth stuffed, he garbled out, "From what I could get, your dude showed up, and Dad told him you were out on a date. No offense, Marcel," he voiced nonchalantly and took another large bite of his sandwich without ever actually looking at the man.

"Caleb, shut up!" Charles exclaimed irritably.

"What!" Bailey's head swung over to her mom. "Lucas? He was here? When?"

"About a half hour ago." Her mom rose and pulled a card from her pocket. She met Marcel's disconcerted gaze as she handed it over. "He asked that I give you this."

It was his white business card. Bailey turned the card over and read the hotel information he'd written on the back. She was completely thunderstruck that Lucas had actually come to Darlington. *He was told that I was on a date.*

"I have to go." She spoke to no one in particular, her heart racing, her brain in disarray. "Mom, I need your keys!"

Nena went off to the kitchen.

Charles shook his head and stood up. "Bailey, don't do this. You're making a mistake here." He pointed at Marcel. "He's a good man who cares about you. He didn't hesitate when I phoned to tell him you were stuck out on the side of the road."

"You knew there was a problem with that truck?" Bailey's eyes narrowed at the infuriating man. "You set the whole thing up, didn't you?"

"Well hell, you'd been home a month and didn't bother calling him. When I phoned to tell Marcel you were back, he was eager to see you."

"Mr. Walters—" Marcel paused at Bailey's light touch of his arm.

She looked up at him and could see he knew what she was about to say. They'd been here in this moment six years ago. She didn't want to hurt him, but what choice did she have? "I'm sorry. I'm in love with him."

"Here you go." Her mom attempted to give her the keys to her Subaru, but her dad snatched them from her hand. "What are you doing? Give Bailey those keys."

"No!" he bellowed. "I seem to be the only one with some sense around here! She's not going!"

"Have you gone mad!" Her mom's voice scraped up sharply. "Give Bailey those keys this instant!"

"Dad, give me the keys. Lucas could leave before I get a chance to see him."

"Let him go!" he barked and stuck the keys in his pocket.

"I'm carrying his child, damn it!"

"Sweet Jesus!" Her dad clutched his chest and stumbled back against the chair behind him, swaying as though he was caught in a spinning pinwheel.

Okay, that's not quite how I wanted to tell him. Quickly taking stock of everyone, Caleb was laughing hysterically to near choking at the sight of their dad standing with his mouth frozen open and his eyes stretched wide as though he'd witnessed something horrific. Her mom simply nodded, her behavior suggested not at all surprised. Bailey wondered if Caleb told her about the pregnancy. And Marcel ... the poor man's reaction practically mirrored her dad's. Right now, Bailey didn't have time to deal with any of them. She needed to get to the hotel before Lucas left ... if he hadn't already.

In a state of panic, she looked at Marcel. *No way.* It wouldn't help her if Lucas saw them together. Spotting Caleb's motorcycle helmet sitting next to him on the sofa, she snatched it up, and raced to the door.

Caleb jumped up. "Where do you think you're going with that?"

"I'm taking your bike." She pushed open the storm door and rushed out.

Nena yelled in alarm, "No, Bailey, you're not! Charlie, give her the keys now!"

"Mom, I got it." Caleb fished in his pocket and pulled out his keys. "She can't go anywhere without these." He went after her. "Bailey, I'll take you," he hollered on his way out.

Chapter Thirty-Three

Caleb pulled into a vacant spot. Bailey leaped off the bike and tossed him the helmet before he could properly set the brake. "Bailey, wait! What room is it?" he shouted as she took off at a mad dash across the parking lot.

"Fifteen twelve," she yelled back. As she passed through the automatic doors, she faintly heard Caleb reply, "If I don't hear from you in thirty minutes, I'm coming up."

She ran as fast as her flip-flops would allow, hurrying past annoyed hotel guests that frowned at her when she nearly mowed them down. There were those that stared at her inquisitively as she picked up the pace when she saw the elevator doors slowly closing.

"Hold the elevator!" she yelled and leaped inside where, thankfully, a man with his young son, held his thumb on the Open button. "Thank you." Working to catch her breath, she exhaled and tried to smile appreciatively at the man's nod while holding on tight to the safety rail behind her for support.

"What floor?"

Bailey blinked out of her thoughts and looked at the man and his son. Both were staring at her. "Oh, sorry. Fifteen. Thanks." Eyes close, she inhaled slowly through her nose and released just as slow to calm her pulse in order to focus.

"Top floor. How do you like the suites here?"

Again, she looked at the pair still staring at her. She was trying to run through what she would say to Lucas in her head, but the man interrupted her mental dialogue. "I've never been inside. I'm visiting ... a friend."

He gave her a once over. She nervously looked away and subtly brushed back the wayward hairs out of her face. Catching her reflection in the shiny brass doors, her hair was a mess from wearing Caleb's helmet. Her face was flushed from both the ride over and the heightened anxiety she felt. She was so nervous over the possibility of seeing Lucas, that butterflies cluttered her stomach to the point she felt she might hurl.

The elevator opened on the sixth floor and the man and his son stepped out. From there, she managed to get to the fifteenth floor uninterrupted.

She jogged down the hall, reading the numbers on the doors as she went, and got to the end of the corridor. The plaque on the wall in front of her read, Room Suites 1511 – 1512, arrows pointing left and right, respectively. Turning right, she rushed the short distance and stood before Lucas's door, trying her best to regulate her racing heartbeat. Circulating a refueling breath through her lungs, she exhaled deeply and delivered a firm knock on the door.

Please be here.

•••

Lucas stepped out of the bathroom with his towel wrapped at his waist. Looking around the so-called suite that wasn't even as big as the great room in his home, he sighed heavily and shook his head, disgusted with himself. *I'm a damn fool. What the hell was I thinking coming here?* The deal he'd made with Sienna was wrong, yes, but with the ease in how Bailey cut things off and then moved on, she was clearly never really into him.

In a hurry to be done with the damn place, he went over to the nightstand for his cell phone to contact his pilot. As he waited for the line to answer, he moved to the sofa and rummaged through his duffel bag for socks and underwear. His hand hit the Tiffany box buried at the bottom. Taking it out, he flipped open the case and stared at the glittering jewels, reminded of the meticulous effort he'd taken in picking the set for her. His pilot came on the line. "Expect to depart in thirty ... shit ... when? Fine," he said and ended the call after his pilot explained that he wouldn't have clearance for another hour.

He closed the case, tossed it back inside his bag, sat down on the sofa, and stared out the window across the room at the cloudless, dusky sky.

She's on a date. Those words were playing on a loop in his head. Minutes ticked by with him sitting there staring through the glass pane as the reel replayed over and over, a constant reminder of just how much of a fool he'd been. Weeks of sleepless nights thinking about her—dreaming—wanting—needing—loving her. He blinked and touched his chin. His fingertips came back wet with his tears. For long minutes, he owned the emotion that took hold of him and allowed himself to release the anguish ripping him up inside. Then, taking in a renewed breath, he exhaled, ran a hand down his face, and rose to his feet to get dressed and get gone, erase her, consider her a glitch in his life's timeline.

He went to the bathroom and washed his face, then returned to get himself dressed. As he reached into his garment bag for his jeans, there was a knock at the door. He went over and opened it a crack. "Ye—" His eyes fluttered for a moment as his brain worked rapidly to untangle the image to register who was before him. She was the last person he'd expected to see. Pulling himself together, he widened the door open without saying a word, simply stared at her flushed face and the wild curls framing her face, some slick at her temples from perspiration. Her long braid that was draped over her right shoulder was half undone.

His anger revved up with clenched jaws at seeing her dressed in a strapless, powder blue cotton sundress, knowing that she'd been out on a date. If that wasn't enough, he could tell she wasn't wearing a bra. The gathered elastic bodice of the dress skillfully showcased her perked nipples and outlined the shape of her plump breasts that kept pace with her rapid breathing, in and out, up and down they went.

She chewed her bottom lip in that cute, sexy way she did when she was nervous, unaware of how much of a turn on it was for him. His attraction to her fueled his rage even more. He struggled with wanting to gaze upon her beauty—he loved and missed her so damn much—and wanting to slam the door in her face—in that moment, he hated her just as much.

• • •

Bailey's eyes fell upon the hard, sculptured pecs and taut abs that greeted her. She forced her eyes up from his magnificent corded physique and swallowed anxiously when she met his fixed glare. He stood there not saying anything, yet saying a mouthful.

"My ... my mom told me you were here." She held up his card, to which he said nothing. "May I come in?" There seemed to be a moment of contemplation before he stepped aside, closed the door and walked past her to the sofa, hardly acknowledging her presence. Her gaze was drawn to the perfect shape of his tight buttocks in the towel and on up his strong, broad back. How many nights had she dreamed of being molded to his beautiful body? *Virtually every night.*

She watched as he pulled out a pair of dark jeans from his garment bag and laid them out across the sofa, all without speaking a word.

"Sienna told me you had my car repaired. Thank you. I'll find a way to pay you back." No reply. "I was hoping we could talk." He still hadn't responded to anything she said. "Lucas?" Finally, he turned around. She could almost taste the raw loathing permeating off him. "Can we talk?" she asked, and instantly his blue-gray eyes darkened to a sea storm of menace.

"Now you want to talk? What is there to talk about? Tell me because from where I stand where you're concerned, there's absolutely nothing."

Bailey flinched at his cold demeanor. "I'm sorry for leaving the way I did."

"You're sorry." He chuckled and shook his head.

"I should have talked things over with you like you wanted. I was upset with Faith and Kevin—" She gasped low on a tremble when he actually growled and took a threatening step toward her. "I made a mistake."

"*You* made a mistake?" A rough chuckle again with lips tight. "Where were you today? Out on a date. I suppose you're going to tell me he was just a friend. Is he another *friend* of yours, Bailey?"

Bailey hesitantly nodded, and his nostrils flared. "I only went out with him because my dad pushed it."

"That's rich. Good one, Bailey," he bit out. "I'm the one who made a mistake by coming here. I've been beating myself up for weeks over what I did. I desperately wanted your forgiveness. I didn't bother you these past weeks to give you the space you wanted. The closest private landing strip is here in Florence. You know what I thought about during that thirty-minute drive to you? I kept trying to think of what I would say to convince you to trust me, come back to me ... want me as much as I wanted you, but you've already moved on to the next unsuspecting fool haven't you, Bailey. That poor chump is like Kevin and me. We're all mere puppets in this game of yours, drawn in by your allure, your beauty," he rambled in obvious hurt and anger.

Seeing the fury in his narrowed gaze, mirroring those emotions, she argued, "You ended us, not me."

"That made it easy for you, didn't it? What is it you get out of it? Do you get some sort of perverted pleasure out of tormenting men?" He ignored her rapid shake of her head and the easy flow of her tears. "It's you who take all and give nothing back. I was a fool for wanting you so damn badly. I guess the joke's on me."

"Lucas, I do want you. That's why when I heard you were here, I came as fast as I could to you."

He scowled. "After you ended your date, of course. Like you say, it's whatever. Frankly, I'm done, done with you, all of it. My plane is waiting, and I need to get dressed. We've talked, now there's the door. Get out." He returned to readying his clothes.

Tears rain down Bailey's cheeks as her nightmare played out before her. She pressed the tips of her fingers to her lips to stop them from quivering in order to say, "I ... we ..." She shook her head when her voice failed her, unable to tell him that they'd made a baby. It was enough that he hated her. She couldn't bear the thought of him resenting their child, knowing it was the last thing he wanted, especially with her.

The pain she felt squeezing the chambers of her heart struck so intense, she could hardly breathe. "I ... I'm sorry," she managed through the tears choking her up.

As she turned to leave, her flip-flop twisted on her foot, causing her to stumble forward. She was able to escape further humiliation by catching hold of an armchair. Surprisingly, out of the corner of her eye, Lucas had moved to catch her. "I'm all right," she murmured, sweeping away fresh tears with her eyes going briefly upward toward the ceiling. *Can't I at least leave with a smidgen of dignity?*

She carried her battered heart to the door, certain that she would never love another man as she did Lucas Marx. *We're good together.* His words she held dear attached to the love she would forever have for him. *I love you.*

She gripped the door handled, twisted, and pulled. "Oh!" It was suddenly slammed shut. Looking up, Lucas's hand was pressed flat against it. She hadn't heard him come up behind her. A renewed streak of fear shot up her spine.

"Say it again."

His voice dripped in anger near her right ear, but she was unsure of what he meant. Assuming it was her apology he wanted, she said, "I'm sorry."

"Not that. What you said after," he gritted.

With her back to him, her heart racing, she rapidly ran through the catalog of their conversation, most of which she'd have liked to forget, and couldn't think of anything that she'd said he'd want to hear repeated. The last thing she'd said was that she was all right after nearly falling on her face. Then she thought about what he'd once said to her while they were making love. That was the precise moment she'd fallen in love with him. Her breath hitched, and she bit her bottom lip hard to gain control of her stricken emotions to avoid bawling her eyes out. Had she voiced it aloud? She would have sworn the words were spoken in her head.

"I need to hear you say it again."

His warm breath caressed her ear with his tone less blistering that time. Bailey willed her body to stop trembling as his hand took a firm hold of the back of her neck. His thumb slipped slowly up and down the side of her throat.

He smelled amazing standing so close behind her. She closed her eyes and inhaled him deep into her lungs to savor and soak up his familiar scent for comfort before voicing low, "We're good together ... I love you." Precious seconds passed in silence as she worried that she'd said the wrong thing. Regardless, it was how she felt, and there was nothing to lose at this point.

Slowly, she turned around within the narrow space between his big body and the door, looked up, and was shocked to see water in his eyes. Thinking that she'd caused this six foot four hulk of a man to show tears, she fought not to cry herself. "We're good together. I love you," she repeated, holding his solemn stare. Her gaze dipped to his smooth lips, on down to his bare, bulging pecs, and then back to his beautiful eyes. "I love you."

"You were with another man," his brows creased as he ran a featherlight index finger along the swells of her breasts that brimmed over the edge of the gathered elastic, "wearing this."

There was blatant disapproval, but she also sensed lust conveyed in his low spoken words. His eyes zeroed in on the deep set of her cleavage as he came in tighter, forcing her back against the door.

Bailey saw nothing wrong with her dress, yet found herself tugging up the bodice. "I went to a festival with an old friend to pacify my dad, that's all." Upset, she raised her chin. "You broke up with me."

He dropped his eyes from hers. "I thought you were ... I lost my head."

"You certainly did. And I did nothing to deserve those ... those," she threw a hand out toward the sofa, "mean things you said to me over there."

"I'm sorry."

"Okay ... well ... you should be."

"I know," he uttered low.

She nodded while studying his handsome features. "You cut your hair." The sides and nape were much shorter, making the natural wave less pronounced.

He ran his fingers through his hair asking, "Was your date one of your two previous lovers? Have you slept with him?" He looked at her then with a scowl.

She vehemently shook her head. "No and never." Telling him Marcel was another ex-boyfriend wouldn't be wise. What's more, she surely didn't consider Andrew and Craig lovers by any stretch, but she wasn't about to get into that with him either.

The heat of his body so close wrapped around her like a familiar warm blanket. She had to scratch her itching palms to tamp down the incessant longing to run her hands over the sleek muscular planes of his smooth, tanned flesh.

The intensity of his eyes on her, she couldn't sense whether it was anger, hurt, or desire he was sending off. Her eyes dipped down between them at the tent formed in the towel between his legs and concluded, it was likely all three. She would take what she could get.

"It was just a festival with an old friend ... nothing more." That seemed to make him frown harder.

"I don't like you having other men, Bailey. I'm a selfish bastard. I don't share. Ever!"

"I don't have other men, Lucas." Boldly, she added, "The only man I want and could ever want is you. I lo—" Before she could utter another sound, he came at her mouth, brutal in his taking, ravenous, tonguing her to the far reaches of her throat. And his hands were everywhere, cupping her face to her neck, shoved down her dress to knead her breasts, briefly sucking on a nipple, and then back to her mouth. His hands raced underneath her dress, gripped, and squeezed her buttocks before tugging at her thong.

"Oh!" Bailey gasped against his demanding mouth when, with a sharp twist and wrench of his hand, the left side seam of lace ripped apart. He shoved the torn scrap of fabric down her right thigh, dropped his towel, lifted her leg, and rammed her pussy fully to the hilt. His plunge was so swift, hard, and deep that she saw stars.

She couldn't get her bearings fast enough as he pressed her against the door, lifted her other leg, brought her knees up at the bend of his arms, spread wide, and began pistoning her with a punishing force that sent her skyrocketing to the quickest orgasm imaginable.

"Oh shhh," she panted, clinging to his shoulders.

"I don't share," he grunted the words at the side of her neck as he continued relentlessly pounding into her body against the hard surface.

She linked her arms tight around his neck and held on as she clamped her wet sex onto his deliciously rigid thickness, relishing in his rough and greedy insistence, allowing him to take her however he wanted, understanding that he needed this just as much as she did.

Pressed to him with his penis burrowed deep within her, he held a firm grip of her buttocks, drew back and stared with a hard intensity into her eyes. "You're mine. Say it," he growled.

"I'm yours." Before she could catch her breath, with their bodies still tightly joined, he carried her to the bed and brought them both down to the mattress. He planted his palms flat on the bed beside her shoulders, split his knees wide to keep her legs opened and anchored and continued his quick paced thrusts. She took his delicious pounding, wildly turned on by their shared primal need, by the powerful strength of her beautiful and feral lover.

He abruptly pulled out, left the bed, and went over to his duffel bag. She watched him take out some sort of cream in a small tube before he ripped open and rolled on a condom in record speed. This wasn't the time to tell him just how unnecessary a condom was at this point.

Returning to the bed, he dropped the tube beside her and frowned at her dress that was bunched around her waist and the scrap of lace twisted around her thigh. Both were quickly yanked down her legs and tossed over his shoulder. He reentered her, resuming his magnificent assault on her pussy.

"Yes!" she panted, feeling her orgasm pick up from where he'd left it. "Lucas, just like that. Don't stop." Unfortunately, that's exactly what he did. *Damn it!* Frustrated, she slapped the bed.

He lifted her right leg to turn her. "Come up on your knees."

Apprehension quivered in her stomach of his intentions, yet she went along without question. He brought her knees forward a bit more and pushed gently at her back until her head met the pillow, leaving her opened and displayed before him.

Two thick digits entered her pussy, thrusting deep, and then he glided his wet fingers over the puckering ring of her anus.

She looked over her shoulder at him. He draped his frame at her back, came in close to her face, kissed her behind her ear, and ran his warm tongue along her earlobe while fingering her clenched rear. "I want you here," he voiced softly, and she stiffened, but hesitantly nodded once.

He slipped his cock into her sex and gave it several deep strokes. Her pleasure purrs and moans built with the momentum of his thrusts. Then he withdrew from her again. She didn't blink as she watched him liberally coat the condom that covered his penis with lubricant before he pressed the head carefully, slowly against her tight ring. Feeling her tense up at his initial breach, he spoke softly while gently caressing a hand up and down her spine, "Relax for me, and don't move." He continued to push slowly into her tight, rear sheath and stopped about midway. Softly, he said again, "Don't move."

Bailey was afraid to breathe let alone move. She'd barely mastered regular sex. Anal sex was something she'd never considered.

Not sure what to expect, she braced herself, afraid that he would take her harshly. Still unmoving inside her, he undid the rest of her braid, and tender fingers pushed her hair aside, exposing her neck. An arm encircled her waist, his chest came flush against her back, and he brushed his lips at her ear, his warm breath caressing as he said, "I'm sorry for the things I did, for hurting you." Feather-soft kisses skated at the back of her neck and along her shoulders. She closed her eyes on a sigh, feeling the tension in her entire body fade away.

He began moving with deliberately slow, controlled pumps. Surprisingly, it wasn't painful, just felt a bit strange at first.

His fingers circled her clit with the same measure, methodical movements as his cock in her rear, bringing about a throbbing in her channel from the rocking motion.

Heavy breaths escaped her as two fingers entered her pussy, thrusting in and out before a third was added, making her shudder from the pleasure combination of being filled in both orifices.

As his free hand captured a breast, his lips trailed kisses along her back and shoulders, all while he continued his slow, even strokes in both her vagina and her rear.

She never imagined she'd enjoy this form of lovemaking. The level of intense pleasure was nearly unbearable.

With her body on the verge of climax, Bailey pressed the side of her face into the pillow and closed her eyes briefly to relish in the sensation of his closeness.

Rocking his hips, he nipped the back of her neck, then brought his face in close to hers. "How is it?" he asked.

Awkwardly, she shook her head against the pillow, unable to express the clutter of emotions overtaking her, and a tear escaped her closed lids.

He froze. "Shit, I'm hurting you!" He moved to pull out, but she gripped his thigh, not wanting to lose the warmth and contentment of his nearness. "You're crying." He kissed away the wetness on the bridge of her nose.

Opening her eyes, Bailey met his gaze and tried to put into words how she felt. "My leaving ... I hurt you. I'm sorry." Her eyes shut again. "I love you and could lose you. That's what hurts me," she said, releasing an endless flow of tears.

"Bailey." He eased carefully out of her and then helped her turn over to her back. She was unsure what he intended to do next.

He rolled off the condom, tossed it to the floor, and then came down slowly on top of her, sheathing himself in her wet sex in an unhurried glide forward, clearly not asking permission to go bareback. A hand cradled the back of her neck and the other went around her hips as he began that same controlled, yet determined thrusting.

She rocked her pelvis, meeting his determined thrusts with her own. "Please don't stop this time." Her ankles linked at his back in an effort to cage him within her body.

"I won't ... so good with you," he grunted into her hair, kissing the side of her neck.

"We're good together, Lucas."

"We're great together, Bailey." He nipped along her throat, upward to her gasping mouth, sucking in her pants and moans, their tongues reacquainting as their bodies undulated rhythmically with backs arching, taking, giving.

With a quick flip, he situated her on top of him, and she sat up, reached back, and gripped his thigh to ride his cock like a rodeo pro. "Shit yes!" he hissed and leaned forward to capture a breast that he flicked, sucked, and tugged before he returned to her mouth.

Again, he rolled her to her back with a restless urgency and brought her arms above her head, entwining their fingers. "Come for me, love. Let me feel it. I need to feel it." His hips pumped faster, and she could hear the wet smacking sounds their combined sex made from the cream of the onset of her orgasm.

She brought her arms down and embedded her nails in his clenching buttocks to hold him inside her as her body spiked, quaking blissfully over the edge. Seconds after, he bit out a cursed breath with his body going rigid.

"I need to pull out," he breathed heavily. With each clenching wave her orgasm provoked, his jaws locked in reaction. He hastily reached back to try to unlock the vicelike hold of her legs at his back. "I'm about to come. Damn, I've missed you."

"I've missed you, too. Come inside me."

He looked at her. "You're on the pill?"

"It's fine." She nodded.

With one last hard thrust, he took his release deep inside her. They briefly crashed chest to breasts in exhaustion, and then he rolled them to their sides. Their limbs wrapped tight around one another, each needing to hold the other close.

Brushing back the damp strands out of her face, he kissed her lips, and she ran a palm across the glistening sheen at his forehead, then stroked his back. They stayed that way for long minutes, simply gazing at one another, a loving, quiet sharing of souls.

Chapter Thirty-Four

With his feelings for her nearly overwhelming him, and that rapid thumping in his chest starting up again, damn, how Lucas wanted to say it—how ridiculously in love he was with her. But with how easy it was for her to walk away, and then to discover her out on a date with another so-called *male friend*, he was deathly afraid to chance his heart to her.

Heaven help me. He had never in his life been at this emotional place before where he banked all that he was on three simple words. Letting out a breath mainly to gather nerve, he decided to throw all his cards in, allow his heart to lead. "I love you, Bailey."

Her eyelids fluttered. "Lucas." Tears slid down her cheeks, and his lips quickly kissed them away. "I love you with all my heart," she said, and kissed him hard, long, and deep, conveying the depth of her words.

There was a knock at the door. Caught in the basking of their love, they chose to ignore it.

Still burrowed inside her, Lucas could feel himself getting hard again. Rocking leisurely, his shaft stroked her silky inner walls as they lay in each other's arms kissing and caressing. He brought her on her back and continued an unhurried thrusting.

The knock came again with more force. "Damn it," he grumbled against her soft lips, and she hooked her legs around his calves. "I should see who it is." She groaned on a nod and unwrapped herself from around him. He rose up and witnessed his semen spill out of her. In that moment, there was a wild urge to beat his chest like a Neanderthal who had just claimed—marked—his female.

With a kiss on her thigh, he left the bed and scooped up the used condom from the floor en route to the bathroom. After a quick wash of his hands, he threw on his robe and opened the door by the third hard roll of knocks. "Yes!" Lucas barked, irritated by the disturbance.

The man tilted his head to the left to check the room number on the door. "Are you Lucas?"

"And you are?" Lucas countered, then quickly realized that it was Bailey's brother, Caleb, having recognized him from the pictures he'd seen at her home ... which must have been severely out of date.

Wearing black Doc Marten shit-kickers, faded, low slung jeans, and a black T-shirt that appeared to be suffering under the strain of accommodating the overabundant muscle mass of chest and arms—arms with tribal tats covering the swollen biceps—the young man eyeing him sharply *at eye level* was about as big as he was himself.

"Caleb, I'm fine," Bailey called out, reassuring him from inside the room.

"I'll determine that," Caleb yelled back while keeping an acute stare planted on Lucas. "You're not what I expected, but it's all good. An ass kicking is an ass kicking if I see one damn tear in my sister's eyes."

"She—" Lucas attempted to tell her brother that she was fine ... and indisposed, but the young man shoved past him into the room.

"Aw damn, Bailey." Caleb swiftly turned his back to her sitting up on her shins in bed with a sheet wrapped around her to shield her naked body, blissfully smiling, her hair wild, and her face rosily glowing.

He turned to Lucas and shook his head. "Dude, you could've warned me."

Lucas cleared his throat to suppress a smirk. "I tried, but you rammed in before I had the chance."

"You all right?" Caleb asked her over his shoulder.

"I'm fine. We're fine." Bailey smiled at Lucas. "I love him."

"No shit," Caleb came back sarcastically and shook his head again. He then hard-eyed Lucas, which suggested he expected to hear it reciprocated.

"Like she said, we're fine. I love your sister."

"Glad to hear," he nodded, "but, I'm not fine. I'm gonna have to find a way to keep my food in my stomach after witnessing this."

Bailey laughed. "Grow up. It's not like you haven't had sex."

"Don't use words like *had sex*, Bailey, damn! You want me to have nightmares?" Caleb stuck out his hand to Lucas. "So you're the dude she's been boo-hooing over since she got here."

Shaking Caleb's hand, Lucas raised a brow over at Bailey blushing on the bed. "I was unaware."

"I tell you, I was about ready to find you myself if you hadn't shown up. I don't like seeing my sister cry."

"I don't want tears in those beautiful eyes of hers either," Lucas replied.

Caleb nodded again. "So Bails, have you told—"

"Caleb, it's time for you to go," Bailey rushed out. "Tell Mom and Dad I'm fine, and I'll see them—"

"She's leaving with me," Lucas stated firmly. A look at the clock. "Shit, I need to have my pilot move the time back." He went to his cell phone sitting on the sofa.

"Pilot! Dude has a pilot, Bailey? Who are you dating here, a prince or something?"

"Caleb, shut up."

Caleb turned to her then and walked over to the bed. "Are you really okay? You know ..." His eyes dipped, giving her a peculiar look over, which Lucas noticed as he watched them.

"Yes," she voiced somewhat low with a glimpse and smile over his way.

"Cool. I wish you would've given me the heads up before you said," Caleb side-eyed Lucas talking on the phone, "what you did. I could've videotaped Dad's reaction for YouTube." He bucked his eyes, staggered, and clutched his chest, laughing. "Priceless."

Watching the young man, Lucas cringed, concluding that it was Mr. Walters's reaction to him dating Bailey.

Bailey laughed and playfully punched her brother's middle. "You're evil, you know that."

Caleb bent down and gave her a hug while whispering something in her ear. He then straightened and turned to Lucas now standing behind him. "Well, I guess I'll be going. I don't have to tell you to look after my sister."

"I got it covered." Lucas stuck out his hand. "Good meeting you, Caleb. You're always welcome at our home." They both looked over at Bailey upon hearing her suck in a breath at that.

"I was admiring that R6 parked at your house."

"Yeah, I'm working on it. Right now, I'm riding my Suzuki R1100. You ride?" Caleb asked.

"Use to. I have a Buell 1190RS custom that you're welcome to anytime."

"No way! There were only one hundred of those made. I'll definitely have to come check it out." Caleb grinned wide at Bailey. "The man knows bikes. He gets my vote."

Bailey sucked her teeth with a shake of her head. "Boys and their toys. Caleb, time to go."

"Looks like you two have a lot to talk about. And I do mean lots." He winked at his sister, then headed for the door. "I'll let myself out."

"Bye, Caleb. Love you."

"Love you, too, baby girl."

When the door closed, Lucas raised a brow at her with a grin. "Baby girl?" He stood next to the bed and brought her up on her knees in front of him.

Bailey shrugged. "It's what my family calls me. Caleb is two years younger, but I've always been treated as the younger sibling. I don't know why."

"Maybe it's because your brother's a freaking tank." Lucas stroked her smooth, bare ass. He loved her tight ass, her legs, the honey coloring of her silky skin, her beautiful green eyes, and her soft lips ... he loved her. And it scared the hell out of him. It wasn't his love for her he feared, it was hers for him.

He controlled everything about his life, and that included his relationships from start to finish, but knew he'd lost control of that part of his life the day he met Bailey Walters. She could strip away his entire world in a blink of an eye if she chose to leave him. That was what he feared most. He had to find a way to hold on to her, and he knew his open line of credit wasn't the answer.

"You two are about the same height, and you're just as big," she remarked with a squeeze of his biceps. "Now, about this *our home* thing you mentioned."

"You're not leaving my sight, Miss Walters." His brows slanted inward, and he added, "You're sure as hell not living across from Kevin."

"Sienna told me about you and Kevin."

Lucas sighed. "I shouldn't have let him get to me. I tried to apologize a few days later, but he slammed his door in my face. I know he's your friend and—"

"And it's a shame that he can't accept that I'm in love with you." She kissed his tight lips that gradually softened to her nibbling. "About me not leaving your sight ..." With quick pecks upon his mouth and neck, she slipped a hand inside his robe and took hold of his cock, applying a firm stroking. Feeling it rapidly thicken in her palm, looking up at him, she smiled sweetly, "I can stay at my place." Her eyes lulled as she massaged his sac and nipped across his chest, flicking a nipple.

"Bailey, if you think you can persuade me by what you're doing, it ... shit!" Lucas hissed a curse at the feel of her firmly caressing his balls. She opened his robe, kissed her way down his body, and nipped along his pelvis to end with her closing her mouth around his dick. Instinctively, his hips bucked. She pulled back, leisurely suckled the head and swirled her tongue over and around the sensitive slit before she slid him in all the way to the back of her throat.

"Fuck yes, Bailey!"

He tangled his fingers in her hair and pumped in and out of her hot, wet mouth as she swallowed his cock, taking him deep. Her tongue kept a consistent pressure on the sensitive, thick vein along the underside to the base, while her hand continued a firm massage of his balls. She showed no mercy as she squeezed, kneaded, sucked, rolled her tongue, and even nipped, bringing him quickly to the brink. "I'm going to come, love."

"Then come," she mumbled around his now swollen length filling her mouth, taking him so far down her throat that she had to breathe through her nose.

"Now, love! Shit!" Shuddering, he held her hair tight as he emptied into her mouth. She swallowed and continued to suck him off until she'd taken every drop, then released him, and sat back on her shins.

Spent raw, Lucas's knees buckled, forcing him to sit before he collapsed. Never before had he come so quickly from a blowjob. It was the best head he'd ever received. *Merciful heaven, how will I survive this woman?*

Eyeing her beside him, she was licking her lips and smiling. *She enjoyed it.* "Come here." He pulled her onto his lap. "You're amazing, you know that, princess?"

"Did you like it? I've never done it before." Seeing his look of surprise, she smiled shyly. "Did I do it right?"

That fact astonished Lucas, considering how skilled she seemed. He was overwhelmingly thrilled that he was her first ... and damn sure would be her only.

"Again, you never cease to amaze me. Like it? Woman, I believe you've spoiled me." He kissed her and got a taste of the residual saltiness from his come on her tongue. "We need to shower and get dressed. Our flight leaves in," a quick glance at the clock on the nightstand, "forty-five minutes."

"But I don't have any of my things—my laptop and my phone ... and you ripped my panties."

"I'll buy you more things ... no arguments. And you won't need panties. You owe me for not giving me a chance to touch you in that dress you wore at the art event. As your punishment, no panties until I say so."

"If that is what you wish, Mr. Marx." Cutting a smirk, she nipped at his chin.

Lucas stood up with her in his arms and carried her to the shower.

"That is what I wish, Miss Walters."

Chapter Thirty-Five

"Good evening, Mr. Marx. Miss Walters." Lucas's steward welcomed them with a polite incline of his head. "Dinner has been prepared when you are ready."

"Thanks, Miles," Lucas said and guided Bailey over to a leather loveseat. "Relax, love, while I speak to the pilot and make a few calls. Then we'll eat. Are you hungry?"

"A little." Bailey looked around the luxurious aircraft that looked more like a flying apartment than an airplane. The entire cabin was done up in deep-cushioned, camel-colored leather furnishings, ivory interior walls with light maple wood trim, and ultraplush, dark brown carpeting.

She sat in what would be considered the lounging area. There were leather chairs and ottomans spread about with side tables beside each and a large, wall-mounted flat screen positioned for optimal viewing from all angles. A conference table that seated eight comfortably was stationed opposite the entrance door of the plane. Additionally, two maple wood doors were stationed on either side of the cockpit door. One was likely the lavatory, and the other could have been the galley. It was where the steward went after he spoke about the meal.

Lucas had driven the Mercedes right up to the plane that had a bright blue letter *M* inscribed on the side of it. He'd handed off the car keys to an attendant that seemed more than happy to take on the task of seeing to the car. There was no Dollar Car Rental drop-off happening, that's for sure.

It hadn't registered to Bailey just how wealthy Lucas was until now. She looked behind her at a pair of double doors.

"It's our bedroom and bath en suite."

Bailey turned her head back around to Lucas standing in front of her. "So this is how you roll." A stroke along the soft leather seat. "Not too shabby."

"Glad you approve." He sat down and lifted her onto his lap. "Love, you look tired."

"I haven't had a good night's sleep since I've been home." She curled herself against his warm body and rest her head upon a strong, formidable shoulder.

"Dinner will be out in ten. I'll feed you and then put you to bed."

The food arrived precisely ten minutes later. Lucas insisted she remain seated on his lap, and to his word, he fed her in between eating from his own plate.

"Lucas, I'm not so drained that I can't lift a fork." He held the fork before her mouth, and she took it in. "I think I can manage it."

"I enjoy caring for you."

He fed her another bite and then brought her glass of water to her lips. Bailey had adamantly declined the wine, even though he explained that it would help her sleep. She wouldn't chance it with the baby.

• • •

Having finished off most of her meal, she pushed the fork with a piece of chicken and asparagus perched upon it away from her mouth. "I can't. I'm full."

Lucas stuck the fork in his mouth, and then stacked the plates on the side table. "Let's rest. We'll land at LaGuardia before long."

Bailey cocked her head. "LaGuardia? We're not going home?"

"I'm taking you to New York to visit Sienna tomorrow, but first, I'll take you shopping."

"I get to see Sienna!" Excited, she straddled his lap. "Lucas, thank you. I really miss her."

"Sienna was just as thrilled when I phoned her earlier. When you mentioned on the ride over that Sandra fired you, I thought this might lift your spirits. I have a penthouse in the city where we'll stay for a couple of days. I've arranged for us to meet her for dinner tomorrow evening, and then we fly to California for my sister's pre-wedding dinner."

"You're so good to me." Palming his face, Bailey kissed him. One arm circled his neck, and the other hand stayed planted against the chiseled angle of his cheek as she tilted her head to take his mouth fully with long, tongue-stroking caresses.

She still wasn't wearing any panties and could easily feel his cock rapidly swelling at the apex between her legs. He once said her kisses turned him on. He wasn't kidding.

He ran his hands up her thighs, underneath her dress to her bare buttocks, and gently squeezed as he forced her hips to rock back and forth, causing her pussy to rub against his growing erection through his jeans. She broke the kiss and smiled to his wicked grin. "You bad boy."

"You're sure you want to sleep, princess?" He took hold of the back of her neck and captured her lips, catching her soft moans in his mouth in reaction to his persistent massaging against her exposed sex.

"I beg your pardon, sir."

Bailey jerked a look over her shoulder, and the steward respectfully gave them his profile. Her back stiffened. She gaped at Lucas, and he merely delivered her a peck on the mouth, unfazed by the intrusion. Immensely embarrassed, she remained unmoving, straddled upon him as he calmly spoke to the man, while his hands stayed underneath her dress, stroking her bare ass cheeks. "What is it, Miles?"

"Is there anything else you require, sir? More wine? Or dessert perhaps?"

"That's it for tonight. Thanks." Miles retreated. Lucas chuckled and kissed her puckered brow. "You can relax now."

Bailey released the breath trapped in her throat. "Oh my God!" she groaned and buried her face in the side of his neck. "That man must think I'm a slut. Here I am groping you right here out in the open for everyone to see." She tried to get off his lap, but he held her in place.

"I believe I'm the one doing the groping, and he's paid well to do his job and maintain nondisclosure with whatever he's exposed to in my employ. My business requires that I keep around only those I can trust. Now let me take you to bed." He carried her into the bedroom and helped her undress.

With a wide yawn, she stretched out on top of the thick, navy-blue velvet comforter. "This is comfortable. I'm really tired."

"Then you'll rest." With a quick strip out of his clothes, he hit the light switch, then joined her beneath the cover, their naked limbs entwining.

Bailey didn't want to tell him that she couldn't sleep because her mind was cluttered with a thousand different scenarios on how he'd take the news that he was going to be a father.

A kiss atop her untamed curls. "Comfortable?"

"Very." Snuggling heavenly against his warm skin, tomorrow, she would tell him about the baby. They both would be well rested. He'd likely take the news much better after a good night's sleep.

"I love you," she voiced sleepily into his chest.

"I love you, too. Get some sleep."

Chapter Thirty-Six

"Kara has set everything in place. I have a quick meeting and should be back in about an hour."

Bailey nodded. She stood with Lucas inside the shoe boutique. Kara had arranged private appointments the entire morning.

The blue sundress had finally been chucked for a soft yellow pinstripe, sleeveless linen sheath dress.

They'd hit up several specialty shops for handbags and toiletries, essentially buying everything Lucas could think of that she'd need to stack her side of the closet. He even purchased her a set of luggage for their upcoming trip to California. All that was left were shoes, and she had to admit, she was looking forward to it.

Lucas held her around the waist as the owner of the store approached, his muddy-brown eyes glinting behind black wire rim glasses. They shook his hand.

"Mr. Marx, Miss Walters, welcome to COS. I am Paul Cosworth, the proprietor. Your private room has been set up upstairs."

Bailey looked up at Lucas. "I don't think I need a private room." She glanced around the boutique at the few ladies casually walking about, studying the array of very expensive shoes that were displayed like priceless artifacts. Several eyed her and dissected Lucas's gorgeous form dressed in his tailored, navy-blue suit. "Really, Lucas, it's just shoes," she murmured.

"You are to be pampered." Stroking her back, he addressed Cosworth, "I trust that you will see to it that Miss Walters is kept satisfied."

"Absolutely, sir. And Miss Walters, I have two of my best staff ready and eager to assist you." Cosworth gestured a hand up to the second floor where the ladies stood wearing bright smiles.

"Thank you," Bailey replied, feeling that once again, Lucas had gone overboard in getting her a private service simply to purchase shoes.

Lucas turned to her. "You have your new phone if you need to reach me." At her nod, he gave her a quick kiss, turned, and left. She watched him through the glass door get into his limo and drive off.

"If you would, please follow me," Cosworth said behind her, and she turned around. "We have selected an array of styles for your consideration."

She walked with him up the stairs to the two ladies that smiled cheerfully as he introduced them to her.

"Tammy and Kate will see to you." Paul Cosworth addressed the ladies, "Take great care of Miss Walters." He turned back to her. "If there is anything you require, please do not hesitate to ask. Enjoy." With a polite smile, he headed back downstairs.

Tammy and Kate led her into the private room where a large table was set up with shoes on display.

Wow! Mystified, Bailey walked over and lifted several from their shiny chrome plinth, turning each this way and that way. *I've died and gone to designer shoe heaven.* There were designer names that not even she, a self-proclaimed shoe aficionado, recognized. And they were all size seven and a half—her size. *Lucas doesn't miss a thing.*

"Would you care for a glass of wine or champagne?"

Bailey turned around to Tammy. "Water would be fine, thank you."

Kate gestured over at the white leather loveseat. "Miss Walters, please make yourself comfortable. We hope you like the selection we've chosen for you."

Bailey took a seat on the couch. "They're all very nice. It will be difficult for me to choose." Tammy came over carrying a bottle of VOSS and a water glass. "That's where we come in." She half filled the glass and handed it over.

"Thank you." Bailey took a sip of water and smiled. "Okay, I guess we should get this party started."

Over the next hour and a half, she was indeed pampered by Tammy and Kate. They were very good at helping her pick out a variety of styles, and in the end, they each held a shopping bag of her shoes.

She felt guilty that she'd spent so much money. There wasn't a pair in the entire store that cost less than five hundred dollars.

Tammy and Kate were tickled by her lack of self-control. They worked on commission with a 25 percent gratuity. As a waitress, Bailey understood what it was like. That fact took away some of the sting of spending Lucas's money.

On her way downstairs, she spotted Lucas sitting on one of the white leather couches, talking on his cell phone. A Middle Eastern–looking man dressed in a fine suit was doing the same directly across from him. The man nodded to an attractive Middle Eastern woman that waved a pair of red stilettos in front of his face.

Bailey took note of a blonde woman casually sauntering back and forth in front of Lucas, slowing just long enough to catch his eye. While continuing his phone conversation, she observed his quick look up at Blondie as she made another sweep past him. His eyes then shifted from Blondie to her across the room. A smile formed upon his mouth as he stood up saying, "I'll call you back." She keenly observed how Blondie then turned somewhat abruptly and faced him, looking rather confident that she'd finally hooked her fish. Lucas walked forward straight in line with Blondie, who was prepped and ready to reel him in. Throwing her golden locks over her shoulders, the woman smiled bright and straightened her spine to draw attention to her noticeably fake breasts as he drew closer. "Excuse me," he said and sidestepped Blondie with his concentration still fixed across the room.

My man, Bailey cheered.

She was a bit shocked when Lucas came up to her, hooked his arm around her waist, his hand at her nape, and kissed her affectionately on the mouth ... with tongue right there in the middle of the boutique, not caring that they had an audience, Blondie included. Long seconds later, he drew back, tenderly stroked her cheek with his thumb, and uttered lovingly, "I've missed you," then gave her another good long kiss before letting go. He then looked past her to Tammy and Kate. Each held a shopping bag of her shoes.

As Bailey slowly recovered from his passionate lip-lock, she peered briefly over at Blondie and met her fixed stare. *That's right, all of this is mine.* Her arm was snaked around Lucas's waist, staking claim to make her point. Dismissing the woman, she lifted a foot to show off her five-inch wedged, lemon-yellow Louboutin sandals. "You like?" she asked him.

"They're lovely. They go well with your dress."

"That was the intention." She grinned.

Paul Cosworth walked up. "Miss Walters, is there anything else we can do for you?"

Lucas then asked Bailey, "Were you pleased with the choices here?"

She could see Mr. Cosworth, Tammy, and Kate holding their breath for her answer. "Yes, and they were all very helpful." She addressed the ladies, "Thank you. I would still be up there trying to decide what to get if it weren't for your assistance in helping me choose."

"How many did you select?" Lucas eyed the bags in their hands. Bailey bit her bottom lip. "Uh, seven. I know it's—"

"Only seven?" He cut a hard look between Mr. Cosworth and the ladies.

And here she thought she'd grossly overspent. "Tammy and Kate were wonderful. I got exactly what I needed." He nodded, and Mr. Cosworth along with the ladies visibly relaxed.

They all walked to the door. Lucas took the shopping bags from Tammy and Kate. Mr. Cosworth handed over his card to Bailey. "Please call if you are ever in need of additional items. We can even come to you."

"We will keep that in mind," Lucas replied.

"Thank you again," Bailey said. Lucas held the door open for her, and she walked out to the limo parked directly in front. The driver stood with the trunk open. He stepped forward, prepared to assist them with their bags, and Lucas was about to hand them off when Bailey stopped him.

"I want to show you what I bought." She climbed in, and Lucas followed. "You don't mind, do you?"

"Not at all. Show me your shoes, princess."

He sat back as she began pulling shoes from boxes. A pair of leather Burberry sneakers and Kate Spade loafers were presented and quickly tossed aside. She eagerly opened several more boxes, and he picked up a shoe—Jimmy Choo, eggplant purple, double ankle strap, six-inch spiked heel with about a one-inch platform.

"Oooh, I think those are my favorite." She took the shoe from his hand. "Or maybe these." A silver pair of Manolo Blahniks were held up before him.

"I believe all are your favorite." He chuckled, and she snorted a laugh in agreement. Taking note of the pointy toe, red pumps at his feet, he pointed at the pair. "I want you to come to bed tonight wearing those and the red lace panties you purchased."

His request made her eyes flutter, and a slow smile curved his mouth, unveiling a hearty dose of mischief.

As his hand slipped beneath her dress and stroked her inner thigh, she looked down at the Giuseppe Zanotti stilettos and back at him with a smirk asking, "So, I get to wear panties again?"

"For the ten minutes that you'll be in them, yes." His cool blue-grays swept over her, as if recalling their earlier naughty escapade.

During their visit at the lingerie boutique, she'd attempted to put on a pair that she'd purchased, but he'd stopped her. As her punishment, he fingered her right there in the private dressing room up against the mirror, pumping his fingers swiftly in and out of her pussy, his thumb working her clitoris with excruciating skill, and captured her moans in his mouth as wave after wave crashed over her body in exquisite bliss. A shuddering breath had left him at the look in her eyes as he brought her to climax.

Just then, the ring of his cell phone in his inside coat pocket brought her out of her thoughts. "What about the matching bra?" Bailey asked as he retrieved it and checked the display.

"Only the shoes and panties, princess." He winked, and she gave him a smile in eager anticipation of whatever he had in mind as he answered his phone, "Hello, Mother."

"I thought you'd be here by now. You're still coming, aren't you?"

Lucas held the phone away from his ear perhaps to not break an eardrum; the woman practically yelled into the phone. "Mother, you can speak at a normal pitch. The sound of the ocean waves doesn't encumber your voice on this end. I can hear you just fine. Why do you insist on calling me when you walk along the beach anyway?"

Watching Bailey, he grinned at seeing her try on two different shoes and then extend her legs out with a dancer's point to admire them on her feet. Pulling the phone away from his ear, he whispered to her, "I see you truly love shoes."

"I do."

"I'll remember that if we should ever argue," he whispered back with an amused look.

"Lucas, are you listening? The family has arrived, except you. What's going on with you? Sandy's here. She said you're seeing a black waitress you met at some sort of night lounge. Sandy said—"

The phone shot back to his ear. "Mother!" he roared, and Bailey's spine stiffened. Her head swung over with her eyes gaping wide at him. Her nostrils flared in anger at the thought that Sandra would speak so ill of her to his mother, but the feeling quickly turned to hurt and disappointment over his mother's apparent objectionable tone regarding her race. *And it's a café, not some skeevy back-alley dive.* That swung the pendulum of her emotions back to anger.

Staring back at her, Lucas said to his mother, "I suggest we end this conversation before I say something you will surely find offensive." He took hold of Bailey's hand and gave it a light, reassuring squeeze as he supplemented, "I wouldn't disappoint Chelsea. My lady and I will be there tomorrow. If she's shown even the slightest disrespect—"

"Lucas, why would you—"

"Good-bye, Mother." He ended the call. Immediately his phone started ringing again. He turned it off. "Sorry about that."

"You should've let her finish what she was about to say." Bailey tapped her chin with her index finger. "Let's see, she might have said why would you stoop low with a black waitress when you could have Sandy? Or, why would you even consider bringing a black woman to our home. Or maybe—"

"It doesn't matter what she was about to say. I love you. I wouldn't bother showing up at all if it weren't for my sister. I'm surprised by my mother. I don't expect you to believe it, but she's usually very freethinking."

Pulling her hand free from his, Bailey shrugged. "Whatever." She slid away from him, and his brows furrowed. "I think you should drop me off in D.C. on your way to California."

"Like hell I will! You're coming with me. You'll have to meet my family someday. It may as well be now."

"I'm not going anywhere where I'm not welcome, Lucas. I need to go home anyway. I still have my job at Nuagé, but I need to start looking for a day job. I have bills to pay. Go to your sister's wedding dinner party."

"Bailey, don't do this. I want you with me."

There was a hint of alarm in his eyes at the sight of her obstinately shaking her head as he watched her irritably shove her shoes back in their respective boxes.

"If you don't go, then neither will I."

Her head jerked to him. "What? Yes, you most certainly will go! You'll not give your family another reason to hate me."

"Then don't fight me on this. Come with me." He reached for her hand, but she tucked it close to her side and inched away.

"It's your sister's dinner party meant for family. I'm just the woman you're currently seeing."

His breath hitched; a look of anguish flashed across his features. "That's what you think this is?" He peered over at her. "Or is it that for you, this is temporary?"

It wasn't how Bailey felt at all, but she was too upset to deal with his feelings after learning that her baby would likely be spurned by his or her grandmother. "I can't go. I've been away from my evening job far too long already. It's all I have right now. I have to get back to the real world." Dismayed, she crossed her arms at her chest and brought her focus out her window. *It's going to be a real treat when your mother finds out that you knocked up the black waitress.*

"Real world, huh," he muttered. "I guess your real world doesn't include me." His head turned to his window.

Bailey didn't rebut it, and no more words were spoken between them.

Chapter Thirty-Seven

They reached the penthouse with neither saying a word during the entire ride. Bailey set the bags down by the door and walked over to the floor-to-ceiling windows that looked out over Central Park.

She'd hoped Lucas's mother wouldn't have a problem with her race. *Freethinker, hah, yeah right. A lot of people consider themselves freethinkers, open-minded progressives until an issue lands on their doorstep.*

Though her dad took issue with her being pregnant and unmarried, there was no doubt both her parents would accept Lucas and love her baby wholly.

She'd have to somehow accept the horrible possibility that she and her child may not be welcomed by Lucas's mother and likely others in his family. It was very disconcerting.

Lucas set the shopping bags on the floor and draped the garment bags over the back of the sofa, then came up behind her and gingerly ran his hands up and down her bare arms. She tried to move away. "Don't, love." His voice was barely above a whisper as he encircled his arms around her middle and held her close in apparent need of the contact.

He kissed his way from her right temple to her neck, along her shoulder blade, and back up. A light grip of her chin angled her head back to capture her mouth as her name breached his lips on a low, throaty whisper. She reached back, snaked her fingers in the soft waves of his hair, turned, and brought her arms around his neck. Her lips parted, allowing his tongue to mate with hers. It was a small sign of her love for him to latch hold to, aligning her askew emotional grid.

He brought the zipper down at the back of her dress, and then a hand glided up her inner thigh, cupping her sex. The heel of his hand massaged her clit before he eased a finger inside her.

"Bailey, I need you," he murmured against her mouth.

She understood that he wasn't referring to just sex. She needed him just as much and spread her legs to give him better access to her sheath's opening.

Staring into his beautiful eyes, she palmed his face and uttered softly, "I'm sorry. I didn't mean what I said. I need you, too, Lucas. I love you." He responded with a greedy kiss, and a second finger was added to the one readying her body to receive him.

Hooking her right leg at his hip, riding his fingers, she tugged at his suit coat and tie, desperate to feel warm skin. Her need near urgent, she yanked at his belt, pulled his shirt free of his slacks, and went to work unzipping his pants.

"*Dios mio!*"

Bailey's hand froze midzip from the stark shriek that resonated around her. *Dear lord not again!* The sound of a woman's accented voice stopped her cold, and Lucas swiftly withdrew his fingers from her body, hastily straightened his clothes, and then turned around.

As he spoke to the stunned-faced woman—his housekeeper apparently; she wore a pale blue maid's uniform—Bailey tried to keep her dress from falling off.

The woman held a taut grip on the strap of her black handbag with her censorious gape meeting Bailey briefly and then shifting down to the floor.

"Rosa, I didn't know you were here." Lucas buttoned his suit coat and linked his hands in front of him to minimize the telltale bulge of his erection.

"Ex ... excuse me, Mr. Marx. It was my day to work. I finished and was about to leave. I'm sorry, sir." With the sudden rush of color flooding the woman's face at having caught them on the verge of intimacy, still avoiding eye contact, she directed her focus on the shopping bags. "Packages arrived today for the Miss. I put them in your closet. Should I put these away as well?"

"I'll take care of it. How is Julieta?" Lucas asked her.

Rosa's eyes brightened, and she smiled wide. "She is still bouncing off the walls with excitement over her acceptance to Harvard."

"So she chose Harvard over Stanford, I see."

Rosa nodded. "Thank you again for writing the recommendations. Oh, and Julieta and I were told at our interview that you and Mr. Wilkes had an enjoyable luncheon." Her gaze softened; a wealth of appreciation glowed in her brown eyes. "Her merit scholarship will run the entire four years. Thank you, Mr. Marx, for helping my baby."

Lucas glanced over, and Bailey smiled lovingly at him as she observed his flushed cheeks brought on by what they had been doing a few minutes ago, but more likely from embarrassment over the reverence Rosa was showering upon him. Such a loving, caring man he was.

"I won't keep you. Have a good afternoon," he said.

"Yes, sir." Rosa sprinted out the door.

He turned back to Bailey with a chuckle. "Another minute and she would have found us naked."

"So you worked some of your magic and helped her daughter get into Harvard? That was really sweet of you." She noticed his cheeks colored more. He wasn't one that basked in praise.

"Julieta is very bright. She earned it. Now where were we? Oh right, Rosa cut short my finger play." He laughed as his hand moved up her inner thigh again.

"It's not funny." Shaking her head, she pressed her head back against the window. "Your entire staff will think I'm a trollop. I hope they don't report to your mother."

"My mother has no involvement in my affairs, and as I explained before, you don't have to be concerned about those who work for me." Seeing her ready to argue, he lifted her up and carried her through the labyrinthine halls of his home to the bedroom. They quickly undressed and got in bed.

He brought his mouth down to her stomach and kissed along her hip on down her legs as he stretched out with his head at her feet. Soft kisses soothed her arches, on up her calves. Then he shifted onto his back and brought her over him to straddle his shoulders.

Bailey looked back and saw him smile and lick his lips as he stared at her spread sex like it was the most decadent treat he'd ever gotten the pleasure to indulge. Without warning, he gripped her hips and pulled her to his mouth, burying his face between her thighs.

"Oh ... Lucas," she moaned. Both arms circled her hips to hold her steady as he once again ate away at her sex. The reverse angle of his mouth on her was unbelievably incredible. "Lucas," she panted, breathless. "What ... what you do to me." The pleasure was so overwhelming—her vision blurred briefly with her becoming lightheaded—that she fell forward upon his stomach.

Gazing at his wondrous cock that just about stretched to his navel bobbing near her face, she encircled the rosy crown between her lips, rolled her tongue around the head, and licked down the base. His body shuddered against hers when she took him deep into the back of her throat. As she suckled, precome trickled onto her tongue—salty sweet.

She drew in one testicle between her lips, and he growled a breathy hiss and sucked her clit harder. She then took his shaft back between her lips while continuing to massage his balls. His cock throbbed in her mouth as more fluid dripped onto her tongue. He would come in her mouth. Anticipating it, craving it, she worked her mouth and tongue upon him faster, deeper. His reaction was a deep guttural growl that reverberated against her sex, causing her womb to tighten from the onset of her orgasm quickly climbing. "Yes, right there, Lucas," she breathed out and rocked against his mouth.

• • •

"Your pussy is so sweet; I could lick you for hours." Lucas nibbled, sucked, and licked, trying his best to maintain focus on pleasing her. She was just so damn good at giving him head, he felt his balls rapidly turning to stones. "Bailey—" He tensed up and locked his mouth on her clit, trying his damnedest not to come. He didn't want their lovemaking to end too quickly. If she continued swallowing him, that's exactly what would happen.

Reaching down, he dislodged his cock from her amazingly skilled, warm, wet mouth. She groaned her disappointment, followed by a loud shrill with her nails sinking into his thighs at the thrust of two fingers inside her. He pressed his tongue flat against her clitoris, ran it back and forth, over and over in time with his quick thrusting fingers until she cried out, "Yes! Yes! Yes! Oh, yes!" and clamped her thighs on the sides of his head as her body quaked for long seconds. He loved how expressive she was in bed, unabashed in letting him know how well he pleased her.

Withdrawing his fingers, he slowed his tongue to aid her descent. Her legs went limp at his shoulders as he lapped up her honey, then rolled her to her back, and kissed his way up her body to settle between her thighs.

A fine sheen covered her skin, her breathing was ragged, and her eyes were glassy and heavy, looking completely satiated.

He brought her arms above her head, twined their fingers, and took possession of her mouth as he entered her wet pussy slow and easy. They began moving together in their familiar choreographed tempo.

"Don't ever leave me," he whispered through kisses.

"Never, Lucas." She reassuringly squeezed their entwined fingers as her knees came up and her inner muscles greedily clenched and relaxed around his cock.

The temperature from their joining rose so hot that their limbs were drenched in sweat, easily gliding wet skin to skin.

She kept pace with his rocking, rotating, and thrusting until his body delivered a fierce jerk, and he called out her name as he filled her full of his hot seed.

Breathless, he buried his face in her hair at the side of her neck and kissed her moist skin, loving her. She slipped her hands free from his to stroke his back as she continued her slow rocking until her inner walls' throbbing finally stopped. Their lovemaking seemed to get better and better with each joining.

"I love you," she voiced softly.

"I needed to hear that." Lucas rolled to his side and brought her with him. He tucked strands of hair behind her ear and brushed her cheek with the back of his fingers as he asked, "Will you come with me to California?" He loved her so much and was completely unprepared for the power she had over him. "Say you'll come with me, love?"

There was a slight hesitation before she gave him a nod.

"We'll rest a bit before we meet Sienna for dinner. Woman, you wear me out."

She gasped. "I wear *you* out?" He kissed the smirk on her lips and then slipped free of her body to retrieve the remote from the nightstand. The blackout blinds between the double-pane-glass windows lowered. He brought up the light coverlet from the foot of the bed and draped it over them. Exhausted, he sighed in complete contentment as he drew her tight within the curve of his body and buried his face in her curls, easily drifting off to sleep.

Chapter Thirty-Eight

Bailey awoke to the weight of a heavy arm and leg strung across her body. She needed to pee. A glance at the clock on the nightstand showed they'd been in bed about two hours.

Earlier, she'd tried to rise to go to the bathroom, but Lucas grumbled something in his sleep amid pulling her tighter within the shelter of his brawny frame. Now her bladder felt ready to burst at any second.

Shifting, she felt the stickiness between her thighs from the runoff of his semen. That brought to mind the baby issue that still had yet to be revealed.

Trying her best not to wake him, she lifted his arm off her breasts and carefully brought it down to the bed, then got free of his leg, eased over slowly, and quietly started to rise.

"Where are you going?" he asked sleepily.

She retrieved the remote to bring up a little light in the room and looked over her shoulder at him. His eyes were still closed. "To the bathroom," she answered. As she got up, he nodded and rolled over to his side. There weren't very many places she could go.

His confining, yet lovingly warm cuddle was another reason why she couldn't sleep. Every time she moved, he would mumble something incoherent and tighten his hold on her. It was as if he thought she might get up and walk out the door.

Returning from the bathroom, the moment she got underneath the blanket, he rolled over and pulled her back into his grasp. *Oh well.* This is how it would be.

Shifting around within her confined cocoon to get comfortable as best she could, she closed her eyes and tried to silence her brain on the baby issue once again. After thirty minutes of staring out over the room, she decided that now was as good a time as any to tell him she was pregnant. Only then, after getting it out in the open, and accepting the fact that he wouldn't be thrilled by the news, at the very least, she'd be able to free herself from the stress of it.

She noticed the way his long dark lashes fanned his closed lids. His lips were slightly parted where his light snoring blew warm air across her face. His expression was so serene; she was almost jealous.

Here it goes. Releasing a quiet breath to brace herself, she spoke softly, "Lucas?" He didn't budge. She tried again, raising her voice a tad, "Lucas?"

"Hmm?"

His eyes were still closed, and his deep breathing sawed in and out through his nose.

Spit it out. Looking up at the ceiling, she said, "I'm pregnant," to which he again droned out a breath. Taking a peek at him out of the corner of her eye, she knew he was still asleep. She brought her eyes back to the ceiling, lightly cleared her throat, and said again with a slightly raised timbre, "I'm pregnant." His deep breathing suddenly stopped. Anxiously, she waited through several racing heartbeats and received no response. Slowly, her head turned and faced his eyes—opened wide, unblinking, staring back at her. She swallowed hard.

"You're on the pill."

His eyes were fixed on her face. She shook her head and swallowed even harder in order to speak, but her throat locked up on her.

He rolled to his back, stretched, and relaxed his right arm above his head. "So you weren't honest with me." His head turned to her, and she looked away. "You can't know you're pregnant already. It hasn't even been twenty-four hours since we started having sex without a condom."

"Technically, I didn't lie. I'm four weeks late ... well, five now. I took a second pregnancy test the morning you came to my home," she explained, and he turned his head to her, giving her a puzzled stare. "We didn't use a condom in the shower, remember?" Silence. Her heart fell to her stomach.

"Pregnant," he mumbled through a deep exhale with eyes fixed on the ceiling.

"I'm not looking for anything from you." Bailey told herself she wouldn't cry. She knew this wasn't something he wanted. A tear rolled out anyway. "I have everything under control." *Not really.* His head jerked to her, and she looked away again, not wanting him to see the tears in her eyes. "I thought you had a right to know."

"What do you mean you're not looking for anything from me? You just told me you're carrying my child."

"I have it worked out. I plan to find another job, and I'll find a sitter so that I can continue on at Nuagé." She tried to subtly wipe her face by rubbing it against the pillow. "I'm okay." There was nothing else to say, except that her heart hurt.

"You're not working at Nuagé or anywhere else for that matter. Until our baby is born, you're going to rest and concentrate on staying healthy. That will be your sole job. Afterward, we can discuss whether you should return to work. Frankly, leaving our baby with a sitter at a young age isn't wise."

"It's done all the time. Babies aren't cheap. Not to mention, I have to maintain my other obligations."

"I settled your student loans," he said.

Bailey's head swung to him. "What? You ... how did ..." She was utterly befuddled. *Good heavens!* The man had essentially set her debt free. "How?"

"It's been taken care of. Your car by the way has been fully restored. I suggest you donate it. You'll need something bigger for the baby. Take the Bentley or get whatever you like. And to argue that you don't want my money would be a moot point, since you can't change any of it. Now your primary focus is our baby." He rubbed his hand over his growing five o'clock shadow in thought. "Maybe a driver." He nodded. "Yes, that would be best. I'll speak to Isaac. He may know someone reliable."

Bailey simply stared at him as he worked the matter out with himself. There was nothing she could say to that.

"You're okay with this? The baby?"

He pulled her into his arms and kissed her cheek; a thumb swiped at the wetness beneath her eyes. "I'll admit it was a bit of a surprise, but don't think for one second that I'm not happy that you're carrying my child."

"You said you don't like kids. I saw how you recoiled at the mere sight of those children on the Mall."

"I said no such thing, and they weren't *my* kids. It feels different with it being my flesh and blood, my child. I want a girl," he blurted, eyes bright, a wide stretch of straight white teeth.

She laughed. "You can't order a girl like some take-out."

"I know, but I want our first to be a girl that looks exactly like her mother. You were a beautiful baby." At her perplexed look, he explained, "The baby pictures at your home."

"What if it's a boy?"

"I'll love him, and we'd try again."

"Again?" Bailey's eyes about popped out of her head. She was still trying to come to terms with the one growing inside her, and he was casually talking about having another one.

"Uh, let's get through the birthing of this one—girl or boy." He shrugged, and she pulled out of his arms to get him to release her breast that he was now sucking. "I doubt your mother would be thrilled by the news."

"It would be her loss if she chooses not to be a part of her grandchild's life. Do your parents know?"

"I sprung it on them before I came to you. My mom seemed okay, but my dad, not so much."

"No surprise. Your mother told him I was your boyfriend. He wasn't pleased by that."

"Only because he figured I wouldn't stay in Darlington if we're together. It wasn't because you're white, if that's what you're thinking." He gave her a disagreeable look. "Trust me, your race had nothing to do with it."

"If you say so." He didn't look at all convinced.

"So, you're okay with this? Really?" Bailey studied him closely, looking for any sign of reservation.

"The woman I'm in love with is having my first child!" His sudden shout out startled her, the boom bouncing off the walls like an antenna net, and then began tickling her. "She's having my baby!" he sang out. His joy over the news filled her full with relief and happiness.

Bailey squirmed to escape his hands, screeching with laughter. "Okay, I believe you!"

Sobering, his loving gaze set upon her. "How could I not be okay with it?" Gentle kisses grazed her stomach. "Your fate is sealed, Miss Walters. You're stuck with me now. Let's celebrate." He grinned, a floppy wide grin as he settled between her legs.

"It's more like you're stuck with me." Receiving his thick member, Bailey focused on relaxing her inner muscles to allow her body to stretch around his tremendous girth.

"I wouldn't have it any other way. I love you, Bailey." He pushed up, seating his cock fully, and began making love to her.

Framing his face in her hands, she clenched her channel, holding him tight. "I love you, too, Lucas. Always."

Chapter Thirty-Nine

"Sorry we're late. Girl, I've missed you." Sienna came around the dinner table to Bailey, both ladies hugging tight.

"I've missed you, too. It feels like forever. And what do you mean by we?" Bailey asked.

"Gavin's been here in New York with me."

Bailey gave her a long look, then she smiled. "You two—" Her friend's hand came up, palm out.

"No." Getting a questioning look, Sienna made clear, "I seemed to be stumbling over him everywhere I go. He's been at my art showing the entire week."

"And that's a bad thing, why?" No answer.

"We would've been on time, but I couldn't pull Gavin off the phone." They sat down adjacent one another. "I see you have a similar problem. We came upon Lucas standing outside talking on his cell." Sienna sat back for the waiter to fill her water glass. "Thank you," she told him, and Bailey did the same. When he moved on, she continued, "Gavin's with Lucas now. There's some sort of problem or something with a deal they're working on."

"Yes, I know. Lucas works constantly. I guess that will change if he'll be as involved with the baby as he claims." Bailey smirked and took a sip of water while eyeing Sienna over the rim.

Sienna frowned. "What baby?" At Bailey's nod and gleeful grin, she jumped up and hugged her tight again. "Oh my God!"

"Sie, you're squeezing me."

"Oh, sorry. Did I hurt the baby?" Sienna stroked her shoulders.

Chuckling, they sat down. "No, we're good. I took the test a few days ago. I'm still digesting the fact of it myself."

"And Lucas? How did he take it?"

"Surprisingly good. I was really afraid he'd freak out. I expected that he would own up and support it, but I never dreamed he'd want to share the responsibility in its full sense. He wants me to move in with him."

"Girl, do it. I'll miss you like crazy, but you two will be a family." A warm hand embraced hers that rested on the table, giving it a light squeeze. "Bails, he loves you and wants you and his child in his life. Don't pass that up. I'm so happy for you."

Bailey palmed her other hand atop that earnest hand. "Thank you." Wanting to delve more into the previous topic, she asked, "So you don't see anything happening between you and Gavin? As you would say, he's a hottie." Bailey grinned.

A heavy sigh. "You'll get no argument here."

"Then what's the problem? He obviously likes you." She tilted her head, studying her best friend. "Sie, talk to me."

Their stare held, then finally, Sienna sighed again. "I'm a struggling artist. I have nothing to offer a man like him."

"Don't say that. You have a hell of a lot to offer. You're beautiful, intelligent, funny, and very talented. He would be lucky to snatch you up."

"Well, I'm not giving him the chance. I know my lane, and I don't need the drama."

"Sie, I nearly lost Lucas because I was afraid." Bailey gripped her hand tight. "Like you told me, think long and hard before you make that decision. You don't want it to be the wrong one." They both painted on smiles upon seeing Gavin approaching.

"Look at him, Bails. He's so freaking hot," Sienna murmured out the corner of her mouth. "Even the way he walks with that easy swagger makes my mouth water."

"Yep, and he's yours for the taking," Bailey murmured back. He claimed the chair directly across from her.

"Good evening, Bailey. It's good to see you again."

"You as well, Gavin." Bailey smiled warmly back at his charming grin. "So, did you guys fix the problem with your business deal?"

"Lucas got it in hand. He settled his gaze upon Sienna. "I've missed you, lovely." A kiss was planted on the back of her hand.

Sienna rolled her eyes. "You were hardly out of my sight five minutes."

"Five minutes too long." A kiss on her palm followed.

She pulled her hand free and subtly pointed a finger. "Who's that?"

Bailey followed that weak aim across the restaurant and saw Lucas talking to a tall redhead. She immediately recognized the woman from the Internet picture she'd seen where Lucas's arm had been intimately tucked around the woman's waist.

"Well, Gavin, who is she?" Sienna pushed.

"Uh, she's an old acquaintance." Gavin cleared his throat and took a sip of his water.

Bailey tried to keep her expression blank, her jealousy contained. The woman had the nerve to walk with Lucas as he made his way to the table. *Are you kidding me!* Standing but a foot away from her, Miss Redhead cut her eyes down to the table and then back up to Lucas. His forearm was given a light, yet intimate stroking. *Seriously!*

"You'll call me?" the woman asked Lucas.

Bailey's raised brows just about reached her hairline at the audacity of this bitch. Both Gavin's and Sienna's eyes flashed to her for a reaction.

Lucas moved to Bailey's side. His hand went underneath her hair and held her at the nape. Obviously aware of the tension mixed with irritation she felt, his thumb and fingers soothingly massaged up and down as he responded to the woman's bold request, "My lady here would have a problem with that."

That brought a turned-up lip to Miss Redhead's already snooty expression. Bailey thought the woman's eyes would pop out of their sockets when Lucas leaned in and kissed her, using his tongue to check her tonsils. Long seconds later, he released her mouth, met her eyes, and ran the pad of his thumb lightly over her lips. "Hmm, I never get enough of these sweet lips of yours," he uttered in that all-consuming, deep, toe-curling baritone. "Sorry for taking so long, love." Another quick peck on the mouth was delivered before he took his seat across from Sienna with Miss Redhead still standing awkwardly beside the table.

"Uh, Lucas, it was great seeing you again."

"You, too, Morgan," Lucas replied impassively without so much as a glance her way. His set gaze remained squarely on Bailey in a way that said he only had eyes for her. The last thing they both needed was more drama to come between them.

As she stared at Morgan sauntering away, Lucas kissed the back of her hand. "Sorry about that; she was a long time ago."

Bailey turned to him and smiled. "Not a problem. We all have a history. You had a life before we met."

"Yes, and it now centers on you and our child." Deep affection reflected back at her in his steel-blue gaze.

"Child?" Gavin's head bounced between them, and then over to Sienna. They all wore bright smiles back at him. The waiter came by and stationed a wine caddy between Lucas and Gavin. Once he was gone, Gavin asked, "What's going on?"

"Bailey's pregnant," Sienna happily supplied.

Gavin regarded Bailey's brilliant smile, then settled on Lucas's proud grin. "So, you've finally found someone who can tolerate your ass other than Kara and Isaac. She even gifts you with an offspring. It's about time," he teased and stood up. "Bring it in, my brother. Congratulations."

Lucas stood, and they shook hands in a bro hug.

Looking on, Bailey watched as Gavin took his seat and brought his focus over to Sienna. There was something ... *longing* glowing in his ice-blue eyes.

My goodness, is Sienna blind?

Chapter Forty

As the elevator made its way up to the top floor, Bailey inhaled deeply, blew out a long breath, twisted, and rolled her neck from side to side, all in an attempt to release the tension that strummed tight throughout her entire body.

"You keep that up and you're liable to crack something." Lucas drew her close. "Relax, it'll be fine." He centered the trillion cut, sapphire pendant necklace at the dip in her throat, undoubtedly pleased that he'd finally got to see her wear the jewels. The moment she put them on, he stripped her naked, except for the jewels, and fulfilled his fantasy. It was the reason they were a bit late for the dinner party.

"Easy for you to say. You're not the one who's about to meet a woman who hates you."

"She doesn't hate you." He tenderly stroked her back. "I intend to have a talk with my mother, and if you feel the slightest bit uncomfortable, we'll leave."

"No. She'll surely place blame on me for that. We stay. Oh no!" Bailey gasped. "You didn't tell her I'm pregnant, did you? My being here could ruin your sister's evening."

"No, and love, you have to relax for the baby's sake. We will tell my mother together. I'll stress that she not say a word to anyone."

The elevator doors opened. They stepped out and made their way across the lounge area to where a maître d' stood at a podium checking reservations.

Lucas removed his arm from Bailey's waist and linked their fingers. "Good evening, we're with the Marx party." The man nodded with a respectable smile.

"Of course, sir. Your party is in the Marina private dining room. Let me get an attendant to escort you." He picked up his phone, but the door behind him opened, distracting him from his task.

"Lucas, there you are! Finally. I've been checking periodically for you." His mother rushed over and gave him a tight hug and a kiss on both cheeks. "I was afraid you weren't coming. Chelsea would have been heartbroken to not have her big brother here."

Lucas brought his arm around Bailey's shoulders, and his mother's eyes homed in on the gesture, then set her focus on Bailey. "Chelsea's the only reason I'm here. We need to talk before we go inside." With Bailey at his side, he walked over to a cluster of leather chairs and loveseats out of earshot of the maître d'.

"Mother, this is my lady, Bailey Walters."

Bailey pushed down her anxiety and shook his mother's hand. "I'm pleased to meet you, Mrs. Marx."

Unlike Lucas's dark features and blue-gray eyes, hers were a startling light gray to almost clear, and surprisingly, Bailey found them warmly staring back at her.

Dinah Marx was quite attractive, slender, but not very tall. Bailey's five-inch stiletto sandals had her looking downward slightly to meet the woman eye to eye.

Her chin-length, platinum blonde hairstyle with a slight upsweep at the tips suited her oval face.

"It's nice to meet you, Bailey." Mrs. Marx looked up at her son. "Lucas, I—"

"She heard what you said, Mother," Lucas interjected. He caressed Bailey's back saying, "I won't have you disrespect my lady, ever. This woman right here will be in my life for as long as she'll have me. If you want me to continue coming around, I suggest you get used to it. Where I go, she goes."

Bailey tensed up at his declaration, while his mother remained quiet as her son chewed her out. When he finished speaking, his mother asked, "Are you done, son?" Then she took a small side step to stand directly in front of Bailey.

"First, Bailey, what I said, I meant no disrespect. May I ask, are you African American and a waitress?"

"Mother!" Lucas glared a warning.

Bailey took hold of his hand. "Lucas, it's all right. I'm proud of both, and I'm not ashamed that I work hard to support myself." She brought her attention back to his mother and raised her chin proudly. "Yes to both of your questions, Mrs. Marx. I waitress in the evenings at a café. It's how Lucas and I met. I'm also a college graduate and a damn good interior designer, but for now, I'm an excellent waitress, if I do say so myself."

Dinah nodded. "Well, I didn't say anything that was untrue. Maybe it came out a bit untoward, but the truth, nonetheless. You are African American and a waitress. I—" Lucas cut her off again.

"We're done." He scowled and pulled Bailey away. "I thought I knew you better, Mother."

"Wait! Let me finish." Dinah followed quickly after them.

Bailey stilled Lucas's stalk to the elevators. "Let her speak. I'm actually curious."

"No, we're leaving." He tugged her forward.

"Lucas, let your mother speak." Bailey turned back. "Go ahead, Mrs. Marx. I want to hear what you were about to say. I have a feeling I already know, but I'd like to hear it from you." She stood surprisingly calm as she waited for the woman to call her all sorts of derogatory names.

"Thank you," Dinah breathed out. "If Lucas would have let me finish before he so rudely hung up on me and then refused to take any of my calls—"

"Mother," he gritted irritably.

"Well, I was about to say, why would you not tell me that you'd found someone special? I worry about you, Lucas, out there all alone with no one to care for you. It was the reason I pushed Sandy at you. Things ended so quickly between you two. I thought you may not have given it a chance. I just wanted peace of mind, to know you were not alone. With your father gone, I know how lonely it can be." She shook her head and looked away for a moment, then back at them. "When Sandy mentioned that you were seeing a *black waitress*—" She held up her hand in defense of Lucas's venomous look. "I was merely repeating what she said, nothing more. She had some other choice comments about you, Bailey, but knowing my Lucas the way that I do, I knew they couldn't possibly be true."

Bailey and Lucas looked at one another, both realizing their severe error in judgment.

Dinah's brows pinched. "I cannot believe you would think I would have a problem with you," she waved her hand out at their linked hands, "with this. Dear God, Lucas." Tearing up, she shook her head in disappointment. "That you would think so ill of me—"

"Mother." Lucas stepped forward and embraced her. "I see that I was wrong. I'm sorry."

Bailey followed. "Mrs. Marx, let me apologize as well. I assumed the worst. I'm sorry."

Dinah faced Bailey. "You don't know how happy it makes me to see Lucas in love."

Bailey took Lucas's hand in hers as she said, "Mrs. Marx, I love your son very much." Feeling Lucas's light squeeze of her hand, she looked up at him. "He means the world to me."

Dinah brought her into a tight hug and then drew back, studying her face. "She's adorable, Lucas. Now I see why Sandy's envious."

Lucas sighed. "Okay, Mother." He pulled Bailey over to him. Their eyes met, both understanding what was next to be revealed. "Mother, we would like to share that Bailey is pregnant." His mother gasped sharply and clutched her chest. She started to sway on her feet. "Mother!"

"Mrs. Marx!" Seeing her on the verge of collapsing, they lunged for her.

Dinah nodded her head rapidly as she tried to catch her breath. "Oh my good lord, Lucas, this is wonderful news!"

Bailey let go of the air she'd trapped in her lungs. The woman's initial reaction mimicked her father's.

"Nearly having a heart attack means you're happy to hear that you're going to be a grandmother?" Lucas asked with a light chuckle.

Dinah exhaled and fanned her flushed face with her hand. "I'm immensely elated by it. Quite honestly, I didn't expect I would have any grandchildren from you, son." She addressed Bailey, "When are you due, dear?"

"In about seven and a half months, I would guess, but I'm not exactly sure yet. I have an appointment scheduled next week."

"You call me the moment you find out." She kissed Bailey's cheek. "I'm so excited! You're having my first grandchild!" Let's go join the party. Lucas, your sister will be thrilled."

"Tell no one," Lucas ordered.

Dinah gasped. "Why not? Chelsea will be overjoyed by the news and the family's all here. It's the perfect setting."

Bailey looked up at Lucas. "It's okay if your sister knows."

"Only tell her, Mother, no one else. Make it clear she is to keep it to herself. Perhaps Landon as well, but I doubt he would care much about such things."

Seeing his mother's disappointed look, Bailey supplemented, "It's early still. I would like to wait a bit. And this is Chelsea's evening. I wouldn't want to draw attention away from her."

She smiled warmly and palmed Bailey's cheeks. "Such a sweet thing you are. I understand. Let us go inside. Call me Dinah, by the way. You're practically family." His mother linked their arms, and they headed toward the restaurant's double doors. "So, Bailey, tell me about yourself. You know, you're the first young lady Lucas has let me meet. Promise you'll come by in the morning for breakfast. We can chat and get to know one another better. Lucas, you be sure to bring her by tomorrow. If the baby is a boy, the Marx family has a tradition that the first born male's name begins with *L*."

Bailey listened to Dinah chatter on. She glimpsed over her shoulder at Lucas walking behind them. He winked and smiled as if to say, you wanted her to like you—be careful what you wish for.

Chapter Forty-One

The Marina dining room had a magnificent view of the Pacific Ocean. A long, rectangular table was elegantly dressed with crystal, fine china, and sterling silver utensils for the thirty or so guests from the Marx and Fielding families milling around the room.

Bailey was introduced by Dinah to Chelsea and Landon. Chelsea, whose features closely resembled her mother's, practically screamed her excitement when Dinah whispered to her Bailey's condition. For such a small frame, the girl hugged Bailey so tight she just about cracked a rib.

Like Lucas, Landon inherited the darker features. He wasn't as enthusiastic about the baby news as Chelsea, but what twenty-one-year-old male would be? All the same, he was genuinely welcoming toward her, administering a comfortable embrace and sincere congrats. He immediately went off in search of his big brother.

Bailey's acceptance by Lucas's family was surprisingly wonderful. Each individual she met seemed to be sincere in welcoming her into their fold.

She caught Lucas in her peripheral and turned to see his eyes trained on her from across the room. He stood with Landon and two of his cousins, to whom she'd been introduced earlier, Camden—he preferred Cam, he'd said—and Justin. She waved back at the three young men now smiling and waving at her. Shifting her gaze back to Lucas, she smirked at his playful wiggling brows, watching his mother make the rounds with her to all his relatives, proudly telling each one that she was Lucas's girlfriend. To Bailey's embarrassment, Dinah made a point of stating with a hard wink to expect to see a lot more of her ... *with Lucas*, she would add for good measure.

• • •

"She's a slam piece, cousin."

Lucas gave the young man a sharp look. "Do you want me to break your other arm, Cam? Watch your mouth."

Cam brought up his right arm encased in the cast that rested in the sling. "One's enough for me, thanks."

"Yeah, Cam, watch it," Landon put in and then tagged it with, "But she *is* super hot, bro, you know that. I'll have to trip it more often to the East Coast if that's what I'll find."

"I hear you," Justin added beside him as the three young men smiled and waved again at Bailey across the room. "Lucas, does she have a sister or a friend as hot as she is?" Justin asked.

"What's it to you, Jus?" Cam questioned. "You have a girlfriend."

"No, I don't ... not really."

They all laughed, including Justin. Cam then asked, "But seriously, does she?"

Lucas grinned impishly at the young men as he pulled out his cell phone from his inside coat pocket. He did a quick search online and found a picture of him and Sienna that was taken at the art contest. He showed it to the trio. "This is her best friend." He chuckled as they all spoke at once.

"Oh hell yes!" Landon said.

"Is she a model? I love models," Justin remarked.

"I call it! That's the rule, dudes," Cam told them. "Lucas, what's her name? I can connect with her on Facebook and Twitter."

"Sienna Keller." Lucas grinned and stuck his phone back into his pocket while commenting, "I'll be sure to tell Gavin you all want to hook up with his lady." It was a lie, not for his buddy's lack of trying.

The young men's eyes widened.

"Fuck! That's Gavin's female? Cam, dude, you're in trouble," Landon voiced, shaking his head.

"Yeah, Cam, Gavin's not gonna like that shit. Glad it's not me. I have a girlfriend," Justin made clear.

Cam laughed nervously. "Lucas, I was just fucking around. You know how I am. I don't want that crazy Irish thinking I was trying to get at his woman. He might put a hit out on me or something." Cam looked around. "He's not here, is he?"

"You better not let him hear you say that." Few knew of his best friend's mafia connection. Lucas chuckled at the anxious look on his cousin's face. He chose to tease him a bit more. "He's not here, but he is in town. I should have him join us for dinner." He pretended to reach for his cell phone.

Cam tensed up. "Damn, Lucas, man, I was kidding. Why would you—"

"Relax." The young man looked ready to piss in his pants.

"I'm starving. When do we get to eat? Look, there's a waiter with appetizers." Cam sprinted off. His cousins were close behind him.

Amused, Lucas shook his head at the three of them now in hot pursuit of the hors d'oeuvres. He enjoyed teasing the young men. In a flash, his playful mood dimmed at the sight of Jack Callaghan coming up to stand beside him.

"Evening, Jack."

"She's quite stunning if I do say so myself. Lucas, it's good to see you. I read about your recent DoD, R&D acquisition. Congratulations."

"Thanks," Lucas said dryly as he watched the man eyeball his lady.

"Your father would be proud of all you've accomplished in such a short span of time. It was also his wish that you and Sandra unite the families," Jack stated bluntly, evidently not interested in mixing words.

"My father didn't concern himself in my personal affairs."

Jack turned and faced him. "On the contrary, Logan and I spoke at length about the benefit of such a union."

Lucas wasn't daft. Along with wanting majority control of Callaghan Textile back, the man looked to get a foothold in MVC by way of a marriage to his daughter. California was a community property state, and if there was to be a wedding, which there sure as hell wouldn't ever be, Jack would see to it that Sandra got her chunk.

"Look, Lucas, even I've enjoyed my fair share of caramel candy," Jack said and took a glimpse at Bailey over his shoulder. "With a body like that—"

"Careful, Jack," Lucas warned, his eyes narrowing.

Jack held up a hand. "Who could blame you? Hell, I envy you. Our nighttime diversions keep us sane," he winked, "but in the light of day, we all must get back to what matters," and then leaned in and whispered, "Sandy understands the way our world works. Who said you couldn't keep that sweet treat under your pillow?"

Lucas clenched his jaws tight for restraint as he said, "Out of respect to my lady, and my mother and sister, not looking to ruin their evening, they're the only reason I haven't laid you the fuck out." The man's eyes stretched wide. "I suggest you step the fu—" He paused at the sight of Jack's wife and Sandra approaching.

"Why the serious faces you two? No talk of business tonight," Nancy Callaghan said as she stepped before them with her daughter beside her. "Lucas, it's good to see you. Sandy mentioned that her company completed your home renovations."

Lucas worked at cooling his temper. "Good evening, Mrs. Callaghan." His eyes met Sandra's, then shifted back to her mother. "Sandra's designer did a superb job in fulfilling all of my needs, and even those I hadn't foreseen." He smirked, and Sandra's lips thinned, catching his meaning.

"I hear you and Sandy attended an event in support of the arts as well. It pleases me to see you two back on even ground again," she commented, and he noted her eyes shift across the room at Bailey for a brief moment.

To that, he merely nodded, then gave a glimpse at Bailey and observed how her previously cheerful features were now muted as she watched him.

"Your mother mentioned that you'll be in the area for a couple of days. You can join us for dinner before you leave?" Nancy looked between him and her daughter. "Perhaps Sandy could accompany you on your plane when you two head back east."

Again, when no reply was returned, her narrowed eyes drifted across the room, betraying her fixed smile before she said, "Don't forget, I want to see you before you leave. Come along, Jack."

As the couple walked away, Lucas gave a look at Sandra and noticed how she held a scathing glare on Bailey. Bailey was no longer looking his way. She'd been pulled into a discussion with his mother and his mother's sister, Aunt Patricia.

"Lucas, I may have misjudged Bailey." Sandra stepped over to his side. "Tell me something, is she splitting her time between you and that hot, sexy man she was hanging on at the art competition?" Seeing the tendon flex in his jaw, she cracked a corner-lip grin. Evidently there was no sense in her playing nice anymore. Bailey was here, which meant her pursuit of him was pointless.

"Is next weekend the other guy's turn with Bailey?" she asked with a taunting smirk.

"Tread carefully, Sandra. And I suggest you break the news to your parents to not put any stock in us becoming the happy couple they envision." A brief scowl crossed her features, before she returned her bitter grin.

"I see you've stuck your poor mother with the task of entertaining Bailey tonight. That's cruel." She tsked and shook her head. "Lucas, I understand your intrigue, really I do. She's a novelty for you, one might even say exotic in a way, but she doesn't know you the way I do, how fast you bore of your female toys. You forget how well I know you."

Lucas cut her a hard side look. "You just can't help being a bitch, can you?"

A hint of a shrug. "There was a time you didn't seem to mind."

"A man would tolerate just about anything when getting his dick swallowed."

She glared at him with a tight smile. "Once the novelty of having black pussy wears off, Bailey will learn rather quickly. You know where to find me when she does." Her hand came up to touch his shaven cheek, but he caught it, and squeezed. She winced, yet maintained a smile. "I won't even hold this lapse in judgment against you."

Lucas dropped her hand and smiled back. "Sandra, that's very magnanimous of you. By the way, do you like the jewels Bailey's wearing? It was painstaking selecting just the right stone for her. It took me damn near an hour. I'm rather pleased with my choices. You know, Gavin reminded me that I was in my teens the last time I personally chose a gift for a woman of interest." Lucas dipped his eyes to the diamond studs in her ears and then back at her narrowed glare. "Kara is very efficient. She does a great job handling tasks with which I care not to concern myself."

"You bastard!" Sandra hissed low through tightly clenched teeth. "I guess you know I fired your little bitch," she jeered. "I'll see to it that no firm will want to hire her. You'll see."

"The only one who will lose is you," Lucas shot back. When Bailey mentioned that she'd been fired, he was ready to snatch the damn company away from Sandra and hand it over to Bailey. Discovering that Bailey was pregnant was the only reason he stayed his hand ... for the time being.

"You forget that I practically own your father's company, which includes yours. If I discover that you've tarnished Bailey's professional reputation, I'll handle things, and you know I'm damn stellar at handling things." With a smile, Lucas straightened his tie, saying, "Um, Bailey did say she was interested in starting her own interior design business. There may be a client list that she's already familiar with." He turned before her and came in close. "Don't ever think to fuck with me or my lady," he warned with razor sharp firmness, and then his smile easily returned. "I believe dinner is about to start. I should go collect my lady before my aunt talks her to death."

"Fucking asshole," Sandra hissed, seething in anger. "Bailey will find out soon enough."

"And yet, you still want me. Enjoy your dinner." Lucas grinned and strolled off.

Chapter Forty-Two

Bailey was enjoying herself. The lobster melted in her mouth. The vegetables were steamed just right. Lucas's family as well as Brad's were very welcoming. Everything was perfect ... except for the cold, crossed looks she was receiving from Sandra and her parents across the table. Why were they here anyway? It was a dinner party meant for Chelsea's and Brad's families to get to know one another. According to Lucas, the Callaghans had no family ties to either side, though they strived for such a bond with the Marxes. Bailey being here put a large kink in their chain.

"Let me put them out."

Hearing Lucas beside her, she pulled her eyes away from Sandra's venomous stare. The woman looked as though she was imagining slitting Bailey's throat. "It's not worth it." She took a bite of her three-layered lemon streusel crumb cake. "Let's just enjoy the evening."

• • •

Lucas gave the Callaghans a sharp look, to which they each immediately looked away, understanding clearly his intentions. He wanted to tell them to get the hell out, but Bailey didn't want him to draw attention to the situation. Dismissing the ass-hats at the other end of the table, he brought his attention back to his lady beside him. Though he wanted to crack the bastard's skull for ogling her, Lucas had to admit that Jack Callaghan was right, Bailey looked stunningly beautiful tonight. Hell, she'd look gorgeous in a potato sack.

During their shopping trip, he'd insisted that she find a dress similar to the one she'd worn at the art competition in order to wear the jewels. This one had thin spaghetti straps and, unfortunately, no side slit, but was otherwise similar in color and design.

His index finger lightly traced the outer curve of her left ear to the large, sapphire trillion-shaped stone wrapped in diamonds at her lobe and dragged a finger featherlight on down the side contour of her delicate throat, skating along the fine chain holding the matching pendant resting upon her silken skin. She pushed his hand away with a shy glance over at his mother across the table who winked at them.

He knew that his PDA was making her uncomfortable in view of his family and Chelsea's intended family, but he couldn't keep his hands off her. He was drunk-stupid in love, unable to imagine his life without her. That now included the child she would bear him. The very thought made him damn near giddy with joy. Abruptly, he pushed back his chair and dropped down to one knee, acting exclusively on his feelings, his love for the woman seated beside him, carrying in her womb his first child. The entire room fell silent.

Bailey's eyes widened. "Lucas, what are you doing?" she whispered and looked around the table. Utensils were held paused in midair and conversations were halted midsentence. Everyone's expression matched hers—shocked.

Taking hold of her shaky hand, he adjusted the tennis bracelet on her wrist before he kissed the back of her hand. "Bailey—"

"Oh my!" she breathed out, gaping back at him.

"I know this isn't the right time and place for this." Lucas looked at his sister.

Chelsea bounced excitedly in her seat. "Yes, Lucas, right place, right time." She shooed him with her hand, beaming happily. "Go on, go on."

He met Bailey's glistening eyes that brimmed with what he hoped were happy tears. "When I didn't know where you were, it was as if my life had been stripped bare down to my very soul. Those weeks without you were the worst of my life. I never want to experience that feeling of emptiness ever again."

Several around the table asked one another what he meant by that, for everyone was intently listening to him on the verge of proposing to her.

"I want us to build a life together. I want to wake up every morning to your beautiful face and for it to be the last that I see before I close my eyes each night. My life, my soul, and all that I am I offer to you. Bailey, will you marry me? What do you say, princess?"

"I say yes, Lucas! Yes!" With tears spilling over, she threw her arms tight around his neck and kissed him. The entire room stood, clapped, and cheered. His mother rushed around the table, kissed, and hugged them. Chelsea cried happily and was held by Brad. Landon, Cam, and Justin ceremoniously let out screeching whistles and hoots.

Lucas noted Bailey's attention was fixed where Sandra and her parents sat—the seats were empty.

Chapter Forty-Three

"I'm thinking doves." Nena smiled on screen. "One hundred white doves would take flight just as they exited the church and white rose petals covering the walkway to their white limo."

"I was thinking more along the lines of paper lanterns on the beach," Dinah said. "Thousands of colorful sky lanterns lit up over the ocean upon the moment they have their first kiss as husband and wife." She smiled dreamily. "It would be beautiful, Nena."

"Dinah, you can't very well see lit lanterns in the middle of the afternoon."

"It's an evening wedding," Dinah told her.

"No, it's an afternoon wedding. I've already reserved the church. Picture it, Dinah, my idea will be lovely."

"Imagine, Nena, the moon casting down." She sighed with a look heavenward. "So beautiful. And a band! An entire orchestra ensemble."

"Yes!" They both screeched and laughed, heads thrown back.

Bailey sat at the table beside her future mother-in-law, her head slumped, propped up by her hand in front of the computer screen as they FaceTime chatted with her mom. She looked on while they debated over her wedding arrangements. *Her wedding.* A sigh. They were turning her special day into a three-ring circus. It was getting out of control. They'd been at it for over an hour. A wide yawn of exhaustion could no longer be contained as they started discussing menu choices. Warm hands came down on her shoulders. She looked up and smiled. With eyes closed briefly, she rubbed her cheek against the back of Lucas's comforting, supportive touch.

"Hello, Lucas, dear," Nena said on screen with a cheery wave.

"Good evening, Mrs. Walters."

Dinah looked up at him. "Have a seat, son. We're discussing the wedding arrangements."

"I can see that. I'm going to put my fiancée to bed. You ladies carry on."

With a look at Lucas, Bailey rose from her chair and mouth silently, "Thank you," then turned back to the computer screen. "Night, Mom. Love you."

"Love you too, sweetheart, get plenty of rest." Her mom blew her a kiss on screen.

"Good night, Mrs. Marx."

"Good night, darling."

Receiving a hug and a kiss upon the cheek, Bailey soaked up the genuine affection felt from her future mother-in-law.

"Good night, Mother," Lucas said and kissed her cheek.

As they headed up the stairs, Dinah called, "Bailey, remember we're going shopping with Chelsea in the morning, so rest up."

"Okay."

Settled in bed, she stared up at the ceiling, her mind racing with thoughts of the elaborate wedding plans. She took a breath and exhaled slowly to try to wash away the tension and the weariness along with it.

Lucas drew her into his arms. "If you'd rather not stay here at my mother's, we can go to my place ... our place. It's only about thirty minutes from here."

"No, this is fine. She lifted her head from his shoulder. The blinds were up; the moonlit night filtered in soft light and shadows. "I like sleeping in your old room. It's kind of special in a way."

"Then what's on your mind?"

His hand caressed along her stomach. He'd been doing that a lot lately as if mentally soothing his child. "It's these wedding plans. Doves and sky lanterns and orchestra bands. It's way over the top. I would just as soon go to the courthouse and be done with it."

He drew back, brows lifted. "Be done with it, huh?"

"I don't mean it like that. I just don't need all the fanfare. She shifted and slid on top of him, stretching out upon his heavily muscled frame. I just want to be your wife. I don't care about all the extreme hooray."

"Then do what you want. Don't you ladies say it's your day to have as you see fit?"

Arms crossed upon the bare expanse of his chest, she rested her chin on her hands. "Yes, but—"

"Why is there a but? You should have the wedding you wish."

"You would be okay with that? A courthouse ceremony, I mean?"

"Woman, I would marry you in a grass hut," he said as his fingers threaded beneath the satin string of her thong and circled the rim of her vagina opening before thrusting in a finger.

Bailey rocked her hips on his skillful digit as she asked, "What about our parents?"

"What about them? They had their weddings." As he pushed her panties down her hips, he added, "Our wedding isn't about them, love. Have the type of wedding you want."

She slid off her panties and lifted her body just enough for him to peel out of his boxer briefs. Then he reached between her legs and guided his cock into her slick channel. Straddling him, she sat up, pulled her tank over her head, and began a slow ride upon his length as she said, "Let's do it."

Chapter Forty-Four

On a beautiful California morning, just before ten, Bailey stood before the magistrate, holding Lucas's hands in hers. Sienna stood behind her as witness. Behind Lucas were Landon, Gavin, Daxton, and Sean—his brothers. Lucas had not chosen one best man. He'd said each one of those men were just that.

Bailey gave a look over at her mother, father, and Caleb, then Dinah, Chelsea, and Brad. All wore expressions of joy. That said, her mom and Dinah weren't happy that they wouldn't get to throw the wedding of the year. *They'll get over it once the baby comes*, Lucas had told her.

Him dressed in a perfectly tailored dark gray suit and her in a simple white dress and matching pumps, they listened to the magistrate as he began.

"Bailey and Lucas, today, surrounded by your friends and family, you celebrate one of life's grandest moments as you join together in a vow of marriage.

"Lucas Grayson Marx, do you take Bailey Elaina Walters to be your wife, to love, honor, cherish, and protect her, forsaking all others and holding only unto her?"

"I do." Without the slightest hesitation, his cool gaze remained steady upon her.

"Bailey Elaina Walters, do you take Lucas Grayson Marx to be your husband, to love, honor, cherish, and protect him, forsaking all others and holding only unto him?"

"I do." She felt Lucas's light squeeze of her hands in his.

"Rings please," the magistrate said. Bailey turned to Sienna who handed over Lucas's smooth platinum band, while Lucas retrieved her ring from his inside coat pocket.

The magistrate looked at Lucas. "Please repeat after me," he began. "With this ring, I thee wed."

Lucas repeated his vows as he slid the seven-carat, canary-yellow, princess cut solitaire surrounded by white diamonds on her finger.

It was Bailey's turn. She repeated the words as she slipped the band onto Lucas's finger.

"With the power invested in me, I now pronounce you husband and wife. You may kiss the bride."

The magistrate's last words were redundant as Lucas had already pulled her into a forever-long kiss. When he finally drew away, he whispered, "You're all mine now, Mrs. Marx."

Bailey smiled. "Mr. Marx, I wouldn't want it any other way."

Epilogue

Lucas came awake to the sound of his private line ringing on the nightstand. He glanced at the digital clock next to it, its numbers illuminating bright blue: 1:31 A.M. Bailey was asleep, half draped over him with her leg wedged between his. Her wild curls covered her face and fanned out across his chest.

They'd spent the day at his mother's, where Lucas caught up on work while his mother and sister insisted they take Bailey shopping for baby things. Bailey had stated it was too early in her pregnancy to start shopping, but it was like his mother and sister to not take no for an answer. Following their shopping spree, having purchased enough baby items for triplets, the trio visited the spa and ended the evening with dinner. They wore his wife out.

Holding her to him, he checked the phone display. *Sienna.* "It's three thirty in the morning, East Coast. That's late even for you," he answered sleepily.

"It's Kevin."

Lucas flinched, jaws clenched. *If this bastard is trying to get to Bailey ...* He wanted to reach through the phone and give him another ass kicking. "That explains how you got this number, but not why you have Sienna's phone," he sharply grated, and Bailey stirred at his gruff tone. He stroked her back, and she snaked her warm, nude body tighter around him. Her soft skin rubbed against the hairs on his body, kindling a heated friction that got him aroused. Caressing her smooth buttocks, he gritted into the phone, "Well?"

"I've been trying to reach Bailey."

"I have to hand it to you, Kevin, you have fucking stones calling me for Bailey," Lucas growled.

"And you need to stop thinking the world revolves around your ass!" Kevin barked back.

Lucas could hear someone tell Kevin to keep it down. "What do you want?"

"Look, Sienna and Faith are in the hospital."

"What!" He looked down at Bailey when she stirred again.

"Lucas, who is it?" she mumbled sleepily. He rubbed her back, and she released a deep sigh, nuzzling against his chest. "Babe, we need to sleep. Get off the phone." Her lean body stretched out practically on top of him.

Gently untangling their limbs, he got up, padded quietly to the bathroom, and closed the door.

"Kevin?"

"Yeah, I'm here. Sienna and Faith were shot."

"Shit!" Alarmed, he raked an anxious hand over his head to the back of his neck. "What happened? How are they? How's Sienna?" Lucas braced himself, fear welling up tight in his chest.

"They'd moved her from ICU to a standard room now that her condition has been upgraded from critical to stable. Faith's room is located one floor up. Her injury wasn't life-threatening. The bullet passed straight through her shoulder into Sienna, getting lodged in, and cracking one of her ribs. It's what prevented Sienna from suffering more internal injuries. The doctor said that had the bullet been a few centimeters higher, it would have hit Sienna's heart. Basically, her rib saved her life."

"Shit." Lucas scrubbed his fingers back and forth across his forehead.

"I'm here with Sienna now. She woke up a few minutes ago groggy from the meds, but she's resting now. I was able to get her to tell me the passcode to her phone before she fell back asleep. That's how I found your number. The shooting happened around six yesterday evening in Sienna and Bailey's apartment."

"A home invasion?" he asked.

"From what I understand, it was Faith's boyfriend. I heard a noise and went over to see if Ba—" Kevin cleared his throat. "The dude jetted out of their apartment. I've only gotten bits and pieces on the details because Faith's been sedated. She yanked out her I.V. twice and kept kicking and screaming, saying that she killed Sienna just like she killed her mother. The staff tried to tell her that Sienna pulled through, but she wouldn't listen. She lost it. They had to knock her out."

"Have they caught the bastard?" His panic now rested just above his rising fury.

"Not yet. In between going bat-shit crazy, Faith managed to give the police some information, and I was able to identify a mug shot they showed me, but they still want to question Faith further and Sienna when she's able. The detective said the dude's mixed up with some heavy players in the drug scene."

"Damn. You're sure Sienna's okay?" Lucas asked with grave concern.

"She pulled through the worst of it. The hospital won't divulge much more. They want to speak to her next of kin. Sienna would want Bailey here for that." Kevin sighed. "Anyway, that's why I called. Uh, yeah, tell Bailey when she wakes up that I tried to call her right after it happened, but she didn't pick up. I didn't have her parents' number. I guess that would've been a wasted effort."

Having apparently heard Bailey's voice, Lucas heard the undertone of discontent filter through the man's tone. "She's been out all day; her phone died. We're in California. We'll be heading back within the hour. I'll have her call you from the plane."

"I'll text you the hospital's address."

"Thanks. And, uh, thanks for letting me break this to Bailey. This will really upset her."

"Yeah, I'll be here. If Sienna wakes before Bailey gets here, I'll tell her that she's on her way."

"Later." Lucas hung up. *Damn.* Sienna and Faith shot by Faith's boyfriend. He thought back to Faith at his office, how she'd intended to blackmail him for money. Sienna getting shot was his fault. Had he given Faith the money, Sienna would not have been nearly killed.

Gavin. He had to let him know what happened to Sienna. Gavin was at his penthouse not very far away. He was in California visiting the company's Silicon Valley office. Lucas quickly scrolled through his contacts and hit Gavin's name. After four rings, he expected it to go to voice mail, but the line picked up.

"What?" Gavin answered, his voice gravelly.

"Get to the plane."

"Do you know what time it is?"

"It's Sienna."

He yawned out, "What about Sienna?"

"She's been shot." Lucas's stomach constricted at the thought that Bailey and his unborn child could have been at the apartment.

He detailed to Gavin all that Kevin had told him. "We'll meet you at the plane."

"I'll be there."

Acknowledgments

I would like to express my sincerest gratitude to my amazing editor, Jessica Verdi, for her invaluable guidance in helping shape this book, her tremendous support, and for giving me the opportunity to share Lucas and Bailey's story. You're truly wonderful! Also, thank you Julie Sturgeon for helping me through cover development. You made the process fun. And many thanks to the entire Crimson Romance/Simon & Schuster team for all the hard work put in to helping bring my dream to fruition.

To my agent, Brittany Booker, thank you for your continued support that kept me moving forward.

Thanks, Laurie and Marnee, for giving me your undivided attention whenever I needed advice or just a few words of encouragement. So glad our roads crossed. You ladies have been such great friends.

To my husband, thank you for being immensely supportive as I stepped out on this journey. And with love and giant hugs to my A-team, my wonderful children. Thank you for your understanding and patience, despite the many hours in which my writing and deadlines absorbed all of my attention. I dedicate this book you.

Finally, I am forever grateful to you, dear reader, for giving my story a spin. Thank you from the bottom of my heart. I hope you enjoy getting to know my characters as much as I loved creating them.

Author's Note

Though inspired by Washington D.C. landmarks, please note that some events and locations mentioned in this book are fictional and are meant solely for you to escape and enjoy.

About the Author

Michele Arris is a Romance Writers of America Golden Heart® award-winning author. Her work is edgy and downright steamy with a melting pot of strong, diverse characters. When she isn't stationed in front of her laptop spilling her wayward imagination onto the page, she's jotting scenes in her head. "It's enjoyable to write stories where two people are guaranteed their happy ending."

Michele loves to hear from readers. To see what happens next in the Tarnished Billionaires Series, please visit her website at www.michelearris.com. While there, please subscribe to her occasional newsletter for information about upcoming books.

Visit her Author Profile page at simonandschuster.com.